WHEEL OF FORTUNE

The Tarnished Crown
Book One

C. F. Dunn

Also in The Tarnished Crown series:
Sun Ascendant
Degrees of Affinity

WHEEL OF FORTUNE

Published by Sapere Books.

24 Trafalgar Road, Ilkley, LS29 8HH

saperebooks.com

Copyright © C. F. Dunn, 2025

C. F. Dunn has asserted her right to be identified as the author of this work.
All rights reserved.

No part of this publication may be reproduced, stored in any retrieval system, or transmitted, in any form, or by any means, electronic, mechanical, photocopying, recording, or otherwise, without the prior written permission of the publishers.
This book is a work of fiction. Names, characters, businesses, organisations, places and events, other than those clearly in the public domain, are either the product of the author's imagination, or are used fictitiously.
Any resemblances to actual persons, living or dead, events or locales are purely coincidental.

ISBN: 978-0-85495-615-9

For Alison King

ACKNOWLEDGEMENTS

As ever this is one of the hardest parts of writing a book, especially one written over a decade or more, and I have incurred debts of gratitude to many people. There have been those there right from the beginning — my family and close friends — without whose support, enduring patience, and infinite wisdom this book would not have been created. For my husband and friend, Richard, whose depth of historical knowledge is equalled by the breadth, and who readily, joyously, shares his expertise on all things military, architectural, and naval. Our daughters, who have grown up with this book, continue to indulge their mother's obsession with great good humour as I write the series. My mother, who let me watch historical TV series when still a tot and who bought me the Ladybird *Warwick The Kingmaker* and a library of books. My father, for taking me to every medieval edifice I could find and who guided me through my first forays in fiction writing. Little did they know where it would all lead. My friend and grammar guru, author S.L. Russell, who unstintingly takes the time from her own writing projects to read mine.

I wish to thank those who have offered endorsements — my friend and historical novelist Elizabeth Chadwick, on whose candid opinion I can always rely; Matthew Lewis, writer, medieval historian, and chair of the Richard III society; Toni Mount, author and speaker — all who have so generously given their time to read *Wheel of Fortune*.

In addition, I thank my wonderful editor Amy Durant at Sapere Books for her eagle-eyed guidance, and the editors and proof-readers, the artists and all those involved in honing and polishing the manuscript. An especial vote of thanks goes to editor and author Liz Carter (E.M. Carter), whose inspiring and creative designs always make books stand out from the crowd.

I am indebted to the countless historians, re-enactors, medieval specialists, archivists and museum curators, the enthusiastic attendants at heritage sites and knowledgeable church wardens, all of whom have indulged my quest for knowledge.

Nor can I neglect the many historians, writers, and academics whose research and analysis — condensed and attainable through their own books and papers — have saved me many years of work. It is impossible to represent the value they have collectively added to unearthing and understanding the complex historical record of the period. You are too numerous to mention here and, even if I did, there would be many more I have unjustly neglected.

To Alison King, whose unique skills and specialist knowledge have enabled me to see beyond the veil, and for this gift there can be no limit to my heartfelt thanks.

Lastly, I cannot end my acknowledgements without thanking my readers for taking time out of their own busy lives to spend it with Isobel. Where would she be without someone rooting for her? And where would I be without my books being read? In my garden like Isobel, no doubt, dreaming up plots. But without readers those plots would remain nothing but a figment of my imagination. It is only when someone picks up a book and turns the first page that stories spring to life and make an author's daydreaming reality.

HOUSE OF LANCASTER

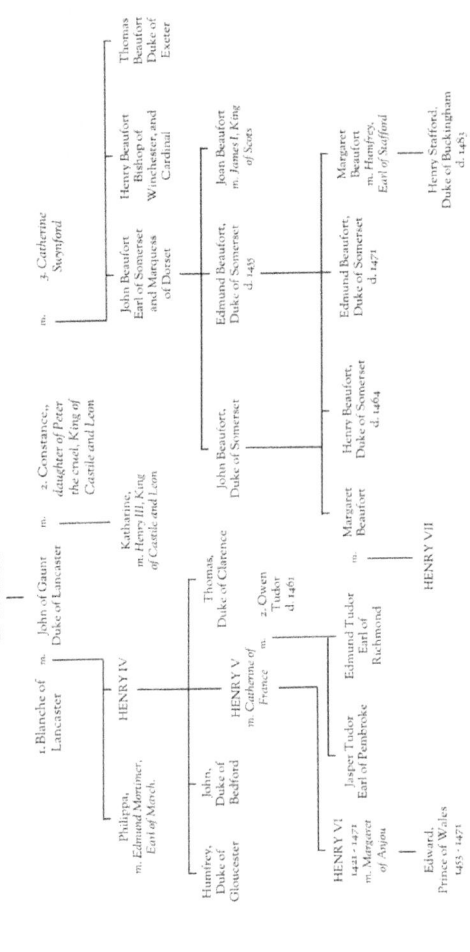

EDWARD III
|
John of Gaunt, Duke of Lancaster
- m. 1. Blanche of Lancaster
- m. 2. Constance, daughter of Peter the cruel, King of Castile and Leon
- m. 3. Catherine Swynford

From 1. Blanche of Lancaster:
- HENRY IV
  - Philippa, m. Edmund Mortimer, Earl of March
  - HENRY V, m. Catherine of France
    - (2. Owen Tudor d. 1461)
    - HENRY VI 1421–1471, m. Margaret of Anjou
      - Edward, Prince of Wales 1453–1471
    - Edmund Tudor, Earl of Richmond m. Margaret Beaufort
      - HENRY VII
    - Jasper Tudor, Earl of Pembroke
  - John, Duke of Bedford
  - Humfrey, Duke of Gloucester
  - Thomas, Duke of Clarence

From 2. Constance:
- Katherine, m. Henry III, King of Castile and Leon

From 3. Catherine Swynford:
- John Beaufort, Earl of Somerset and Marquess of Dorset
  - John Beaufort, Duke of Somerset
    - Margaret Beaufort m. Edmund Tudor
  - Edmund Beaufort, Duke of Somerset d. 1455
    - Henry Beaufort, Duke of Somerset d. 1464
    - Edmund Beaufort, Duke of Somerset d. 1471
    - Margaret Beaufort m. Humfrey, Earl of Stafford
      - Henry Stafford, Duke of Buckingham d. 1483
- Henry Beaufort, Bishop of Winchester, and Cardinal
- Joan Beaufort, m. James I, King of Scots
- Thomas Beaufort, Duke of Exeter

HOUSE OF YORK

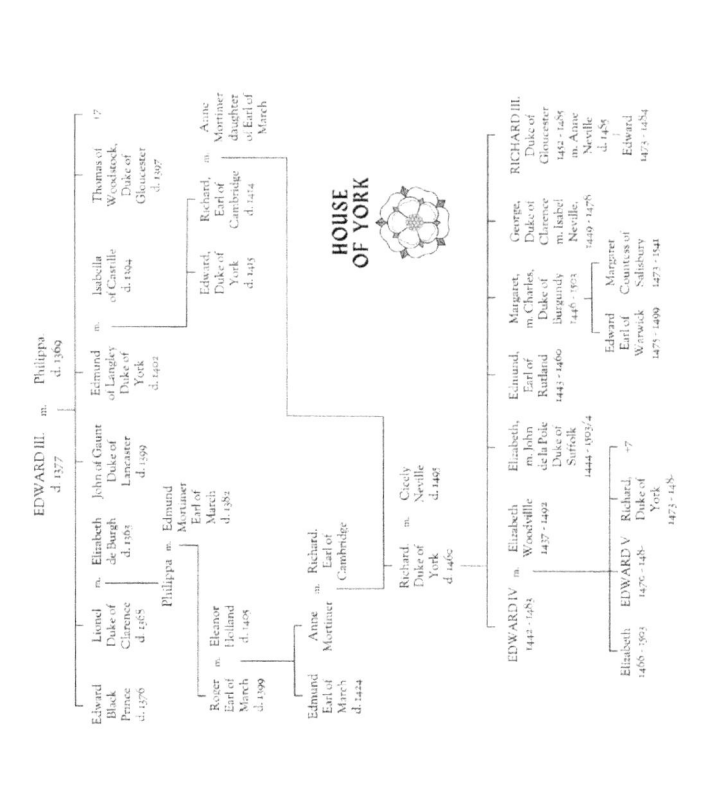

EDWARD III. m. Philippa
d. 1377   d. 1369

- Edward Black Prince d. 1376
- Lionel Duke of Clarence d. 1368 m. Elizabeth de Burgh d. 1363
  - Philippa m. Edmund Mortimer Earl of March d. 1382
    - Roger Earl of March d. 1399 m. Eleanor Holland d. 1405
      - Anne Mortimer m. Richard Earl of Cambridge
      - Edmund Earl of March d. 1424
- John of Gaunt Duke of Lancaster d. 1399
- Edmund of Langley Duke of York d. 1402 m. Isabella of Castile d. 1394
  - Edward, Duke of York d. 1415
  - Richard, Earl of Cambridge d. 1414
    - Richard, Duke of York d. 1460 m. Cicely Neville d. 1495
- Thomas of Woodstock, Duke of Gloucester d. 1397 m. Anne Mortimer daughter of Earl of March

Children of Richard, Duke of York and Cicely Neville:

- Anne ?
- EDWARD IV 1442-1483 m. Elizabeth Woodville 1437-1492
  - Elizabeth 1466-1503
  - EDWARD V 1470-1483
  - Richard, Duke of York 1473-1483
- Edmund, Earl of Rutland 1443-1460
- Elizabeth, m. John de la Pole Duke of Suffolk 1444-1503/4
- Margaret, m. Charles, Duke of Burgundy 1446-1503
- George, Duke of Clarence m. Isabel Neville 1449-1476
  - Edward Earl of Warwick 1475-1499
  - Margaret Countess of Salisbury 1473-1541
- RICHARD III. Duke of Gloucester 1452-1485 m. Anne Neville d. 1485
  - Edward 1473-1484

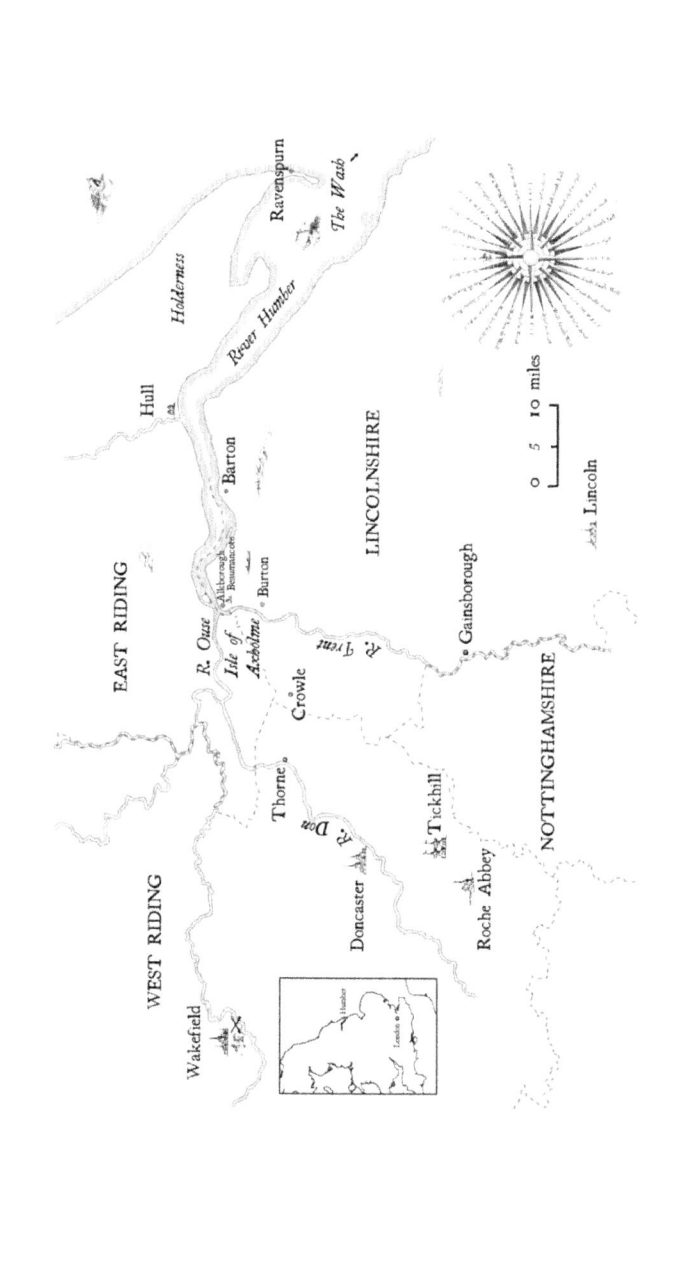

LIST OF CHARACTERS

THE LANGTON FAMILY:
The Old Earl — died in battle
Duarte Langton — his eldest son — died in battle
The Earl — his second son
Robert Langton — his youngest son
Duarte — the Earl's son
Felice — wife and countess to the Earl
Elizabeth (Bess) — their eldest daughter, married to Lord Dalton
Margaret (Meg) — their second daughter
Cecily — their youngest daughter
Langton retainers and servants:
Nicolas Sawcliffe — Master Secretary to the Earl
Hyde — the Earl's steward
Louys — the Earl's esquire
Alun — groom to the Earl
Godfrey — Sawcliffe's clerk
Martin — Robert's esquire
Edgar — groom to Robert
Master Clay — Master of the Kennels
Lady de la Roche — Mistress of the Nursery and aunt to Felice Langton
Joan — chief nursery maid
Alice — nursery maid and maid to Isobel

THE FENTON FAMILY:
Sir Geoffrey Fenton
Lady Isobella Wray — his wife — died
Isobel Fenton — their daughter

Buena — her servant
Arthur Moynes — their steward
Jack — kitchen lad
George — sergeant-at-arms
Adam — sergeant-at-arms
Oliver — the reeve
John — head gardener

THE LACEY FAMILY:
Thomas Lacey — betrothed to Isobel
Henry Lacey — his father
Lord Ralph Lacey — Thomas's uncle

THE PLANTAGENETS:
Edward IV — Edward Plantagenet, King of England and eldest son of Richard, Duke of York
George Plantagenet — Duke of Clarence and younger brother of the king
Richard Plantagenet — Duke of Gloucester and youngest brother of the king
Elizabeth Woodville (formerly Grey) — wife and queen to Edward IV
Henry Plantagenet — Henry VI, King of England
Margaret of Anjou — wife and queen to Henry VI
Edward, Prince of Wales — their son
The Neville family:
Richard Neville, Earl of Warwick — cousin to Edward IV
Isabel Neville, his elder daughter and Duchess of Clarence — wife of George
Anne Neville, his younger daughter and wife of Edward, Prince of Wales (son of Henry VI)
John, Marquis of Montagu — his brother

PROLOGUE

Spring 1465

"Well?" From the amber stone of the tower parapet, Sir Geoffrey Fenton made out the distant blur of movement on his land. "Who are they?" he demanded.

His sergeant-at-arms strained forward, shielding his eyes from the fine mizzle falling from a shrouded sky. Men — armoured men — were riding hard, earth tearing beneath iron hooves. "Less half a score, my lord, and no banner. They make for the ferry."

Squinting, the older man ground his fist into his weakened eyes. "Curse these; I would see for myself. Even a half-score will bring trouble if they head this way. Muster the household. Isobel, go to your mother."

Close to her father's shielding arm, Isobel hesitated as a shout, more a cry, rose on the air, and the group turned like silver fish and headed up the rubbled rise of the road that led to the gatehouse on which the watchers stood. One, two … seven men in full harness; swords, a poleaxe, their visors raised but too distant to make out their faces. The sergeant-at-arms urgently sought that which had thrown the riders off their course towards them.

"Shut the gate!" Fenton took hold of his daughter and pushed her towards the stair. "Isobel, get inside."

"My lord!"

Distracted, Fenton turned, his child forgotten, and followed the sergeant's pointing finger. From amidst the bare-branched spinney, more horsemen crashed out of the undergrowth onto open strips of barely greening soil, merging as one as they found the track. Sensing victory, they accelerated, churning tilth in a plough of hooves as they rode hard on the heels of the hunted. Standing on tiptoe and peering through the battlements, Isobel could just make out the faces of the small band as they neared, eyes wide, lips pulled back over teeth clenched so tight the air could barely pass through, now staring forward, now casting over their shoulders, driving their horses on. Haunted, hounded animals. Prey.

Isobel tugged at her father's mantle. "Let them in, Fader, let them in!"

As one, the small band of desperate men veered towards the church, which stood proud of the village and apart from the manor by a bowshot. Horses stumbled on the new-turned clods and furrows before finding surer footing on the way-worn paths.

Echoing her words, the sergeant said, "They seek refuge. My lord, will you allow it?"

Mounting a rise where the strips, ploughed before Michaelmas and plush with winter wheat, made firmer ground, the pursuing horsemen curved in an arc seeking to cut off the men's flight to refuge. Within his sight at last, Fenton followed the chase, his face burning with a hunger Isobel had not seen before, his mouth pulled into a grim smile of recollection. He stabbed a finger in the direction of the hunting party. "Look — they're driving them towards the cliff edge. Hah! These men know this land. Can you make them out now?"

With the riders too far away to make out distinguishing marks, and without colours to denote their affinity, the sergeant shook his head.

Isobel watched as the hunted scattered in confusion, their escape blocked, their horses floundering in the marshy ground besieged by recent rain. The river cliff cutting off their retreat, the little group of men, exhausted by flight and fear, had no option but to turn to defend themselves. Dragging their horses around, they faced the onslaught. A confusion of cries from animals and men came to the watchers across the land — faintly, like children playing — as steel clashed on steel. Men called out and then fell silent.

For a moment the watchers remained still, reading the movement at the cliff edge, then Isobel's father spoke quietly. "They come this way. Take what men we have and place them on the outer wall in plain sight. Reinforce the gates and put bowmen on the walls to cover the road. Is the message took to the village to make ready? Look to it!"

The sergeant shouted to the waiting men as his lord scanned those remaining of his household who had not yet been called to serve in the recent unrest — too young, too old; wanting in years, or too many, they were willing but no match for the victorious knights now riding towards them.

"Will you take your armour, my lord?" A boy proffered the padded jack.

Taking the sword held out to him by his young squire, Fenton shook his head. "No time. Arm yourself — these lords will not spare your youth, nor none else here. Not in these times." He secured the broad leather belt around his waist, adjusted the lie, and loosened the sword in its scabbard, feeling the welcome weight of it in his hand. Only then did he see his daughter, overlooked until that moment. "Isobel!" He reached out to pull her towards him, but she flinched from the unaccustomed anger in his face. Surprised, he said more gently, "I told you to go to your mother. It is not safe for you here. Go — *now!*"

She turned and ran diagonally from the gatehouse's wall-head to the door of the stair turret, down the narrow spiral where, hearing men rising the steps to take up positions on the parapet, she pushed into the door arch to the sergeant's chamber to let them pass. Unlatched, it swung open. Glancing to see if any would notice, she stepped inside. The shuttered windows stole light from the dull day and, safe from view, she paused to catch her breath, listening for the sound of challenge and answer from the heavy gates guarding the entrance beneath her. Unseen, heart jangling, she waited.

Isobel heard a shout from outside: "Will you not give way to your lord, Fenton?"

Her father's voice replied. "Open the gate. Open the gate for the Earl!" Then she heard him descend the same stair as she had done, passing by her hiding spot.

As his footfall faded, Isobel nipped across the chamber and slid onto the deep window embrasure facing inwards on the courtyard. She inched the plain-faced shutters open, adjusting her eye to the crack she had made just wide enough to see through without being seen. Metal hooves struck worn stone as men and horses, ducked and bunched by the confines of the gate, now spread in a fan into the courtyard, and came to a standstill some yards from where she watched yet close enough for her to see the horses' breath in the cold air curling like dragons' smoke.

She heard her father's voice before he came into view, tight with tension and breathless from haste. He bowed as low as his stiff limbs allowed. "Forgive me, my lord."

The man in front of him swung his metalled leg over his horse's back and landed with a greater degree of grace than the mired armour suggested. He allowed his squire to remove his helm and arming cap, revealing crow-black hair cut short.

"Has it been so long that you no longer recognise me?" A hand taller and still in the vigour of youth, the man came close and stood looking down at her father. "It has been too many years, Fenton." Then, abruptly, "There are matters to attend; you'll like as not thank me when done. We have old wounds that need scouring before they can heal." He gestured and the two men on horseback, hands still bound, were dragged from their saddles. His plated foot catching the high pommel, the younger of the two fell heavily against the stone, his horse shying at the metallic clash. Isobel's curiosity gave way to pity. The two men were forced to their knees, their heads hanging.

The Earl spoke, nodding in the direction of the older prisoner. "He became separated from the rest of his household. We've tracked him since dawn. He sought to make the river before the tide turned, perhaps take refuge in Hull and thence to France. They've removed all identification, but I never forget a face, nor the injury done by it."

"You bring war to my demesne, my lord," Fenton said.

"I bring you *justice*." In a stride, the Earl reached the nearest prisoner and, with his fist thrust under the man's chin, forced up his head. "Recognise him?"

Blood from a wound above the man's eye obscured part of his face, but Fenton drew back, his shoulders straightening. "Why have you brought him here?"

"Identify him."

No longer cowed but defiant, the wounded man looked up, his lip curling, and Fenton's demeanour changed. "Ralph Lacey."

"And his crime?"

"This is the man who killed your father, the Old Earl, I would swear to it."

"And gave you the wounds you now bear."

"Aye, and those, too." Fenton grimaced.

With a jerk of his head, the Earl indicated to the men-at-arms and the prisoners were shoved lower, exposing their necks.

"Not the boy. Not my nephew!" Lacey, rough-voiced from exhaustion, struggled to free himself from the metal foot against his back. "In God's name, mercy for the boy; I ask none for myself."

The Earl bent his head close to Lacey's face. "You showed none for my father," he hissed. "You cut him down though he lay wounded and cried out for quarter. You took his life when mercy was yours to grant and made a mockery of his state." Blue-grey eyes burned despite the ice in his deliberate articulation. "I will wipe your blood from the face of this land, and none shall remember you except your bastards, and they will curse your name." He stood and indicated to the men standing behind, but Fenton stepped towards the Earl and, bowing his head, spoke swiftly and earnestly and so softly Isobel could not hear. The Earl threw a look at Fenton, then at the kneeling pair, and gave the briefest of nods.

Now Fenton addressed Lacey directly, his bass tones gruff and strong with authority. "It pleases my lord Earl to grant the boy mercy on condition he hereby forswears allegiance to the former King, Henry Plantagenet, and his son, and he and his heirs will take an oath of fealty to King Edward, the fourth of that name, witnessed here by the grace of God and in the name of the king."

"By whose authority?" Lacey demanded.

"By my own hand as King's Justice of the Peace for these parts."

The prisoner cast a vicious look at the Earl, and then to the boy said, "Do it, Thomas."

The boy looked up and at that moment Isobel's head swam in recognition of the wide-eyed and ash-faced gangly youth. It was Thomas Lacey, her friend. Her own skin paled as he stumbled over the few phrases that would bind him to life without tasting the flavour of his words. When he finished, he turned his head from his uncle, biting his lip.

Lacey said, "You do what you must, Thomas." And then to the Earl: "May you live long enough to reap what you have sown."

As the long sword swung high, Lacey deliberately looked around him at the courtyard, the great hall, the tower, as if imprinting them on his memory. Then he raised his head skyward, his eyes squeezed shut, mouth moving silently. In the instant he opened his eyes, Isobel fancied he looked directly at her, and as his lips curved in what might have been a smile, the sword fell. His severed head struck the ground and rolled to a leaden halt, leaving the body upright and kneeling for a few seconds longer until falling forward, spilling its lifeblood — red against yellow — across the rough stone flags. It pooled in the hollows, gathered in the joints, and turned new grass livid. Mesmerised by the sightless eyes that continued to stare, Isobel clutched her hand and repeatedly pinched the flesh between thumb and forefinger until she controlled the fear that welled unbidden.

The Earl pursed his mouth, considering the carnage before him. "Bag it and take his head to the king. Send the body to his widow."

"And the lad, my lord?"

With dispassion, the Earl looked at the boy still kneeling by his uncle's body, lank, pale yellow hair damply clinging to cheeks rounded with youth and not yet stubbled with manhood.

"What do I care for the boy? He bears his family's shame. He is *nothing*." The Earl turned his back and stood for a moment with his hands on his hips contemplating the blank face of the sky. Then he breathed out. "It is done," he said. "Justice is served."

PART ONE

CHAPTER ONE

Four years later: Spring, 1469

"Alfred, you are crushing the plants! Get off and take your smelly bone with you!" Isobel hauled the long-limbed dog off the cuttings' bed, and he loped onto the path, showering soil from his shaggy fur. She surveyed the damage — a few bent tender stems that would recover as they grew — decided the dog would be forgiven, and turned back to where her gardener was fumbling a cutting. "No, John, not like that, or it will fail to take root. Like this." Isobel took the blade from his big hands and cleanly sliced at an angle through the stem, narrowly catching the expression on the young man's round face. "And you need not look at me that way."

She handed back the knife and sank the new cutting into the fresh-sifted soil of the raised border sheltered from the east wind by the high brick wall. "Water it well; this warm weather will help it take." She brushed specks of soil from her hands and wiped them on the coarse cloth of the gardening apron protecting her skirts.

"Buena," she called, and an older woman, once dark-haired and handsome, appeared around the side of the trellised arbour, carrying a woven basket. "Have you the seed?" The woman, her pronounced cheekbones and sallow olive skin making her gaunt, indicated the basket and small bundles of twisted cloth, lying among strips of green bark and the gloves Isobel should have been wearing. "Give them to John. He can sow them when he has finished here." Isobel heard a barely audible sigh from behind her. "After he has taken his dinner," she added, trying not to smile and already leaning towards the other woman to inspect the contents of the basket.

She picked out a vivid strap of bark. "With the sap still green, these will have much potency, so my lady mother would say," she murmured.

The older woman grunted a response meant to comfort, but Isobel turned away at the sound of a two-note whistle — high then low. A tall, fair-haired youth, of perhaps a few years her senior, stooped under the low-arched gateway to the garden, raised a hand in greeting, then lowered it awkwardly on seeing Isobel's surprise. Leaping the woven willow hurdles separating the narrow borders each side of the path, he came to a breathless stop in front of her, his taut doublet bearing witness to broadening shoulders as he strained to control his breathing.

As Isobel rose, a strand of hair loosened by the breeze tickled her ear and she used the back of her hand to brush it aside, leaving a smudge of mud on her cheek. "Thomas. I did not expect to see you today."

"Sir Geoffrey said you were in your garden." He frowned at her soil-smeared apron. "He said that I might speak with you."

Replacing the bark strips in the basket, she said, "Why?"

He noticed her caution. "And why should I not? Come, I would speak with you alone." He took her hand and pulled her towards the greater seclusion of the arbour, where buds broke the reddened stems of the twisted plants covering it. Picking up his bone, Alfred followed them with his loping gait.

Once inside and free from the curious eyes of the gardeners, Thomas bent to kiss Isobel, but she broke away laughing before his lips made contact with her own. "You said you wanted to talk, Thomas!"

He grinned and pulled her to sit by him on the broad stone seat instead. He smelled of horse and leather, and the damp air of the river.

"Where have you been?"

Removing his riding gloves, he reached inside his close-fitting doublet and withdrew a small packet. "To our manor across the river and thence to Hull, to get you this." He pressed a silk-soft bundle, warmed by his body, into her hand and held it there longer than he needed. Isobel eased her hand from under his to look at what lay there. "It's Genoese silk. As the ship brought it into harbour, Queen Elizabeth herself was said to be so desirous of it that the whole consignment was bought before it reached land."

Isobel let the length of blue-green ribbon, the colour of rue and woven with silver, unroll in a lustrous fall in the half-light of the arbour. "It *is* beautiful. How came you by this if the queen bought it?"

Stretching until his toes touched the sunlight at the arbour entrance, Thomas reminded Isobel of a sandy-coloured cat, all skinny-bellied and smug as it spread out in the warmth of a good hearth. "I have some influence. The ship's master was pleased to do me this service."

His nonchalance failed to impress. Isobel poked his stomach. "What influence? Come, tell me."

He caught her hand. "A kiss first, in payment."

Pushing him away, she became conscious of his greater strength and ducked sideways under his arm to stand up. "A gift requires no payment, Thomas, and I cannot be bought."

Still sitting, he tried to grab the ribbon from her, but she snatched it and hid it behind her back.

Thomas held out his hand, trying to look serious like his father, but failing. "Give me the ribbon back, then, and I will find another sweetheart who will wear it for me."

Isobel stuck out her chin, dangling the ribbon in front of him. "So I will," she declared, handing it to him, and immediately regretted it as his smile faded and his eyes dulled. "No, Thomas, it is mine and I am thankful for it." She bent down and kissed him swiftly on his cheek. "There, now you know I am. Tell me what influence you have in Hull?"

His fingers briefly caressed his cheek where her lips had lain before he looked at her again and she saw herself forgiven.

"I merely mentioned your father, and the ship's master made this little gift to me." He hesitated at her expression. "Why should I not? It is nothing; I thought it would please you…"

"The ribbon — or that you used my father's name to secure it? Thomas, how *could* you? My father holds his office from the king and will not see it abused. Is the custom paid?" She ground her teeth when he didn't answer. "He will be furious. What did you think to do?"

He rose to his feet. "I wished to please you. Isobel … do not tell him. It is a trifle. I wanted you to have something only the queen would wear."

"I am not the queen," she answered, angry, "and nor are you the king to use my father's name so. Here — take it." Shoving the silk into his hand, she turned her head, not daring to look at him in case she saw his rejection and softened.

He moved closer, trying to see into her face. "You shall be my queen, Isobel. Look at me, be not so harsh."

Within the confines of the arbour she backed away and thorns snagged her hair. She put up a hand to free herself but pricked her skin instead. Cross, she sucked at the bead of blood and Thomas smiled at her familiar impatience.

"Wait, be still." He unwound the threads of her shining hair, smoothing it with his palm, his touch becoming a caress.

She twitched away. "Thomas, don't…"

He tutted in the peculiar way he had of pressing the tip of his tongue behind his two front teeth. A slow tut, and one he had taken to using lately when showing his displeasure. He withdrew his hand, looking disgruntled. "You should cover your hair. It is not seemly to have it loose; the men were watching you."

Her mouth pressed into a stubborn line. "It is of no import to them and anyway, I am unwed, and this is *my* garden. I will do as I please."

Puffing out his chest, he assumed his full height and as much dignity as he could muster in such a small space. "When we are married, you will do as *I* please." The cat had become a cock, fluffed up and vivid in his fine feathers of red wool fastened with silver.

Isobel imagined his next words might be crowed and her lips quivered on the verge of laughter. "We are not even betrothed," she reminded him.

He forgot to be haughty in his eagerness. "But soon will be. That is what I came to tell you. My father wishes to make a contract now I have reached my majority, and will talk to Sir Geoffrey. Isobel, we can be wed this side of Michaelmas — in the summer, perhaps."

Her inclination to smile evaporated. "Not until I am eighteen, Thomas. I cannot marry until then and that is two years away."

"You can persuade your father; I know you can. He will do anything you ask of him."

"My mother made him promise —"

"Isobel, your mother is dead."

Isobel turned her back on him and fiddled with a rose stem loosened by a winter storm.

"I mean that she has been gone, may she find eternal peace, for nigh on two years —"

"One and a half."

"One and a half years, and might there not be room to reconsider? Did she not wish you to make a good match? And you want it too, don't you, Isobel?"

Isobel found the tattered end of the twine and re-secured the stem without answering.

"Leave that be, and tell me," he pressed.

She followed the stems upwards with light fingers, curving the tips around the thorns, feeling the roughened bark of the old wood and the silk-skin of the new. "She planted this rose with her own hands when she bore me and tended it every year that I can remember. She said that I and the rose would grow together."

Hardly glancing at the plant, Thomas saw nothing but bare wood and spite. "Isobel, you think more of your garden than you do me."

She came back from her memory and looked at him, saw the growing manhood in the shadow on his jaw, the brash shock of hair the colour of yellow clay, eyes as light blue as the sky before sunset. She had known his face for much of her life and never thought twice about it. Now he was asking her to make it part of her future and the twist of uncertainty she felt disturbed her.

"But I might not wish to marry," she announced, watching him pale and then flush as he saw she teased. "I might enter the convent and live out my life as a nun."

Before he could answer, she danced out of the arbour into the welcome warmth with the dog bounding in front of her, and down the narrow path between borders where new shoots ruptured the earth as they pushed towards the sun. Thomas caught up with her, slipping his arm around her waist. Isobel was aware of Buena's watchful gaze. The woman had not moved from where she stood before.

"You are not meant for a nunnery," he whispered into Isobel's ear, squeezing her hip through the thick cloth of her skirts. "You are not obedient enough to be a nun. I'll tame you, my Bel." He let go abruptly as Buena approached, returning her resentful glare. "And you will have a more suitable servant woman when we wed."

Isobel bristled at his use of her fond name and at his threat. "I have Buena; I need none other."

"You will be my wife, and you will have what I give you. You shall be Lady Lacey, and when I inherit —"

"You are too ready for your father's death!"

"Though it please God he remains in health," he continued, "*when* my father dies, I shall inherit my uncle's title. And together with your lands —"

"And you are too eager for my father's," she snapped. "I wonder if you think of aught else."

"It is not *all* I think about." Isobel pushed past him, but he caught her by the elbow and lowered his voice. "Do you not think of it, too? The king's wife is nothing compared with you. Be queen of my bed and my heart."

She did not know what to think. Since childhood they had been used to each other's company until Thomas had been sent to train in the household of his uncle, and then everything had changed. She pushed aside the memory of his terrified face and the grinning death-head of his uncle lying in the courtyard. Now the boy she once considered a brother spoke of land and love in a way that made her feel he knew much more about them both, a world with which she had yet to become familiar. Isobel felt a flutter of regret at the passing innocence of their friendship.

"Thomas, take a care how you speak of the queen. My father will not brook any treason, no matter how slight."

"Treason? How can it be treason if none but us hear it? And you will not speak of it, will you, Isobel?" His voice had taken an edge and she glanced at him, uncertain for the first time, but he unfurled the ribbon, wrapping it around her hair in an attempt to pull her close to him.

"I must ensure my father takes his dinner," she said quietly and, gathering her skirts and taking the ribbon from her hair, started to make her way down the paths towards the gate in the wall.

"He is in good health?" Thomas called after her.

"He is well enough," she said without looking back.

"Fit for a queen," her father remarked, holding the length of ribbon to his good eye and feeling the quality slip through his scarred fingers, "and for my daughter. What did young Thomas want in exchange for this treasure?"

With thyme-scented soap, Isobel concentrated on removing the ingrained earth from around her nails, watching it dissolve and fall to the bottom of the copper basin. There would be little point in prevaricating. She avoided the subjects of the attempted intimacy and the method by which Thomas had acquired the silk, as she thought her father would have suspicion of both, and she would not insult him by refuting it. "For me to talk to you."

"Ah, I wondered."

She dried her hands on the fringed linen cloth, handed it to Buena, and plucked the silk from her father. In her chair by the solar fire, she proceeded to roll the ribbon, pressing it against her thigh as she did so. Sitting stiffly, Geoffrey Fenton stretched his damaged leg before the hearth and watched her. Alfred finished cleaning his paws and, in laying his greying chin upon them, gazed at his master from beneath whiskery brows.

"Isobel, you have only to ask, you know that."

She finished her task and had nothing else to occupy her hands, so studied them instead. "I know, Fader, but my lady mother wished I should not marry until I am eighteen."

"Your mother had her reasons, but I must look to your settlement and your future." The last of the sun slipped from the windows and with it the warmth of the spring day. Fenton watched the sky pale through the uneven glass. "Do you have your doubts about this young man?"

"As much as you do, Fader."

He grunted a laugh. "Aye, well, you are my daughter there at least — if not by looks, by inclination. My caution is bred of too many years watching men climb over one another's backs to be surprised by it when I see it in my neighbour. But treachery … that is hard to forget in a man even though he would have me do so."

"Why do you let Lord Lacey court your favour if his brother fought against the king?"

Fenton paused before answering. "There are many wounds this conflict has so lately wrought, and we must heal them or see them fester and destroy us all, Isobel. Ambition need be no curb to a match between the families; it has its place. Would you say Thomas has ambition?"

"I think so."

Fenton nodded slowly. "I see as much. His family served the old king." He lifted his hand to stop Isobel's protest. "Nay, it is not treason to say so, child. They had reason to be loyal. The

Laceys prospered under King Henry. All these lands south of the river — including our own — were owned by Ralph Lacey, and a title with them." He eased his bones, drawing the edges of his long robe over his calves to trap the warmth.

Isobel remembered the years Thomas spent in the service of Lord Lacey when still only a child, how he returned home following his uncle's treason — changed, older, with an unvoiced motivation — but still Thomas for all that.

"Ambition," her father continued, "will keep Henry Lacey to heel and young Thomas keen to serve. Lacey has the wits to know which king will best provide, and he has sought King Edward's favour since his brother's attainder."

"But the king does not trust him?"

"His Grace is counselled against it by those who bear the wounds of Lacey's betrayal hardest." His silver cup gleamed in the light of the fire as he drank. He wiped his top lip with his thumb and held the cup at an angle so that he could make out the noble arms it bore. "Forgiveness, Isobel, is the luxury of those who have nothing to forgive. Or the dead," he added, almost to himself. "Still, he has proved loyal since and has much to gain by it — as have you."

"Me?"

"When I die… Hush, I know, I know, but wishing it otherwise will not change the hours of the day nor the course of my life. When I die, I have no male heir to protect you, or you an uncle or cousin who will offer guidance. We must look to a husband for you, Isobel, one with status and prospect of advancement. You are my child, and I will have you settled before my death because I cannot face it without knowing you have a position of standing."

"I will follow Agnes into the nunnery," she began.

He laughed. "You will follow Agnes because she is your friend, not because you offer service to God, and that is not reason enough. And I would…" His smile softened. "I would be content knowing that a little of your mother still lives in the children you bear, even if I should not live to see it." He bent his head.

Isobel dropped to her knees next to him and laid her hand on his arm. "I miss her, too, Fader."

Tenderly, Geoffrey Fenton kissed his daughter's raised forehead. "Being twice her age when we wed, I did not think to bury her. But she gave me a child and for that I give thanks. You are so like her, Isobel, I wonder sometimes that she does not breathe again in you."

With the dog's contented wheezing accompanying them, they fell into silence, each with their own thoughts, the fire warming their faces as the chill of spring cooled their backs.

Finally, Fenton broke the stillness. "Why did you accept Thomas's gift?"

Startled, she answered before thinking. "I did not know how to refuse it."

Was that disappointment she saw in her father's face, or resignation? But he merely nodded as if he understood her reason, patted her hand, and pulled himself to his feet.

"I have reached such an age that sitting too long is as grievous as standing." He took a few steps to the fireplace and, bracing outstretched arms against the stone hood, eased his back. "I think this marriage will bide a while longer, although I dare say Henry Lacey will press his case. He'll want to secure the match for his son and the lands that go with it as surely as I want to have you safe. I need to move this leg; mind the way there."

Isobel moved to let him pass, taking the crudely embroidered scarlet cushion she had made him as a child to soften the floor beneath her, and watched him pace the room, giving little shakes of his leg every now and then. Idly marking out the stitches forming his device and her mother's dainty flower-heads in a circle around it, she said, "Thomas might marry elsewhere."

"He might," her father conceded, "but he will not. You are a pretty prize with none to contest your inheritance and — if he plays his hand with care — the offices granted by the king. This manor once belonged to his family, as you well know, and only by marriage will it return to them."

Isobel glanced at the painted roundels in the window. The Lacey pike swam in one, while in the other, the Fenton heron pierced a similar fish — hardly a subtle representation of Fenton's rise at the cost of the Lacey family.

"Yes, well," her father smiled, a touch rueful, "fortunes wax and wane as the wheel turns. The Duke of York gave the manor to Old Earl Langton, and he in turn bestowed it on me."

"Why, Fader? I never understood why when he had sons to inherit."

Fenton sucked his teeth, still contemplating the window. "Mmm? Well, let us say that I rendered a service to the Old Earl for which I was well rewarded."

"And is that why you serve his son, Fader, when you could serve my Lord of Warwick, or … or none at all?"

"You must understand the bonds of fealty that tie this family to the Earl, Isobel," he said quietly. "My family have served the Langtons for generations, though more humbly than I am fortunate to do now, and I have been compensated richly for that service."

Isobel snorted less than daintily, startling the dog. "With the loss of an eye and a leg that pains you each time you walk."

"I would have none of this, I would not have *you*, if it were not for the Old Earl. I had been content advising him in minor legal matters until called to arms. He raised me up beyond my expectations, rewarded my loyalty with this manor. And without this manor and the offices granted to me, I could not have wooed your mother and won her. As for this leg —" he tapped it lightly — "it earned me a knighthood and the manors to support it. Aye, I served him well, but I am the richer for it." Lifting her chin with his knobbly forefinger, he kissed her forehead.

"But if the Old Earl served the Duke of York, did not that make him a traitor when the duke took up arms against the king? And…" she hesitated, "…if *he* was a traitor, then … are you also in serving the Earl?"

"If King Henry had been fit to rule, the Duke of York — King Edward's father — would have had no cause to press his claim to the throne."

"Yes," she protested, becoming animated, "but King Henry was still the *king* … still *is* a king now. King Henry and King Edward are both anointed; how can a man serve one king without being traitor to the other? It seems to me that Lord Lacey's brother was only a traitor because King Henry was defeated."

Her father looked sharply at her. "Has Thomas said aught about the matter?"

"No, I do not talk about such things with him; I know it to be a matter of delicacy."

"As your husband, he will expect you to take his part."

"I am not yet his wife, Fader."

"Indeed, you are not. This matter of kingship, of fealty, is grievous." He shook his head. "This division in our land must be resolved or else, like an ulcer, it will keep returning to haunt the peace and prosperity of it."

"If only men were not so greedy for land and lordship."

"Greed? Is that how you see it? God's teeth, Isobel! I am sorry if that is what you perceive because I will have failed to teach you anything if it is so." His face had taken on an unnaturally harsh hue that faded to his usual pallor as he calmed. "It is not your fault. How can you be expected to understand when you are young, and I have kept you from the world?"

"I understand enough. Have you not taught me that honour and loyalty are the duty of all subjects? The Duke of York was King Henry's subject before his son — King Edward — took the throne. When did it become right for the Duke of York to withdraw his service and make his own claim?"

"When King Henry could no longer rule. A king has a duty to rule, just as a lord does. Think of it this way: if I did not govern my lands, what would happen?"

She peered at the ceiling, thinking. "The fields would not be sown or harvested —"

"And?"

"Husbandmen would cut our wood and take our game without licence."

"And?"

"They wouldn't pay their rent. Or their milling dues. Or the customs on fishing rights. And they'd squabble over the common land and who tills what, when. *Again*."

"And who settles such disputes, Isobel?" he asked, softly.

"Oliver Waveney, the reeve."

"And whom does the reeve serve?"

"You, Fader."

"And when Lord Brough decides he will burn John Appleyard from his cot, steal his pigs, and rape Mary, his wife, who will stop him?"

"You will."

"Why?"

"Because you are John's lord, and it is your duty to protect him."

"Why?"

"Because … because he serves you."

He sat back. "Aye, and so it is with the king — any king. It is a king's duty to govern, to make law — and war, when warranted — defend his people; rule with wisdom, strength, and mercy. And collect taxes. A strong king deserves loyalty, demands respect. King Henry could not protect his people from the one thing they feared most."

"What is that?"

"Themselves. People like to be ruled. Oh, they'll pull against the traces, spend evenings muttering into their ale, but while they have ale to drink and coin to spend on it, that's where it'll stop because what is worse than rule, is none at all, and they know it. Look…" He pulled himself forward in his chair, beckoning her to bring the bowl and set it before him on his footstool. "See this earth and sand from your garden?" He swirled the water, the grains caught in suspended agitation at the very centre. "When a country is stirred against itself, the people go this way and that seeking certainty where there is none. They fight, they quarrel — neighbour against neighbour, father against son — until such time as strong lords appear from the chaos — see — there." He pointed to several larger grains that had settled to the bottom of the bowl and a cluster of smaller ones gathered around them. "Strength is certainty, like the walls of this house, and it attracts those who have no leadership in themselves and rely on others to supply it. King Henry's rule failed because he was not fit to lead. The Dukes of York and Somerset — both able men — claimed the right of birth and lordship to provide that leadership, not —" he emphasised before Isobel could suggest it — "through base greed — although the rewards were as great as the stakes they diced with — but to establish rule. Rule. Law. Prosperity. Honour." With each word, he stabbed his wet finger on the arm of his chair, leaving glossy prints that soon faded. "Somebody had to settle the waters of this country, Isobel. York died in the attempt, but his son now sits where Henry once did, and has proved himself able."

"But if King Edward is a strong king, why is there still unrest? Surely people must see he has brought peace to England?"

"Look in the bowl again and tell me what you see."

Isobel peered through the water into the shiny depths, where the fine sediments now formed a thin layer like mist on the bottom, and a few outcrops of larger grit dimpled the silky surface. "There are several bigger grains, quite a lot of smaller ones — of sand, I think — and a layer of fine mud across the bottom."

"And which is the biggest?"

Chewing her bottom lip, she measured each with her eye. "I cannot be certain, but that one looks a little bigger. I think."

"And so it is. After the country is shaken and a great lord has settled to rule, there will be others who, with equal claim, look with envy upon the throne."

"Greed," she stated flatly.

"Greed in some, yes. Envy, perhaps, or a belief they have the ability or right to do better. For many it will be to secure their future and that of their family. Lords are men, and men are fallible, as God in Heaven knows. I serve the Earl; the Earl serves the House of York; and Edward of York is king, long may it please God."

"And, Fader, if another ruled instead of King Edward? Whom would you serve then?"

Any other father might have scolded his daughter for cross-examining him, but hers had taught her to question. He exhaled a sigh. "What would you do, my daughter, if your husband chose to follow a different banner?"

"I would…" She didn't know what she would do. Her father didn't press her for an answer but waited as she turned her thoughts inwards and interrogated her conscience. Alfred wheezed and jerked in his sleep, and finally Isobel looked up at her father. "If I swore fealty to a lord, then by my oath would I be bound."

"Even to death?" he asked.

She regarded him solemnly. "Even to death."

He brought his hands down on the arms of his chair with a decisive *thump*. "So be it. Honour defines this family, my little minnow; let loyalty be its watchword."

He found a space between the dog's paws to place his foot, brought his weight to bear on it, and stood carefully. He stepped over the animal and Alfred snored but did not move. "Eh, I wish I could sleep the sleep of this dog, troubled by nothing but hunting hare in his dreams. Of course," he said almost as an afterthought, except Isobel — watching him put his hands on his hips and easing his shoulders back — knew him better than that, "when you are a wife you must not be so quick with your tongue. Smile little, laugh less. Men do not like women to be so bold with their knowledge that it shows how wanting of it their menfolk are. Keep your thoughts to yourself and remember, not all who smile are your friends. You will know no other politics than your husband's. You will owe your duty to him in all things, whether it be your inclination or no."

Isobel snorted her indignation. "Then his politics had better be *mine*."

"In *all* things, Isobel. In law, you have no status other than your husband's. You are not answerable for your crimes or your debt. In law."

"And in conscience, Fader?"

"Ah, well that, my child, is entirely your own." He evaded Isobel's further questions. "Now, this marriage of which we speak. The boy is fond of you if the number of visits he pays is aught to measure by. I trust he shows you the respect you deserve?"

Isobel blushed, adjusting her skirts and rising to her feet to avoid answering. Alfred shuffled and flopped onto his side, taking up the entire hearth with his ungainly length.

"No matter. With Buena on guard your chastity is safe enough." He laughed. "With Buena in attendance it is a miracle you were conceived at all. Your mother prayed to the Virgin for a child, but it was I that supplied the key to the door and it is the key that won. I will give young Thomas a lock for your chamber as a bridal gift." Laughing heartily, he nonetheless saw Isobel colour, and curbed his humour. "Aye, well," he said, "enough on that matter for now. How fares your garden?"

She told him, aware that he had little interest in it but for the love of growing things she shared with her mother, and for that, he listened intently enough. "But Thomas does not like me to husband the land. He thinks I look like a yeoman's wife."

"Hah, he would not say so of your mother, and few women cultivate learning as you do. Do not mind him. You will become skilled at tempering his mood with soft words, and he will learn when to be master of you and when to allow you to sway him. These are things you will both learn with time. Let me sit again."

Isobel rolled Alfred out of the way so that her father could sit without treading on him. "As you did with my lady mother?"

"Your mother?" He stared into the heart of the fire without seeing. "Your noble mother bettered me in all things. She brought grace and beauty into this house. I could never be master of her; I had not the will to crush her light." His eyes closed at the remembrance and Isobel used the time to study his face. She had not noticed how grey he had become, how his once thick hair had thinned, how the strands of it imitated the lines on his face and the scar creasing his brow to his cheekbone. For all of that he looked well enough, and the fire brought warmth to his skin. He opened his eyes and she smiled.

"And you are the image of her. With her blood, she could have married anyone, but she chose to marry me. My life has been blessed by my wife and my daughter."

Isobel sidestepped his sentiment with a wave of her hand. "My lady mother used to say that about *you*." It was her father's turn to smile and, encouraged by his returning good humour, Isobel went on. "She did — she said that without you she would be nothing."

"She said that? What else?"

Cautioned by the turn in his voice, Isobel hesitated. "Nothing else. Why should she?"

Geoffrey Fenton didn't answer immediately but inspected his daughter's face and found the truth reflected in the steady gaze of her blue-edged eyes. Her mother's eyes. "I expect she spoke out of her illness," he said at last, turning his head and watching the fire consume new wood greedily like a hungry child. Isobel said nothing. She neither believed him nor thought he believed it. But her father never said something without meaning to, and meaning lay hidden behind the measure of his words. Rubbing a hand over his eyes, he blinked once and looked at her. "I am a little out of sorts tonight."

"Does your leg trouble you? I'll make you dwale to ease it and help you sleep."

"My leg? Aye, my leg troubles me right enough."

Isobel looked to the corner of the room where Buena stitched in the light of the cresset. "Buena, my casket," she instructed, taking her father's cup from him and pouring a little warmed wine into the base — ruby against silver. From her ivory casket she took honey, and into a small square of linen tied spices and fragrant bitter herbs as her mother had taught her.

Her father took the cup; she knew he would welcome the ease of sleep it would induce, but it was his bruised heart against which his hand pressed, and for that Isobel had no cure.

CHAPTER TWO

The warm promise of early spring breathed deceit, and during April rain fell, turning fields raw and heavy. Fresh growth drew back into the earth, stunted, to await the sun. The lean gap between the last of the winter stores and the new season's crops lengthened, until fat men became spare and mothers rubbed their children's bellies when they cried with hunger. Rumour grew, and, across the Humber, malcontent.

"Is there truth in the report?" Henry Lacey, long-faced and ever-vigilant, leaned back in his favourite chair making the frame creak and eyed Geoffrey Fenton with a calculating look. Fenton always knew a great deal more than he was willing to say. In his position as Justice of the Peace he had access to information destined for the king. Unfortunately, in Lacey's view, Fenton kept the information close, which meant that he in turn felt obliged to keep the careful man closer.

On this occasion, Lacey hoped to extract a little more than news of the unrest in the north. In his private chambers, where the fire warmed the rich colours of the newly acquired hangings on the walls and away from the curious ears of his retinue, Lacey proceeded to eel his way around Fenton's caution. "So, this rumour?"

Fenton smiled in the frustratingly oblique manner he had. "Little more than that. It will amount to nothing."

"It is said this Robin of Redesdale is in fact Sir John Conyers," Lacey probed.

"Is it?"

"I thought you might have knowledge of it." Lacey scratched at his high steeled hairline behind his ear, a previous fashion he clung to as he did to the memory of better days. "You have risen in the Earl's regard; you hold offices from the king himself and have the noblest connections. And your wife, may she have rest, was the fairest of high-born women, who would have graced Court had she not…" He trailed off.

Fenton smiled. "Had she not married me? Aye, I did indeed make a fortunate match," he concurred. "Which brings us to the subject of your concern this night, if I am not mistaken?"

He was not; Lacey relaxed into his chair. "This marriage, Geoffrey. We have long had an understanding and I would fain see it contracted. My son is keen to wed; his blood is as hot as ours once was, though it is so long ago my body has forgot the memory of it, even if a wench should lift her smock for me that I didn't have to pay for." Using the back of his hand, he wiped spittle from the corner of his mouth and leaned forward. "I would have him sire a son — unite our bloodlines, carry my name, bear the title and honour of the family…" He caught the faintest lift of a grizzled eyebrow but chose not to rise to the challenge. "Thomas will rebuild Lacey honour and our fortunes, be assured of it. If — *when* — he secures a position, he will prove his worth and the king will grant him the title my brother lost." With a note of urgency now, Lacey lowered his voice. "Geoffrey, with your influence, Thomas can find a position in the Earl's household. He needs to make his mark."

"You know the Earl will not be moved on that score."

"For your daughter's sake…"

Fenton seemed to consider that. "I will bring the matter to the Earl should—" he raised a finger to emphasise his line of reasoning — "it be meet to do so. I'll not test my lord if he declines to consider it. I've seen far better men than I fall because of it. But I will speak with him, aye, for the sake of our children — *both* of them."

Lacey leaned back, a satisfied gleam in his eyes. "And the contract?"

"As for the marriage," Fenton said, pushing down against the table and rising from his chair, "sleep will make the timing clear."

Lacey's ringed hand clasped Fenton's arm. "Let us be settled on this. Thomas will not wait so long that his seed loses the urgency of youth. Do you want to live to see your daughter's womb wither? And who will protect her should you no longer be able to do so?"

The implications were not lost. Fenton looked first at Lacey's hand, then into his face, and the man withdrew his hand. "That is a fine ring you wear, my lord. I believe I have not seen it before."

Lacey hardly disguised his impatience. "I am come into some good fortune of late, my friend. Let Isobel share in it; this has been put off for too long. Let them wed and be done."

"Michaelmas?" Isobel dropped the stems into the ewer, barely noticing the pleasing contrast of sulphur trumpets against pewter for which it had been selected, and turned to face her father. "The marriage is to be so soon?"

"It would be sooner if Henry Lacey had his way. As it is, Thomas will be gone from England to Calais for some months to try and seek a position to raise his prospects. You will marry on his return."

In the solar her mother had favoured above all other rooms, Isobel took her time arranging the flowers while she thought over her father's words. .She looked up and saw he had pressed his palm against his chest, his breathing laboured.

"Fader?"

He met her gaze. "It is for the best, Isobel. The sooner you wed the sooner I can rest at night. With this ferment in the north, I would be at ease knowing you have a strong husband and stout walls."

"I have a strong father and the walls here are as stout as any. Besides, Thomas has never been in battle as you have, and Lord Lacey — well, I do not know what *he* would do. Sue for peace with both sides if it gained him a groat and a manor."

He laughed. "I have not lifted a sword since Ralph Lacey's axe took the sight of my eye and a mace the use of my leg at Sandal over eight years ago. I have not had cause to keep more than an ageing sergeant-at-arms and a handful of trained men these past years, and even these walls cannot keep out a sustained assault. There is trouble brewing, Isobel. Men are hungry, and the disease of discontent grows large in empty bellies. This unrest in the north —" he shook his head — "perhaps it will settle with full stomachs. Perhaps not."

Isobel stopped fiddling with the flowers. "Have you word from Hull?"

"Too much that disquiets me and not enough to move on. What reports I send to the Earl are full of rumour, and the king will not act unless his revenue falls short or rebellion is raised, and neither be true at present."

Wiping a stray drop of water from the wood, Isobel returned to setting the stems straight. "Lord Lacey's brother fought against King Edward."

"Aye, and forfeited his title and his life for it. Have no fear, Henry Lacey won't risk it; he has too much to lose and this time the king will not be so forgiving."

With an involuntary shudder, Isobel had an image of a severed head and remembered with an unpleasant surge the stone stained red in her own courtyard. Over the years, the dead man's eyes had come to stare accusingly at her from her imagination as if she should have done more to save him from the vengeance of the Earl and the part her own father played in it.

She dismissed the thought and, picking up the ewer, found a place for it on the cupboard where the spring sun from the window opposite threw its shadow on the wood and burned the petals gold. Yet even such beauty failed to erase the memory. This dread that lodged deep within her, this fear of change unlooked for and without cause or remedy. Who could say what a day might bring? And her father? Who would read to him and ease his loss if her husband forbad it? Who would sit through the night with him and make physic for his pain?

Geoffrey Fenton returned to his chair, arranging the cushion to suit his back. She went to help him.

"Bel, have you taken time with your Latin today?" Isobel pulled a face. "I thought not. Fetch whatever pleases you and I will hear your lesson ere we sup." Her eyes strayed to the window, and he chuckled his throaty laugh, lightly tapping her forehead with the tip of his finger. "Nay, but your garden will wait awhile, child; there will be time enough to tend it. Let us plant some seeds of wisdom in the demesne of your mind while you are young enough to tend them."

Smiling, Isobel went to the reading table where her father kept his books and his stand, calling back over her shoulder as she selected a book, "Thomas dislikes *anything* to do with gardens, especially chives and wild garlic. Nor, he says, should I know Latin. He says that the only proper occupation for a woman of good breeding is to know her husband's needs, but he would not say what they might be." She thought she heard her father choke, but when she returned to his side bearing the book bound in its protective chemise of leather, he was busily examining the frayed tassel on the end of his paternoster and seemed perfectly well.

"I think, my daughter, that young Thomas would do well to look to bettering his own mind rather than trying to curb yours, for which I wish him good fortune if he believes he will succeed. When I tried with your dearest mother, she soon educated me, and I am the richer for it, although I did not say so at the time."

Isobel dragged her chair close to his.

"I must caution you against eating chives and garlic if you want your marriage bed blessed with children."

"But I like chives!" she protested.

"That, my dearest minnow, is not the point. Now, what have you brought to read to me? Ah, a history of Rome; it is well chosen. Pray, read on."

A few days later, Isobel was sitting on the turf bench within the sun-gilded walls of the gardens. She shook her hair free of the confines of her headdress, and raised her face to the sky. Buena clicked her fingers in disapproval.

"Just a little while, Bayna; it is not yet so hot, and no one is here to see. Besides, I do not know if I will be able to do so when I marry. Lord Lacey has no need for a pleasance and Thomas has no interest in maintaining one." She pouted her displeasure and squinted in the light. "He talks of love but has feet of iron; he crushed violets underfoot when we walked by the river and laughed when I chided him."

A shadow cast across her face as Buena came between her and the sun.

Isobel leaned sideways to find its warmth, once more turning her hair to burnished honey. She pulled on the leather gloves Buena insisted she wore to protect her hands. "I asked him if he will let me have my garden, but all he wanted to talk about is when he leaves for Calais and what he hopes to do there. And I am not interested in Lord So-and-So or whether a position might be found here or there although he says I must be." She plucked a stray stem of grass from between two stones. "I do not like to be told '*must*' or '*shall*' or '*will*', or with whom I should talk and how to wear my hair."

Here, in her private garden separated from the manor buildings by high walls all of its own, Isobel breathed deeply, letting the tensions of the past few weeks lift and fade. Lightly touching the other woman on her arm, she peered into her face. "And you shall be my servant, Buena. You will always have a place with me."

Breaking the watchful lines of her face, Buena smiled, brown eyes slanting upwards in deep creases, skin tautened over prominent cheekbones already darkening at the touch of the sun. Bending down, she kissed Isobel on each cheek.

"Now," Isobel declared, standing suddenly and shaking free of her mood, "we have much to do. The chamomile is barely grown, and the season is so late I wonder if we can catch up with the loss. Are the strewing herbs taken to the house? When John finishes sowing his field, he is promised here, and none too soon."

Lifting the scent of apple blossom from the garden orchard, the increasing warmth of the day grew round and soft, but the bell from the nearby church rang for mid-morning prayers and dinner. With some reluctance, Isobel gathered the last of the early herbs and placed them in the flat-bottomed basket next to the flowers. Together she and Buena made their way up the cutting garden's narrow paths, past beds of grey-green lavender basking in the sun, and through the door in the wall to the world beyond. Picking up speed now as she heard the urgency of the bells, she became aware of a different rhythm and saw John's sturdy form pounding its way up the path from the manor. He came to a halt in front of her and, panting, bowed.

"John, you make haste in the wrong direction," Isobel said, nonetheless pleased he seemed so eager to tend her garden.

Red-faced and breathless, John managed, "My lady, a fine company is come."

She blinked, surprised. "None is expected."

"'Tis a great noble party, my lady."

"Is my father returned?"

His round, good-natured face puckered in anxiety. "Nay, m'lady, and the noble lord 'as taken injury; the grooms say there is much blood."

For a heart-stopping moment, Isobel visualised metalled men and the heaving flanks of horses, marled mud, and gore. Then she recovered her wits. "Where are they?"

"The great hall, m'lady. The steward is still abroad wi' thy lord sire. The sergeant asks will you 'tend?"

If she hesitated it was because, in her sixteen years, Isobel had never before been called upon to exercise such a duty, but with her father absent and their steward, Arthur Moynes, with him, it fell to her. The bell had stopped its tolling as if waiting for her response. She removed her apron, neatened her hair with the flat of her hand, and took the basket from her maid's arm.

"Buena, fetch my casket. John, go to the kitchens and have them boil fresh-drawn water and bring it to the hall. Be quick!"

The courtyard swarmed with unfamiliar faces bearing weapons of the chase: long-limbed hunting dogs in wide metal collars strained on leashes or lay panting in the shadow of the wall. Liveried men in yellow and blue, huntsmen in Lincoln green; and her own household — drab in comparison —

carrying water from the well to men and dogs under the watchful eye of the fewterers. Hastily tethered to a wall ring, Alfred bayed at the strangers as horses, tended by stable lads, trod the stone of the court. From one, the carcass of a roebuck was dragged, its antlers scraping the ground. The noise and smell of it filled her head, the foreign voices of man and beast, sweat of horses, and, upon the steps to her own great hall, blood browning in the sun. Voices, uncowed by their surroundings, unsolicitous and without restraint, came from inside the great hall.

Isobel entered the passage, pausing by the door of the screen wall, and peered around the edge. George, her father's sergeant-at-arms looked up to see Isobel's cautious eye, and his own widened with relief. He hurried over and gave a short bow.

"My lady, you are come," George said needlessly, his weathered features glistening with heat. "With my lord away, I knew not what else t' do." He indicated to the group of men gathered by the fireplace and the new-lit fire, two dressed for the kill, another wearing black and a fixed smile. One, sitting in her father's great chair with his back to her, cradled his forearm in his other hand.

"Who are they?" she whispered. "What do they want?"

He cast a furtive glance in their direction. "It's the Earl, m'lady."

"The *Earl?*" Her hand twitched to her throat. "Is he injured?"

George nodded in confirmation. She debated retreating to the garden until they gave up waiting and went away, or perhaps her father would return and deal with the Earl himself; but George had that expectant look that said she could do neither, so she had to do something.

Setting the basket aside, Isobel took courage with both hands, and entered the hall. Conscious of the voices dying as, one by one, the men noticed her presence, she kept her eyes lowered, sinking into a deep curtsy as she neared the Earl, and stayed there. One of the men laughed. Movement came from the chair as the Earl turned. She imagined him examining her day gown, unruly hair and stained fingers, finding her wanting in manner and bearing. Then he spoke — assured, cool, and with a touch of arrogance, making her instantly nervous. She was unaccustomed to feeling nervous, not here, not in her own home.

"Such courtly deference as would befit the king; I wonder what His Grace would make of it?" More laughter, this time with an edge. "Rise, lady, and tell me your name."

Isobel rose as bidden, still keeping her eyes lowered until she heard a breath, sudden and sharply indrawn. She raised them to find the Earl staring at her: hard eyes, the grey made brighter by the dark lashes surrounding them, eyes she remembered from the darkest of dreams. They burrowed under her skin until she blanched beneath his gaze and felt her tongue pinned to the roof of her mouth.

"My lord asks your name, lady," his big-framed companion reminded her, although not unkindly.

"I know who this is," the Earl said almost to himself, continuing to flay her with his eyes until she felt raw and exposed and she looked away. "Where is Fenton?"

Isobel swallowed the knot encasing her throat. "My father presides over the courts baron, my lord. He returns today." She couldn't tell whether that annoyed the Earl; his face remained immobile.

"And he leaves a child to run his affairs and no one to attend me. I might take offence."

Was he jesting? Resisting the urge to twist her hands, she clasped them in front of her. "I will attend, my lord, if it please you." She heard her voice falter, become thin, and sought iron from somewhere inside her to give it strength.

His look became appraising. "And how will you do that?"

She gestured. "Your arm, my lord; I have a little skill."

There was a slight lift to one side of his mouth. "I am sure of it. Here, tend it if you will." He moved his hand from his forearm for her to see. A ragged tear in the fabric of his sleeve, stained darker than the surrounding cloth and about four inches long, marked the site of the wound. "Come closer, I will not bite." Again, there was low laughter, as if he had made a joke.

She did so and then more boldly as she saw a slow drip of blood form on the end of his finger and fall to the floor where it soaked into the plaited rush matting. Another joined it, more quickly this time, running down his hand, pausing at the dyke of the great ring on his finger, mounting, and flowing to the tip.

Isobel parted the torn cloth and the reddened shirt beneath. Bloodied skin oozed. She looked around for Buena and saw instead one of the kitchen staff bearing a heavy jug, another with a bowl and folded strips of linen cloth.

"Place the jug in the fire, the bowl here on its stand on the table by me. Be quick! Where is my casket?" Exasperated, she turned again to find Buena watching from the door to the stair, the ivory box in both hands. Isobel frowned, beckoned, but Buena handed the casket to the returning kitchen servant and withdrew into the shadows.

Stemming her annoyance, Isobel resumed her task. She washed her hands, discarded the water, then had the bowl filled afresh to which she added vinegar from a flask. With careful fingers, she folded back the loosened sleeves of silk, wool, and fine linen, revealing the Earl's muscled forearm, the dark hairs matted with drying blood. Dipping folded cloths into the water, she carefully worked the area until it lay clear for her inspection. "What made this, my lord?"

"The roebuck we pursued had no wish to be caught."

"Nor his throat cut, hey, my lord?" a jocular voice enjoined from the heavily built man, his broad back to the fire. He nudged the fair-haired youth next to him and winked.

Isobel glanced at the Earl's quilted doublet tarnished with the animal's lifeblood, then regretted raising her eyes as she met those of the Earl's, darkly mocking. She hurriedly lowered them. "The animal's teeth made this injury?" she asked, forgetting to address him with proper dignity.

"Its antler. It made poor sport."

Beef-voiced and built like a butcher, the genial man guffawed. "Not like the he-boar you wrestled last winter, my lord. Tore its tusk near clean from its head before you let the dogs to it. That made a fine show." He made a wrenching motion with his hands, making the rich brocade he wore flap and the folds of loose skin of his jowls shudder.

The Earl didn't answer and instead watched as Isobel focused on drawing fragrant items from the intricately carved ivory casket now beside her on the table. Acutely aware of being observed, she scooped a heavy golden liquid from a jar, added drops of pale vinegar and a scattering of flowers and spices, and proceeded to grind them together using a short, twisting motion that released a sweetly astringent perfume to scent the air. The resulting paste she spooned onto a square of thin cloth, placed another over it, and the whole over the wound, binding it in place with linen strips.

She felt the muscles of his arm flinch as the plaster made contact with his open flesh. About to apologise, Isobel opened her mouth, but closed it as she met the Earl's challenging gaze. "It is done, my lord," she said quietly, and backed away to the side of the table to pack the casket.

"And it is done well," he said, standing and examining the neat bindings. Then, lifting his arm, he flexed it.

"Do not move it so!" Isobel exclaimed, flushing as his mouth hardened. "My lord, please, it needs to heal," she added in helpless mitigation.

Outside, dogs erupting in a fury of barking saved her from censure.

Slowly the Earl looked away from her face to follow the interruption. "Ah, Fenton is returned."

Sure enough, her father made halting progress towards them, the edges of his riding cloak catching around his legs in his haste. Breaths came hard to him as he bowed low. Careless of his bound arm, the Earl strode forward, clasping Fenton at each shoulder in greeting.

"Well met, Sir Geoffrey. I am come to beg a little of your hospitality, if you will entertain it, and offer redress for straying on your land." He held his arm aloft. "The roebuck has already exacted its revenge; I ask you to show me more mercy."

Fenton's brow creased. "You are injured, my lord?"

"No longer; your daughter has cured all — except my thirst."

Isobel, colouring at her omission, attempted to remain still when all she wanted to do was run back to her garden and hide.

Fenton nodded sharply to the steward who barked an order, then, placing his hand over his breast, inclined his head. "You honour us with your presence, my lord. Forgive my absence and accept what little hospitality I might offer. My lord Langton." Bowing again, he addressed a man standing alone by the window whom Isobel had failed to notice before now. Hair the colour of old oak gleamed in the stronger light as the man tilted his head in acknowledgement, but he did not smile, and returned to his solitary occupation of studying the sky.

"Lord Raseby, Lord Dalton." Fenton addressed the other men — the genial butcher and the bored youth. To the dark-haired man, whose lips curved permanently upwards but whose eyes failed to reflect the humour of his mouth, he merely said, "Master Sawcliffe." And then, "I will send for my physician to attend you, my lord."

The Earl demonstrated the use of his damaged arm. "You see that I have no need of a physician. I am ably enough repaired and the better for it."

"I thank you, my lord. My daughter has neat hands and a way with healing, as she has oft shown. Rarely does she fail to restore to health that to which she sets her mind."

"My lady has a touch of magic about her," the oil-smooth man with the enduring smile slid in, waving away the wine cup offered to him without looking.

"Nay, Master Sawcliffe," Fenton said sharply, "there is no magic in this house, may it please God."

Sawcliffe angled an eyebrow over his heavy-lidded eyes as if he begged to differ, and, sensing her father's rising anger, Isobel quickly interjected. "The wound is no more than a scratch. A child would barely notice."

"The little lady believes you make too much of your injury, my lord!" Raseby laughed.

Flustered, Isobel shook her head, dislodging her hair. "I meant only that my skill is not so great —"

"Ah, so it is by Divine Grace that you heal?" Sawcliffe slid in.

Isobel didn't know whether he made fun of her or posed a serious question as nothing about his permanent smile indicated either way. "No…"

"Then by other forces."

Raseby tut-tutted. "Enough of this, Master Secretary; your jest wears thin and my hunger waxes great."

Still smiling, Sawcliffe inclined his head. "As you wish, my lord."

The Earl had said nothing during the exchange, but seemed to be contemplating the casket, his brows drawn together, his thoughts elsewhere. Robert Langton left his vigil by the window and joined them. He threw a scant look in Sawcliffe's direction. "Your hospitality is gratefully received, Fenton, if we do not outstay our welcome. Perhaps your daughter will grace us with her company?"

With her hair astray and dress barely more than scruffy, Isobel felt conspicuously unkempt. "My lord, I am not fit to dine!" she said, before her father could answer.

"Now, now," Raseby said, "your dress is of no moment and my lord Langton wishes it. A little gentle conversation will soften our blood, is that not so, my lord Earl?"

"Let it be so," the Earl replied.

"But, my lord…" Isobel tried again, before her father placed a cautioning hand on her arm. The Earl's expression had noticeably darkened.

"Forgive my daughter, my lord, she is young and my only child and not accustomed to noble company. I have indulged her when many fathers would have chastised."

"So it would seem. Mark well, my lords, when women govern, from their mouths pour empty thoughts and little learning. It is a man's place to rule and a woman's to obey."

Isobel opened her mouth to reply, but Alfred, freeing himself from the grasp of his keeper, launched between them. He then sat on the Earl's booted foot, raised his rear leg, and proceeded to scratch mightily at his flank.

"Alfred!" Isobel chastised, dragging him off, leaving a swathe of dried mud and fur in his wake and making him the reason to excuse herself from the room.

"There you are!" she exclaimed, spying Buena in her yellow dress, hair respectably coiffed, standing unseen in the inner hall where the light was poor and none but household staff had reason to go. "Why did you not bring my casket when I called? No matter. Alfred's disgraced himself again and my lord expects me to dine. But I am not meet to be in such company. Get me my ribbon; at least *it* is fit for an earl." Buena did not respond. "Did you hear me? The ribbon. Now, Bayna. Without delay." Isobel tucked wayward strands of hair behind her ears and smoothed her gown into a degree of respectability.

Buena made no move; something in the hall seemed to have caught her attention. She backed further into the shadows. Isobel saw nothing other than the throng of men talking, and the commanding figure of the Earl, who — rather than joining the conversation — watched the doorway where she stood. She then saw her grim-faced father pacing towards her with the ivory casket under one arm.

"Fader, I did not mean —" but he silenced her with a warning look.

"Go to your room, Isobel," he said quietly, taking her arm and ushering her towards the stairs.

"But, Fader—"

"Do as you are told. I will make an excuse to the Earl for your absence. Take this and go to your chamber. And, Isobel..."

"Yes, Fader?"

"Cover your hair."

CHAPTER THREE

Isobel sat on the high window seat looking onto her garden and the fields that lay beyond, kicking her heels against the stone and not caring if they bruised or the paint scuffed. The wall already bore the marks of years of frustration. That is where she wanted to be, not sitting inside having been sent to her chamber like a chastened child. Giving a particularly hard kick that hurt, she slid off the seat, hobbled for a second, and then stalked over to her table, still avoiding Buena's sombre gaze. She picked up her mirror, viewed her distorted reflection with distaste, and threw it back with little care.

"Why would Fader not let me stay?" she grumbled, although it was not what bothered her most. Swivelling on her stool, Isobel faced her maid. "I called for you, Bayna, but you did not come. I needed your help. What if the Earl were badly hurt? I have not the skill to heal deep wounds and he would have bled to death all over the mats and where would we be then?"

Buena shook her head, drawing her brows together.

"Fader might be accused of letting the Earl die and the king would send his officers to make enquiries. He might even be arrested…" Isobel's imagination had her father condemned for treason and executed before she could rein it in, his head rolling haphazardly across the flagged courtyard of her home. Pinching the soft pad of her hand until it hurt, she brought her thoughts back under control. "I needed you," she said, "but you were not there." She felt Buena's hand on her back and looked up into the older woman's broken face. "I know you do not like to be seen, but I will protect you."

Buena's face crumpled into a smile, and she held Isobel against the lavender-scented wool of her dress until Isobel's fear slid away and strength returned in the set of her shoulders.

"I mixed cockeburr and rue with mint and yarrow, but they have lost much of their potency, and the myrrh is all gone. Was I right to use a covered plaster?" Chewing her lip, Isobel gave it some thought. "But the herbs might sit in the wound and fester if it were not covered, so it must be so. Should I have used clove?"

Buena wagged her finger and opened the lid of the ivory casket sitting on the table beside her. Exotic scents rose from the camphor-lined box as she removed a selection of jars and small drawstring bags and proceeded to demonstrate a series of instructions accompanied by complex hand gestures and grimaces.

After watching each stage of the process with intense concentration, Isobel sighed. "I pray my cure will not be found wanting. Tending the Earl is not like treating John's boy, or the miller's rash. I do not want his wound festering until it becomes green and putrid, and his flesh falls off." Plucking at imaginary gobbets of rotting skin, Isobel pulled a face, and Buena gurgled in her throat. "And do not be caught laughing or I'll not know how to explain it." She rubbed her stomach. "And I have missed my dinner and my prayers; see how cross it makes me?"

Buena patted Isobel's stomach, making her strange throaty sound again, imitating a fevered eating motion, and rounding out her belly.

"I am not fat!" Isobel exclaimed, pushing her towards the door with a laugh. "Well, not very. Go to and find us something to eat if aught is left after the Earl's men have feasted and left us stripped like Egypt after the plague of locusts."

"The years have been hard on you, Fenton," the Earl observed, waiting as the older man reached the top of the main stair, bending a little to catch his breath.

"Yet, kind or not I have had them, for which I offer thanks to Almighty God — and to you, my lord." The Earl offered his arm, but Fenton held up his hand. "My thanks, but a day spent in court on a hard bench and in a harder saddle has left me feeling my years in every bone I possess, and my gratitude to you does not extend to letting them get the better of me. I am not yet in my grave, although my body might call to it. Hark, it would deafen me."

The Earl's mouth rose into a wry smile. "Your wit has not withered with time, I see."

"Unlike my body? Yea, it is all that is left to me. Ah, my private chambers — here we are."

He stood aside to let the Earl enter the solar, noting as he did so the ease with which the man moved despite hours spent on horseback since early that morning. The Earl looked as vigorous now as he had a decade before. Only a few pewter flecks in his dark hair betrayed his age for everything else about him remained young, and his eyes as clear and sharp as ever. Fenton briefly attempted to recall former days when he did not ache, but the memory eluded him.

Standing with one hand on the hilt of his dagger, the Earl took in the proportions of the room, the Turkey rug on the table, the arras decorating the walls. "The chamber has a fair aspect. You do well here, I think."

Fenton longed to sit; his leg throbbed and his back shouted in competition. He allowed himself to lean on the back of his chair. "Passing well, my lord. The new office of cranage affords greater comfort than I could have hoped; I thank you for commending me to His Grace."

"The control of the river brings valuable revenue and information, and the king rewards loyalty." The Earl fixed him with steel eyes. "As do I."

Fenton held his gaze steady, then bowed his head in acknowledgement. To his relief, the Earl chose to sit and Fenton, easing himself into the other chair, offered up a silent word of thanks and an audible one as his esquire lifted his leg, carefully lowering it onto the footstool. He could have done with one of Isobel's physics to ease the pain, but he would make do with the wine now being served.

If the Earl's injury caused him discomfort, he hid it well as he stretched out, hooking one riding boot over the other and resting his arms along the wooden arms of the chair. "You presided over the court these past days; anything I should know?" Business-like as ever.

"My clerk prepares a report for you as we speak, my lord. Much of the same: fines levied but not paid; a dispute over a field boundary; a sow trampling a cottager's cabbages. But ... I have concerns, yes."

"Oh?"

"A case of an unwed girl taken from her brother's house by youths."

"And?" The Earl raised the cup to his mouth, drank, waited. "She lives?"

Fenton held his cup between both hands, contemplating its depths. "She lives, but will be no man's wife."

"The brother sues for compensation, then? It is a family of consequence?"

"None of note." This case had played on Fenton's mind since it had been brought to his attention. The girl of fifteen had been presented to him by her outraged brother, the assault still evident in the bruising on her face and her stilted gait. She had not raised her eyes once and wore her shame like a shroud. He took a mouthful of wine. "It is not the first case and I suspect others unreported. You have heard of the troubles in Dijon, my lord?"

"I have — bands of youths with nothing to occupy them but the pursuit of maids and widows. What of it?"

"The city authorities in Dijon fear it will spread to the taking of respectable women from their homes, and public disorder, and have licensed further brothels in the hope it will curb the excesses of unwed young men; but the numbers have swelled, and it is like a disease…"

"And you fear contamination?"

"Aye, my lord. With our commerce with France and the recent disturbances in our own land…" His hand rose and fell in explanation, and he let the pause do the rest.

"I will ensure His Grace is made aware of it. Have any of the youths been identified?"

Fenton shook his head. "They wore hoods. It was dark and the girl threatened beyond her wits." Leaning forward, he dropped his voice. "My concerns go beyond this girl; it is the lawlessness that precedes a wider malaise stemming from malcontent and fuelled by hunger." If Fenton had ever doubted the Earl's complete attention, he did not now. "The king does not have the loyalty of all in this region, and there are those who hold to previous allegiances. Old roots run deep in these soils, and there are those who seek to harvest them."

The Earl leaned forward. "You have names?"

"I have suspicion of names. Word travels upriver, and trade is not just in wool and wine, my lord, but in whispers and promises."

"I want names, Fenton. His Grace will want names. He seeks peace, and while the old king lives to contest the throne, it is my duty to ensure that peace is maintained and yours to help me do so."

"Within the law, my lord, *only* within the law. His Grace would have it no other way."

"His Grace will secure it in whatever way he can, be sure of it. Until he has an heir there are men who see their fortunes made in the other camp, and the old queen Anjou will make promises of our titles and manors to sweeten them. Do not think we will keep our heads if the tide should turn against us."

"My lord, I know it well enough."

"And so you do."

Divided by slender columns of stone, the sun, now past its zenith, had found its way to the oriel window. Smudges of blue, red, and yellow decorated the floor where light shone through the roundels of coloured glass bearing the arms and devices of the previous occupants, as well as — more recently — Fenton's own.

The Earl followed his gaze and rested on the snout-nosed fish in the oldest glass. "We are all the beneficiaries of the treachery of others," he remarked wryly. "Yet Fortune is fickle, and I would fain be the one that turns the Wheel for fear that another control it."

"Amen to that," Fenton muttered.

"And as to that, my brother Robert will take horse to Hull and make his lordship known to the good company of aldermen and burghers there — lest they choose to forget it. He will also look to this matter of the youths; he is in need of distraction, and this will serve his purpose, as well as the king's."

"Lord Robert seems disconsolate, my lord." The growing ache in his lower back nagged Fenton to get up and move about, but the Earl showed no sign of standing, and Fenton resigned himself to surreptitiously lifting one buttock at a time under the cover of his long gown.

"My brother fears the death of another child. His lady has miscarried two already, and the third was stillborn. She is weakened by her loss, yet the child she now bears is near to birth."

"The death of a child is hard to bear. I will pray to the Virgin for safe delivery."

The Earl's mouth twisted downwards. "Pray it be a boy; the death of an heir is hardest of all."

Fenton cared little whether the child be male or female; he had but one child and for her enduring health when his own failed, he gave perpetual thanks. The Earl had three daughters still living, yet he mourned the death of his only son, and with the countess past her best years, no more were likely.

"How does the countess? She is blessed with good health, my lord? And my ladies?"

The Earl came back from his dark thoughts, cloaking his mind. "She is well enough; my daughters also."

God's teeth, this man was hard to read. Without warning, the Earl rose, went to the window, and opened the casement. Where the chair had scraped the rush mat, the sweet scent of crushed herbs lingered, stirred by the new air from outside. Fenton stood more slowly, wary of the man's sudden mood. He waited.

"I had word of your own loss, Fenton."

Fenton's heart cringed at the mention of it. Shallow breaths eased the cramp a little, but not the pain. He hoped the Earl did not expect an answer; indeed he appeared to be watching something intently from the window.

"She has the likeness of her mother," the Earl remarked, softly to himself.

Joining him, Fenton lurched as he saw Isobel crossing the court on her way to the garden, although he had given her servant instructions to keep her to her chambers. At least she now kept her head covered. Buena was nowhere in sight.

"My daughter is my comfort and my joy in this world, my lord; I seek none other."

Isobel reached the arched doorway that would take her on the path to the garden and disappeared.

The Earl turned from the window. "Who is that woman your daughter spoke with before we dined?"

"Woman, my lord?"

"Yes — or are you so far gone in age you no longer know a woman when you see one?"

Fenton grimaced. "Not so far gone, my lord, but more in need of comfort for my spirit than my bed."

"So?"

"A woman of the household, my lord, of no consequence."

"I thought I recognised her. She served your wife?"

"She serves my daughter."

"Do not play games with me, Fenton, or I will believe that you have something to hide."

"My lord, my manors and household are open to your scrutiny. She is nothing but a wretched serving woman in want of a tongue."

"She cannot speak?"

"She cannot, my lord."

The Earl appeared appeased, but Fenton knew all too well that once roused, his lord would harbour suspicion until the truth of it was found wanting — or exposed. For now, however, he seemed content to let the matter lie, but every now and again, as they talked of old times, he looked to be turning his grey eyes inwards as if searching for a memory once known, and now lost.

CHAPTER FOUR

Isobel had given Buena an errand and the slip and skipped out of her chamber and down the back stair as soon as she was able. Not that she resented her maid's ever-watchful presence; Heaven knew she had been her constant companion and guide since her mother's death, and her mother's faithful servant before that. Buena had been part of Isobel's life for as long as she could remember and, despite Thomas's threats to the contrary, she aimed for her to be part of it for as long as they both lived. But Isobel wanted time alone to think. More than that, she needed to be free of the burden of expectation her status and growing adulthood demanded. This unexpected visit by the Earl had set her day about her ears, and she sought to make it right in the only way she knew how — in the solace of her garden and her own thoughts.

The garden was conspicuously empty and for once Isobel forgave John's late return to his work, though what he found to occupy him at home to take him so regularly back there each dinnertime, she could not imagine. Not yet married these two years and his wife already carrying their second child, his devotion made for an attentive husband, but a poor gardener. She would remind him of this fact when she next saw him, but for now she would be content with her solitude.

Checking the hidden nook behind the loosened brick by the door, where her mother and Buena had sometimes left a sweetmeat or sprig of lavender to delight her, Isobel felt a little flurry of grief at the empty space. She pushed it to one side. Beyond the walls, she could just make out the occasional shout from women weeding the fields and the faint cries of children picking stones and driving crows from the new-sown crops, but the space inside remained hers, and she made regular inspection of her domain with as much thoroughness as her father did their lands. This was her world and she its master.

Drunk on nectar, a fat-furred bee lay on its back, buzzing furiously. Isobel offered it a leaf and, lifting carefully, transferred it to the throat of a nearby flower. She watched the bee's solitary progress as it negotiated the depths of the purple iris, then set about her own task. Intent on pulling stray seedlings from around tender shoots, she heard the door to the garden protest on its rusting hinges but did not look up until the alarmed call of the thrush brought her to her feet. She craned her neck to see clear of the lattice of tumbling roses, heavy in bud, and saw the door swinging shut, but no evidence of who had passed through it. Fully suspecting John making his tardy return to work, she opened her mouth to call, thought better of it, and instead tiptoed around the trellised bed to surprise him.

She stopped dead in her tracks. The broad back facing her was not John's, nor any of her household. The figure moved, and the broadcloth of his tight sleeve gleamed red-purple in the sun as he reached out to break the long neck of a columbine. Isobel took a step back, and the hem of her gown caught a twig. The dry snap had the man spinning to face her, hand on his dagger. His guarded defence was instantly replaced by one of surprise. Restricted by the narrow path, Isobel sank into a shaky curtsy, tried to rise, wobbled, and would have toppled sideways had his hand not shot out to grasp her by the arm to steady her.

"Faith, lady! I could have gutted you like a hog!"

Isobel stammered an apology and found herself staring at the nodding head of the blue columbine he held in one hand rather than at the exasperation in his eyes.

His tone moderated. "Perhaps it is I, who comes like a thief to your garden, who should apologise. Here —" he held out the flower — "I could not resist such beauty; I thought to take a little healing of this place to my lady wife. I return it to its rightful owner and ask forgiveness." He bowed — not the shallow nod she might expect from one of her own station, nor the awkward slouch from a servant, but deep and elegant, borne of years at Court and an abiding confidence in his status. "Robert Langton," he introduced himself.

She received the flower, holding it self-consciously and, not knowing whether he mocked her, felt heat colouring her skin. She closed her mouth, remembered her manners, and managed to curtsy in return without falling over this time. "Isobel Fenton, my lord. And the columbine is yours. If you wish it." She proffered the flower, the stem's graceful head bowing in demure supplication. It seemed such a ridiculous thing to say, but he received it gravely.

"I thank you for my wife."

"What ails Lady Langton?" Isobel asked, hoping she didn't seem impertinent, but curious anyway. Lord Langton's expression became blank.

"Nothing that a safe delivery will not make right." He gathered himself. Holding the flower so that the sun encased the indigo petals in pearl, he asked, "Eagle or dove?"

"*Columba* — dove," she answered without hesitation, glad that he had changed the subject.

"But the eagle is the noblest of birds; should this not be *aquilegia* in tribute?"

She regarded the winged petals guarding the gold-tasselled heart and thought it apt, but, "*Columbine* is the name my mother called it, and so shall I. It is ... was ... her favourite flower."

"Then *columbine* it shall be in honour of Lady Fenton, the gentlest of noblewomen." He spoke with genuine warmth and she lost a little of her awe.

"You knew my mother, my lord?"

"I met her once when not much older than you are now; she showed me great kindness."

Isobel waited, but Robert Langton did not explain further, instead marking her closely with a consideration she found disconcerting. "You are very like her."

She managed to stop herself from rolling her eyes. "Everyone says how much I take after my mother, although my hair is darker and I am smaller. *Everyone*," she emphasised.

"No, I meant that you are kind."

"Oh." She looked away, confused.

"You do not recall our meeting?" Isobel shook her head before she remembered it was not considered courtly and stilled it. Lord Langton almost smiled. "Nor why should you? You were a child." He walked a few paces away and pointed at the orchard at the far end of the garden, where the ground dipped away so that the crowns of the apple trees in spring appeared covered in pale pink snow. A few late blossoms remained, full of bees. "I found you under the trees, crying —"

"I never cry!" Isobel blurted indignantly before she could stop herself.

"You were crying," he insisted. "A young rabbit had frozen, and you wrapped it in your mantle and held it to you to warm it although you trembled with cold yourself."

Isobel reached back down the years searching for recollection and found somewhere, in the halls of her childhood, an impression of anguish. Snow had lain on the ground in hard ridges under her feet, the sky lifeless and grey. She remembered being confused and frightened.

Despite the sun, she hugged her arms about her body. "It was cold. I remember the cold. Men had come to the house, and I had been sent into the garden. I found the coney. It still lived and its eyes were open, but it wouldn't wake up. A man came — a man with blood in his hair." Her own hand touched the side of her head. "He took the coney from me and … and broke its neck." Isobel looked up, seeking recognition. "That was *you*, my lord? You killed the rabbit!"

He detected an accusation. "I believed it the merciful thing to do."

"I thought you were a thief come to steal my mother's flowers, but you stole my coney instead. I think that I might have been very angry."

One side of his mouth lifted in amusement, making him look like a broader, younger version of his brother, the Earl. "You were; you shouted at me, called me *villein*, and kicked my shins. I was grateful you were not wearing pattens to add to my battle bruises, although your feet must have been like ice."

Isobel writhed with embarrassment. "I wonder that you are here now if such is your memory of this place. And as for calling me *kind*, I see no evidence of it, only a girl who deserved a beating for her insolence."

His face softened. "You were but a child and, as for kindness, you showed mercy to a creature despite your own distress, such as your mother did for me."

Isobel pictured herself crying over the animal, cradling and singing to it, willing animation back into its listless body. She found herself recalling the tall, steel-clothed man who appeared at the edge of the bare-leaved orchard, first standing and watching her, then ducking under a low branch, taking the rabbit from her arms although she fought him. She remembered him running his gloved hand over the animal and then, in one swift movement, breaking its neck. *Crack*. But the only distress she recollected was that for the coney, not for herself. Her confusion must have shown on her face because he tilted his head, inspecting her with interest.

"It is not something I would have thought easily forgotten — the day we brought your father home."

Standing in the garden in the sun, that cold, dismal day seemed another lifetime, another world away. She had not connected the two. Heat, trapped beneath her tight headdress, became suddenly overwhelming and Isobel longed to rip it from her head. "That was then? Oh!" She frowned. "Oh."

"This heat has made you pale; sit in the shade awhile."

Riding the top of the turf bench nearby, plush camomile provided a welcome seat between two lattice panels crowned with roses. Isobel sat gratefully and he perched nearby, crossing one long-booted leg over another. He leaned forward and undid the first buckle, releasing the well-worn strap from its metal ring. He seemed to be thinking. "Forgive me; it is so clear in my mind that I did not doubt that it would be so in yours." Isobel allowed herself a quick shake of her head. "No, of course, you must have been but six or seven years of age."

She found her voice. "I had seen eight winters, my lord, but was small for my years and so must have seemed younger." Her fingers twisted the cloth of her skirts. "My mother would not speak of that day, and my father —" she smiled thinly — "would not risk her wrath except to jest about it. There were men — many men and horses ... the courtyard was full of them. But what I remember most — why I thought it a dream — was the quiet; they made no sound. I remember their silence."

Isobel closed her eyes, feeling a knot of fear as she saw her mother's face, her eyes unnaturally wide, her mouth opening and shutting as if giving orders, but out of which no sound came. Her father on a litter borne by men in blue and yellow — more red than yellow — unmoving and as sightless as her coney. The stench of blood, of sweat and horse leather, of damp wool and the mire of mud-mangled men, made more noise than those spectres did.

She opened her eyes. "They were like ghosts." She looked up at him. "I thought they had brought back the ghost of my father." She jumped as the garden door slammed open and Buena appeared, her head covering askew, a curl of hair sticking to her forehead. Spotting Isobel, she crossed the garden, carelessly trampling the young plants in her haste.

Still caught in the past, alarmed, Isobel rose. "My father…?" she began, but stopped at the anger in the woman's face. Buena raised her hand as if to strike. Instead, she grasped Isobel's slender wrist and pulled.

"Ow!" Isobel said, as much in surprise as at the force used. She tried to free her wrist. "Bayna, let go. Let. *Go*!"

Buena released her and stood breathing rapidly, glaring at Isobel.

"What do you think you are doing? Show my lord proper respect."

The look Buena shot in Robert Langton's direction could have felled Goliath; his expression changed from bemused to displeased.

"*Now!*" Isobel barked.

Buena bent her head in token deference but continued to glower.

Isobel tugged at her sleeve and pushed her in the direction of the door. "Go!" she ordered, then turned to Robert Langton, sinking to the ground. "My lord, I beg your forgiveness." She didn't rise until she heard him exhale.

"Sweet Mother of God," he remarked mildly. "I pity you your servant; I need chastise you no further."

"You humiliated me in front of Lord Langton." Still fuming, Isobel tore off her headdress and threw herself across her bed, face flaming from the sun and her embarrassment. She kicked her legs and groaned into her grass-green bedcover. "It is bad enough you treat me like a child, but to show such disrespect… what did you think to do?"

Thwack. A hand came down by the side of her head, making the embroidered covers bounce. Isobel stared at Buena's creased brown hand lying in front of her, then into her servant's face and saw anger melt into desperation. She sat up. "What have I done?" she asked, bewildered.

Buena curled her hand like a spider and ran her fingers across the wool sward decorated with flowers.

Guiltily defiant, Isobel shrugged. "Yes, I went to my garden; what of it?"

Buena's two index fingers formed figures, which bowed and nodded to one another.

Isobel frowned at the mime. "I talked with Lord Langton. And?"

The fingers swayed, bent towards each other, entwined.

Isobel's face darkened. "How dare you!" Swinging off the bed, she faced her maid, hands buckled into fists, squeezing words through her teeth. "You insult me. You insult *him*… I can have you beaten. I should have you whipped and sent from here. Thomas is right; you are not fit to be my servant. I will... I will..."

Grabbing Isobel by the shoulders, Buena shook her roughly then she lifted her fingers and once again let them dance in the fragments of dust suspended in the air, making one fall on the other, crushing it until it lay still beneath. When she saw Isobel understood, Buena nodded once and backed off.

Isobel sat heavily on the edge of her bed, suddenly cold in the stuffy room. "I would not let any man touch me, Bayna. I would defend my honour." She smoothed the lily-of-the-valley and daisy-covered cover beneath her palm. "And Lord Langton is an honourable man; he is the Earl's brother."

Buena snorted, held a finger up in warning, and slowly wagged it from side to side, shaking her head at the same time.

Isobel pursed her lips, looking pained. "Very well, if I can't go anywhere without you following me, I might as well allow you to stay in my service. But remember, you are my servant and I expect you to behave like one."

Buena replied by picking up Isobel's hand, kissing it, and briefly holding it to her forehead.

"Hmm, and don't think that you can win me over so easily; my lady mother would not have allowed you to curb her so." To her surprise, the look Buena gave her was neither compliant nor vexed, but briefly sad. "Come," she said more gently, "bring me my bowl and water and help me ready for this evening. My fine gown might have been eaten by moths since I last wore it, and I am an inch taller."

Distracted by the sound of voices through the open casement, Isobel drifted back to her conversation in the garden. "Lord Langton spoke of the time Fader was brought back home after the battle. I had thought it a dream — a bad dream — but now I think I have woken up and I do not want to. I do not wish to remember what that day felt like." Somewhere a dog barked, and she started, then smiled. "How silly. That day is long past, and Fader is well, and all is right with the world." She hopped to her feet. "And if it is to continue so I must remove these stains from my nails and be the lady my mother meant me to be." She pulled a face and crossed her eyes, making Buena laugh.

CHAPTER FIVE

Fenton was relieved when the Earl rode to Barton that afternoon, taking his brother and the closest members of his retinue with him. The fewterers with their greyhounds and brachets who had accompanied the Earl on his visit to Lord Raseby's manor had returned to the castle at Tickhill and taken their noise with them, leaving the courtyard ringing and empty.

This interlude gave the household time to prepare food and chambers fit for the noblemen upon their return. The venison would provide meat enough for the numbers expected, with coney from the warren and squabs from the cot; but their steward, Arthur Moynes, had been obliged to send to the village for additional supplies, and Christ in Heaven knew that there was little enough in these lean times as it was without stripping it for their table.

The Earl's business kept him overnight in Barton, but he returned before noon and in time for dinner. As Arthur Moynes consulted with her father over the seating arrangements in the great hall, Raseby turned his attention to Isobel. She had been trying to look inconspicuous in one corner away from the Earl's retinue, but Raseby beckoned to her to join him by the fire.

"My lady wears a pretty ribbon such as my own daughters would be pleased to own. Did not Her Grace the Queen sport such a silk when we were last at Court, my lord?"

The Earl's eyes grazed Isobel's veil, beneath which the strand of ribbon fought to contain her heavy hair. "I did not pay heed to the Queen's form of dress." He looked away and continued to give instructions to Sawcliffe, who — Isobel had learned — was the Earl's secretary.

Raseby leaned forward. "Come closer, little lady." He peered at the barely visible blue-green frond. "Hah! Now I am certain. Where did you come by such a delight? I shall make a present of it for my chicks."

"It was a gift, my lord."

"Well, well, and a fine one at that. Dalton," he addressed the bored young man, "would not the Lady Elizabeth like such a trifle?" He did not give the youth time to answer, but seeing the steward approaching them, gave a hearty slap to his own stomach. "Ah, we are called to dine. Let us see what fare your good father has ordered today."

Dalton had turned his back on Isobel, and she was left standing while the men drifted towards the dais and trestles. She felt movement beside her.

Tall, thin, and raven-dark, Sawcliffe hovered close. His mouth curled. "I heard rumour that Her Grace's consignment of Genoese silk measured a little short by about … mmm, the length of a ribbon. Does Sir Geoffrey not control the customs on these waterways?"

She darted a glance towards the dais, which had been decorated with an embroidered blue canopy. The Earl was being shown to the high-backed chair her father used when addressing his retinue on manorial business, now softened with fat cushions.

Sawcliffe whispered close to her ear. "I believe the ship made port somewhere north of the Wash, perhaps Hull? But then, how would you have such knowledge, you are but a maid."

Isobel stared fixedly at the floor. "It was a present."

"From your doting father, perhaps?"

"No."

"An uncle then?"

"I have no uncle, sir."

"Well, it is a gift of some remark, so I suspect a degree of affinity. Or perhaps you have a sweetheart?"

Isobel flushed.

Sawcliffe moved so close the light veil she wore lifted in the passing air. "I thought so. A fine gift from a sweetheart to gain favours." He smiled. "Or perhaps pay for them…?" he slid in, so quietly Isobel thought she might have imagined it had his look not spoken as much.

"No!" she said, too loudly and then, lowering her voice as her father frowned in her direction, "You do me dishonour, sir!"

"Honour? What is that you say, Sawcliffe?" Raseby called, heaving himself into a chair behind the lord's table that complained loudly as flesh and exuberant green and gold brocade filled it. "Come now, speak up."

"Mistress Fenton has been honoured by the gift of a ribbon, my lord, for he who gave it risks much in the giving should the queen become wise to it."

"Well, there is no fear of that, little lady, for none here will speak of it. And were I a younger man I would consider the honour mine to risk. Come, sit by me." Raseby patted the plain chair next to his own, and Isobel did as bidden, glad to be rid of Sawcliffe's uneasy attention.

Raseby winked, adjusted the fall of his wide-sleeved gown, and pressed his meaty, scarred hands together in supplication as the chaplain blessed the meal. Still smarting from Sawcliffe's slur against her father's integrity and her own chastity, Isobel mouthed the prayer without heed, crossed herself habitually, and resigned herself to hours of men's banter.

Since her mother's death they had entertained few guests and none of such status as the Earl and his company. She did not include Thomas's father, Henry Lacey, whose frequent visits rendered them mundane and his conversation predictable. In the past, her mother's presence had always ensured utmost etiquette was maintained, and none who came into her aura ever left without comment on her grace and beauty.

A poor imitation of her mother she might be, but Isobel folded her hands and straightened her back as she had been taught, determined to appear neither overly interested nor bored, smile when required but not too much, nor laugh too loud — a mirror to the men. She would make no political comment other than to become her father's cipher if required, and when — invariably — the general conversation turned to comments she did not fully understand, she would assume a bland mask behind which she would disappear.

She did so now, allowing Raseby to ladle compliments on all that came under his cheerful eye while slipping in anecdotes about the four daughters he obviously adored. She had nothing to say and found her attention wandering to the rest of the company arranged in a long 'u' behind the cloth-covered trestles, in decreasing order of precedence the further they sat from the dais.

She ate a little venison pasty; rinsed her hands in the bowl of scented water held for her; considered a squab pie, but found her appetite reduced by Sawcliffe's comments and more than made up for in Raseby's obvious enjoyment of the fare. And every now and again she raised her eyes to find the Earl watching her, and she averted them again.

The venison was a little tougher than Geoffrey Fenton might have liked and would have benefitted from being hung for longer, but the dish, encased in fair pastry, had made a splendid entrance when brought before them in the great hall, and the Earl seemed pleased enough. The stew made with fish fresh from the manor was, however, a triumph. Fenton would ensure he remarked on it when he next saw his cook.

"What matter is this you wish to discuss?" The Earl rinsed his fingers in lavender-scented water and dried them on the linen offered to him.

Caught off-guard and chewing carefully, Fenton took a moment to answer. He swallowed the piece of meat. "My lord, it is of some delicacy." He waited until the remains of the venison had been removed and replaced with coney in gravy and tiny fruit pies made from the last of the winter preserves. He spoke quietly so that the Earl was obliged to lean towards him to hear above the general hubbub of the room. "It concerns the settlement of my daughter."

Not for the first time, the Earl glanced sideways to where Isobel sat. She had eaten little and, apart from a few words, spoken less. Robert Langton seemed equally preoccupied and had resumed the air of one waiting for ill news. Fenton had timed his moment well. The Earl, easily irritated, would no doubt see Fenton's concerns as trivial, but supped and wined as he was, would be in better humour for it, and more inclined to benevolence.

With hard eyes scanning the assembled diners, the Earl said, "Go on."

Now that it came to it, Fenton struggled to find a form of words in which to describe his case. "With your lordship's permission, Isobel is contracted to wed at Michaelmas. She is my only child and has no kin to defend her should I be taken from this life ere she is married."

Ringed fingers thrummed impatiently. "And? Bring the match forward; is she not of age?"

"She is, my lord, but the lad is in France until Michaelmas, and I am in need of my daughter's company for a little while longer."

The Earl finished the fruit pastry and followed it with the best wine Fenton held in his buttery. He savoured it, drank again. "It is but several months hence, may you be spared to witness it. Might the boy's family be entrusted with her care until then, should God choose otherwise? Who are they?"

Fenton dodged the question, instead bringing it back to his original purpose. "If I should die before September…"

The Earl replaced his cup with a thud. "What is it you ask of me, Fenton, if it is not to grant permission for this match since you seem to have settled it upon yourself to do so?"

Why should the Earl concern himself in the petty affairs of lesser men? Fenton rubbed weary eyes and wondered if he had misjudged the situation. He had seen little of the Earl in more recent years and the bond they once shared had frayed. He would have to play this with a greater degree of caution than anticipated.

"It is so lately agreed I had not the time to bring it to your attention, my lord, and it is of such little consequence."

A chill note crept into the Earl's tone. "When has the marriage concerning the estate of one of my most loyal servants not been a matter for my lordship? What is the family?"

This was not going as well as Fenton had hoped, and he had yet to broach the question that had played on his mind since he agreed the match.

"Well?" The Earl's voice echoed in the hall, and Fenton regretted bringing up the subject when so many ears were present and straining to hear their conversation.

"The boy is ... Thomas Lacey, my lord."

His brows forming a sharp 'v' and his hand crushing the fine linen cloth, the Earl looked ready to explode. "Lacey? *Lacey*? Kin to that traitorous whoreson, Ralph Lacey?"

"His nephew."

Robert Langton leaned sideways and said something inaudible to any but his brother, who grunted, "Very well. We will continue elsewhere." The Earl stood abruptly, forcing the company to their feet. "Alone," he added, gesturing to Fenton to follow him.

"Have I not always been a good lord to you?" the Earl demanded when they reached the seclusion of the solar. What constraint to his temper that had been in force no longer remained, and the Earl made no attempt to disguise it.

"You have, my lord."

"Then you will know that I will not countenance such an alliance."

"It is agreed upon —"

The Earl stabbed a finger on the rug-covered table hard enough to jar the wood. "Not without my permission, and I do not grant it."

Keeping his tone even and his movements calm, Fenton moved to where he could see the Earl's expression more clearly through his good eye. He wished he had called for more light when they had entered the room, but his mind had been elsewhere. "My lord, let the past rest. The boy is not subject to his uncle's treason; his loyalty is not in question —"

"Unlike yours."

Fenton counted to five, slowly and silently. "My lord, in all my years of service I have *never* given you cause to doubt my loyalty."

The Earl took himself to the far end of the room where the fire cast shadows but not enough light to enable Fenton to read the man's mercurial temper. He stood in the oriel window where earlier they had watched Isobel cross the court on her way to her garden. He stared through the casement into the blank night, biting the knuckle of his thumb. "Did Henry Lacey broker this match?" he asked eventually, turning sharp eyes to focus on Fenton through the gloom.

"He did."

The Earl smiled without mirth. "Why does that not surprise me? What else does he want?"

Fenton debated the wisdom of answering the question, but he had promised Henry Lacey and would abide by his word. "A position for his son."

"In *my* household?"

"If it please you, my lord."

Like hog fat on a fire, the Earl's temper flared. "It does not *please* me. *You* do not please me." Turning his back on the man, he clasped his strong hands behind his neck, regretting it as his injured arm stung. "*Bastard —*"

"My lord…!"

"Henry Lacey is a sorry bastard son-of-a-whore and I'll see him damned to hell before his whelp takes any service in my household. I'd not have him sleep with my dogs lest he gave them mange. Has your brain softened that you let him court your favour? I forbid the match."

Fenton spoke slowly and deliberately. "I let him, my lord, because marriage to Thomas Lacey will give Isobel the position she deserves, and a title she would have had if her mother had not married *me*."

Swinging on his heel, the Earl marched towards the table and, leaning over it, brought his face close to Fenton's. Had the older man wished to, he could not have avoided the direct stare of his lord, nor have misinterpreted the venom of his words, the vengeance behind his eyes. "I — will — not — allow it."

Fenton gazed back calmly. "My lord, you owe me this favour." It could go either way. He had seen the result of men who had ventured to push their luck with this man for less than he now asked, and they had not survived to regret it. White-knuckled, the Earl continued to lean on the table, crushing the fine wool pile. Fenton added, "It was what her mother wanted."

The Earl drew back, lips compressed into an unyielding line; but rage had given way to something else — guardedness, perhaps. When he spoke, it was with scorn. "Are you so easily bought with a title?"

"Are you, my lord?"

For seconds longer, the Earl burrowed into Fenton's eyes, then he straightened, turned his head, and concentrated on adjusting his dagger on its elaborate belt so that it hung true to his hip. He seemed to have found something trapped between the gilt embellishments and the leather. Intent on removing the strands of deer hair, his apparent lack of attention was meant to disarm. "If you are determined to pursue this, I will not prevent it. But be aware, I will make your daughter a widow should her husband or *any* of his house even so much as raise piss in the direction of Lancaster. Do you understand? And who will protect her then, Fenton? When the forces of Anjou and Henry the dotard come beating on her doors, who will protect her then?"

Fenton braced himself. "You will, my lord."

"*What?*" The Earl ceased plucking.

With great effort Fenton kneeled before his lord. Taking his hand in both of his, he pressed his forehead to the ring he had taken from the lifeless finger of the Old Earl, whom he had tried to defend, and failed. "I beg your indulgence, my lord, and ask one thing more in the name of the trust you have shown me. If I should die before she is married, take Isobel under your protection and make her your charge."

The Earl jerked his hand away. "You ask too much."

Fenton continued to kneel although his leg berated him and his back yelled. "She is all I have left. My lord, for the love you once bore me, protect my child and see her safely wed." He remained in supplication, guessing that the Earl calculated the odds of having to fulfil this duty between the months of May and September.

"And you entrust me with this task knowing my will is against the match?" the Earl said slowly.

"Aye, my lord."

"And is your child aware of the legacy she carries to this marriage?"

"She ... is not."

"So be it. You tell her nothing and I will protect her — it is my word."

Staggering a little as he found his feet, Fenton placed his right hand over his heart, inclined his head, but could say nothing of the gratitude that had his throat close and his eyes prick with relief.

*

Isobel thought her father looked more drawn when he joined her in the solar once the Earl had departed early the following morning. Fog had crept up the river overnight and still lingered along the banks and ditches when the Earl swung into the saddle. Huddled in her cloak, Isobel watched from the steps, trying not to shiver. Hatless and with hair as silver as the mist and as thin, her father approached the horse, his head level with the Earl's knee, and bowed. The two men exchanged words, the Earl momentarily scanning the windows of the tower as if he expected to find someone watching there. Pulling his horse's head free of the groom's hand, he wheeled about, took one last look, and was gone in a cascade of metal hooves, taking the tension with him.

Now in the familiar comfort of their own company, Geoffrey rested his eyes for a moment while Isobel made his favourite concoction of ale warmed with spiced milk, sweetened with honey. Behind his eyelids, he pictured his wife bending before the fire, her head silhouetted by the light, her fair skin warmed when she turned to him and gave him his silver cup. Her cup. Their cup.

He heard the hollow tap of the horn spoon against the side of the cup and opened his eyes. Isobel had said something.

"Did you remember to give Lord Langton the herbs for my lady's laying-in?"

She was so like her mother, down to the slight gap between her two front teeth, and her green eyes surrounded in a circle of blue as if it had been drawn to prevent the sea of her eyes spilling over and drowning him. And her smile — always, always her smile.

"Fader?" Only her hair was different — darker, like his — but long and thick and lustrous as the honey it resembled. Men would covet her honey; she must always cover her hair.

She placed her small hand over his own, gnarled and scarred by age and war as it was. "Fader, did you remember?"

"You must always cover your hair, Isobel." He blinked, patted her hand. "Yes, yes, I remembered; as you commanded so I obeyed. My Lord Robert bade me give you his thanks for your gifts and asked that the dove should forgive the eagle his transgressions." He frowned. "I did not understand his meaning; perhaps you do?"

Geoffrey waited, but Isobel squeezed his hand and, rising, went to the jug sitting on its stand, warming by the fire. Dipping her little finger to test its heat, she said, "The Earl makes me uneasy. I do not know if I like him."

"It is as well to be cautious of great men, my Bel, they have much to lose and far to fall and it makes them difficult masters to please. I have known the Earl for many years — have I ever told you how I served the father before I served the son?"

"Yes, you have, and how you lost your eye and the use of your leg defending him, and how the king himself knighted you in reward for your loyalty…" She stopped, looking troubled.

"What is it, minnow?"

"Lord Langton reminded me of when the Earl brought you home. I believed the day to be a dream, but I remember now." She did not say how the image of her father lying so still — his face bound in bloodied rags, his leg askew and seeping — made her feel, as if the recollection made his mortality real, and in making it real, imminent.

"But I lived," he said gently. "By God's good grace and your mother's healing, I lived, and each day I am reminded of the fact when I see you. Then, and when this old ploughshare I call a leg wakes me at night." He cuffed his thigh. "Is that ale ready yet? It is all that keeps me from taking an axe to it and finishing the job properly. Aye, well." He rubbed it ruefully. "The man paid dearly enough, though his pain was brief and mine long." He might have said more but he remembered his daughter had been but a child and knew nothing of the execution of Ralph Lacey he had sanctioned. He closed his eyes again.

"I still do not like the Earl," Isobel muttered to herself, adding a scrape of nutmeg and a pinch of precious saffron to the brew.

Her father coughed and opened his eyes. "Never court the Earl's anger, Isobel, his vengeance is swift and final. It was not always so; time and circumstance have made him that way. He might have been a different man had he not…" He pulled a face. "Well, that is a tale best left untold. It does nothing to rake over old embers; you can never tell who might end up burned."

"Fader, what did the Earl say to you before he left? Did he say you must ride out to put down the rising in Yorkshire?" She poured the sweet ale into his cup, tasted it, and handed it to him. His hand shook as he took it, and he held the cup tightly before she could notice.

"My lord Earl?" Sitting back, he concluded with a degree of satisfaction that the chase had proved more successful than the venison it procured. "No, my minnow, I'll not be riding out. He assured me of his good lordship."

"And what did you say to him?" she asked, astute as always.

"And I assured him of mine." He smiled, closing his eyes again and resting back in his chair.

PART TWO

CHAPTER SIX

Late August had baked heat into the stone walls and bricked the soil of the fields, and Isobel sat in her father's chair in the relative cool of dawn. Through the open door at the end of the hall, she thought she caught the faint call and response from the boy at watch by the gate and, moments later, Arthur Moynes entered, the linen of his white shirt already limp at his neck, his skin reddened by the sun. Today, Isobel thought as he bowed before her, his bagged eyes drooped even more towards their outer corners, mirroring the downward bow of his mouth and making him look even more like a scent-hound than ever.

Even so, he attempted to lift his face into a smile of encouragement. "My lady, it is time."

A few months ago, Isobel might have come back with a quip about the fragrant herb of the same name, and his serious face would have looked a little bemused. Now, however, she had nothing to say. She rose, allowed Buena to place her light travelling cloak around her shoulders, and followed her steward through the screens and along the passage to the wide door for the last time. Here she hesitated, sensing the finality of her next steps. Somewhere in the pit of her stomach, the gulf that had opened on the day of her father's death yawned wider than the gaping Hell Mouth on the wall of her church. The serried ranks of the damned knew nothing of the void that filled her now.

Buena touched her arm, and Isobel walked the few paces to where her father's household servants stood waiting silently in the pale dawn for her to bid them farewell. Most she had known all her life and she greeted them by name, finding a few words to say to each. When she came to one of the young kitchen lads, she stopped.

"How is your finger, Jack, is it healed?"

He held up his hand in his eagerness to show her. "Aye, 'tis right fair, m'lady, and straighter now than beforetime."

She smiled faintly. "Good, and remember to keep your hands free of the spit-iron chain next time or you might not have a finger left to mend."

He grinned, then remembered to bow.

She spotted an awkward figure fumbling his hands at the end of the line. "How is your wife, John? And your babe?"

"God bless you, my lady, both well. My wife says she is stopped bleeding with the physic you sent, and the child is not so colicky of nights. She slept right through the last an' that be the first. My wife … she says…" He mumbled something Isobel did not catch, and then pressed a small, hard object into her hand: a wooden bead the size of an oak-gall, crudely carved into an acorn and with a twist of copper forming a loop at the top. "From the abbey, m'lady. It's for your chaplet, if you'll take it. My wife had it blessed." It would have cost them to do so, and with his wife but lately churched and free of pain from a difficult birth. This was more than Isobel expected, and she felt both her voice and her resolve thin. She gave a quick nod of thanks, felt her lip wobble, and reined herself back.

"Look after my garden, John Appleyard. Let not the weeds seed and remember to remove the spent flowers on the roses or they will weaken the plants." He looked away as tears grazed her eyes.

His rough chin quivered. "May God and all the Saints bless thee, my lady."

The steward's calm voice saved her from herself. "My lady, the Earl's man awaits and must be away to reach the castle before nightfall."

She nodded, not trusting her voice, then managed, "Bayna, is my casket packed?"

Buena confirmed with a grunt, as she had done three times before over the course of the early morning, and followed her mistress to where Isobel's pretty palfrey waited, flicking its tail against flies. Her baggage was already suspended on the sturdy packhorse nearby. The familiar weld and blue livery appeared brash in the shallow light as — throwing the horn cup back into the bucket — the stocky man wiped his mouth on his sleeve and pulled his knee-length cote straight.

Alfred panted expectant drops of drool that gathered in shiny pools by his paws and was rewarded with the remains of the man's early breakfast. Isobel resisted kissing the dog's wiry head and patted him instead, avoiding the brown eyes that reproached her desertion. "I will see you again soon," she whispered, and then to the man, "We are ready."

He gave a short bow. "Your pardon, I have orders to accompany only one."

Isobel looked surprised. "Yes, of course. I expect no other." She motioned to Buena to mount her pony and made ready to do the same.

The man thrust out his arm, stopping Buena. "One only, mistress. The Earl commands it."

It took a moment for it to sink in. "Buena is my servant; I will not leave without her."

Arthur Moynes stepped forward. "My lady cannot travel without a servant. It is dangerous enough as it is."

The man shrugged. "As you wish; but none'll be allowed in the castle."

For an instant Buena's eyes flared. Isobel stood her ground. "I must have Buena; it is not seemly for me to attend without my own servant."

The man looked as if he cared neither one way nor the other. He spoke with a mid-country accent from the south and west of the Trent, the whine in his voice making him sound insolent. "My lord made plain his command. Take it up with him if you wish but I have orders to fetch only one, and only one will I fetch. Let another make the journey if you desire, but my lord Earl will admit only you, mistress; the other will have to return."

Arthur's normally placid features hardened as he brought himself menacingly close to the other man. "This is outrageous! Sir Geoffrey would not allow it."

"Then let Sir Geoffrey take it up with the Earl."

Arthur's fists balled, and Isobel intervened before he could use them. "Leave it, Arthur. George will go with me as far as Tickhill. He can stay there and return on the morrow. None will bother me; I am of no importance. Buena —" she turned to the woman — "there must be some mistake. I will beseech the Earl and send for you as soon as I may. Stay here and wait for me; it is not long till Michaelmas." She could not bear to go on and, bringing her mouth close to Buena's ear as she embraced her, said, "I will miss you; keep safe."

As she let go, Buena grabbed her arm, a sudden fire in her eyes. She lifted two forefingers in a swift, obscure dance before Isobel's face.

"Yes, I will take care," Isobel assured her. "May it please God, I will keep safe."

Isobel did not look behind her as her light-footed palfrey took the dust-dry track from the manor towards the river. She did not dare. She kept her eyes fixed on the griffin on the man's blue and yellow back glowing in the strengthening day as he rode ahead of her. She barely registered when George questioned why they weren't taking the ferry upriver, nor the man's stunted reply that "he didn't hold wi' water" and George's gruff response. Instead, they followed the river's course past the stripped fields until they came to the woods and the trees separated her from view of her home. Beyond the woods lay the boundary to her demesne lands.

Loss blunted grief. A numbness had invaded her heart the moment her father's had stopped. She had left him one evening, his servants dismissed, contentedly sitting by the open window listening to the late song of a robin as the light faded from the evening sky. And there she found him early the following morning, asleep or so she thought; but his wine cup lay haphazardly on the floor, its contents, brown like blood, spilled from its lip on the wide oak planks.

Barely had she seen him encased in lead and stone and lain next to her mother in the pale-yellow church than the messenger arrived from the Earl. True to his oath, he summoned her into his protection. But she had known nothing of the agreement, and the shock of learning of it added to her misery. Ever since she'd first seen him, this man had represented death.

Within spitting distance of her home, of Buena, of her parents in their stone-hard tomb, Isobel already missed every part of it. She even missed Thomas, gone now to France for the better part of the summer with no word. His father had attended the requiem mass with eager solemnity and a new gown. Oozing insincerity, he assured her of his heavy heart and fatherly intentions, and made no mention of the inheritance and manor he banked on her bringing his son, although it lay behind his every word.

Mesmerising, the griffin's red-forked tongue licked the man's back as he rose and fell in his saddle. Isobel watched it as they passed the crumbling cross marking the end of her land and thought that if her horse were to stumble or bolt, she might fall, and then there would be no option but to turn back. George, in a moment's distraction as he touched his beads to his lips in brief prayer, looked away. She loosened her grip on the reins. Sensing change, the horse shot forward, but the sergeant grabbed Isobel before she could slip from the saddle. She murmured her thanks, resigning herself to his vigilance and the long journey ahead.

They crossed the Trent at the Gunness ferry by noon, the journey made easier by the hardened tracks, but it was late when at last they rode clear of the numerous copses marking boundaries, and Isobel found herself confronted by the castle rising out of the ground like thunder over the town crouching at its feet. Within the encroaching night, lights like yellow glow-worms in grassy banks marked the distant houses lining the streets and along the course of the deep-cut dykes, where water ran silvered by the moon.

Before long, Isobel rode into the gathered heat of stone walls embracing tight houses crowding narrow streets off which winding alleys ran. The empty cobbled road echoed to their horses' hooves and the occasional strident bark, quickly cuffed to silence. Above them, jettied windows opened to curious faces, spilling light briefly before being closed against insects battering the glass — *tck*, *tck* — breaking bodies in a senseless onslaught of fragile wings.

Putrid heat lay trapped between the walls, stifling, choking. Isobel covered her face with her cloak to stop herself from gagging. Riding so close that their knees almost touched, George kept his voice down. "Not far now, my lady." He pointed ahead into the darkened way. "West past the butter cross in the market square, then south t'castle's barbican. The barbican's gate'll be closed now, I'll mark."

Her voice muffled in the folds of cloth, she asked, "You have been here before?"

"Aye, wi' your father on the Earl's business when you were a lass and he more able to get about. It's a swapping great place and right fair, and the great hall is the finest here 'bouts. But make no mistake, the Earl knows how t'keep a tight ward; he's rebuilding the barbican and opened shot loops in t'great tower. When done, it'll hold in a siege and then some." Neat stacks of sawn stone and timber lying against the castle's wall bore witness to recent defensive measures against uncertain times. George saw her looking. "Aye, and wi' the king not rightly knowing whether he be comin' or goin', I reckon the Earl is right."

"My father used to speak fondly of his service here."

"Aye, the Old Earl was a good lord, as your father were mine." Just in time, he ducked under an opened casement muttering something Isobel thought better not to hear and giving her a thankful moment in which to subdue the swell of emotion his praise of her father had evoked. Instead, she said, "You'll rest and find lodgings for the night?"

"I have letters for the Earl from Master Moynes. I'll not leave till they're delivered safe. But I've left the manor to nowt but an old man and a bag o' boys, an' I'll want to see it well defended in case o' further trouble."

"Trouble? Do you think there *will* be trouble?"

"With the king abiding at the Earl of Warwick's pleasure these last months, how can there be otherwise?"

"But Arthur said the king is visiting with my lord Warwick. You make it sound as if he is his prisoner!"

George gave her a slanted look. "I reckon tha' Master Moynes wished to save thy bones from being afeared. What good would it do thee to know the truth, eh? Wi' your goodly father gone what matter is it to thee who's king?"

A surge of voices and a shout of laughter invaded the night as a door opened and shut, and a shambling figure stumbled out of an alley, almost colliding with his horse. A swift oath and George had drawn his sword before the man recovered his balance. He stared, blearily surprised at the blade inches from his face.

"Pardon." The man belched loudly, and fumbled with his disarranged hose. "Takin' a piss," he offered in explanation, waving a hand perilously close to the tags of shirt barely covering him. Isobel forgot to be startled and looked anywhere else, rather than risk the man exposing himself.

George kneed his horse forward, forcing the drunk out of the way. "Get back!" he growled, and to Isobel, "Ride on, m'lady; there's no harm in him that sleep won't cure. The barbican lies ahead."

CHAPTER SEVEN

Isobel woke the next morning to a blunt stabbing sensation. A child's face — half obscured by an unruly mess of hair — hung suspended a few inches above where Isobel lay on a low truckle cot by the bed. The child extended a finger and jabbed Isobel in the stomach. "Wake *up*!"

"Cecily, stop that!" a disembodied voice called from somewhere in the room.

The little girl pulled a face. "But she won't wake up. Who is she?" The child rolled out of view. "I'm hungry, Meg; tell her to get my food."

"Shhh. She's not your servant. She arrived late yestereve when you were asleep."

The girl's face reappeared, frowning. "Then why is she down there? I don't know her. Tell her to go 'way."

The journey had been long and the road to the castle rough. Isobel relocated her aching limbs and began to sit up. She squinted at the untidy peat-coloured mop and the startlingly blue eyes that stared from beneath it. The child stuck out her tongue and rolled across her bed, releasing a slight whiff of urine, to go and stand by an older girl combing her thin straw hair by the open window. It must still be early. The sun had risen perhaps an hour before, but it was low on the horizon and had not yet brought warmth to the day.

Disorientated by the late night and unfamiliar surroundings, Isobel rose stiffly and stood feeling disjointed and out of place in her smock. The older girl, of perhaps eleven years, stopped combing her hair.

"Cecily does not mean to be rude; she is only a child and has a tendency to peevishness." Her clear voice carried an unnatural maturity at odds with her thin, pale face dominated by large hazel eyes. She looked a sombre little thing next to the buoyant, wriggling child. "I heard you come in last night and that there was nowhere else for you to sleep. I am Lady Margaret Langton, and this is Lady Cecily." She inclined her head and nudged her sister to do the same. The child stuck her thumb in her mouth and gazed over the head of a yellow-haired poppet she clutched to her.

Feeling ridiculous in her smock, Isobel nonetheless dipped a quick curtsy to the younger daughters of the Earl. She longed to wash and dress and arm herself against the newness of the day and her surroundings.

"The cot is not very comfortable." Lady Margaret indicated the truckle bed. "Alice usually sleeps there, and she always complains. But it must be better than sleeping in the servants' hall." She returned to drawing the comb through her hair, wincing slightly as she encountered knots.

Hugging her arms about herself in the morning air, Isobel looked around for her clothes and saw them piled more or less neatly where she had abandoned them in the dark of the night before. Her throat felt dry, and she had not supped. Her stomach ached with hunger, and she longed for the comforting sounds and smells of home.

Cecily sucked hard on her thumb and squirmed. "I want Alice," she declared. "I want to piss."

Margaret gave her sister a gentle shove in the direction of a door set in the wall. "Go then, you do not need Alice; you are old enough to take yourself."

Cecily's thumb made a popping noise as she plucked it from her mouth. She stamped her foot. "I want Alice. I want her *now!*"

"She's not here."

Cecily grabbed her sister's arm and her voice rose. "You do it, Meg. Come with me. Come *on*…"

"Cecily, no —"

"What is this noise?" The rising chorus gave way to the sharp reprimand of an older woman dressed entirely in browns and coiffed as a widow. She bustled into the room bag-eyed and bellicose. Both girls stopped their tugging and stood still. "Well?"

Margaret took Cecily's plump hand firmly into both of her own. "It is nothing, Aunt."

Pinch-mouthed, the woman looked around. "Where is Joan? She should be attending you."

Dark and defiant, Cecily twisted with urgency. "But I want Alice. I want to go piss."

Eyes bulging, the woman glared at the child. "Go to and take your nonsense with you."

The girl's mouth trembled. Pointing at Isobel, she said, "She can take me."

The woman turned and saw Isobel still standing by the bed, unkempt, unwashed, and bewildered. "Well? What are you waiting for, girl? See to it."

Crossing the room under the baleful eye of the older woman, Isobel took the child by the hand and let herself be led towards the corner of the room.

Cecily pointed to the door. "It's through there."

Isobel turned the iron handle and pulled the door open. The unmistakable stench of a privy in summer met her. She held her breath and waited for the girl, but Cecily held back.

"You go in."

Isobel went in, breathing shallowly and letting her eyes adjust to the dim light from the uncovered slot that served as a window. Sweeter air filtered through from outside; she took a lungful. The girl peered around the doorway, dashed forward, lifted her night smock, and plomped her bare bottom on the wood slab seat. She kept her eyes squeezed shut and, as soon as the desperate stream slowed, jumped up and raced from the room. Isobel followed more slowly.

When she entered the bedchamber, the other woman was admonishing a sullen-faced girl of about Isobel's age, who she called "Joan" and whose buoyant breasts strained to escape a hastily donned kirtle. Joan bobbed her head in acquiescence, then, as the woman turned, thumbed her nose at her back. She saw Isobel looking and challenged her with a stare. Scooping up her clothes, Isobel made for the screened end of the room where she had hastily changed the night before.

"Where do you think you are going? Come here!" the older woman called after her.

Isobel bristled. The last time anyone had spoken to her like that she had been seven years old, and her mother had caught her lurking on the main stair outside the great hall after the merrymaking company had woken her. She considered ignoring the order, then thought better of it and slowly faced the woman. She tried to look as dignified as she was able, given her state of undress.

"What is your name?"

"Isobel Fenton, madam."

"Your father?"

Isobel steadied her voice. "Sir Geoffrey Fenton."

"A *knight*." Her tone said it all.

Rattled, Isobel raised her chin. "My mother was Lady…" But the woman had turned her back and was giving the nursery maids instructions to dress the girls, and Isobel whispered her mother's name to nothing but the air. Ignored for the time being, she slipped behind the screen and quickly dressed, unwashed and in linen grimed with the previous day's journey.

When she emerged, with hair finger-combed and hidden beneath her hennin, the woman whom the girls called "aunt" had vanished and the Earl's daughters were washing their faces in a large bowl. At least Margaret did — quietly and diligently — but Cecily protested against the cloth scrubbing at her face.

"Stay still!" Joan pleaded. "The countess might visit, and you are not fit to be seen." But Cecily escaped, diving under the bed where only her pink feet could be seen flapping the edges of the covers until they, too, disappeared from view.

"My lady, *please*…" She threw her hands in the air as Isobel approached. "She never does what she is told," she complained, and bent sideways to speak to the void beneath the bed. "Come out of there or I will have a beating to be sure."

The only answer was a giggle of non-compliance. Cecily reminded Isobel of her own childhood, when she was less biddable than the kittens in the stables, and not as sweet. The child now hummed a song beneath the bed. Joan kneeled and was about to try to grab the nearest limb when Isobel tapped Joan on the arm, put a finger to her own lips, and beckoned her away. Her raised voice carried across the room. "I did not sup last night, and I am *so* hungry. Might food be had to break my fast? Soft, warm manchet bread and a little butter?"

Joan pushed her plump lips into a puzzled expression, making her look like an annoyed fish, but Margaret — face still shining with water and lit for the first time with mirth —

jumped in. "I like manchet dipped in warm milk with cinnamon and honey. Cecily likes that too, but not today. She's not hungry today."

The humming from under the bed stopped. The tatty doll thrust from beneath the hangings. "Nan's hungry, too."

Margaret, standing thin and skimpily clad with damp wisps of fair hair curling at her forehead, bent down and patted the doll on the head. "Then Nan had better come out or she'll miss her meal."

Nan danced a jig and vanished again. The humming set up beneath the bed; occasionally a toe stuck out and wiggled for attention only to be withdrawn seconds later. Margaret gave up and went to the dressing screen where a pale green gown had been put out for her.

Joan made a grab for a foot but missed. She lifted the edge of the hanging. "I'll be telling Lady Roche about you if you make us late to mass," she grumbled, but straightened as Alice, a cheerful girl with buckle teeth, whom Isobel had met briefly the night before, came into the room.

"Where've you been?" Joan grumped. "Lady Roche'll dine on your liver if you don't hurry yoursen."

Alice took no notice and instead said to Isobel, "What comfort did you make of my fine featherbed?"

"It was better than the floor and stayed more still than my horse, so I thank you for it."

"But only a little better." Alice wrinkled her nose and laughed. "You did me a service: I slept like a queen and have already breakfasted like the king."

"Which one?" Joan muttered. "Henry or Edward?"

Alice's smile became uncertain. "*The* king, of course. *Our* king."

"Don't be so sure of it if the Earl of Warwick has his way. If King Edward is his *guest*, who's king anyway, him or Warwick?" She placed an imaginary crown on her head and did a little strut. "King Richard Neville; there's a thing. What will the countess make of *that*, I wonder?"

Alice darted a look at the screen and then at the door. "Shh, don't speak of such things. If the Earl hears of it…"

Joan flicked a hand at her. "Well, he won't, will he, unless you tell him, and how are you going to do that with the Earl gone awhiles, unless you have Master Sawcliffe's ear?" She slid a look at Isobel. "Or you. Will *you* tell?"

Isobel met her hard eyes and held them. "My father taught me that loyalty is more precious than virtue, and true loyalty as incorruptible as gold."

Joan appraised her for a moment, then shrugged. "Eh, well, just so you know — you don't go blathering, you hear? Then we'll get along fine enough. Now you're here, you can give us a hand." She thrust the fresh smocks into Isobel's arms.

Isobel had never been in the position of dressing someone before. With Buena kept busy making physic to ease her mother's pain, Isobel had once helped brush her mother's hair when she had been too ill to do so herself. This was different. This placed her in the position of a servant, and she felt suddenly, unnervingly, out of control.

"Will you not bathe, my lady?" she asked as Margaret held up her arms to receive her smock.

"I have washed my face and hands."

"No more?" Isobel asked somewhat hesitantly.

A squeal from behind the painted and carved wooden screen alerted them to Cecily's capture and confinement.

"Lady La Roche says that it is not necessary to cover myself with water daily. She says that it lets the humours rise in the body and corrupts maidens." Margaret raised her skinny arms and the fine, light linen kirtle settled over the smock. With the amount of bathing in which she had indulged during her life, Isobel considered that she must be thoroughly corrupted by now. If that were corruption, she thought, she wished more would seek it and save her senses every time she passed the stinking... pure.

Margaret stepped into her gown and Isobel fumbled the laces, ruefully considering how simple a task Buena made it on a daily basis, while here she was managing to make a brier's nest of it. She stood back to survey her work.

"What do you call *that*?" Joan remarked, emerging from behind the screen followed by a sulky-looking Cecily, clothed and recalcitrant. "Here, let me tie it for you, my lady." She undid the laces and swiftly re-secured them. "What household have you been in that you don't know how to lace a gown? Sweet Mary, what a mess!" Isobel didn't think it that bad. "Well? Where have you been?"

"Been? I haven't. I stayed at home."

"A situation couldn't be found for you? My brother managed to find a place for me here when he came to serve. He's done right well. Shame your father couldn't do the same for you beforetime."

"He did not wish to," Isobel said, indignant. "My mother taught me French and music and all I need to maintain a household, and my father schooled me in history, Latin, and law, and matters of our estate, so what need I to seek a place elsewhere? I had no need to serve," she added. "My father was a knight."

"O, aye." Joan screwed her eyes into narrow wedges. "And what makes you think mine's not?"

The uncomfortable gap that followed was broken by a bell filling the air with its urgent call to morning prayers. Joan flapped. "I've not combed Lady Cecily's hair and it won't stay hid for long even if I cover it and secure it with glue and trenails. Lady Margaret, you go; your sister will be along, and if any ask, she is taken with an ill humour which must be expelled ere we leave." Her agitation made fuel for the child's entertainment. Cecily darted under Joan's extended arm and would have hidden under the bed again except Isobel caught her around the waist as she fled, and secured her, kicking and protesting, against her own body. There was nothing for it but to hang on until she exhausted herself or gave in.

"We'll be late, and I'll be flayed," Joan complained. "You see what I have to put up with." The child's limbs beat desperately, reminding Isobel of the struggle of a frightened animal more than the protestation of a wayward child. From her childhood, she recalled a lullaby and softly, in the depths of her throat, began to sing.

Standing with her hands on her hips, Joan huffed, "What do you think *that* will do?" But gradually the child's movements slowed, lessened, until Isobel felt her resistance dwindle, and she carefully put her back on her feet. She half-expected her to bolt, but she stayed, still transfixed, and Isobel kneeled before her, looking earnestly into the child's face. The thumb had found its way back into her mouth and with the other hand she scratched at her head.

"I do not know the way to your chapel, will you show me?"

"She'll not do anything *you* ask," Joan declared. "And take that thumb from your mouth, my lady, or I'll take you to the barber-surgeon and have it cut off." She tried hooking the offending thumb from between Cecily's lips, but the girl shrugged her off and instead took Isobel's hand. Warm and sticky, this simple act of trust caught Isobel unprepared, and she felt her heart move.

Joan tutted. "Your hair is a right sight, make no mistake…" She started to fuss around Cecily's unruly curls, but Isobel quickly interjected as the child started to pull away.

"My lady's hair is the prettiest colour and as soft as feathers; leave it be for now." Still holding Cecily's hand, she stood, almost fearful she might startle like a jittery colt, but the girl turned and, tugging Isobel's hand to follow, marched determinedly towards the door.

What Isobel had seen of the castle the night before had been obscured by a weary darkness and cloaked by grief. In daylight, and with the sun cutting dazzling wedges into the pale-washed stone as they passed pinched windows along narrow passages, she felt a surge of excitement at the unknown.

Cecily stopped in front of a larger door, ornately carved and hung with rich cloth. It had been left slightly ajar and from beyond it came a faint voice raised in incantation. Heady and thick, sweet incense seeped at the hinges and from under the door.

"You can't go in," Joan hissed to Isobel. "It's my lady's chamber and only the family and her favourites are allowed in there. She usually goes with her sister, but Lady Cecily'll take herself, won't you, my lady?"

But Cecily had other ideas. A 'v' formed between her eyes, and her mouth opened as a small pink cavern.

"No, don't start!" Joan pleaded as Isobel looked on in astonishment. "She always does this if she doesn't get her own way. Come on, my lady. I'll snike caraway comfits from the confectioner when he isn't looking; you like those, don't you? Or an apple fritter."

Cecily closed her mouth, narrowed her eyes, and seemed to be considering the proposition. Movement from beyond the door suggested morning mass might be drawing to a close.

"Quick!" Joan flustered. "Before my lady notices…" Taking Cecily by the shoulders, she propelled her towards the door.

Letting out a scream of defiance, Cecily's small hands grasped the side of the door frame with surprising strength and refused to budge. But it was too late. The door opened inwards in a gust of perfumed air, and Isobel saw Lady La Roche bearing down on them like a tidal surge blown with brown fury.

"You are late, and Lady Cecily is a disgrace. Get back to the chambers and I'll deal with you anon. I have a mind to have you dismissed." She left with the girls subdued and trailing behind her.

"Sweet Mary," Joan breathed, "I feared the whip but got her tongue, and that's bad enough, make no mistake. We must get back before she changes her mind." When Isobel didn't follow, Joan stopped. "Where are you going?"

"I must find my possessions." Isobel made to continue in the opposite direction, but Joan tagged her sleeve.

"You mustn't go wandering around the castle by yourself; there's all sorts here now the garrison's swelled. Even some from Kent and they're a rabble so they say. Best stay with me." She looked back the way the girls had gone, nervous to be after them. "Come," she beckoned, "I'll send one of the maids to look for your things later."

By the time the girls had returned, the chambermaids had prepared the table and tidied the room. Margaret took Cecily to one side and was helping her dress her poppet in russet wool with a girdle of twisted yellow threads. The window had been closed and the air felt tight.

Lady La Roche emerged from the pallet room. "You idle girl!" she said to Joan. "The countess is deeply displeased at your failure to present Lady Cecily for morning prayers. It is a wonder you are not to be sent back in shame to your father. Instead, you are to be fined for your slackness. Any repetition and you will be beaten. Is that clear?"

Joan bobbed low. "Yes, m'lady. Lady Cecily was in ill humour, m'lady, and would not obey."

"It is of no account. Cecily is a child and will do as she is told, as will you."

Feeling out of place, Isobel had taken herself to the corner of the room where the children played. Margaret talked quietly to her sister, but every now and again raised anxious eyes to where her aunt continued lashing Joan with her tongue. It seemed to Isobel that the girl carried a burden of care beyond her years. Cecily appeared unaware of the trouble she caused, or that Joan had all too readily sought to shift blame to her young shoulders. Again, Isobel felt a tug of pity. The girdle was proving to be troublesome, and Isobel kneeled beside the girls and showed them how to slip the braid into a knot that would stay. She longed to be free of this place and the tension that leached out of every stone and found herself missing Thomas.

Growing tired of her tirade and the bland submission offered by Joan, and with her long paternoster beads snapping at her ankles, Lady La Roche snorted like an enraged bull and left the room to find entertainment elsewhere.

"Is she not responsible for the nursery? How can Lady La Roche talk about duty when she fails in the observance of it herself?" Isobel said indignantly when she had gone.

"You're not used to the ways of court, are you?" Joan said. "Been too long on your own manor. Let me tell you, if Lady

La-ruddy-Roche tells you to walk into the mouth of Hell you do it, because the countess is her niece and will be there with a pitchfork waiting for you if you don't."

Isobel didn't know whether she felt more shocked by Joan's acceptance of the injustice meted on her, or her lack of respect for the countess.

"Look," Joan leaned close, "I don't know where you come from and I don't rightly care, but I intend leaving this castle well-wed or not at all. I'm not going home to a sag-arsed husband too boiled in his own piss to raise it, whether my father thinks so or no." She might have said more but the door opened to a maid preceding two scullery knaves bearing food on large trays. They brought with them smells of fresh bread and animal fat from the kitchens, making Isobel's stomach grind with hunger. Joan prodded the food, found a loosened piece of bread, and took it.

"Don't eat it, don't eat it!" With a scurry, Cecily ran to the table, barging past Joan to grab a handful of bread.

"Watch yourself, my lady," Joan remarked, but otherwise didn't seem too bothered by Cecily's grimy fingers dipping in and out of the milk before anyone could stop her.

Horrified, Isobel blurted out, "She hasn't washed her hands!"

Helping herself to bread, Joan glanced at the girl. "Don't you worry about that, there's time enough to wash her ladyship after. Mind, I'll have to sit on her."

Isobel watched Cecily cram soggy bread into her mouth, indifferent to her sister's admonition or the dribble of milk that ran from a corner, down her chin, and soaked a translucent patch on her kirtle.

Joan tutted. "I do my best, but she's got the devil in her —"

"How can you say that!" Isobel exclaimed.

Joan shrugged. "It's not what I say, it's Lady La Roche that says it. The child doesn't mind; she's in her own world most of the time and doesn't hear half of what's said and does less than half of what she's told. Don't you, my lady?"

Cecily stuffed a piece of bread into the pouch of her cheek and drank from a cup with as much gusto as a blacksmith after a day at the forge. She still managed to hum to herself, but otherwise seemed oblivious.

"Lady La Roche is meant to oversee the children, but she's oft with the countess and when she's here, she'd rather be somewhere else." Joan shrugged again, the idle movement pushing her kirtle forward to reveal the deep cleft between her breasts. Isobel drew her own kirtle upwards a little. "I call her La *Roach* because she is slippery as a fish," she confided. "Of course, it makes more work for me, but better she were gone than meddling, I say."

"Does the countess not care?"

Joan's lip curled unattractively as if Isobel had said something which would have been blindingly obvious to anyone else. "My lady," she said, "has her position to keep. Or she did. She served the queen, and there's not many in my place that can say that." Glancing at the children, she dropped her voice. "'Course, she's not there now, not after … you know." Her raised eyebrows were meant to convey a message, but Isobel was none the wiser.

"After what?"

"Where have you been? Don't you hear anything where you're from? They say the king took a passing fancy to Lady Elizabeth — the Earl's eldest girl — and the queen was so angry she dismissed her, not that she had any reason to, I'd say, though I would have given her some." She sniggered. "Have you *seen* the king?"

Yet again, Isobel shook her head.

"Well, I have, and I'd be happy to oblige His Grace if he should ask, make no mistake." Joan blew out her cheeks and made a show of fanning them with one hand. "That's if he's still king. Don't know what the Earl'll make of it if he's not. Can't see him changing his allegiance, not him." She shook her head and, reaching for the bread, tore a piece. "So, you weren't sent to a household?" she asked with her mouth full, resuming the previous conversation. "Didn't you want advancement, you know, meet my lords and their ladies, perhaps find a husband? What need of Latin when you have a husband's bed to warm?" She dunked bread into the milk, seemingly forgetting whose fingers had been there not so long before.

Carefully removing the fingered outer layer of bread, Isobel considered her options: life at Court at the bidding of others whose lives made her head spin, or on her own manor with her husband oft away and time to be spent at her leisure in her garden. Her choice remained simple and nothing she had seen persuaded her otherwise.

"I have a husband, or I will come Michaelmas."

"You're to be wed? You have a sweetheart? What's he like? Is he handsome?" Joan pronounced the word 'andsom', giving away her origins somewhere in the West Riding. Isobel suspected this to be a favourite topic of the young woman because she licked her lips and, keeping an eye on the door, lowered her voice. "I have a sweetheart, but don't tell anyone." It appeared she didn't count Margaret or Cecily. "His name's Jon; he's esquire to old Crook-Nose, you know…" she said, but Isobel shook her head. "The steward. He keeps him tight, does the steward, won't give Jon an inch and works him hard. Still manages to give him the slip, though. He's a right one, my Jon." She winked.

"When will you wed?"

"Wed? Nay, we're not betrothed, not yet at any rate so don't let on. My lady would have me thrashed and thrown out if she thought I had taken a fancy to a man. She won't allow it — not in her household. The daughter of Lady Forest got with child and when my lady found out, she had her banished there and then from the castle, and she ended up at the nunnery with naught but her chaplet and the clothes she stood in. The child died and she might as well have."

"What about the child's father? Would he not marry her?"

"He was already married, and her own parents wouldn't have her back — spoiled goods can't be sold, can they? Though I dare say a match might have been made with a third son of a poor merchant and a big enough dowry. Blood is what it is, and some'll overlook a bastard child, but not many, and her life wouldn't be worth the living neither being one thing nor another. I pity her."

"What do you mean?"

"Well, not being with her own kind, and not belonging with her husband's, would make for a lonely life, I'd say. So, not a word about me and Jon."

Isobel shook her head. "I'll say nothing. I'll be gone soon anyway."

"Aye, so you said," Joan muttered.

"And when you do marry," Isobel continued, "you will have your own household."

"Jon's not able to wed — not for some time yet. He'll not chance to lose his position here, nor will I ask him to. You might have the means to live but we don't. With four brothers and two sisters my dowry's as thin as small ale and Jon looks to not much more. His father wants a better match than I can afford him, and mine is looking for a widower to feather my bed and his own, and I'd rather eat maslin and wild garlic for the rest of my life. It'd be like bedding with my own father and, sweet Mary, I'll not be doing *that*." She pulled such a comical expression that, despite everything, Isobel let a smile through, and Joan, liking her more for it, warmed a little. "That's enough about me; what's your story?"

Isobel wasn't sure she wanted to disclose anything about Thomas to Joan. She couldn't be certain that anything said in front of her would remain between the two of them. It was not something she had needed to consider with Buena, not because she had never spoken, but because even if she could, Isobel felt sure that she wouldn't. Loyalty often lay in the mind of the beholder, and discretion — her father had taught her — could be the difference between keeping one's head and losing it. Not that her betrothal could be considered disloyal in any way, but her father had avoided the subject of the Earl's disposition towards the match and his silence had spoken more than his words ever could.

At the thought of her father, Isobel felt her throat close, and she made pretence of removing a lash from the corner of her eye. She had never felt lonely, not even after the death of her mother, whom she had missed like a limb. This was more; this was her world laid waste and her father and Buena were part of its foundation. Without them she thought she might sink into sand and be swallowed by the earth.

"So...?" Joan pushed.

"My father died recently. He charged the Earl with my care until I am wed."

"At Michaelmas, you said." Joan sniffed. "Nobody charges the Earl. Only the king *charges* the Earl. Why would my lord allow it?"

"My father never said," Isobel replied, but she wondered the same. Why did she feel that the Earl had an obligation towards her father, and what could have led to it?

The sun had moved beyond the window and the room became stifling. Going to the casement, Isobel opened it and leaned to catch the faint breeze that rose from the river below. The air smelled different here — warmer, rounder — and even the river carried a new scent, its clear dark waters moving glass upon which the sun played.

Kneeling on the cushioned seat, she stretched as far as she dared, following the course of the river where it embraced the walls of the castle, curving in an arc to enclose it securely. Beyond lay the town and the road down which she had travelled the night before. The road home. At home, John would be gathering the first of the sour apples and the last of the plums. The skeps would be replete with honey, the combs full of gold. The broad, brown-brindled river would be cooling the air and it would be silent down by the water where the heron waited for silver eels. She wished she were there now and closed her eyes, but the cries from the town, the barking of the dogs, and the complaint of oars in the boats by the small town dock were insistent and, try as she might, the quiet of her home eluded her.

"You can shut that window," Joan called. "Lady La Roche doesn't like the window to be opened in case foul air from the river infects the room."

"The only foul air I can smell is in here," Isobel muttered crossly. "Lady La Roche has an excess of choler and might benefit from bathing to cool her liver." She eyed the water. "I can suggest a quick route down to the river."

The room behind her had become very quiet. Isobel turned from the window, blanched, and scrambled to her feet. The woman who stood at the threshold of the room was no more than middling in height, but Isobel felt her presence like a blow, and sank in submission. She watched the richly patterned skirts held in a fall of silk, revealing glowing underskirts beneath and the tips of scarlet shoes. Other feet, partly obscured by skirts or robes, moved behind and around the woman in a multicoloured dance. Isobel felt herself examined but dared not look up.

"Who is this?"

A pair of brown shoes came to a standstill by the red. "Isobel Fenton, my lady," a soft-voiced man answered.

"Stand," and as Isobel did as bid, the countess marked her movement openly. "Who is her father?"

"Sir Geoffrey Fenton, my lady, of Beaumancote. A gentleman made knight in service to the king."

"I have not heard of him, lord steward; he is not at Court?"

"No, my lady. He held offices in the region of the Humber and Trent. He is lately gone from this world." He looked an odd little man, with a permanent stoop thrusting his head forward and a nose that looked grafted from the knobbly stump of a tree.

"Why is the girl here?"

"She has no kin, and my lord Earl has taken her under his charge until her marriage. She has a little learning and my lord bid me place her with my ladies until such time as she is wed."

The countess's mouth became tight. "My lord did not think to ask *me*. Can you read?" she asked Isobel directly.

"I can, my lady."

"Can you converse in French?"

"Yes, my lady. I can speak and write both French and Latin."

"I did not ask if you have Latin. If I wanted a clerk, I would procure one. In which household were you placed?"

"My own, my lady."

The countess spent moments more than Isobel could bear scrutinising the state of her dress, and Isobel saw in the pursed lines of her mouth her evident displeasure. Isobel folded her fingers inwards to hide nails stained by the blood of her garden, her hands wind-chapped and roughened by the sun.

"Your mother neglected her duty, as women of her degree are wont to do. You would do well to learn what you can here in the presence of women of estate before you make the same mistake with your own daughter."

In all her years, Isobel had never heard her mother referred to in such a demeaning manner. She could only stare dumbfounded, unsure whether her face burned with anger or shame. The countess spoke to the steward. "Hyde, the girl can help Joan. She can quarter here."

Isobel at last found her voice. "My lady, I have not come to serve. My mother was of noble blood, the daughter of the Earl of —"

"I see no evidence of it. You are what your father made you, no more. If you lie under this roof you must expect to pay for it." Only then did the countess appear to notice her daughters in the corner of the room, Cecily's thumb stuck fast in her mouth as she half-hid behind the slight body of her sister. Their mother motioned them to join her. Cecily clung to her sister's skirts as Margaret lifted her face to her mother. The countess inspected them like horses. "Cecily has lice." Then, taking a handful of Margaret's sparse hair, she squeezed it, dismissing the limp strands with a twist of her mouth. "Keep Margaret's hair veiled; it will not be so noticeable."

Margaret remained subdued after her mother flowed from the room in a wave of damask rose. Lady La Roche busied about, alternating scolding Joan with chiding the maids and instructing Isobel on her duties. Margaret sat by the window with her back to the room, the embroidery on her knees unworked.

"I expected worse than that," Joan declared as Lady La Roche relieved them of her presence. "I feared she'd stir it with my lady for the sport of seeing me beaten. Looks like you'll be bedding down here after all." She rubbed her hands together. "I reckon they'll leave us be for a bit. You stay here with my ladies, and I'll find my Jon. He wasn't with old Crook-Nose, so he'll be in his chambers I'll warrant." Pinching her cheeks and pressing her full lips together until they ripened, Joan plumped her breasts and, with a wink, left Isobel alone with the girls.

Cecily had become absorbed in feeding her poppet tiny beads from a toy spoon and making her drink from a pewter beaker, singing and talking all the while. Stepping around the child so as not to disturb her play, Isobel opened the window wide again, and sat opposite Margaret. The girl didn't look up. Isobel held her hand out of the casement, feeling the brush of air against her sun-struck skin.

"If I were at home on a day like this, I would be in my garden. John Appleyard would be tending the beds, and Buena — my servant — would be fussing about me wearing my hat." She withdrew her hand. "Is there a pleasance here, my lady?"

Margaret nodded but kept her head down. In the distance a dog barked, and below them and on the other side of the river, a group of long-legged hounds were being run on leashes. Isobel smiled. "Alfred — my father's dog — keeps digging holes in the borders to bury his meat bones and John scolds him, but he never takes any notice. If bones were seeds my garden would be full of flowers, he has planted so many."

A small sniff and a sigh. "I know what you try to do, but it matters not."

"Your lady mother did not mean anything by it."

"Yes, she did," Margaret said with resignation. "My mother thinks me ugly. She allows my sister, Lady Elizabeth, to attend her, but she keeps me here where I cannot be seen. When Bess was but twelve winters, my mother brought her to her chambers, and I am a year older and still I share a bed with Cecily."

Pale and watery, Margaret reminded Isobel of a limp new stem of angelica growing long and thin by the river's edge. "Perhaps you would like to walk by the river, my lady; it will be cooler there."

"It is not allowed."

"The pleasance, then?"

Margaret considered for a moment. "Joan does not like to walk abroad; she says it is unhealthy." She gave a quick smile. "But I do."

"And Lady Cecily?"

"She will follow," Margaret said, leaving her embroidery on the window seat. Sure enough, when Isobel looked behind her as they left the room, Cecily trotted after them without a word.

If it had been hot in the chamber of the Earl's youngest daughters where the window opened onto the face of the sun, here between the high walls leading to the pleasance, the heat intensified. By the time the girls had led Isobel through passages and down stairs, through high-ceilinged chambers and close-boarded doors, she wished for nothing more than to bathe her feet in the river and swim among the fish.

Cecily danced ahead of them, hiding behind pillars and walls and jumping out at them until Margaret could maintain her composure no longer and pursued her sister as they ran bursting into the pleasance.

The girls skipped across an enclosed courtyard and disappeared down a long allée of pleached linden trees, leaving Isobel alone in a court whose roof of interlaced branches sheltered her from the blistering sky. She could see nothing other than the trunks of the trees, but she could hear laughter.

Isobel picked up speed, emerging pink-faced and panting to find startled doves rising and the girls around a tiered fountain, splashing each other with water from cupped hands. Margaret's hair had come undone, and Cecily had lost a shoe, but on seeing Isobel the older girl stopped and hissed something to the child. Margaret's head drooped, waiting for admonishment, so she didn't see Isobel lean forward and scoop water from the fountain until she felt it against her skin.

Margaret gasped, looked up, and, seeing the challenge on Isobel's face, her eyes widened and a smile of cautious delight seeped across her thin face. Reaching out, she splashed the water, sending fine drops like beads of glass over Isobel. Small patches bespeckled her gown. Isobel looked at her dress, cocked her head, and stepped swiftly forward, raising her hand and then cuffing the surface of the water. *Smack*. With a squeal, Cecily hit the water and within seconds all three of them were in a melee of water and arms and laughter.

Tired at last and wet through to her smock, Isobel flopped to the ground. Her light wool gown hung unevenly, clinging to her hips, and she spread it out around her in the sun to dry.

"You smell doggy," Cecily sang, dancing in a puddle on the glistening grass.

Isobel looked around the garth properly for the first time. On all four sides trees provided dense privacy to a square garden made of quarters of grass. She had never seen a sward like it, smooth and sleek, not burned by the sun into scabby patches as hers was wont to be in summer. Instead of paths, channels ran from the fountain down which water flowed towards big urns of gillyflowers and roses standing at each intersection like graceful guards. The air smelled sweet.

Selecting a dry patch of ground, Margaret sat down.

"Doggy, doggy, dog, dog," Cecily chanted.

"This is a fair garden, my lady," Isobel observed, ignoring the antics of the child.

Margaret looked puzzled. "It is but part of the pleasance."

Cecily had given up and now jumped in and out of the narrow channels. Her other shoe lay abandoned to one side, and the hem of her gown dragged around her ankles.

"The rest is beneath the tower on the other side." Margaret pointed to the opposite side of the garden from where they entered. "It is the wilderness garden; we do not go there."

It sounded wonderfully enticing and Isobel was about to ask why, when a shout went up from the allée. Startled, Margaret jumped to her feet and Isobel followed more slowly, searching the shade of the trees for the source of alarm.

Lady La Roche stalked towards them, finger wagging. "What do you do here? You know this is forbidden to any but your noble maman and those privy to her pleasure."

Isobel took a step towards her, partly shielding the girls. "Lady Margaret wanted to show me the garden, and Lady Cec—"

"I did not address *you*." The woman focused a baleful eye on her, then turned her attention to her nieces, taking in their state of dress. Margaret's gown was drying in patches where the sun made the green silk pale on the tops of her shoulders and at the edge of her bodice, but the little girl continued her game of kicking water, making rainbows of the spray. Lady La Roche's face became puce, her lips thin and drawn as she spat out, "Get to your chamber, I will deal with you there."

Her headdress slipping, Isobel dragged it from her head as they made the final ascent towards the girls' chambers. Hearing distant voices, Cecily finally managed to wrench her hand free of Isobel's and, like a stickleback, darted around the corner. Isobel approached the mural passage with caution. Cecily talked animatedly to a man on one knee as he listened intently to her prattle with a grave expression. He looked up as Isobel hurried forward, and only then did she recognise him as his eyes widened in response, his mien changing from serious to bemused as he took in the state of his nieces' dress, and her own. Aghast, Isobel barely skimmed the ground in a curtsy as she took hold of Cecily's hand and all but pushed past Robert Langton as she made for the nursery.

Shoving the door closed behind them, she leaned against it, chest heaving, sweat glazing her neck and, holding out her hands in front of her, she found them to be shaking. Squeezing her eyes tight, she drew her fingers into fists until they stopped trembling. After a moment, she opened her eyes and saw Joan staring at her, hands on hips, looking none too pleased.

"I don't know where you think you've been, but I've had the Roach tearing my ear off looking for you. The castle is in a right wasps' nest, and I've been given more errands than I've hands for." Taking in the children's disarray, and Isobel's unkempt hair, she sucked her teeth. "Holy Mary protect us, what have you been doing? I'll deal with Lady Cecily. You," she addressed Isobel with a matron's rebuke, "had best be about your dress lest Lady La Roche see you."

"Too late," Isobel said, hopping as she removed first one sodden shoe, then the other.

Several chambermaids were scuttling around the room like mice. An air of urgency accompanied them.

"What's happened?" Isobel asked, moving out of the way as a maid bobbed past her to get to the door.

Joan threw a look over her shoulder and tutted. "Haven't you heard? The king's been released, and the Earl is returned."

CHAPTER EIGHT

The castle was awash with rumour. Men with loud voices, brash with tension, flooded the outer ward and crammed the passages. The Earl had returned with news of King Edward's release from Warwick's enforced hospitality, and he now awaited further developments. From the town walls to the gatehouse, efforts were redoubled to protect the castle from attack, and Isobel watched as beyond the river wicked tongues of flame spread along the far bank, stripping the remaining undergrowth and laying the land bare of any cover from which enemy eyes might watch.

"It's an ill omen," Joan warned, viewing with repellence the char-headed crow stalking the ground, her temper soured now Jon was kept busy and she short of gossip. She threw a last look at the bird before turning her back on it. "The king might be free, but no good will come of it, mark me, not until there be but one king on the throne. And what of the Earl of Warwick? What if he were to push a little harder, eh? King Edward might not walk free next time and then we would be in a pretty state. What would our Earl do then? Change colours if he has any sense, or lose all this and us with him." She nodded to the room and to his children bent over Isobel's casket investigating the contents.

Isobel finished filling the coarse linen square with crushed oats, leaves of sage, and purple lavender, brought the ends up to form a bag, and secured them neatly with thread. "The Earl won't do that," she said, keeping her voice low. "He'll not betray the king."

Joan took a bite of the pastry saved from dinner and wiped her mouth with the back of her hand. "Then he's more of a fool than I took him to be, though I'd not let him hear me say it."

Isobel frowned in the direction of the girls. "Shh, not so loud. The Earl is loyal to the house of York, as his father before him."

Joan waved her hand, scattering crumbs in an arc. "What of it? What does it gain a man if his fealty ends on a scaffold? Look what happened to the queen's father and brother. If they'd played their hand aright and given Warwick the wink, they'd not be in their graves, would they? Loyalty's only as good as the end it serves, no more, and you're as much a fool as the next if you think otherwise. Now, the Earl of Warwick — *he* has the power to break kings: first the old, and now the new." She raised her brows as if she spoke a universal truth and severed the end of the pastry with a definitive bite.

"And you would be happy if Jon changed allegiance, is that it?" Isobel probed, trying to disguise the disgust in her voice.

"I'm not saying that," Joan said slowly, viewing Isobel as she chewed. "He will serve." She stood suddenly, brushing crumbs to the floor.

One of the Earl's greyhounds had found its way into the girls' chamber. Fine-limbed, it snuffled around looking for scraps on the floor with Cecily's veil flapping around its neck. Isobel held out her hand and the dog came to her hopefully. Unwinding the veil, she stroked its silky head and was rewarded with dark gold orbs of adoration until Joan found a flake of pastry trapped in her kirtle and flicked it to the floor. Scenting food, the dog left Isobel's hand and she watched it for a few moments before remarking almost to herself, "If dogs serve only the ones who feed them, I fear for the world, for none shall know who is the master and who the dog."

Joan stopped brushing herself down. "Eh? I don't know about that, but Lady Cecily's been scratching again, and I'll know who's master all right if I don't put a comb through her hair. And I'll tell you one thing," she said, pushing the dog out of the way and checking she couldn't be overheard. "I'd sooner serve a king like ours than old Harry; and as for the Earl," her brows fluttered expressively. "Well, you know…"

Joan pulled her mouth meaningfully when Isobel didn't respond and leaned so close that Isobel could smell the soft cheese on her breath. "He's only to ask. Not that it's likely," she added, standing. "Not with the countess around. Should think he's done a bit of wenching since he's been away, he and the king. Oh, my lady knows, of course she does, so do all — but he keeps it from his nest, so to speak. They keep separate chambers — he in the great tower, she here in the new apartments he built when they wed." Joan indicated Cecily with a nod of her head. "She'll be the last, and there's no heir. Not now."

Joan fetched the lice comb from the cupboard and, as she passed Isobel, who had resumed fondling the dog's ears as Alfred had liked her to do, she paused, tapping the ivory comb against her hand, thinking. "That dog there — my noble lords part with manors and fall over themselves to have a pup whelped by one of the Earl's bitches. If Warwick can't bend the king to his will and His Grace falls, who's going to want one of the Earl's daughters, you tell me that? I'd rather place a bet on the dog's chances."

Gathering the little oat bags, Isobel stood up without answering.

Joan waited for a response, and when none came, piqued, said, "And what do you mean to do with those, might I ask?"

"Lady Margaret can use them to bathe and keep sweet."

"What'll she be wanting them for?" Joan scoffed. "A dog doesn't ask if a bitch is clean, does it?"

Cecily had been fractious all morning. She had spent days pent up in the nursery and the thunderous weather, laced with heat, had made it worse, so she had stripped to her smock and kicked off her shoes and hose as soon as they returned from morning prayers. Joan's conversation became increasingly raw and, by the time Lady La Roche had stormed through the rooms with a bellyful of bile, Isobel had to bite her tongue to stop snapping back.

In an attempt to cool their fraught nerves, she made a balm of rosemary and lavender, and now Margaret sat in front of her as she gently combed the mixture through the girl's hair. Margaret held a book at arm's length to prevent drops splashing the precious surface, and slowly worked the Latin text, picking out the words she recognised from her last lesson. She learned quickly, and Isobel praised her, pointing out that she had been a reluctant scholar at the best of times as she would rather have been in her garden. She ceased combing for a moment, caught up in the memory, until Margaret touched her arm lightly and Isobel saw concern in the girl's face, and continued her task.

Margaret held the book out again. "I like to learn; I like to understand what people talk about and why it matters. If I were a boy it would not seem so strange."

"If you were a boy, my lady, things would be very different." Joan brandished Cecily's fine-toothed comb, weighing her chances of catching the child unawares as she stood next to her sister in her smock, watching, thumb in mouth and poppet dangling from one hand. "Your tutor would have you at your lessons nigh on half the day, and the other half 'd be spent at arms. You wouldn't want that, now, would you?" She made a grab for Cecily and missed.

"Why not?" Margaret said. "I have learned to read and write; I can dance and draw thread. Why can I not learn Latin and law and to figure numbers?"

"Because it is not needed. You'll be no merchant's wife, my lady, nor a lawyer's." Joan thrust out a hand and managed to secure Cecily long enough to force her on her knee, and began roughly combing her hair. "And you will have a steward to run your estates and a secretary to write your letters and no need for learning. Such knots and tangles; stay still! You cannot be seen like this."

Cecily writhed on Joan's knees but couldn't escape. "I want to see him! I want to see him!"

"Well, you can't; the Earl doesn't want to see *you*."

"Joan, be gentle!" Isobel exhorted, hearing Cecily's hair stretch and snap and the child squeal; but Joan continued her relentless onslaught.

"No, Latin's not what you need, my lady," Joan reiterated. "Just a noble husband and strong sons." Still fighting the tangles, she didn't notice Margaret's mouth twist.

"If a husband can be found for me."

Cecily writhed from Joan's knees, across the room, and under the bed. "There's no worry about that," Joan said, giving up on the child. "Looks are not what count in a maid, and a good dowry will make up for want of beauty, you can be sure of it."

"Be quiet," Isobel hissed, but Margaret shook her head, making her slight body vibrate.

"Joan is right. I have neither the benefit of beauty nor the privilege of being a boy. But I can learn. Perhaps I can persuade my father to let me enter the convent? I could pray for my family and the king."

Joan ploughed on. "And not have a husband? The Earl will want to make a good match for you, and he is a powerful ally for any family, especially with King Edward's favour. Besides —" she winked — "think of what you'll miss."

"That's enough," Isobel snapped, and Joan looked at her in surprise.

"I only said —"

Isobel thumped the comb on the table. "You have said enough. Leave it."

Margaret pulled her long hair over her shoulder and tugged dejectedly at it. "I think *mon père* will have to find a blind man to marry me. My hair is horrible. It's all dry. It is not like Maman's hair. She let me touch it once — it felt like silk. She's so beautiful." She fingered her own strangled hair with its dry ends split into a confused mass of dull yellow strings. "I told you, it is horrible," Margaret wailed.

Isobel scooped the hair back and loosely braided it. "Perhaps a little time outside will let the sun warm your hair and take up the balm," she suggested. "Is there anywhere we are allowed to go?"

"There is the wilderness garden…" Margaret hesitated.

"You are not permitted?"

"Nay, it is not that." Seeing the eager light in Isobel's face quickly doused, Margaret added, "But if you would like to see it? Cecily," she called, "we go to the Far Court." Then more quietly, "She ran away once and became lost. We found her there. Our father was very displeased."

Conjuring the Earl's level frown, Isobel could quite imagine the lasting impression his anger must have made on his daughters. She could feel his cold eyes even now and darted a look at the door before she could stop herself.

The Earl was still on Isobel's mind when she found herself looking up at the sheer walls of the great tower where he kept his private chamber. The heat of the day bleached the sky pale blue, but in the tower's shadow, she felt a chill.

"Do you see much of the Earl, my lady?" she asked Margaret.

"Little. He is oft with the king. King Edward trusts his counsel in matters of state." Margaret sounded quite matter of fact, and Isobel wondered if she understood the implications of what she said.

"And have *you* seen the king, my lady?" Isobel asked as they entered the garden through an arch. Cecily dawdled, chasing butterflies.

"Oh, yes, and his brothers, the Duke of Clarence and the Duke of Gloucester, but not often, and only at a distance. Maman never allows us any closer. She lets Bess, though. She is her favourite. Bess was lately at Court, but she is returned now." Margaret sighed. "Cecily, come *on!*" They waited as her sister hung back, trailing wetly like a reluctant slug.

They found themselves on the edge of an expanse, and any awe Isobel might have felt at Margaret's casual disclosure became lost in the revelation before her. Between the glowing walls of the castle rising into the sun above them, and a bend in the slow-flowing river that made up the moat, a great garden stretched in informal idleness.

"I don't want to go," Cecily grumbled behind them as she caught up.

"I do," Isobel breathed, eager to follow the bricked path lined in swagged roses and plush bushes of lavender. The flower heads had long been cut, but the bruised leaves between her fingers released their pungent scent. Isobel forgot her changed circumstances and the daughters of the Earl and inhaled the magic of things green and growing. Partly hidden, temptingly close, the further garden called. Intoxicated, Isobel's feet moved of their own volition.

Cecily's cry broke the spell — "*No!*" Margaret dragged her protesting sister behind her. "I don't *want* to, Meg."

"We cannot leave you alone; remember what happened last time? I'll go first if you like."

Isobel turned back to the girls. "I'll tell you the names of the plants," she offered.

"Don't care," Cecily all but shrieked, and taking a shoe, threw it as hard as she could.

Isobel caught it before it vanished into a hedge of roses. Red-cheeked, the child crossed her arms, scowling and determined. Isobel crouched in front of her. "Do you not like flowers?" she asked, but Cecily didn't answer, her mouth open in horror, her eyes wide and fixed on Isobel's dress.

Isobel looked down. She smiled and held her palm open, and a fat sandy-brown spider crawled onto it, leaving a trail of silken thread across the wool. "Is it not pretty?" she said, holding her hand to the light as the spider investigated her palm. "Can you make out the cross of Our Lord on its back? There — can you see?" She held it out for Cecily, but the child flailed wildly, knocking the spider into the air. She fled to her sister, and Margaret soothed her, stroking her curly hair.

"She's frightened of spiders. Many flowers are tall, and she is so small that she cannot see beyond them. She hates what she cannot see, like the webs of spiders."

Looking around her at the long stems and solid-leaved hedges garlanded with webs, Isobel could understand why. "Forgive me, my lady," she addressed Cecily gravely, "I did not know."

"She is — we are — not permitted to be frightened." Margaret looked down at her sister a little sadly. "She ran away from her nurse one evening and was not found until the following day, over there." She pointed to the far side of the garden where the head of a tree rose. "She did not speak for two days, and she has feared spiders ever since. We only come here when we must, but ... but *I* like it here even though…" Her eyes drifted towards the river. "But I *do* like it," she finished with a hint of defiance.

Isobel considered for a moment. "If my lady will allow me to carry her, we shall be giants and the spiders will fear our might and run away." She held out her arms and to her surprise Cecily came to her and Isobel swung her onto her hip. "I expect your nurse must have been right glad to find you," she said as they began to explore.

Margaret answered for her. "She would have been — she was very kind to Cecily — but we never saw her again. Joan says she was beaten and sent from the castle in disgrace. Our aunt was given charge of us. She is not so kind."

That was understating the truth of it, Isobel thought sourly, recalling her brief encounters with the woman and the lasting impact they had made.

With Cecily's eyes tight shut and her small fists screwed into Isobel's dress, they moved along paths and through arches of vines, past hedges sculptured into fanciful creatures and raised pools where tiny insects skimmed the water. Isobel named each plant she recognised, wondered at those she didn't, and explained how this or that made into a potion or plaster might be used to ward off a chill, soothe a bite, or heal a low spirit. So long had she been the pupil, and her mother or Buena the teachers, that Margaret's attention came as a welcome change, and Isobel found herself enjoying the girl's questions and the challenge of fashioning an answer.

Crowning what appeared to be a rise in the ground towards the centre of the garden, a single apple tree rose, offering welcome shade. In this part of the garden, grasses grew taller, the hedges less kempt, and unswept leaves baked crisp by the heat blurred the line between grass and path. The area beneath the tree looked cool and the grass shorter. Nearing it, Isobel could see fruit already colouring red and green like particoloured hose. Cecily wriggled to be let down and ran towards the tree. Throwing her arms about it as far as she could reach, she hugged it.

As Isobel and Margaret drew closer, she seemed to be talking to herself, but it soon became evident that she chatted to something on the tree, which she stroked and patted. Winding around the slender trunk curved the form of a serpent.

"Oh!" Isobel exclaimed. She touched the hand-smoothed surface carved from fruitwood, each scale so perfect it might have been real. Once the snake would have stood proud of the trunk but over the years the tree had grown and filled until snake and bark were one. She ran her hand up the trunk until she came to the head and looked into eyes of black glass. Cold and emotionless, they reflected her face and, despite the heat, Isobel shivered. There seemed something odd about the creature. She stepped back to survey it and saw that the snake's long head had the features of a woman's face and, below where the neck might be, two swellings materialised as scaled breasts: a Lamia — destroyer of innocence, devourer of children.

Behind her, Margaret frowned. "It makes me uncomfortable, but Cecily likes it; this is where they found her when she became lost."

"Lady Snake," Cecily whispered, and continued to tell the serpent her woes, her fingers tracing the curves as if it were a chaplet, and the scales each a bead.

Isobel considered it an unwholesome creature for a child to like, and a strange, unnerving thing to have in a place of beauty. "Who had it fashioned?" she asked.

Margaret was busy removing her shoes and hose. She wiggled her chalk-white feet in the sun. "It has always been here. It used to frighten me; I believed it could see my thoughts, but now I know it is only made of wood and glass."

It might be, Isobel reflected, but if wood and glass could express meaning as surely as this did, who knows of what the messenger himself might be capable? After all, it was not the point of the sword which created the message, but the man who delivered it.

Margaret went on. "Lady La Roche will not allow Cecily to talk to it; she says she is feeble-minded." She tapped the side of her head and crossed her eyes. "But I do not think so, do you?"

Isobel had not yet formed a judgment, so instead, glancing at the aspect of the sun, said lightly, "It is nearing noon. We must get you changed before you dine, or your lady mother will not wish to be seen with you!" She turned to smile at the girl, but found her looking blank, and realised her error. "I meant only that —"

"Did you dine with your mother?" Margaret interrupted.

"Yes, always, until she became too ill to eat, and then I sat with her instead, and read from the romances." Isobel looked at the sky, seeing it had enriched to a blue the colour of the

Virgin's robes. "And when she died, I dined with my father when he was not about the king's business or the Earl's, and he would have me read to him, only he was not interested in romances; he had me read Latin texts and histories." She felt her smile wobble and tracked the progress of a small flock of doves towards the great tower rather than look down.

"I am sorry for your loss," Margaret said, and went on quickly, "I would like to read more."

"Would you, my lady?"

Margaret nodded and Isobel smiled at the eagerness in the girl's face.

"My father has wonderful books, my uncle also."

"Your uncle?"

"Lord Robert," Margaret clarified. "He is often here now that Lady Ann is…" The next word was lost as the bell for noon rang and the doves erupted in harried confusion from the tower, and she just said, simply, "He is more often here."

"And we must be away," said Isobel, noting Margaret's hand brought quickly to her eye before she thought it seen. She turned towards the tree. "Where is Lady Cecily?"

"Cecily?" Pulling on a shoe, Margaret looked up in alarm, but Isobel spotted the child at one side of the sward where roses massed over a deep bower. Thumb in mouth, she stared into the shade.

"What do you see, my lady?" It took a moment for Isobel's eyes to adjust, and then heat rose to her skin, and vanished as quickly. "Come away," she said briskly, taking Cecily's hand in her own and walking in the opposite direction.

"The man is hurting the lady," Cecily protested, pulling back.

"It is time to eat now," Isobel said, firmly walking towards Margaret, "and we will be late."

"She made noises." Cecily tried turning around to look again. "Meg," her high voice rang as they neared her sister, "she made noises, like this," and she moaned like a dove.

"Who did?" Margaret said, but Isobel located the path from which they had entered the garden and, scooping Cecily into her arms, found the way they had come.

CHAPTER NINE

The pattern of days became monotonous. Isobel heard nothing from Thomas, nor from Arthur Moynes, and frustration grated her patience as much as the relentless heat. She made do without Buena's help, but she was reluctant to ask for Joan's assistance in lacing her gown every morning in the pallet room, and felt more like a servant each day that passed. Sometimes she wondered whether there had ever been another life and found herself longing to see Thomas and all with which she had been so familiar. In the nursery, real life passed them by while the world outside their rooms rumbled with confusion and overheated rumour. She longed for the days when her father discussed politics with her. Here she felt ... overlooked. She wanted something to happen. Anything.

She went to a window and threw it as wide as it could go, but the heavy morning clung to her throat and did nothing to alleviate her temper. Behind her Cecily gave a particularly piercing scream and Isobel heard a squawked oath and, on turning, saw the comb fly from Joan's hand as she tipped backwards, and a flash of Cecily's bare legs as she escaped from the room.

Frantic barking drew Isobel across the bailey and towards the great tower, where she caught sight of Cecily's small, white-clad form racing up the open stairs. The child pushed between the trunks of men's legs as they descended, greyhounds snapping excitedly at her heels.

"My lady, no!" Isobel called.

Too late. Cecily was lost to view under the covered stair leading to the iron-bound door. Breathless, Isobel reached the top step as the door opened, and Cecily, avoiding the guards on duty and flitting through the narrow gap like a shaft through an arrow-loop, disappeared into the tower itself.

Isobel could hear small feet pattering up the curving stair within the thickness of the wall, and then exclamations of surprise from unknown voices. Seconds later, Isobel burst into the first-floor chamber and slid to a halt. From the assembled body of men came not a murmur, and at the head of the lord's table around which they gathered, sat the Earl.

Oblivious, Cecily trotted up the line of men towards her father. Not knowing what else to do and with her pulse rattling her ribs, Isobel collapsed into a curtsy. One of the lords coughed. She remained bowed, feeling their eyes on her, until she heard the Earl's irritated command to rise.

As the initial shock wore off, faces resolved into several she recognised: Lord Raseby, big, broad, and amused; Master Sawcliffe, appraising her with his permanent smile. And Robert Langton. His face was unreadable. He stood over a map spread on the table in front of his brother and had been in the middle of saying something because he still pointed to a mark blacked in ink upon it.

Cecily managed to climb onto her father's knee and was even now trying to turn his head towards her with little hands. Stone-faced, he took her hands from his face and motioned to Isobel and, finding her wits and legs, she moved to take her from him.

Clutching her poppet, Cecily wrapped her arms around Isobel's neck in such a simple gesture of trust that Isobel felt a rush of warmth to her heart in the icy atmosphere of the stuffy room. She murmured, "All is well," into the child's ear and, seeing the faintest smile ghost Lord Langton's mouth, fled the

Earl's council chamber red-faced, pursued by exchanged remarks and low laughter.

"Idiot girl!" Lady La Roche appeared shortly afterwards accompanied by distant thunder from the lowering sky. "You made me look like a fool." She jabbed a warning finger at Isobel. "Do not think I shall forget this. And you —" she swivelled sharply, bearing down on Cecily's frightened upturned face and taking her roughly by the arm — "will learn to obey." She thrust the little girl into the corner of the room, where she slid against the hard wall, bumping her head. "Stay there until I tell you otherwise. Move and you will have a beating."

"You've made an enemy there," Joan remarked with a slight swagger once the woman had gone. "And you'll be wishing you were back at home if the countess hears of this, be sure of that."

"I never wished to be away from it," Isobel said, kneeling by Cecily's curled-up form.

"Eh, didn't you hear what the Roach said?"

"She said Lady Cecily is to stay here, not that I cannot be with her." Isobel placed a hand on the child's arm and, meeting no resistance, settled down beside her. "Here is your poppet, my lady; she is missing you." She placed the doll in the cradle of Cecily's arms, and she clutched it to her.

Joan sniffed. "Don't take any notice of her; she'll come out of it. It'll be time for dinner before long and she'll be wanting sommet to eat soon enough. Now, Lady Margaret, we'll have that hair dressed before your lady mother comes visiting and catches you looking like last year's strewing reeds after a Yule feast. Where's the comb?"

The sky growled again and a faint breeze from the window lifted the edge of Isobel's veil, breathing scents of newly damp earth into the room. Raising her face to the freshening air, she welcomed the promise of rain. "John Appleyard, my gardener, will be pleased with this change in the weather. He will not have to water the flowers and it will keep the dust down on the paths."

She looked at Cecily: her nose dribbled, soaking the poppet's wool hair, and she snuffled quietly. Taking her kerchief, Isobel tried to wipe Cecily's face, but she buried her head in her arms, crushing the doll to her. Letting her hand rest on Cecily's head, Isobel gently stroked the curls apart, finding the reddened bump. "I have a little physic for your poppet's head. Shall we see if she likes it?"

Cecily didn't answer, so Isobel uncurled her legs and, having fetched the casket, sat down again and opened the lid. A wary eye peeked over the top of her arm as Cecily watched Isobel prepare a sweetly scented lotion. "Perhaps it would be better if you put this on her bump?" she suggested, placing the tiny mortar by the casket and beginning to pack the flowers and bark away.

From the corner of her eye, she saw Cecily sit up and peer at the liquid. A small pink finger dipped quickly into the pot, then, with great care, dabbed at the doll's head.

"Does she feel recovered?" Isobel ventured, but Cecily shook her head vehemently and repeated the action, beginning to hum as she tended to her doll. Isobel took her own kerchief and, dipping it into the potion, soothed it onto the child's developing bruise. "What is your poppet's name?" she asked.

Creating a pause in her humming, Cecily said, "Nan."

"Nan is a pretty name."

Her hair freshly rinsed and smelling of lavender and rosemary, Margaret came to sit with them. "'Ann,'" she said. "Cecily called her 'Ann' after our lady aunt, only she was too young and could only say 'Nan'. She gave me this comb; it was hers when she was my age, but our uncle, Lord Robert, gave her one with their devices carved on it when they wed, and she wanted me to have this one." She glanced over her shoulder to where Joan was busy telling off one of the maids while instructing another on laying the trays of food for dinner. "Will you comb my hair for me?" She wriggled around so her back faced Isobel.

As she drew the comb through Margaret's hair, Isobel smiled to herself. "I loved my hair being combed. Buena always used the wide teeth first and worked each section from the bottom up, so it never pulled. And, although she did not speak, she would keep a tune in her throat, like this." She set up a deep resonance in her chest in imitation of the strange notes that had sounded like the call of a far-off country.

Cecily stopped her humming and, leaning against Isobel's arm and with Nan held close, watched Isobel comb her sister's hair. Outside, large drops of heavy rain began to fall.

Isobel waited until the girls were abed before taking up her chaplet and making her way to the castle chapel. The outer wall formed part of the castle's defensive face against the world — bleak and blank; but inside the bailey, the delicate tracery of the high-arched windows glowed with the armorial colours of the earldom in the evening sun. She had chosen a time when she could be certain few would be at prayer in the chapel or idling in the courtyard before it. Even so she waited until the small groups of men with foreign voices moved on before she crossed the open space. Stilling the sound of the beads as they clacked against her hip in its purse, she eased open the blue and yellow painted door and slipped inside.

Thick and resinous, incense clung to the slender stone columns forming a central nave. Between them lay tombs of such intricate delicacy that Isobel, in reaching out to touch a crisp pinnacle with gilded tips as bright as the sun, thought it would melt as ice under her hand. She stood on tiptoe and made out the form of a sleeping knight, immortal under his fragile canopy of stone. She barely breathed in case she should wake him and left him to his eternal slumber. Beyond the rood screen separating the choir and the nave, the figure of the priest mumbled his prayers. Without making a sound, Isobel made the sign of the cross and, kneeling where she would be unnoticed, bent her head.

She had left her father's soul to the care of their own priest and daily she offered up prayers for his salvation. But she dared not see him in her mind's eye, nor conjure his scarred face before her own. In quieter moments, she thought she heard his voice or saw the back of his head among many, and for a fleet second almost believed him to be alive, only for a stranger to turn and hope to dissolve. Such moments brought loss, and with loss, weakness, and she could not, would not, weaken.

She let her thoughts wander from their church to their home, and from her home to her garden, and she found her hands shaking as she gripped her crucifix, and the stone with which she had encased her heart crumbled a little. Crossing herself and blinking away tears, she stumbled to her feet, and the hand she put out to steady herself met iron.

In the fading light an enclosure of metal worked into ornate scrolls appeared unfinished, the raw unpainted iron almost indistinguishable in the dusk. Within the space, alone and to one side, a young child lay. She moved closer, imagining he might wake at any moment.

Taking care in case the gate squeaked, she entered the enclosure. He must have been little older than Cecily when he died. He had been painted to resemble life: an earl's coronet rested by his fair head, his skin warmed by the sun. At his feet slept a greyhound, and in his hand — tucked under the fold of his ermine-edged robe — a knight rode a toy horse. With careful fingers, Isobel touched the child's cheek.

"He was my brother's son."

Isobel started back, striking the railings and making them echo with alarm.

"He died in the river; he drowned." Robert Langton moved into the remaining light, his face pale, his eyes as dark as the water that took his nephew.

"I ... forgive me, my lord," Isobel stuttered.

"Why?"

"I should not be here."

Lord Langton looked down at the child. "Is it possible to trespass against death?"

She was unsure whether he expected an answer, feeling like an intruder trapped within someone else's grief. She wanted to leave the enclosure, but he stood in front of the gate, and she saw that the skin under his eyes seemed puffy and he looked drawn.

"I am sorry," she said again, and this time he looked at her. "For your own loss," she added softly.

"I thank you." He nodded once and opened the gate to let her pass, closing it behind them. For a moment, he stared back through the bars.

"When the time comes, this is to be my brother's tomb."

Isobel looked at the gleaming stone stacked to one side awaiting a mason's touch to transform it into air and light.

"Even now he prepares to lie next to his son. I pray God it is not yet." He lifted his head and mouthed "*not yet*" towards the ribs and arches in the blind dark above him. Almost in answer, the ceiling bosses of gilded angels bearing flaming suns flickered into life. He looked over his shoulder to where the priest and his boy hurried towards them carrying lighted candles.

"My lord! Your pardon!" Puffing like a duck, the man waddled to a standstill. "I did not know of your noble presence —"

Lord Langton raised his hand. "It matters not — the dead need no light. See that this lady is accompanied to her chamber; the dark is not safe for her to walk alone." He inclined his head towards Isobel and left her standing with the priest and his boy as they watched him reach the chapel door and retreat into the night.

Later that evening, as Isobel soberly measured the depth of her own loss, she wondered whether it equalled that of the pain she had seen in Robert Langton's eyes as he had searched the vaulted heavens of the church, and thought, perhaps not.

CHAPTER TEN

With the breaking of summer, Isobel made efforts to replenish her casket, and sought the castle physic garden set aside for the growing of plants of healing. On her return to the nursery, Joan announced starchily, "You have a visitor," and jabbed her head towards the corner where a fair-haired man stood.

"Thomas!" Isobel threw her arms about his neck, nearly knocking him off balance. He had grown since she had last seen him. His thin neck had thickened into broader shoulders, giving him a slender waist in his fashionably short doublet. "I did not think I would see you!"

He returned her embrace after a second's hesitation, and cleared his throat, grinning awkwardly. "I have but recently returned from France. Did you not get my message? I sent it two weeks ago."

She shook her head, too pleased to see someone she knew to say anything.

Joan had stopped shuffling and Thomas glanced in her direction. "Is there somewhere we can talk privily?"

"Have you seen Buena?" Isobel asked as soon as they were beyond earshot in the little pallet room. "And Arthur Moynes? Have you word about John Appleyard and his family, and is Alfred still digging up my garden?" She counted the weeks in her head. "The apples must be harvested and the mulberries all gathered…" She heard his little snort of frustration and she smiled guiltily. "And how does Lord Lacey?" she enquired, dutifully. "He is in good health?"

Thomas inclined to redden when peeved. "I am gone these several months and you ask about your people and my father's health. Do you not wish to know about my business? About me?"

"Of course I do. Come and sit by the window and tell me what you have been doing. You look very well."

He brushed his hand over his fur-trimmed doublet, making the little silver bells decorating the sleeves tinkle. It looked new and expensive. Nor did she recognise the dagger with the silver-gilt mount and elaborate pommel he wore at his side. He took her hand in his, quite firmly, so she could not withdraw it if she had a mind to.

"I will be better when we are wed." His lips became moist, his pale eyes heated, and she remembered the arbour in the pleasance and the soft moans of the woman. She had nowhere to go except lean backwards against the shutters and accept his kiss. She thought she owed him that at least for her error of omission. He took the first kiss when she did not resist, and then pressed for more, his tongue seeking entry to her mouth. Grabbing her chin, he held her when she struggled against him, and he grew hot, his hand finding her breast through her dress, and squeezing.

"Thomas, no!" Scrambling to her feet, Isobel broke free. Pulling her gown back into place and putting the single stool between them, she glared at him. "You are too bold."

He grinned, tasting her lips on his. "You'll not say *no* on your bride night, and you'll not want to when I've done." Although he smiled, she saw no humour in his eyes and something about the way he said it sounded almost like a threat.

She folded her arms over her breasts. "Well, that is not today."

He jumped up, barely contrite. "Ah, Bel, do not be so cross; I meant nothing by it. I missed you, and you must have missed me because you wear the ribbon I gave you." He bent his head to look into her face. "Say you missed me a little?"

She kept her arms firmly crossed and admitted, "A little."

"Good!" He swung away. "You will not believe the lords I have met and the favour they have shown me. Even now, my Lord of Warwick has entrusted —"

"The Earl of Warwick?" she interrupted, forgetting to punish him with her silence.

"Yes, the Earl of *Warwick* himself," Thomas glowed, "has trusted me with a task of great import."

"Why? What has he asked you to do?" Isobel said, seeing him ready to explode with the news if she didn't ask.

Thomas lowered his voice to that of a conspirator. "You must promise not to tell any other of it. Do you take that oath?"

"How can I if I do not know what it is?"

"You must promise," he insisted, and, taking her silence as acquiescence, went on. "Warwick has given me a letter to give to the Earl."

"A letter." Narrowing her eyes, she asked, "Why?"

"He has honoured me with this great task, Isobel, do you not see? My Lord Warwick trusted *me* above all others with this. And if this, what else?"

"What is Warwick doing sending the Earl secret messages, Thomas?"

"How would I know the business of great lords?" he parried unconvincingly.

"Because you make it your business," she stated bluntly, "you and your father."

"It is *our* business, Isobel — yours and mine, or soon will be."

"Thomas, you cannot serve two lords; the Earl serves the king, but Warwick serves himself. If you bear letters from Warwick, your loyalty might be called into question."

His smile dropped. "I would serve your Earl if he gave me leave to do so, but he would not see me. You could make my suit plain to him. You bide here with my ladies so you must have found favour with him. Have you spoken with the Earl, Bel?"

She remembered with an awkward twist of her stomach the incident in the council chamber. "I am nothing here, Thomas, no one. I am shown no favour and I do not bide with my ladies; I serve them."

"But your father was held in esteem by the Earl — trusted by him, entrusted with the king's business…"

"Thomas, my father is dead, and any influence he might have had with the Earl died with him." Had he been paying attention he might have seen the flash of pain across her face, but he was too intent on finding a path to the Earl.

"Do they not know who your mother was? Surely the countess would advance your plea."

Her cause or his? Isobel thought. "They neither know nor care. I am the daughter of a new-made knight and my mother's noble birth is of no consequence to the countess and her ladies. She made that quite clear."

"Then I must find a way," he muttered, "unless the wind changes and blows another way, and then chance might find me."

"What do you mean?" Isobel said sharply. "*One* master, Thomas, and if the Earl believes you to be courting another it will not be favour he shows you, but the edge of an axe."

"So, my Bel does care for me a little," he teased. "Or is it because she wishes to marry me and escape to her manor and her garden and the dark witch she calls servant?" His hands had found their way to her hips, and she wove her way out of reach before he made further inroads on her chastity.

"Buena is not a witch," she said, cross. "And you had better not be found here or I will be disgraced."

He slipped his hand back around her waist. "At least be dismissed for something than for naught," he hummed, eyeing the pallet. "Let me take a little on account, and I will repay with interest when we are wed."

She unwound his hand and gave him a push, trying to keep a straight face despite her annoyance. "Usury is a sin, Thomas, as is what you suggest. Faith, you do press your suit a little too much. You used to be more patient."

"The closer to Michaelmas, the more impatient I become. Besides," he said almost as an aside, "I knew not what I missed."

She opened her mouth to ask him what he meant, but he grinned as if he intended it as a joke and backed out of the room, compelling her to follow him, almost knocking into Joan bent double by the door as she made busy sweeping the poppet's tiny beads into a pewter pot. He assessed her briefly as she curtsied and dismissed her with a glance. He puffed his chest, looking like one of the Earl's doves but not as pretty. All he needed to do was strut.

"I will send my men to escort you, and your new servant with them. I picked her myself — the daughter of Sir Francis Cunningham, as will befit your station as my wife."

"I would rather George came for me, and I will have no other servant than Buena."

Cecily appeared, yawning, and stood in the doorway to the bedchamber rubbing her eyes with a knuckle and looking suspiciously at Thomas.

Bending down to speak to her, Isobel said quietly, "This is Thomas Lacey, my lady. I will wed him soon."

"I don't like him," she declared, her lower lip protruding ominously. "Tell him to go 'way."

"Thomas, I think you had better go," Isobel warned.

He grinned. "Three weeks, Isobel."

Thomas left the chamber in a buoyant mood. Isobel's unaccustomed affection had caught him off guard, but he was no less pleased for all that, and her mouth had yielded long enough to know what he had to look forward to on her bride night. She had filled and rounded over the summer, and her girlish features softened with womanhood. His fingers curved and clenched in memory of her breast, and he smiled at the recollection of her struggle against him and the thought of the resistance he would need to overcome. He would show her who was master in their marriage. Humming a French bawd's song, Thomas came to the long stair to the tower. He stopped and looked back as he heard the strutting voices of two men crossing the bailey towards him. Bright silks and heavy collars denoted men of quality and Thomas bowed. One of the men glanced at him, inclined his head, but made no other acknowledgement and continued their conversation. Thomas bristled. Turning his back on them he drew himself to his full height, broadened his shoulders, and placed his foot deliberately on the first step.

"Sir Thomas Lacey?" a voice said from above him. A thin man standing on the short landing under the covered stair, wearing the Earl's griffin on his blue felt hat, bowed shortly. "My lord bids you attend him." It was the last thing Thomas had expected and the most he could have hoped. "This way, my lord."

Thomas followed, tugging his doublet down at the back and hoping his braies weren't on display over the top of his hose like a slack-arsed churl, not that a knave had the right to wear a doublet let alone afford the fine-woven hose to display his legs. He adjusted the lie of his hat and trusted he didn't smell of horse; surely Isobel would have said.

Instead of being taken to the great chamber where the Earl conducted estate business with notable visitors, Thomas was shown a smaller room to one side, simply furnished with a table placed to catch the light from the single window, several stools, and an unlit fire. A figure stood in the embrasure, splendid in vermilion and cloth of silver. He had his back to Thomas and, in hands clasped behind him, twitched a piece of paper repeatedly.

Thomas recognised the broken seal and his blood thinned. This had nothing to do with his advancement. He bent low and kept his head bowed as he swiftly ran through his options and, seeing he had few, decided to brazen it out. He rose to find the Earl assessing him and felt all warmth driven from his bones. But when he spoke, the Earl's voice betrayed nothing of the cool contempt of which his eyes spoke; a voice eerily calm and beguilingly low.

"Thomas Lacey. I see the resemblance to your uncle; I trust there is none in your loyalty."

Sweet Jesu, the man didn't waste time. Thomas bowed with a flourish. "No, I … I mean yes, my lord."

Flick, flick the letter beat against the palm of the Earl's hand. "You are of age, and shortly expect to come into the title forfeited by your uncle?"

Thomas licked his lips. "Yes, my lord, when my father dies and if it pleases the King's Grace to make grant of it."

"And do you?"

"My lord?"

"Do you please the king, Lacey? Do you serve His Grace in all matters?"

The letter had become a whip cracking Thomas's semblance of calm. Sweat broke the surface of his skin and he darted a glance at the paper in the Earl's hand. Did he know? Had he guessed? His mouth dust-dry, Thomas barely managed, "In all things." Then shot out, "As I would, my lord, if you will entrust me with such a duty that I might prove myself worthy."

The Earl did not answer and instead held out the letter like an accusation. A dark-robed man with a fixed smile hurried forward and took it from his outstretched hand with a bow, while the Earl's blue-grey eyes continued to scour Thomas. "It is my understanding that you intend to wed the daughter of Geoffrey Fenton at Michaelmas and that, on your marriage, his entire estate and the manor of Beaumancote will be yours."

Blinking rapidly at the sudden change in direction and the Earl's detailed knowledge of his affairs, Thomas swallowed. "Yes, my lord, although…" He had been going to add that the manor of Beaumancote had been in the Lacey family long before his uncle's loyalty to the old king had called into question his loyalty to the new. He had no need to say anything because the curl of the man's lip said it all. Thomas shut his mouth.

"Then you will be aware that Isobel Fenton is in my charge until such time as I deem fit."

The hairs on the back of Thomas's neck prickled with heat and tension. "Until Michaelmas, my lord, as her father desired."

"As I see fit," the Earl repeated. "And that time is not now."

"But, my lord…!" Thomas protested, what dignity he tried to maintain dissolving in the realisation that he had none where this man was concerned. He felt the heat rising to his face.

The Earl's voice hardened. "Until I allow it. Isobel Fenton will stay under my protection." He turned his back. "You may go."

The Earl waited for Thomas Lacey to all but stumble from the chamber, then released an almost inaudible sigh. "We will see what comes of this," he addressed the back of the room.

"And do you?"

"Do I what?"

Robert Langton pushed himself away from the wall where he had gone unnoticed during his brother's exchange with the Lacey boy and moved into the subdued light that was all the rain-laden clouds emitted. "Do you trust him?"

Pulling thoughtfully at his top lip, the Earl said, "Would you?"

Robert scanned the letter that had had his brother blistering with fury not an hour before. "Do you think Lacey knows the content?"

"Undoubtedly. Possibly."

"Yet he asks for your lordship. If you do not let him marry this girl you will make an enemy of him. Is it not better to keep him close? Give him the offices he desires, show him your favour — he might yet be won and his loyalty secured."

"He is already our enemy, Rob. He is his father's pup, tainted with his uncle's blood, and will no sooner serve us than bite the hand that gives him meat. Warwick chose him to run this errand because Warwick knows he is a bought man, and I will not trust him. I cannot trust him, and Warwick will use him to create discord between us. If Lacey marries Isobel Fenton, his lands will stretch from the Isle of Axholme to Hull. And if he gains Fenton's offices as well, he will have control of the river all the way from the mouth of the Humber to the Trent. I need not tell you what that could mean to our security and that of our sovereign lord."

With a humourless half-smile, Robert Langton shook his head. "Then you intend to prevent the girl's marriage to Lacey for as long as it takes to keep him to heel. Or make a match that will ensure her lands do not wed into the wrong hands. You would break your oath to Fenton…"

"Perhaps." The Earl surveyed his younger brother. These recent months had worn heavily on him, and he looked older than his twenty-six winters, the joy snuffed out of him by his wife's death. He wouldn't welcome the reminder, but time was not on their side. "Robert, we must look to a marriage for you —"

"Not now."

"Yes, *now*, Rob. Ann's death — may she have eternal peace — was beyond our control, but your remarriage is within it. You are my heir, and sweet Jesu, we know not how long any of us have before we are called before God's Judgment."

Robert threw a sharp look at him.

"Yea, as you well know. As do I." The Earl moved closer to his brother, imparting an urgency. "I saw our father's life cut from him and our victory with it, when life should have been *his*. Who can say how long either of us might have before a treacherous whoreson decides to control his own destiny by taking ours? Without an heir, all this —" he cast his eyes over the room and beyond the window to where the sun now shone once more across the bailey — "all this will count for nothing, and what our forebears fought for will put meat upon another man's table." He faced him now. "I will not father another son by my wife."

Robert looked at him. "Cecily is but four winters, there is time enough. And Bess will make a good marriage and you have the choice of sons…"

"And our name will be lost to his. Felice is almost beyond the bearing of children. Besides," the Earl grunted as if at a private joke, "I fear I am almost beyond the begetting by her. Nay, do not look at me like that; I have done my duty, more perhaps than you will ever know." He smiled bitterly and slapped his brother's shoulder. "Now it is your turn. I am away to York to meet with the king, may God grant us both safe passage. I leave my castle and my family in your charge, brother. Think on what I have said." He pulled a piece of parchment towards him, picked up a quill and, dipping it into the inkwell, prepared to write.

"What of Isobel Fenton?"

"I will see her before I go. I am her lord whether she thanks me for it or no."

"And what reply will you give Warwick?"

The Earl looked up. "Ah, now that is something to which I will have to bend my mind lest he try to do it for me. Warwick is not an enemy I wish to make in haste, and we were friends once, when we both backed the same cause, but he sheds his loyalty more readily than chastity a soldier's whore. It credits him nothing and gambles all. It is not a path I will take to the dishonour of this family, and we are in too deep with the king to make others believe it should I do so."

CHAPTER ELEVEN

Preparations for the Earl's journey north to meet the king had been made and his horse now waited in the bailey with a company of men swelled by knights and men-at-arms who owed him fealty. He was under no illusion that this uneasy truce between the king and Warwick would last, any more than the unseasonably warm weather would bide until Yule. The wind would change once more and with it would come a blast from the north in the form of either Richard Neville, Earl of Warwick, or the bitch queen, Anjou, and her poppet of a king. Which would be anybody's guess.

Isobel Fenton gave a nervous curtsy when brought into his presence, and he almost regretted what he had to tell her next. He hadn't seen her since she had burst into his council bringing a vital brightness he had found difficult to ignore. He detected a change even in those few short weeks, and more since he had first met her last spring, and it irritated him that it should matter.

He told her of his decision in measured tones, and she kept her eyes downcast and her face immobile, but her lips trembled and her hands, folded in front of her, blanched white where her fingers bit into her skin. He briefly wondered whether telling her the reasoning behind his decision would make the knowledge of it any easier, but dismissed it. His lordship gave him responsibilities beyond her understanding and station, and her duty was to accept it. He would protect her inheritance and she would continue to benefit from the monies he saw fit to release to her; the rest he would retain until such time as she married someone of his choosing.

Looking at her now, head bent, he thought she would not accept what he had to say even if he were minded to tell her. She was young and there was more to look forward to in marriage than a husband to protect her estates, and he had disappointed her of that. She would resent him for it and, to his surprise, he found he minded.

"You will continue to bide with Lady Margaret and Lady Cecily, and the countess will oversee your education. I doubt that you had the opportunity to learn the latest dances when at Beaumancote?" She didn't answer, nor did she look up, and he pursed his mouth, frowning. He wasn't used to dealing with women the same age as his oldest daughter. "And my lady will instruct you on the ways of court, fashion, dress, and such baubles as women value — you will not wish to appear ill-mannered and without grace." Small creases appeared between her eyes and her lips tightened; he was making it worse as he blundered about like a drunk among swine. What was he supposed to say to the girl? "You will instruct your servant —"

Her head whipped up and she looked him dead in the eye. "I have no servant, my lord; you would not let her attend."

He felt himself change in the look she gave him, growing young again, and unsure. His colour rose and fell and, within the confines of his chest, his heart wrenched. How long had it been since he had last been that way? Too long. Not long enough. How dare she answer him thus; how dare she raise in him the swelling emotion he had learned to crush nigh on twenty years before. The Earl forced the muscles in his jaw to relax and controlled his temper. He wanted to turn his back on the girl and walk away as he had done once long ago, but pride prevented him, and instead let stone replace blood. "You will accept the servant appointed to you and you will bide here."

"How long, my lord?"

For as long as it took to bring the Lacey cur to account or for a stranger of his choosing to wed and bed her and bind her lands to a noble cause. He took his time pulling on the long blue gloves embroidered with his griffin entwined with the white rose of the Royal house, thankful he no longer had to look at her disappointment.

"Long enough."

Isobel barely noticed the probing glances Joan gave her when she went back to the chambers, past the girls, and straight to the pallet room. She sat on the edge of the window seat where only a few hours before Thomas had spelled out his desires for their future life together in the force of his kiss and the ambition of his plans. Without explanation, the Earl had exercised his rights as her overlord and removed from her the one chance she had of returning home.

In her mind's eye, she saw Buena reflected in her looking glass, her features warped by the uneven surface, brushing out her hair and smiling at some observation Isobel had made. She thought of Alfred digging in the borders, and John shouting at him and then stroking the dog's wiry head when he thought she wasn't looking. And her father, more alive in her memory now that time had stolen him from her, sitting in his favourite chair, cup in hand, listening to her read to him with the look of tender patience he reserved for such private moments.

Crushing her thumbs in the vice of her closed fists, she shut her eyes, squeezing hard, but tears found the valleys of her face and fell onto her hands — summer rain, salt and warm — and she could hold them back no longer.

"Is'bel?" Cecily held out her grubby poppet. "Nan's hungry."

Isobel ran her sleeve across her eyes, attempting to focus on the doll. "Is she?"

"Nan's belly is empty, here." She patted her own stomach, dark curls framing her wide eyes in an unruly halo. Cecily peered under the shadow of Isobel's short veil. "Your face is wet."

Isobel found her kerchief, dried her face, and wiped her nose. "Yes, I expect it is." She took in the anxious frown of the child. "Are you hungry, too? Shall we wash Nan's hands and ready her to dine?"

Cecily nodded vigorously and took her hand. Controlling the well of tears that simple act of trust evoked, Isobel went with her into the children's chamber, where Alice was handing Margaret a towel and Joan hovered near the table laid with dinner.

Thankful for something to do other than answer the curious stares of the woman, Isobel helped Cecily onto her stool and restrained the hand that would have grabbed the first pastry she could reach. "Nan needs a wash," she whispered, not yet trusting her voice, and placed the bowl of scented water next to her. She turned up the edges of the child's sleeves, and Cecily dipped the doll's wooden hands into the water and assiduously washed them with the small oatmeal bag Isobel handed her.

"Well, I warned you right enough," Joan remarked when she grew tired of waiting. Isobel didn't answer, but handed Cecily the towel to dry the poppet, before washing her own hands. "Didn't I say the countess would have you dismissed if she thought you'd been dallying?"

Taking her chaplet from the bag on her belt, Isobel kissed the cross and, enclosing the beads between steepled hands, closed her eyes in silent prayer. Crossing herself, from the corner of her eye she noted Margaret doing the same.

Joan helped herself to a fragrant pottage of meat and beans, taking in the blotched skin beneath Isobel's eyes. "You've nowt but yourself to blame for it," she huffed like a hen, breaking a wafer and scattering crumbs onto the white cloth. "Be thankful you've got a husband to go to; marrying will take some stink out of the dung, if you get my meaning." She dipped the wafer into the stew. "But muck'll stick where you roll in it and that's the truth of it, mark me. You just pray it goes no further and the Earl doesn't hear of it; he won't be forgiving of such disgrace. When do you leave?"

Waiting until the girls had been served, Isobel took a little pottage and gazed bleakly at the fat cooling in pools on the surface. "I am not leaving," she said eventually.

"What's that?" Leaning to take a small pie from the centre of the table, Joan almost dropped it.

"I am not leaving," Isobel repeated. "I am to remain here."

Joan's evident disappointment was matched only by the delight on Margaret's face.

"What of your marriage? Have you been forsworn by your Thomas? Eh, I know not what is worse: to be disgraced afore your marriage or for lack of it. Who'll want you after this, that's what I want to know?"

Isobel could have done without her false pity, but more than that, she couldn't be certain whether her own reaction resulted from the shock of remaining at the castle, or her thwarted desire to return home. And where, in all that, did she place her feelings for Thomas?

Having listened to the short exchange, Margaret wiped her fingers and, clearing her throat, said, "*I* am glad you are staying, and Cecily is, too."

Cecily wobbled her head, her mouth too full to answer, and instead made Nan dance up and down in a jig.

"You'll not be wanting that thing at the table, my lady." Joan tried to take the doll from her, but Cecily danced Nan away and sat her next to Isobel's cup where the doll smiled blandly up at her with a smear of food making it lopsided and absurd.

Picking the poppet up, Isobel carefully wiped the doll's face and somewhere, deep inside, felt a trickling despair.

PART THREE

CHAPTER TWELVE

Summer's back had been broken on autumn rain, and roads mired with a season of horse and man ran with their stink until cleansed of the reek. The Earl remained with King Edward as unrest along the Scottish border rumbled like an incipient storm, and the castle held its breath until, at last, remaining men were called to arms, and marched north to join him.

Isobel wrote to Arthur Moynes, explaining she would not be returning to the manor for the foreseeable future and instructing him to ensure its safety in the face of the continuing unrest. Her steward replied almost immediately, voicing his regret, but not surprise, and Isobel suspected that he already knew. He assured her that the manor remained in good order and gave brief tidings of her people and her garden. He made clear his lasting regret at her father's death, but voiced faith in the Earl's good lordship. But of Buena he said little except she tarried with them, and Isobel wondered whether hers were the only eyes to see the letter. She cautioned herself against revealing her thoughts to any other than God.

A little of her loneliness abated under the relentless demands of Lady La Roche and Isobel's own determination to serve the daughters of the Earl as best she could. She saw little of the countess and what she did, she did not like. Her infrequent visits left the girls stung by her indifference and rattling with friction. Joan, by contrast, was full of the news of Court, gleaned from Jon and passed around until she swelled with the noise of it. With uncertain times ahead, the countess courted favour where she could and sought the most advantageous matches for her daughters.

By the end of September, Warwick had joined forces with King Edward, and together they crushed the northern rebellion, whereupon a wash of relief flooded the castle bringing hope of a lasting peace. Gradually men returned from the north with tales of the vanquished Lancastrians — no doubt embellished by victory — and the castle filled and overflowed into the inns of the town.

Tired of Joan's incessant gossiping, Isobel took Cecily into the wilderness garden where they could be alone. Running narrow and bold with recent rain, the river churned the banks, turning the water tan; but between the water and the castle walls, the air was liberated of conflict and marriage, and Isobel breathed freely. Margaret had been summoned to her mother, and Isobel, having persuaded Cecily to leave Nan asleep in her crib, had taken a soft leather ball, and together they sought an hour's sunshine and peace outside.

The ball fell between Cecily's stiffly outstretched arms. She ran after it, heels bobbing under the edge of her dress like a rabbit's tail. She returned pink-cheeked and threw it in Isobel's direction. From somewhere in the castle grounds a high-pitched yapping and a shouted command competed with the river.

"Like this," Isobel called, holding her hands in a cup-shape as she caught the imaginary ball. Cecily threw the ball again and Isobel leaped to secure it before it escaped, feeling the fabric stretch under her arm. "Try again," she encouraged, throwing it carefully.

This time Cecily captured it between her arms and her body, and Isobel clapped in delight. "Well done!" she laughed as the ball came sailing past her ear, landing a little way beyond her and rolling down a slight slope and out of sight. Cecily giggled and trotted after it, and Isobel bent to pick a golden leaf from the grass to hold it to the light.

Cecily's laughter became a squeal of fury. Alarmed, Isobel looked up in time to see a streak of pale lavender as one of the Earl's greyhound pups made off with the ball. It loped on long gangly legs a dozen yards away and settled down to chew the ball trapped between its paws. It rolled onto its back, ripping the leather with needle teeth. Outraged, Cecily ran to grab the toy from the dog. The puppy twisted onto its feet, lowered its head over the shredded ball, and growled. Furious beyond care, Cecily aimed a kick in its direction.

"Cecily, *no*!" Isobel reached them before the puppy could bite the foot and whisked the child into the air. Yipping wildly, the pup leaped at them, teeth tearing Isobel's sleeve as she tried to protect Cecily's dangling legs. From the corner of her eye, she saw a flash of a murrey doublet, and the puppy was swept out of the way still snapping and growling. Isobel held onto Cecily's protesting form tightly.

"I hate it!" the child screamed, kicking Isobel's shins with hard heels, making her wince.

Shushing her, Isobel said, "It is only a pup; it knows no better." Then, to the young man attempting to restrain the struggling animal in his arms, "You must control your dog, sir!" On seeing his exasperation, she moderated, "It would have bitten Lady Cecily. My lady is upset and rightly so, but unharmed. I thank you for your timely intervention."

"I believe," he said, eyeing the flailing feet, "that the animal had the disadvantage."

"My lady would not have hurt the dog."

"Yes, I *would*!" Cecily screamed in Isobel's ear and kicked out viciously in the direction of the young man. Isobel put her down before she hit her target. Standing with her hands on her hips and a face like Hades, Cecily stamped her foot and shook her finger, sounding fearfully like Lady La Roche. "It is a *bad* puppy!"

The tension left the young man's face, and he now wore a faintly amused expression. Dark eyebrows defined an inquisitive face, one brow irresistibly quirking upwards as he took in the remonstrating child. "Indeed, it has yet to learn to govern itself. The scolding is well-deserved; I must ask my lady's pardon." The pup still in his arms, he bowed.

Cecily shoved her thumb in her mouth and scowled at the dog now chewing the fur-lined sleeve, ignorant of the ire it had evoked.

Isobel could not tell whether the elegant youth addressed her or Cecily, nor whether his comments referred to the puppy or the outraged child, but she sensed humour and thought she owed an explanation. "My lady has a new tooth coming and it makes her out of sorts."

"As I believe it is so with this animal," he said, mildly, removing his sleeve and firmly encasing the pup's jaws in his gloved hand before any further damage was done to the delicate fabric. He looked young — perhaps her own age — and his well-defined chin was yet to be roughened by daily stubble. Going down on one knee, he looked earnestly at the sulking child. "I will ensure he makes amends and sends you a new ball."

Cecily removed her thumb, glistening and wrinkled. "Promise?" she asked suspiciously.

He nodded, eyes creasing as he smiled. "Upon my honour, my lady."

Cecily made no move to forgive, and Isobel bent down before the child caused offence. "It is courteous to thank this gentleman."

With a solemn air, Cecily held her gaze. "I did not chew his dog, Is'bel." Then to the youth, "Nan says you are forgiven," she announced grandly, then she skipped off singing to herself as if nothing had happened.

"Nan?" he queried, standing and tucking the puppy under one arm. It seemed to have tired and appeared content to gnaw on the young man's leather-covered thumb as if it were a bone.

"Nan is my lady's poppet. I think you are absolved, sir."

"Then I am honoured to be so pardoned," he said with a dry smile. "How easily a child forgives; I wish it were so for all." He smiled more widely, the corners of his mouth bending attractively. Quick-eyed, lean, and strappy, he looked younger than Thomas but stronger, as if used to being in command of his body, whereas Thomas had yet to catch up with his.

Finding herself following the movements his mouth made, liking the humour in his eyes and the moderate tenor of his voice, Isobel felt her colour rising and sought to hide it. Keeping one eye on Cecily, who now danced chaotically as she chased early falling leaves, she stroked the puppy's gleaming narrow head. "Is this not one of the Earl's sighthounds? How came you by it?"

"It is … a gift. For the day of my nativity."

"Oh," she said, half-listening as Cecily — having more success catching leaves than she had had with her ball — strayed closer to the river edge, then danced away again. "I thought that the Earl jealously guards his dogs. I did not think he made a gift of one so lightly…" She saw where her sentence was leading and stumbled out of the thicket of thorns she was making for herself. "I mean, it is a lordly gift," she mumbled as his eyes widened.

"It is indeed. Yes." There was a lengthy pause in which neither knew what to say next, and he made no move to leave.

He indicated the sodden remains of the ball with a nod of his head. "I think my lord Earl wishes to humiliate me in the eyes of the very young — and in front of maids — by giving me a wrecking dog." Swapping the puppy to his other arm and tucking its long legs securely, he regarded her with a degree of interest. "You have come recently to the castle, have you not? I do not recognise you."

Isobel had a feeling that she should know who this youth was, but there was nothing that told her whom he served, or his degree other than his well-cut clothes and courtesy, so she erred on the side of caution and if she called him *sir* when he was but a knave, so be it. She reached to fondle the puppy's soft ears. Newly weaned, it found her thumb and suckled it, looking sleepy.

"I have been here since my father's death in August. I am in the Earl's charge, sir." Despite the wrench, she found the pain a little less than before.

The smile faded from his eyes. "I wish him peace and you, solace." Placing a hand on his heart, he bowed his head in such a courtly gesture that Isobel forgot the tenor of their conversation and had to remind herself of it rather than risk the unexpected fluttering in her stomach being reflected in her face. Thankfully, his action stirred the dog and, as its suckling became gnawing, Isobel rapidly withdrew her thumb before teeth broke her skin. It squirmed to escape, and Isobel laughed at the look of consternation on the youth's face.

"It needs a leash. Will this do?" Undoing the rue-coloured ribbon about her neck holding her father's seal, she wound it lightly around the puppy's throat and gave the long end to the man to hold. It tried to bite at it.

"My thanks. He is in want of his collar, but not one as fair as this. I will be hard-pressed to replace it should he succeed in destroying it."

Isobel felt a welter of guilt at how lightly Thomas's gift slipped into another's hands, and how little she cared. She brushed the memory to one side. "It reminds me of Lady Cecily when she is wont to struggle and will not be still for all the scolding or bribes."

"And what do you do with her then?"

"I sing to her." Simultaneously, they looked at the dog. "Nay, I will not be doing *that*!" Isobel exclaimed as she watched the thought flash across his face. "Maybe he is tired and will sleep soon?" she suggested hopefully. "What is he to be called?"

"I have not a name for him yet." He held the pup aloft, canting his head in thought as it gazed at them with liquid eyes. "Perhaps you might suggest one?"

Cecily had come within earshot again, and Isobel called out to her, "The puppy is in want of a name, my lady; can you think of one?"

Intent on hopping from leaf to fallen leaf, Cecily didn't look up. "Nan," she said, continuing her game. Isobel laughed again, watching the man's mouth curve upwards when she thought he wasn't looking.

"Hmm, I hoped this dog might sire some whelps. Calling it 'Nan' might confuse him."

"Ned, then," Isobel suggested lightly. "After the king. There should be no confusion there."

She didn't think it was such an outrageous thing to say given the king's reputation, and she meant it only in jest, but the young man cast a swift glance at her as if she had overstepped the mark. She sobered rapidly, seeing the man in the boy.

"I think not," he said quietly, and then when he saw she meant no harm, "I would give him a hero's name. What say you to Heracles?"

"It is a very big name for a little dog, sir, and he had the fortune of divinity."

"If not Heracles, what?"

Corrugations formed on her brow as she thought back to her father's books and the time spent discussing them. The hours had seemed long then, but so brief now. "Hector. He was but a man, yet his strength lay not only in his great courage, but in his noble desire to act justly and wisely."

The boyish humour returned. "I think you admire these virtues."

Her face lit. "I do — beyond all others. They surpass all rank and can inhabit the lowliest heart. It is what sets Man above creatures."

"And gives him the semblance of divinity you eschew in Heracles?"

She could not be sure whether he tested or teased. Treading carefully, she watched for his quicksilver reaction as she stroked the dog's silky neck in time to her thoughts.

"Man's divinity is merely a reflection of God for which he strives, yet in striving he comes closer to the Divine in this life. Heracles was born divine so knew not what it was to be mortal, and in being mortal, fallible. Is it not better to strive to attain that which we are denied by our very nature than to be granted it by the mere chance of our birth?"

He did not answer and, when she looked at him, she found his direct gaze fixed on her face. He seemed neither angry nor pleased, but to be considering her comments. She had no more to add, so said nothing. Her attention wandered to where

Cecily busily collected sticks, so did not see the puppy's head swivel until she felt its teeth on the side of her finger.

"Ow!" She shook her finger free of its jaws.

Taking her hand in his, the man inspected her thumb, brushing pins of blood from the surface. He frowned. "I will have the Earl to answer to for damaging his charge's hand as well as his daughter's plaything; I shall no longer be made welcome." He held her hand a little longer and Isobel made no move to stop him, and when he released it, she wished he hadn't. He wasn't like Thomas; there was a surety about him that she found attractive, and she had never reacted this way before — not to Thomas, not to anyone. Unsettling though she found it, she liked the way it made her feel.

"I am certain you will be gladly received, sir," she breathed, flushing as he met her shy glance with open interest. It seemed that he was about to answer, but Cecily came running up to them waving a short stick wildly in the air.

"Is'bel, look what I have found for Nan-dog!" She jumped up and down in front of them, almost prodding the animal in her excitement.

"Carefully!" Isobel exhorted, but the youth took the proffered stick and offered it to his puppy, who sank its teeth through the weathered bark, chewing with relish.

"A kindly gift and well given; Hector thanks you. Now, I must be about the day and let you do the same —"

They all looked up at the sound of broken breaths and feet hitting the hollow ground in haste as a liveried youth appeared over the slight rise that hid them from view. He saw them, came panting to a halt, and bent double in a bow. Dangling a braided blue leather leash in one hand off which a collar hung, he managed to stand upright, puce-faced and glistening.

"Faith, Warryn," Isobel's companion said, "you had charge of the animal less than an hour. Here, give me the collar before he is lost again."

"Your pardon, Your Grace…" Warryn panted, "the hound —"

"Slipped its collar. So it would seem."

The collar swung slowly in the sun, light catching the silver boars and flaming suns upon white roses studding the broad blue leather band at regular intervals. Isobel's eyes widened as she recognised the emblems, and everything she had said over the last few minutes became indiscretion. Looking anywhere but at him, Isobel backed away and curtsied.

"Mistress," he said, amusement colouring his voice, and she cringed internally at her blind stupidity.

"Your Grace, forgive me…"

Handing Hector to the youth, the Duke of Gloucester leaned towards her and lowered his voice. "I find nothing to forgive," and he draped the ribbon about her neck as if adorning her with gold.

"Why did that man call his dog *Hector*?" Cecily asked when she and Isobel returned to the girls' chamber. "I said it is called *Nan*."

Her face still burning, Isobel barely listened. "Because it is a male dog, my lady."

"But I want it to be *Nan*," Cecily insisted.

Looking at the cross little face in front of her with the bright red cheek where a tooth struggled to break through the gum, Isobel sighed. "I think your Nan is ready to wake up now. She will want something to eat and we must wash her hands. Alice will help you." She nodded to the cheerful wispy girl. She had been relieved when Alice had been assigned as her servant, and the girl had not objected.

Isobel rose and went to the pallet room to fetch her casket. When she returned, Margaret shut her book and laid it on the table where she had been copying the Latin text. She was quieter than usual, and subdued. "Have you been to the wild garden?" she asked a little tightly.

"There was a man there," Cecily piped up from the other side of the room just as Lady La Roche made her daily appearance to inspect the chambers. Isobel gave an inward groan as the woman turned sour eyes on her.

"A man, you say?"

Cecily carried Nan to the table where she sat the doll propped up with her legs stuck stiffly in front of her as if begging alms. "He had a puppy and he didn't call it Nan and it ate my ball and it tried to bite me. He called it *Hector*," she added indignantly, dipping Nan's wooden hands and her own into the bowl of water Alice held for her.

Lady La Roche stiffened perceptibly. "Who was this? The Earl will have him whipped!"

"My lady, I do not think…" Isobel began, but was drowned out by Cecily's bright voice.

"Hector-Nan ate my ball like this." She made her wet hands into mouths that champed at the air.

"He said he would replace the ball," Isobel interjected rapidly. "No harm was done."

"He should not let his dog roam freely; you know that the Earl forbids it. Only my lord's dogs are allowed in the castle grounds."

"My lady, this was one of —"

"And you should not talk with any man unless it is with the countess's permission. Who was it?" she asked again.

Margaret's eyes looked unnaturally wide, her mouth drawn tight and pale as if stretched like the skin of a drum. "Aunt, it is of no matter if Cecily is not hurt."

Lady La Roche raised her chin, glaring down her nose at Isobel with a haughtiness she reserved for the maids. "I command you to tell me."

Isobel's temper bubbled. This is what she had come to: standing before a woman who had arrogance bred into her, being chastised and commanded like a servant. Michaelmas had come and gone and her hopes of returning home in the foreseeable future withdrawn like a broken promise. She felt deflated, a pig's bladder battered by the boots of the boys kicking it hither and thither, relentless and pointless.

Lady La Roche had turned a peculiar colour. "I am waiting."

She would not lie to the woman, but what Lady La Roche might do with the information she could only guess. Isobel folded her hands before her. "Madam, the pup was the gift of the Earl. He gave it to the Duke of Gloucester. It was His Grace's dog."

Puffing indignation, the woman expanded in front of her. "You lie! His Grace would not countenance talking with a girl of your station. Using his name thus will be severely punished. Such insolence!"

Cecily had been holding a one-sided conversation with her poppet. Now she seemed to be illustrating her encounter with the dog, making little grunting noises and wiggling two fingers like tusks in front of her face.

"Cecily, be quiet!" her aunt rebuked. "As for you, Isobel Fenton, be certain of it, the countess will decide your fate."

Isobel contemplated her hands, smelling faintly of the clove she had used to ease Cecily's sore gum. No longer stained with the lifeblood of her garden, they looked more like the hands of a knight's daughter than a yeoman's wife, which Thomas had frequently pointed out they resembled. But a yeoman's wife — with all the labours expected of her — had more freedom than Isobel did now. And a purpose in life. She had given it little thought, but as Thomas's wife she would have had the running of the estates to oversee in his absence, and his absences would have been frequent if he served the Earl or another great lord as her father had done. And between her duties as a wife and the running of the manor, her time would have been her own. What point was there to thinking about it now? Something else bothered her, something of which she had not been aware until now. Her conversation with the Duke of Gloucester had done more than cause her acute embarrassment because of her own omission; he had looked at her in a way that warmed her from the inside out, like the sun emerging from behind cloud, and she liked it, she liked it a lot.

"What are you doing in there?" Joan's face appeared around the door, unnaturally pink. "My lady's running me a merry dance this evening and she'll not settle without you."

Isobel replaced the tooth powders and little birch sticks and secured the lid of her casket. Wrapping it in her travelling cloak, she put it back on the floor at the end of her pallet where it would be safe. "She likes it if you sing to her, Joan."

"Eh, I'll not be doing that. You do it if you like but my back aches and I have better things to be about than crooning for my lady. If she were more like her sister I wouldn't mind so much as there's nowt to her to bother; but that little devil... The countess must have been right melancholic when the child was begat to bear her as she is. No wonder she sees her so little. I'd disown her, I would; I'd have drowned her at birth and be done with it. What do you look at me like that for? You know it's the truth."

Isobel brushed past her none too carefully and into the girls' bedchamber. Margaret finished saying her rosary, genuflected, and smiled, raising her fair eyebrows as Isobel came into the room and pointing under the bed.

Isobel nodded. "Would you like me to teach you the song my mother taught me, my lady?" she offered, waiting for Margaret to slide between the sheets Alice had warmed with stones wrapped in wool. She pulled the covers to the girl's chin, sat on the edge of the bed, and began to hum the sweet melody. Before long she felt movement by her foot, and Cecily's head appeared.

"*When the nightingale sings,*
The trees grow green,
Leaf and grass and blossom springs,
In April, I wene…"

Without ceasing her song, Isobel raised the bedcover and patted the mattress as the child materialised like a sprite from under the bed, drawn as if by a charm.

"*Between Lincoln and Lindsey,*
Northampton and London,
I know no maiden so fair…"

She sang as Cecily hopped up, her night smock flapping carelessly around her thighs. Small burgundy smudges marked the front of Cecily's sturdy legs just above her knee, as if she had rolled on blackberries. Isobel stopped singing and peered closer, squinting in the yellow candlelight, and rubbed at one of the marks. Cecily flinched. Not stains; bruises.

"How came you by these?"

Cecily stared with round eyes, holding Nan to her face, but saying nothing.

Lowering herself into a chair with a sigh, Joan let her arms flop either side and stretched out her legs. "Like as not from fooling with the dogs, or maybe from all that play about you let her do. You know what she's like — never stops but she starts again. Fair wears me out, I can tell you."

"Did you fall?" Isobel turned to Margaret. "My lady, do you know?"

Margaret's brief nod was hardly perceptible. She darted a look at Joan sitting by the fireplace, then at Alice swapping gossip with the chambermaid. "Cecily wouldn't obey. Our aunt —"

"Lady La Roche did this?"

Again, the quickest movement of her head, as if she feared being caught. Isobel looked at Cecily's legs, then drew the nightshift over the blotched skin and tucked the covers around her. Wordlessly, she left the girls and went over to Joan. "I would speak with you."

"Eh?" Joan opened one eye, saw Isobel's expression, and, hauling herself out of the chair, followed her to the pallet room.

"Did you know about this?" Isobel demanded once they were beyond earshot of the Earl's daughters.

Joan scratched under one arm. "What of it?"

"Have you *seen* her legs? They are covered in bruises."

"Well, she should have done what she was told."

"You *knew*? Has this happened before?"

"What are you getting so tethered about? So, La Roche gives her a pinch or two when she has a mind. Serves the child a lesson she might be mindful of next she thinks of doing nowt but she pleases."

Heat rushed to Isobel's face and her palms itched. She pressed them together. "Do you not care what happens to the girls?"

Joan shrugged. "Care? Why should I? They are not my own." She yawned. "What's it to you? You think any here would raise a hand to aid you if you had need?"

"Then I'll tell the countess, the Earl…"

Joan's lip curled and her eyes hardened. "You'd better not be doing that. My lady won't hear a word against La Roche, and the Earl … well, let's just say he gives more heed to his curs than his daughters, not that I blame him. Without an heir what good is a girl when he's dead and gone, eh? No, keep quiet and bide your time is my advice. A slap won't kill the girl and might do her some good. I had enough in my day, and I've handed out a few to my brothers and sisters when they were out of turn, I can tell you; the runts deserved it."

"Hurting Cecily will teach her nothing; kindness costs *nothing*," Isobel fumed.

"It'll teach her to mind herself. She'd best be learning *that* lesson before she comes of age. Now if *you* don't mind, I have a rest due me and I'll take it by the hearth." Joan shivered. "It's nesh cold in here; you do as you please."

Still seething long after the children slept, Isobel went to bed and let her frustration warm the cold sheets. While she understood the responsibility of an adult to chastise a child for its own good, the bruises on Cecily's legs were the legacy of spite, not justifiable rebuke. She could not ignore it, but to whom should she turn if the countess chose to turn a blind eye and the Earl was still with the king?

CHAPTER THIRTEEN

"Wicked child! You are no better than a churl's brat. Get in there!" Lady La Roche's voice expanded and filled the room. The woman towered over the defiant little figure standing in her stained night smock. "*Now!*"

Isobel took in the damp sheets on the bed, Alice trying to be inconspicuous, and Joan standing with her arms folded on her chest and a triumphant expression stretched across her face. Her look became speculative as she saw Isobel enter the room.

"I will take her, Aunt," Margaret was saying, holding Cecily's hand and pulling her towards the door to the privy.

Cecily grabbed hold of the bedpost and clung to it. "No!"

"You will not, Margaret. She will go alone, and she will go now as she has been commanded."

Wide-eyed, Cecily stared at her aunt but did not budge.

"She does not mean to disobey. She is frightened of the spiders," Margaret cried out. "Let me take her, *please.*"

She might as well have been invisible. Nostrils flaring, Lady La Roche pointed with a short cane towards the privy. "Get in there!"

Cecily's chin wobbled, but her brow lowered perceptibly. "No. I. Won't. I won't. I *won't*." And, to Isobel's horror, around the child's bare feet a pool gathered, spreading darkly across the planks and seeping down the cracks between them.

Nobody said a word. A small smile of defiance crossed Cecily's face, followed swiftly by a flash of fear as Lady La Roche took a step forward and raised the thin whip of a stick.

Isobel dived between them and seized hold of the woman's arm before she struck. "Leave her alone!"

Lady La Roche wrenched her arm free, lips pulled back over teeth like mooring posts in the river as they emerged from the mud of her gums. "You dare oppose me!" She lifted her arm again. *Whack*. The first blow sent shock waves through Isobel, sending her staggering back against the bed. By the second, she had raised her arms to protect herself and Cecily — the child now cowering beneath her shielding arms. The willow whip sliced across Isobel's shoulders and neck, coming perilously close to Cecily's terrified face.

"Stop!" Margaret's cries hardly registered above her sister's screams. "Please, *stop!*" She tried to grasp her aunt's hand but was flung back as the woman raised her arm to strike again. Crying, Margaret ran from the room.

Robert Langton woke, as he did every morning, with a void in his heart. He lay for some moments wrestling with the desire to return to a state of sleep that would give him some respite from the gnawing emptiness, but knew it to be futile.

He swung out of the warmth of the bed and opened the shutters of the window overlooking the pleasure gardens below. He had done so the morning after his wedding night and before he had taken his young wife to their own manor, and nothing had changed except the circumstances in which he viewed it now. He had not anticipated waking once more in the room in which he had spent his youth. Not alone. Not without her. He crushed his lips together and turned his back on the gardens.

His esquire knew better than to ask how his night had fared as he shaved him, for it was the same every night when Ann walked again in his dreams, only for him to relive on waking the moment he learned of her death. He glanced at the boy: at seventeen, fair-haired Martin might have stopped growing, but his voracious appetite for food and life was matched only by his need for sleep, and he looked as if he could have done with another hour this morning.

Robert tried to remember what it was like to be that young and have nothing but sex and food and hunting in mind when he woke to a day. Holding his arms out for his narrow-sleeved doublet, he shook his head at the thought: in the decade or so that had passed, he realised grimly, the memory had eluded him. He felt older than his twenty-six years — older than his brother although nearly nine winters separated them — and now the Earl wanted him remarried and fathering an heir. He jerked the belt roughly around his waist and reached for his paternoster. "Sweet Jesu!"

"My lord?"

He had spoken out loud without realising. "It is nothing. Break your fast; I will take mine when I return from devotions."

He could have taken prayers with the family in their private oratory, but he preferred the anonymity of the chapel, and found some comfort in the gathered remains of his forebears, lying in a state of eternal repose with peace carved into their features. At the manor he had called home for the eight years of their marriage, Ann lay in her yet-unadorned tomb while masses were said for her soul to ensure everlasting life. Before long she, too, would have her likeness formed out of rock, and she would pass from death to immortality at the touch of a mason's chisel.

Although Robert failed to feel its feeble warmth, a cautious sun crept over the roofs of the stables in the lower ward when he left the castle chapel; an October sun, edged with the first promise of the winter to come.

He was organising his day in his thoughts as he approached the door to his chambers when a strangled cry came from behind him. He turned to see his niece, still in her night smock and her face wet with tears, running towards him.

"What is it?" He stopped her before she collided with him, holding her by the arms until she was able to gasp out, "Please, please ... she's hurting her!"

"Who? Margaret, who is being hurt?" She took his hand and, tugging urgently, pulled him in the direction from which she had come.

At first, he didn't recognise the noises coming from the nursery — almost the sound an arrow makes as it strikes the butt, yet thinner, accompanied by a rhythmic grunting. And a sound he knew all too well: the keening cry of fear.

He released Margaret's hand and elongated his stride. Without pausing, he pushed the heavy door open with a bang. Standing over Isobel Fenton, Lady La Roche bore down on her back with a whip as Isobel tried to shield his youngest niece from the indiscriminate blows. Crossing the floor in a few long paces, Robert caught the stick as the woman raised her arm. She spun around, eyes starting from their sockets, foam flecks on her lips. Ready to strike, she stopped dead when she saw his face.

"Enough!" He snapped the whip in two and threw it at her feet, where the pieces rattled to a standstill against her skirt.

Lady La Roche found her voice, still thick with rage. "How dare you hinder me!"

Robert turned his back on the outraged woman. Taking Isobel by the elbow, he helped her to her feet. She rocked slightly but kept hold of the child who had pulled the folds of Isobel's skirts around her like a tent. Bending down, he parted the cloth and examined Cecily's streaked face under her mop of hair.

"Uncle?" Margaret lifted the edge of her sister's smock, revealing the pinch marks on her calves.

His features hardened. Beckoning to Alice, he lifted his niece into her care.

Without Cecily to protect, Isobel swayed, and he steadied her. "Look at me," he told her, but she kept her head bent so he was obliged to turn her towards him. With two fingers, he raised her chin. A thin line of raised reddened skin sliced at an angle from her cheekbone to her jaw. Beads of blood sprang from another on the exposed skin between her shoulder and her neck, staining the edge of her kirtle. With an unsteady hand, she pulled the gown to cover the slash.

"The girl defied me," Lady La Roche blustered. "Cecily refused to do as bidden and the girl prevented me from carrying out just chastisement…"

"Did you?" he asked Isobel, keeping his tone even.

She moistened her lips. "Yes, my lord."

Lady La Roche stabbed a finger in Isobel's direction. "And she would have struck me had I not defended myself!"

From nearby, Margaret gave a little gasp and the maids shifted uneasily. Only Joan didn't react.

"Would you?" Robert asked Isobel again without taking his eyes from her face. She looked at him for the first time: disquieting eyes — green within blue.

"No, my lord." She held his gaze until he gave a brief nod, turned, and addressed the older woman still standing, bunched and belligerent, feet away.

"Madam, you are dismissed from this household."

Lady La Roche's mouth opened and shut like a beached fish. "How … how dare you! I am aunt to the countess … she entrusted her children to my care. Only she can dismiss me."

He regarded her without emotion. "You have betrayed the trust placed in you and are not fit to supervise the Earl's children."

She drew herself to her full height. "I did my duty —"

"Your *duty*," he flashed, "was to oversee the welfare of these children and those who care for them. I see evidence of neither." He turned to Isobel. "Will you take on these offices?"

Isobel hesitated and swallowed. "If you wish it, my lord, and I am able."

The swiftest nod. "Then it is so." He looked at Alice. "See to your mistress's comfort." He turned to Margaret. "Have you breakfasted?" She shook her head. "Then you and Cecily will join me. Mistress Fenton will bring you when you are ready."

"Can Nan come?" Cecily had squirmed out of Alice's arms, and she now stood with one hand wrapped firmly around her poppet, the other hanging onto Isobel's skirt.

"Nan?"

She held out her doll. For a second, Robert looked at it blank-faced, and then forced a smile. "Of course, bring your poppet if you wish. I will see all anon."

"The countess will hear of this," Lady La Roche threatened at his retreating form.

"I will ensure she does," he replied without looking back.

Margaret watched as Alice bathed Isobel's raw skin. "Does it hurt very much?"

Isobel forced her hands to relax. "Not much; it stings a little, but the tincture will soothe it and help it heal. It matters not."

She tried not to wince as the oils found the broken lines across her shoulder, and she subdued the nausea that ensued.

"I don't know why he gave you charge; you've been here less than no time and by my account I should have the position." Joan slammed a dish on the table, making the water jump in the bowl. She had barely spoken since Lord Langton had left the room other than to snap at the maids who scrubbed the floor by the bed. "The countess will have something to say about it when the Earl returns, make no mistake. He'll be a lame cock among hens for certain, and I don't fancy my lord's chances when she starts pecking." She pointed a spiteful finger at Isobel. "And you — don't you go thinking you can lord it over me just because *Lord Robert*," she minced his name, "says so."

Isobel censured her with a look, but Joan was too busy screwing her face in mockery to see.

"Who does he think he is to interfere in my lady's household affairs when he's nothi—"

"That is enough," Isobel cut in, and Joan looked at her in surprise.

"I was only saying —"

"I know what you were saying, and you have said enough." Isobel stood, dislodging Alice's hand. "Thank you, Alice; I will dress now. We must not keep my lord waiting any longer."

A fair-haired youth of about Isobel's age bowed to the girls as they entered a sparsely furnished chamber with little in the way of comfort to soften the masculine edge. From the hearth, an old scent hound opened one eye. Without waiting to be called, Cecily ran to her uncle sitting at a small table by the window on which a simple silver cup reflected the early sun. He murmured something as he lifted her onto the bench by the table, and she giggled, and then he greeted Margaret, kissing her on both cheeks.

Isobel hovered uncertainly by the door, watching with a sudden ache the degree of affection between them. As if he sensed her, he glanced up, smiled, and then frowned as she didn't move.

"If it please you…?" He indicated a stool at one end of the table, and she moved into his chamber and sat self-consciously opposite him. He caught sight of the edges of the livid marks, and she pulled her kirtle to obscure them.

Cecily dumped Nan unceremoniously on the table by his cup. Isobel shook her head slightly, but Cecily tossed her curls, wide-eyed and mischievous. Washing his hands in the bowl held for him, Robert raised an eyebrow.

"Martin, it seems we have another guest."

His esquire looked puzzled. "My lord?"

Robert dried his hands. "The Lady Nan is breaking her fast with us. Bring her a dish so she can join us at the table."

Cecily clapped her hands in delight, grabbed her poppet from the table and waved it at the perplexed esquire. Margaret laughed and Isobel broke into a smile.

The Earl's youngest daughter managed to sit still long enough to fill her stomach before she began swinging her legs and wriggling despite Isobel's cautionary looks. Her uncle replaced his napkin.

"It seems your poppet wants to play; go and show Gryphon, but mind, he is old and inclined to dribble." The hound lounging near the fire rolled and yawned at the mention of his name. "And do not let Nan stray too close to the fire," he added, as she skipped towards it.

Isobel stood up to follow, but Robert stopped her. "Stay. Meg will watch over her. Margaret, ask Martin to show you my books."

"I can read a little Latin now; Isobel instructs me," she said, following Martin to a reading table where several books lay.

He raised his voice so that it carried across the room. "Then you will have wisdom to accompany your grace. It will be a fortunate man who marries you one day and acquires a wife both beautiful and learned."

Margaret, pink from praise, took a book from the table. "I do not wish to marry, Uncle. I want to join the abbey. I am better prepared to serve God if I can read Latin and understand the mass."

He looked at Isobel. "Is this something you have encouraged?"

"No, my lord, it is my lady's own mind."

He lowered his voice. "Then let us pray that it is also the mind of the Earl, although I doubt it."

"She is but a girl," Isobel blurted out and he gave her an odd look. "I mean that there is time yet before she marries, and perhaps the Earl might consider her wishes?"

He leaned back in his chair. "Perhaps." He rubbed the joint of his forefinger against his lips as he considered her. "And will you take the habit and become a nun?"

Uncertain, she sought her father's matrix on the ribbon and did not respond immediately; then she saw that behind his finger he smiled. She relaxed a little. "No, my lord, I do not think I am suited to a convent, or so my father told me."

"I think," he said quietly, "that I would agree."

A burst of laughter distracted them as Cecily rolled against the dog and it tried to lick her. Isobel watched Lord Langton with curiosity. He was not the man she had once met at

Beaumancote. He had grown older, no, weary, since then, and the good humour that always seemed on the verge of breaking out had become subdued, like the flooding of a river over green fields leaving them grey. But even flooded fields greened again, and she found herself wanting to see him laugh as he had that time in her garden. She remembered the warmth of it. It felt a very long time ago.

"So," he said, turning back to her, "you are not one for a contemplative life. What, then?"

"I do contemplate, my lord, but in my garden."

"You find God growing in your garden?"

"I do, my lord."

"And where do you find Him here?" He followed her gaze as she watched Cecily's childish antics and Margaret's quiet repose. "What you did this morning was brave and kind. Perhaps you will have children of your own one day."

"How can I, my lord, when I have been forbidden to marry?"

"Do you think the Earl forbad the match with Thomas Lacey out of spite?" Her look confirmed it. He shifted forward in his chair. "You must understand that there are circumstances beyond your own that compel his actions. He acts in the way he judges fit, and he saw fit to annul your betrothal. You do not need to know why, only that he did so—"

"As my *lord*?" The words were out of her mouth before she could stop them.

He sat back again. "Yes, as your *good* lord."

There was a lull in which Isobel set to playing with the matrix once more. "Forgive me, I meant no disrespect, my lord," she said eventually.

"Perhaps you did not, but nor do you forgive my brother for denying your marriage," he remarked. "The Earl will find a more suitable match for you. He is not insensitive to your needs, and you might grow to love another in time." Cecily was walking her doll across the dog's back. He marked its progress. "My wife," he said with some difficulty, "gave Cecily the poppet. It had been meant for our own child."

Isobel ceased fiddling. "Lady Cecily treasures it, my lord. It gives her great joy."

He nodded and, when able to speak, said, "It gave Ann some consolation; she was passing fond of the girls."

"And they of her," Isobel said softly.

"Is that so?" The lines across his forehead lessened a little. "I am glad of it." He paused, then placed his hands squarely on his thighs and stood up. "I must see what learned texts Margaret has translated. My Latin is a little rusty."

From across the room the door opened, and a sharp voice cut through the chamber with rose-scented anger. "Where is Lord Langton?"

Isobel jumped to her feet, her kirtle grating against her raw skin. She curtsied. With a barely discernible sigh, Robert assumed a mask of courtesy. He bowed. "Madam."

The countess, white-faced, turned winter eyes on him without any pretence at civility. "What do you think you were doing dismissing my aunt from my household like a common servant?" she lashed, her tongue coiling so viciously that even the dog cowed behind Cecily's legs as she stood dumbed and trembling by the fire. "My household is my concern alone. You have no right to interfere."

"Madam, Lady La Roche is not fit to oversee your daughters. Her rule is overly harsh and unjust."

"That is not your concern."

"She beat Mistress Fenton till she bled —"

The countess snorted. "And what of it? The girl attacked her. My aunt had every reason to chastise her."

"That is not so," he said, with an edge to his voice, "and Mistress Fenton is in the Earl's charge, not your household, and she was protecting *your* daughter. Have you seen Cecily's legs? She is covered in bruises."

The countess's lips thinned. "No doubt she fell. The child is clumsy and has a tendency to unruliness. She must be disciplined for her own good. It is Lady La Roche's duty to ensure Cecily does not become host to the devil —"

In a flash of temper, he shot back, "You cannot believe that!"

"I choose to believe what Holy Church teaches even if you do not, my lord. My aunt will be reinstated immediately."

"She will not. I have given Mistress Fenton the care of my nieces."

"That girl?" The countess looked at Isobel, standing to one side, as if noticing her for the first time. "She is of little birth. She is not suitable to bring up the children of the Earl."

"I deem her fit," he replied evenly.

"You do not have the right."

"But I do, madam. While my brother is from the castle, I stand in his stead. I am lord over his household and father to his children."

"You take the girl into your own household if you wish … ah, but I forget; you have no need of a lady's maid, have you, my lord?"

He blanched visibly, and the countess all but vibrated at her little victory.

"Nonetheless," he said quietly, "Mistress Fenton will take this position."

The countess stared at him. "I will speak with my husband when he returns," she said tightly, casting arrows at Isobel.

"As you wish."

She thrust out her hand, a ring of ruby glowing against her long white fingers. He looked at it momentarily, then bent his head close to her proffered hand. She turned and walked stiffly from the room.

Isobel had been breathing so shallowly that she took a gulp of air. Robert waited until the countess left the room, then he looked around for the girls. They hadn't moved. "Margaret, take the book with you; you will have more time to read it than I, and you can tell me about it when we next meet." He bent and lifted Cecily. She had become subdued and was sucking her thumb. "And you, my little maid, must tell me of Nan's adventures when I see you again. Will you do that?"

In answer, Cecily popped her thumb from her mouth and wound both arms around his neck. He held her securely for a few moments, kissed her hair, and put her back on her feet.

"My lord ... the Earl..." Isobel began.

He read the worry in her eyes. "All will be well," he assured her. "All will be well."

Felice Langton folded her hands together in the way she had seen in the painting of St Anne her husband had recently acquired from the Venetian envoy. She had wondered if he had bought it to mock her, then thought it unlikely that he had given her any thought at all. A muscle twitched in her cheek, and she compressed her lips to control it. She turned her thoughts inwards to search for peace and found none, so studied instead the heavy brocade in dark green and gold that spread across her knees and fell to the floor in a terminating band of deep fur. She must ensure she wore it when they came to Court; the Queen would be envious of such a gown as this. She preened inwardly at the thought.

A slight cough broke her little pleasure, and she frowned. Elizabeth cleared her throat again and gave her mother a sideways look — half apology, half fearful — before returning to her needlework, her neck bent gracefully as she had been taught. Such beauty — the culmination of her parents' desire in the first months of their marriage. Elizabeth was everything that might be expected from the union of two of the most handsome heirs of the kingdom.

God's blessing was wrapped in this slender human form; purity that had tempted the king himself. Her own vigilance had saved her daughter's chastity, and a better marriage had been secured for her because of it. The queen knew how to protect her own interests — and those loyal to her — and she had been pleased to broker a match which served them all.

Felice silently glowed in a frisson of pleasure at a game well-played and won, then chilled with an afterthought. With a daughter such as this, why, then, had they been visited with God's displeasure in the years since? She could see the river from where she sat, glinting in the brittle sunlight and hiding in its depths the spark of her son's life it had so greedily consumed.

Sometimes, sitting here, she tried to imagine what their lives would have been like if he had lived, and then quashed the thought as she would a mosquito sucking on her happiness. There was no point in dwelling in the half-life of yesterday. Those left behind had to make do with today if they wanted better tomorrow. The image of the noisome insect made her arm itch and she longed to scratch. She made do with rotating her arm slightly within the tight silk of her sleeve instead.

And tomorrow was what today was all about. She could not afford to let Robert Langton have his way if she were to maintain complete control of her household. For if she allowed this one small matter to slip, who knew what other challenge to her authority she might face? She — and she alone — would rule their estates in her husband's absence. She might no longer occupy his bed, but she would dominate every other facet of their lives until it was wrested from her dead hand. And dead is what she would have to be before she relinquished one jot of the power she had helped him maintain over their years together. She had done her duty: she had given him an heir and three living daughters. But God had taken their son, and of their two younger daughters she despaired.

Her mouth skewed. Margaret would have to be wed beneath a veil if she were to get to the altar, unless the groom be blind or so old he was beyond caring. Or both. And Cecily? Felice involuntarily crossed herself. She might have suspected the work of an incubus had it not questioned her own fidelity, so she had to accept that her youngest child had been visited on her because of her own failings. Was that why she had also failed to secure her husband's affection and faithfulness?

Felice was not used to introspection; it laid her open to thoughts that disquieted her mind and distracted from the needs of the present. From beyond the door of her chamber, she heard voices. She straightened her shoulders.

Elizabeth raised her head, listening. "It is my father. Do you wish me to leave?"

Felice calmed the sudden rush she felt whenever she heard him. "No. Greet your father; it is as well he remembers who you are."

Elizabeth did as bidden, so that when the Earl entered the chamber he so infrequently visited, she was standing in readiness. She curtsied.

"Elizabeth." He kissed her on both cheeks and stood back to see her. "I hear Dalton has made a pretty gift to you; does it please you?"

She dimpled. "Yes, Father, and the silver trappings are so fine. They came from Brabant. The Duke of Burgundy's own master smith fashioned them." Her chin tipped up and she primped her mouth. "There are none to match in all England."

"Hmm, and the palfrey he sent with these treasures?"

"She rides well enough."

"The animal is young and will need to be ridden with care until she has reached maturity. Make your rides short in duration, but frequent, to help build her stamina."

Elizabeth all but raised her eyes heavenward. "Yes, Father, I know. The groom takes her out. Father, have you seen His Grace?"

"The king? You know I have."

"No, I mean the Duke of Gloucester. I missed seeing him when late he was here."

"Yes, what of it?"

"Did His Grace speak of me?" She reddened and dropped her eyes.

"No, he did not." He twitched. "Leave us. I wish to speak with your mother." There was a pause. "What is this nonsense about the duke?" he asked Felice when they were alone. "Has Bess given him cause to enquire after her?"

Felice remained seated. "Do you think I would let her? She likes him. You could have encouraged his interest in her instead of rushing ahead with a match with Edmund Dalton. We might have had a royal duke for a son instead of a…" She bit back her words as he visibly flinched at the mention of a son. "Instead of Dalton," she finished.

"The king has my fealty; he has no need to buy it with his brother. Gloucester can secure a better match elsewhere. I have ambition, but it does not rise to the royal house. Dalton is heir to one of the wealthiest men in the kingdom and his blood is old enough to sit at our table. He has the respect of the merchants and the ear of the king, and Bess will marry him whether she wishes it or no. You were pleased enough with the match as I understood it, and nothing has changed. Did you wish to speak with me, madam? You are well?"

Once, she thought briefly, he might have cared one way or the other; now, his question was a mere salutation demanded by courtesy. He always returned from Court on edge, as if he spent his time there on guard, and she should have known better than to allow their meeting to begin on such a tense footing if she wanted to get her way.

"You are tired, my lord, and I forget your comfort. Be seated and let me pour you wine."

He accepted the wine cup, but not her pleasantries. He remained standing as if he wanted to spend the least time possible with her. It had not always been so. "What is it you want, madam?"

She bristled, tried again, softening her voice and her face. "It is your children — Margaret and Cecily — I am troubled."

"Do they ail?"

"They are well, but it is their moral weal that concerns me. Margaret obeys readily enough, but Cecily is unruly. She is disobedient and…" Felice paused for effect, "…she has been heard talking to her poppet."

The Earl cast dispassionate eyes over her. "What of it? Children talk to all manner of things, do they not? Tell her not to."

"She has been told but she continues. When Lady La Roche reprimanded her, she bit her." The Earl grunted, which Felice took for a laugh. She chose to ignore it. "But worse, one of the attendants attacked my aunt and struck her to the ground in a fit of madness. She would have suffered further abuse had Lord Robert not stopped the girl."

"What is it to me? This is a matter of your own household."

Felice wrung her hands, shaping her face in an imitation of anguish worthy of the Virgin at the crucifixion. "Lord Robert's good nature was misused. The girl told him a wild tale and he believed it. He dismissed Lady La Roche without hearing her speak. *My* household, my lord — a faithful servant and my kin cast out because of the lies of this girl!"

Her husband didn't react immediately, and she wondered whether she had overdone it a bit, but she counted on his sense of duty and rigid adherence to justice.

"Who is the attendant?"

"That Fenton girl. She has an insolent disregard for authority and assumes more than her degree permits."

"Her *degree*, madam? What do you know of her degree?" He exhaled slowly. "If she serves with the loyalty her father showed me, it is enough. She is well-born, and her degree is not in question."

Felice stood and laid a placating hand on his sleeve. "I understand the connection you have to the girl's father and that you act as her good lord. She is your charge, which is why I bring it to you. I would not make a move without your authority. But Lord Robert is too gentle to see through the girl's scheming. My lord, he has given the care of your children to a girl who encourages Cecily to talk to her poppet and to … to … *spiders*. And I have reason to believe she has been instructing Margaret in Latin instead of duties more appropriate to her sex." She allowed her voice to break just enough to make her distress real. "I pleaded with him, but he is set against Lady La Roche and disregards my entreaty. Shall I have no say in who cares for our children? Am I to be cast aside?"

His finger tapped the side of the cup. "My brother appointed Isobel Fenton to take charge of the girls, you say?" She inclined her head and her mouth. "Then he must have had cause to do so." He handed the barely touched wine cup to her. "If that is all you wished to discuss, madam…"

"How does His Grace?" she asked as the Earl moved towards the door. He stopped, one hand on the frame.

"The king fares well."

"And Frances Stapleton?"

He hesitated before saying, "She is no concern of yours. I keep such pleasures discreet."

"She beds with my husband — how does that not concern me? I am still your *wife*, my lord."

He looked back over his shoulder. "If I find comfort under another roof, madam, it is because I long ceased to find it here."

CHAPTER FOURTEEN

Isobel woke as a heavy object landed on her stomach and proceeded to bounce. "Is'bel, wake up!"

Alarmed, she shot upright, shedding her blankets. The air was cold in the small room.

Joan grumbled in her sleep and rolled over.

"Is'bel, look, *look*!"

Isobel climbed off the narrow pallet and followed Cecily to the window where she had scrambled onto the stone seat and was trying to open the shutters. Early snow had fallen in the night, and it lay sparkling under a cold, bright sun. She felt her spirits lift as reflected light flooded the small room. Cecily danced.

"I want to go outside. Can we go? Can we?"

Isobel smiled at her eager face. "But Nan might get cold and catch a fever," she teased, hardly containing her own excitement and pulling her hair over her shoulder to untie the long plait.

"Nan will stay inside and say her pat'noster," Cecily replied grandly.

"Oh, will she, my lady!" Isobel laughed. "And have you said yours?"

"Ye-ees." Cecily twisted her night smock, stretching to see outside and avoiding Isobel's smile of disbelief. "But I have been to the privy by my own and I did a pee."

Margaret appeared behind her, rubbing sleep from her eyes. "She did, I heard her singing to the spiders."

"I sang them their song and they kept away like you said they would, Is'bel." She spun a circle in her bare feet, waving her arms above her head.

Isobel sent a silent prayer of thanks for a plentiful supply of mint and the hard work of the maids, whom she had instructed to scrub the small privy room until their arms ached and the stone gleamed. She entrusted Alice to do a daily patrol to ensure unwanted visitors didn't appear and, so far, it had worked. Even Joan grudgingly acknowledged the improvement, but that was just about all she had done since Isobel had been given charge of the girls. In every other respect she dragged her feet and, what little she did, she did badly. No doubt the countess was keen to see Isobel fail, and she suspected Joan harboured a similar ambition. She pushed the thought from her mind.

Crowding the pleached branches of the lindenwood allées, the sun-softened snow dropped in loose clusters on the girls' heads as they raced towards the garden and the virgin sward of the snake tree. Isobel was relieved — but not surprised — to see that no couples warmed the air inside the arbour, and they were alone. The footprints of a cat patrolled the paths, but the snow around the tree lay pristine. A few apples clung to the highest branches; wizened, corrupted, beyond redemption. Cecily broke away from Alice, skipping to hug the tree, singing her now-familiar song to the twisting form of the snake. Isobel shivered.

Flumph. A wet ball of snow brushed her skirt and fell harmlessly at her feet. Twisting around, she narrowly missed a second snowball, but saw instead Margaret's shining face. Scooping a handful of snow, Isobel held it menacingly aloft, as Alice bent to do the same. Whooping in delight, Margaret made for the shelter of the tree, kicking snow from her heels as she ran. Isobel launched the first missile. It missed its mark, landed squarely on the tree's trunk, and slid onto Cecily's uncovered head. Squealing, Cecily quickly forgot the snake and scampered between the flying snowballs, barking like a dog as she tried to catch them. Soon they became a mass of limbs and pink faces, and Isobel's hair — escaping the confines of her binding and flying loose — became a river of honey against the snow.

She didn't notice the man until she upended Cecily and threatened to roll her into a giant snowball. She heard him laugh and looked up. Leaning against the rose-thickened arbour, Robert Langton watched their play. Bare headed, he looked younger as he came towards them. Then she remembered who he was and bobbed her head. Any attempt at dignity was lost, however, as Margaret took advantage of Isobel's lull in concentration and lobbed a lump of snow in her direction. It shattered into slush against the back of her head, making her squeak in surprise. Lord Langton caught a second ball before it found its mark, reformed it, and hurled it at his niece, who ducked and sprinted away. Brushing snow from his gloved hands, he grinned at Isobel, and she met his warm eyes with an unguarded smile.

"Thank you, my lord," she puffed, breathless and glowing.

"It is as well to know your enemy and guard your rear from attack from an unexpected quarter." He smiled, keeping a weather eye on Margaret, who was forming a snowball as he spoke. "Or else keep a friend close who will watch your back for you." He studied the ground around them as if measuring battle lines. In the sunlight, his dark blue eyes had touches of violet in them. She hadn't noticed before. He turned them on her again and she hoped he believed her rising colour evidence of her recent exertion.

"I came on an errand," he said, and retrieved from his belt, into which he had tucked a round shape, a package bound in vivid red cloth with a scrolled message attached. "Cecily!" he called out over Isobel's head. She came running over, one glove missing, curls bouncing. He held out the parcel. "This is for you."

Cecily clapped her hands and grabbed the gift and then remembered to say, "Thank you," at Isobel's prompting before tearing the binding off the bundle to reveal the contents. She cradled a bright leather ball made of multicoloured segments and big enough to fit securely in her hands. Her eyes became round. She waved the ball and it jingled softly from a secret bell inside. She giggled.

"Hector-Nan gave it to me!" She threw it in the air and promptly dropped it, picked it up, and ran off to show Margaret and Alice.

"His Grace remembered!" Isobel exclaimed, retrieving the discarded cloth and removing the furled message. She opened it: "From your faithful servant, Hector", the duke had written in suitably doggy writing, signed with a paw print, and with his own elegant initials 'R.G.' beneath. Richard of Gloucester. She laughed. "He remembered," she said again to herself, recalling him in an instant and her own ridiculous error of identity.

"His Grace rarely neglects that which he promises, and he seemed to find *you* difficult to forget." His mouth curved at her surprised embarrassment.

"I did not mean to offend His Grace," she rushed.

"Nor did you. That was not why he remembered you…" He stopped, changed tack. "The duke respects honesty and he found your lack of guile … refreshing."

"Oh." She reddened again, but this time with pleasure. The girls were getting bored waiting. A snowball tested the ground nearby, then another exploded on the tree by their heads.

"*Bellum domesticum*," Margaret declared, dancing up to them with a compacted ball of snow at the ready.

Robert Langton held up his hands in submission. "*Pax!*" he shouted, laughing, "*Victis honor!* Let there be peace and honour to the vanquished. Who else can you trust if not your family?" But she strayed too close, and with a quick movement he trapped Margaret within the folds of his arms, disarmed her, kissed the top of her head, and released her scarlet with indignation.

"Uncle! You ... you said ... you should trust your family!" she spluttered.

"Indeed, but always beware the serpent within," he said, throwing the snowball and hitting the thickness of her skirts with a satisfying thud.

"That's not fair!" she protested.

His face straightened momentarily. "Life rarely is." He looked down at Isobel as if he knew she would understand, and his expression changed. "You must be getting cold." Reaching out a gloved hand, he removed fragments of snow from her hair, and something in the way his face softened and the movement of his mouth as his lips bent into a smile made her skin warm. He smiled again, and this time she felt it in her stomach.

From his privy chamber in the great tower, the Earl watched his daughters chase in the snow as his brother and Isobel Fenton talked beneath the skeleton of the apple tree. He saw Cecily rush up to them, take something handed to her, the delighted jig as she realised what it was, and imagined her laughter as she ran back to her sister to show her. Somewhere, deep inside, he regretted being the man he was. Robert would have made a better father than he had been, and his girls deserved more attentive parents than they had. Fate had dealt him and his brother different blows, each bitter in their own way.

Below, in the gleaming snowscape, Robert reached out and took something from the Fenton girl's hair. The Earl imagined her beneath the tree, honeyed hair cloaking her shoulders, blue-green eyes smiling, and they were smiling at *him*. He opened his eyes — "God's teeth!" — and saw Isobel Fenton walking away. His brother watched her for a few moments before slapping the trunk lightly and crossing the snow towards the tower. Robert glanced up and waved his hand. The Earl hesitated, then raised his own in acknowledgement, then hid it as it shook.

"She is fair," the Earl said later, when the brothers supped together in the quiet of his chamber. Robert helped himself from the dish in front of him. His appetite had improved, the Earl noted, and his colour returned.

"Who is?"

The Earl wondered if his brother feigned indifference. "Isobel Fenton," he said shortly.

Robert cocked his head on one side as if he needed to consider the question. "Yes, she is," he replied, and continued eating.

Replacing his knife and wiping his hands on his napkin, the Earl examined his younger brother in the light of the fire. Robert's oak-brown hair was thick and untouched by grey, framing a strong face. His eyes — determined and dark — were unswerving, and he knew to his cost that his brother kept his gaze whether the recipient liked it or not. He was a little broad in the shoulders, perhaps, and would be inclined to carry weight had he not trained his body to hardness from years in the yard and in the saddle, but his open manner appealed to women, if he ever cared to notice, and he had youth on his side. The Earl grunted.

Robert looked up. "And...?" he asked.

"She instructs Margaret in Latin," the Earl said as an afterthought.

"Yes, she does." Robert smiled.

Keeping his thoughts to himself, the Earl selected a disc of sugared fruit and turned it so that the firelight shone through it like a little sun. "How did Cecily like the duke's gift?" He felt his brother's eyes settle on him.

"Better, if you had given it to her yourself."

"His Grace entrusted it to you."

"He probably thought you would give it to one of your dogs." They both looked at the exquisite greyhound lounging in the heat of the fire. As much as there might have been a grain of truth in what Robert said, nobody else could have got away with a comment like that.

The Earl growled a laugh. "Probably." He turned the sun into a crescent with a single clean bite. "As to the duke, how did you find His Grace?"

"Young — but come into his own. I like him well enough."

"More so than his brother George?"

Robert didn't rush his answer. "I know little of George Clarence other than the few times we met at Court. I cannot say one way or the other, except I found him peevish. Clarence can be persuasive enough, but he doesn't know when to stop pushing."

"But Gloucester is proving steadfast?"

"It would seem so."

The Earl paused, then, "The king thinks highly of his youngest brother. It would be as well to align yourself to Gloucester — make your loyalty known, make it felt, make it *count*. For the sake of the family —"

"You do not need to teach me my duty," Robert shot. Then, more moderately, "I know it well enough."

The Earl drank, covering a smile at his brother's flash of temper. He wiped his mouth, threw the napkin on the table. "Your duty, mine — and that of my daughters. With favourable matches for Bess and Margaret —"

"Margaret wishes to enter the convent," Robert stated.

"Then she will have to think again," the Earl replied. "She will reach her fifteenth year come February, and I have several in suit for her hand."

"Who?"

"Cosham. Raseby. Brakespear. Alfrington."

"Alfrington is Warwick's man!"

"I said he is in suit, Rob, I did not say that I would grant it."

"So, you play both sides." Robert found it all but impossible to hide his distaste. "Have you given Warwick an answer to his letter?"

"I have only ever fought for one side, Rob, you know that, and the king knows it. Warwick knows too, but I'll let him go on believing I might bed with him for as long as it serves our family and our cause."

"You will play the whore? Where is the honour in that!"

The Earl had been rolling a walnut in his palm; now he picked up another and deftly circled the pair, favouring neither one nor the other as he contemplated his brother. "I do not have the luxury of declaring my loyalty so wantonly in these times. I am for the king — liver and heart — but if Warwick thinks I might be bought, I'll let him continue in his delusion because it serves the king's purpose to keep him close until he declares himself openly. And then," he said, enclosing the walnuts in the vice of his fist, "honour will be served." He crushed the nuts, breaking them like brittle skulls. He opened his hand, letting the fragments fall onto the cloth, and selected a kernel, corrugated like a brain. "And when the smoke clears and the battle is done, we shall pick over the remains of those who sought to overthrow this king and be the richer for it." He offered the other half of the walnut to his brother.

Robert took it, raised it in salute. "Then, may it please God we win, for the alternative is unspeakable."

The Earl shrugged. "There is that," he said, consuming the walnut.

"Mistress Fenton!"

Isobel stopped. The short figure of the Earl's chamberlain hurried after her, dodging between the small groups of men crowding the great hall.

"The Earl commands you attend him." He turned, expecting her to follow.

"Why?" Isobel called, and then ran to catch up. "Did my lord say why he wants to see me? It must be important if he has sent you."

"I do not know my Earl's mind," he said, somewhat impatiently, and then, stopping for a moment at the foot of the great stair, "I was on my way to see Lord Langton. I chanced to see you, that is all."

Instead of pausing at the entrance to the Earl's great chamber where Cecily had interrupted her father's council not so long ago, the chamberlain crossed the room and continued up another hidden stair to a door she had not seen before. He gave a brief knock and, opening the door, stood back. "The Earl is weary; do not vex him," he warned as she passed him. He shut the door behind her, and she heard his light steps scurrying away until they faded.

The large chamber seemed empty. The remains of dinner lay on the table and a heavy chair, fat with cushions, stood pushed back as if just vacated. Covering one entire wall of the room, wooden panelling, glowing with colour, rose to the ceiling. The painted image of a massive and stately tree grew with spreading branches until the tips touched the furthest panels at either side and subtle, rich gilding picked out the tracery of every delicate leaf.

There was no sign of the Earl. Curiosity biting, Isobel inched forward to get a better look at the panels. From top to bottom, each branch supported a painted figure armoured in tabards of yellow and blue over bright steel, and women in headdresses Isobel had only ever seen fixed in stone on tombs. Between their outstretched hands, they held coats of arms, quartered into so many divisions the detail swam in the uncertain light. Generations in an unbroken line from father to son. At the very top, a large wheel within which sat a woman in robes of blue and ermine. Fortuna herself, and at the summit of the wheel, in splendid ascendance, the crowned figure of an earl.

Isobel followed the trunk downwards and recognised the Earl's features and, next to him, his countess. The space below looked oddly blank as if something had once decorated it but had been erased. She touched the surface and felt the rough brush marks of new paint. A voice came from behind her.

"My kin," the Earl said, materialising through a door to one side as he adjusted the wide sleeves of his gown. He raised his eyes to the painted figures. "My grandsire wanted to make a record of our family." He used his ringed hand to indicate a lifelike portrait of a bearded man. The Old Earl looked determined, like an aged version of his grandsons, and rather grim. "He wished his sons and those that follow them to remember that Fortuna is always ready to turn her wheel. *Fero tui sceleris — I bear your villainy*. As if we could ever forget," he added to himself. "You instruct Lady Margaret in Latin. It was made clear that you were not to."

It was stated as fact and Isobel had nothing to say in her defence.

"You have gone against the bidding of the countess."

Isobel kept her eyes lowered respectfully, but every inch of her body screamed resentment and she pinched the skin of her thumb repeatedly. "Yes, my lord. But Lady Margaret wanted to —"

"It is not for you to determine what Lady Margaret is to be taught, nor for you to encourage her to defy her mother's wishes." He sucked his teeth. "My youngest daughter —"

"Cecily, my lord."

"I know her name! Do you not think I know my own child? Look at me."

She raised her face and met his eyes. She saw a shift in the way he looked at her, a moment in which his brief confusion because a swell of anger. Reaching out, he hooked his hand behind her neck and forced his mouth against hers.

Struggling, she cried out her resistance in her throat, sounding like a frightened animal, and he released her, turning his back on her shocked face.

"Get out."

Blindly, Isobel fled down the dim-lit stairs, almost careering into a figure coming up them. Hands gripped her elbows. "Have a care!"

Robert Langton was the last person she wanted to see. She freed herself and without looking at him ran on, leaving him standing alone on the stairs.

"Where have you been?" Joan demanded as Isobel crossed the girls' chamber and disappeared through the door on the other side without stopping. "There's a letter for you. From your sweetheart, by the looks of it." Joan pulled a face and took herself to the doorway. Isobel had initiated a frantic search of her casket. Joan held the folded letter out. "Don't you want to know what it says?"

Isobel stopped and took it from Joan's plump hand; the seal had cracked, and part of it was missing.

Joan shrugged. "It were like that."

Isobel threw it on her bed and continued her search. She found what she wanted in the bottom of the ivory box. She went to the table where the jug for the morning water still stood. It was empty.

"Alice!" She didn't recognise her own voice. Her servant appeared. "Fetch hot water. Now. Make it scalding," she added as the girl bobbed and took the ewer from her, squeezing past Joan's immovable form that almost blocked the doorway.

"What do you want that for?" Joan nodded at the tiny green fragments Isobel ground into the oats in the base of her mortar, releasing the astringent aroma of thyme. "Eh, you are a strange one, right enough. I'd mind myself, if I were you. The Earl'll not take kindly to your addling ways, not with his children's —"

Isobel didn't let her finish. At the mention of the Earl, her head whipped around and, glaring at Joan, she pushed her forcibly through the door and shut it in her face. She leaned against the broad planks and only opened it to receive the heavy ewer from Alice.

Dipping the herb bag into the steaming water, she scrubbed at her mouth until her lips peeled. Then she flopped onto her pallet and sat, hunched, until her hands stopped shaking. A tentative knock preceded Alice's placid face around the edge of the door. She popped through when Isobel didn't react.

"Mistress?" she ventured. "My ladies have eaten, and they ask for you. Oh...!"

Isobel looked up and saw the dismay in Alice's eyes. Isobel put her fingers to her own lips: they burned, and she could taste the thyme oil on them. It would pass. She would make an ointment to calm her skin and it would be as if nothing had happened at all. The thyme would make chaste that which the Earl had defiled.

"The Earl was here," Alice said as if reading her thoughts. "This morning while you were at mass..."

"What did he want?"

Alice twisted her hands in front of her. "He did not say. My lord spoke to Lady Margaret for a while — in Latin. He did not seem displeased, though, as I thought he might. Then he took Lady Cecily on his knee and talked with her... I have not seen him do that before..." Alice broke off, staring, and Isobel made a conscious effort to appear unmoved.

"And?"

"And she showed him her poppet — made it talk and dance, as she does — and then..." Alice faltered.

Isobel ground her teeth. "What? Speak."

"He laughed right fairly."

The Earl must have made an impression on Alice, because she blushed deeply and made a show of blowing her nose. In Isobel's mind, the dancing doll became Buena's cavorting fingers, and she sickened. She held her hand to her lips until the moment passed, remembered that they were where his mouth had been, and clasped at the chaplet in its bag at her waist instead.

"Go to," she said somewhat sharply, then, less so, "Leave me; I need to think."

The overcast day dimmed towards dusk, and the small room cooled. Isobel pulled the bedcover over her shoulders and from the crumpled wool retrieved the forgotten letter. She viewed it with a mixture of dread and longing, a piece of news long looked for, but whose outcome was uncertain. The remnant of the Lacey seal fell unchallenged from the letter. She recognised Thomas's blunt writing, read the message it contained with a sense of detachment, folded it, and held it motionless between her hands.

Buena was ill, Thomas wrote; he thought she ought to know. She avoided asking herself why he cared enough to tell her and only knew that she had to get away from here; she had to get home. Should the Earl send after her... She shuddered in her cloak. Her father had warned her not to provoke the Earl's wrath. What defence did she have against his will, unless — Isobel's heart almost stopped at the thought — unless she married Thomas and had the protection of her husband?

Her mind raced. Not even the Earl could deny a marriage made before witnesses. She was not his ward, and he had no real legal authority over her except what honour and convention gave him, and he had flouted both in her eyes. She bristled at the memory. But to ensure her marriage was valid she would have to lie with her husband — let him touch her, kiss her, even. The thought was not appealing, but needs must.

"I passed Isobel Fenton on the stair," Robert said as the door to the Earl's privy chamber closed behind him. He could see his brother's back silhouetted against the brightness of the fire as he leaned both arms on the chimney breast, but the rest of the room was unlit in the gloom of the winter day. "She seemed distressed." He wasn't sure if his brother had heard him. "Did you see fit to chastise her after all?"

The Earl pushed himself away from the fireplace. "Why would I do that? You gave her governance over my daughters; I saw no need to countermand that decision."

"Felice…"

"What of her?"

"I thought she might have persuaded you to change your mind."

His brother's mouth lifted in a dry smile. "She has long since failed to do that. Maud La Roche has the balls of a man under her skirts without the wit to know what to do with them, and my wife chooses to remain blind. No, Rob, I am satisfied in your choice. Margaret is acquiring Latin and the grace to use it prettily, and Cecily managed to sit still long enough to talk without either offending my nose or biting me."

"Then Mistress Fenton has served you well in all respects. She will retain her position?" Robert asked.

One of the greyhounds wandered over to the Earl and pushed its muzzle into his hand, and he stroked its soft head distractedly. He seemed to be thinking. He gave the dog a conclusive pat and faced Robert. "There is a matter to which I wish you to attend. In the morning, I would have you tell Isobel Fenton that she can return to her manor." Robert's surprise must have been clearly visible because the Earl raised a hand to stop him speaking. "She has no business here. She'll need an escort, but I am satisfied her father's steward can oversee her affairs until she marries. Or comes of age."

Robert couldn't read his brother's face. He had never known him to go back on a decision made as definitely as he had done with this girl. An uncomfortable sensation lodged in his throat. "You will let Thomas Lacey wed her?"

Sitting, the Earl rested his head against the back of his chair and closed his eyes. "I would not let Thomas Lacey marry the third daughter of my stable jack, but I want her from this place, Rob; I want her gone."

CHAPTER FIFTEEN

The level darkness of the previous day had given way to a clear sky in the early hours of the morning. Without light, Isobel had packed what she could as Joan slept and then lay clothed under her blankets until the castle stilled and all around became quiet. Cradling her casket, she now made her way across the girls' bedchamber towards the door. Sleep had made the girls younger, and in the last light of the fire, Isobel looked at their untroubled faces. She knew she shouldn't risk it, but she stepped over Alice's sleeping form and softly kissed Margaret's forehead, then leaned a little further and touched her lips to Cecily's hair. She said a silent prayer of protection, fought the emotion welling at her departure, and left the sleeping children to their rest.

The night shifted. Somewhere close by a dog barked. Isobel peered around the edge of the wall and made ready to move. The outline of the great tower grew out of the inked sky, and bird voices of the oncoming dawn broke from the roosts of the dovecot. To her dismay, Isobel could make out the dry scratching as the ovens were raked out in the castle kitchens. Before long, new smoke would scent the air. She drew her hood over her face and kept to the walls where night still clung to the stone.

She crossed the bailey without challenge, but the gatehouse was heavily guarded and day crept upon the lightening sky. Already sounds of the town beyond the castle rose on the morning air and from inside the gatehouse great chains raised the portcullis. Outside the gates she had entered in the heat of summer, a whole world existed from which she had been confined. In town, she would be able to hire a horse and perhaps a boy to go with her as far as the old cross marking her lands. She would go home where her own walls and gates would rise around her, defining her identity, defending her state.

From above her, a guard shouted from the gatehouse walls. The gates opened, and the first in a series of carts laden with faggots of wood trundled across the ward. She had lingered too long and lost the obscurity of darkness. She would have to bluff it out.

The carters were taking their time passing under the gatehouse. Despite the cold, the flanks of the heavy horses glistened from the long haul, and Isobel could smell the sweat of the men's labours as they exchanged ribald comments with the porter as each cart was checked by the guard. Isobel pulled her shoulders back and found from somewhere the confidence to make a bold step forward. She walked past the first cart and found her way barred. Although the main gates stood open, the smaller wicket gate next to them was still locked. The porter had his back to her. Quelling an overwhelming urge to squeeze past the heavy carts and risk being crushed, Isobel instead stopped and waited expectantly by the metal-bound door as if she had every reason to be there.

Flicking the contents of his nose, the porter finally noticed her. He hurried over, then slowed as he took in her youth. "Goin' somewhere, mistress?"

She forced a pleasantry. "I have business to attend. Open the gate."

"Right early for a bit o' business. Goin' alone, is you? Got a sweetheart in't town, 'ave ye?" Scratching at the greyed stubble on his chin, he grinned, revealing a staggered row of teeth.

Isobel gave him what she hoped was a haughty look. "Open the gate, I'm in a hurry."

He eyed her, shrugged, sniffed, then slid the greased drawbar back into the thickness of the wall and opened the door. Beyond the vaulted tunnel of the gatehouse and under the teeth of the raised portcullis, the stone bridge crossing the moated river was partly blocked by the last of the carts. It struggled to cross the rutted wooden drawbridge which spanned the yawning gap between the end of the stone bridge and the gatehouse itself. The wheel stuck; men and beasts heaved.

Isobel gathered her skirts and climbed through the door, holding the wrapped casket close to her. It was already heavy, and her arms ached, but, despite the acrid horse urine in the confined space of the gatehouse tunnel, she scented freedom. She flattened herself against the wall as the horse closest to her startled at her sudden appearance. She glanced back to see the face of the porter peering after her. He said something that was drowned out by the metalled hooves striking stone and, to her alarm, stepped through the door after her. She hurried on beneath the blank eye of the murder hole, through the outer gate of the barbican, and into the open.

On the bridge, the carter's boy gave the lead horse a *thwack* on its muscled rump and the animal urged forward, a widening gap opening as it rumbled over the uneven surface. Isobel could wait no longer. She let the horse pass, then darted along the side of the precariously swaying wain.

"Mind yer'sen!" Isobel felt a sharp tug on her cloak, and she almost fell backwards as several bundles of timber narrowly missed her as they fell from the cart and rolled into the moat with a hollow *plonk*. The porter coughed and shot a gob of phlegm after them.

"In a didder rush such as would get yer kill'd, yer glaikit lass." Wiping his mouth on his sleeve, he squinted at her, then at the pale corner of the box protruding from its cover. "What ye got there, then?" He reached out and jerked the cloth aside before Isobel could stop him. Silver-gilt, the sun lifted over the horizon and shone cool beams on the ivory casket in her arms. The creases of the porter's face hardened. "Where d'you get that from? Gi' it me." He tried to take the box, but she held onto it, heart beating against its unforgiving edge.

"It's mine, let me go!"

Keeping one eye on Isobel, the porter called over his shoulder, "'Arry, call t'sergeant; we got a sniping thief making way 'ere."

"How dare you! I am no thief! This is my casket, and you stop me from going about my business."

"Aye, well, we'll see aboot tha'. You'll come wi' me and tell it t'sergeant."

She had little option but to follow the porter back through the gatehouse and into the smoky guardroom. A brazier burned to one side, and a new bundle of sticks sent smoke spiralling to the ceiling where it hung in a fug. Isobel coughed and, wiping her eyes, found several unfriendly faces appraising her.

An ox-chested man slowly stood up from the stool beside the fire. In his scarred hand, he held a piece of bread off which he had just carved a wedge with his knife. He prodded the blade in the direction of Isobel's scared but defiant face. "What's this, then?"

"Caught this lass sniping chest, sergeant. In a hurry t'leave castle she were, but I thought, me, 'Here's an odd'n out this time of the morn,' so I took after her, like, and she 'ad this on 'er." He pulled the cloth from the casket, and the sergeant's expression changed.

"Take that off," he said, indicating Isobel's hood. The porter yanked it from her head before she could do so herself. "Who are ye?"

She tried to remind herself that this man was only a sergeant, and in normal circumstances she would not even speak with him. But these were not normal circumstances, and his bulk blocked out the feeble light from the arrow-loop as he towered over her waiting for an answer.

"She be a spy," the porter suggested with a sly grin.

Isobel flushed with anger. "Do not be ridiculous! I am the daughter of Sir Geoffrey Fenton of Beaumancote." She hoped the mention of his name would be enough. "Let me go my way and I will not mention this to him."

"Oh aye, are ye now?" The sergeant hefted the bread into his mouth, chewing slowly as he appraised her. "You don't liken after him and I knew him right well." He wiped his blade on his sleeve. "An' the Geoffrey Fenton I knew wouldn't 'ave let his lass travel alone. Besides, unless you plan on talking wit' ghosts, you'll have a hard time telling him aught because he's been dead nigh on three month, which you'd know if you were his child."

"I *am* Isobel Fenton! You have no right to stop me. I must get home..." Isobel blurted, feeling her words dry into a thin strand of pleading. "Please, let me go."

"I have the right, mistress. This castle's security is my duty, and I make duty my pride, as your fader would 'ave known if he were still alive to say it, mercy be on him." He beckoned over her head to one of the guards lounging against the back wall. "Take message to t'constable: we have a fledgling here who'd take flight without letter o' transit, but with a fine coffer I don't rightly know is hers."

"I'll pluck 'er feathers for 'ee," one of the men sniggered under his breath from the corner of the room, echoed by another.

The sergeant's thick neck rotated towards the soldier, and the man's leer dissolved. The sergeant addressed Isobel in a low voice. "With these troubles abroad, there be hired men about the castle who'd not be trusted with ye. I'd best take you there myself. You, lad —" he raised his eyes to the soldier — "can take double next watch and allay your lust on t'battlements, or else answer for your mouth wi' Constable."

The open casket sat on the table in front of the Earl in the council chamber. Robert Langton dismissed the constable and came back to his brother. He bent close so the others in the room couldn't hear him. "I do not understand your anger. She was making for her manor; it is what you wanted me to tell her this very day." He checked over his shoulder at the huddle of men by the window. "You have her waiting outside like a felon. Is that what you want? I do not understand why you treat her this way."

The Earl continued to stare at the casket. "I did not give her leave to go."

"What perverse petty justice is this that you punish her for doing your will? Sweet Jesu, you are hard to please and harder to serve."

"My lord." Nicolas Sawcliffe approached the Earl in a cloud of clove. Robert wondered how much he had overheard and turned his back on him, biting his tongue. "The girl is young, but she left the castle without your leave. It might have been mere folly, but…" he spread bony hands in a question.

The Earl looked up sharply. "But, what?"

"The question has to be asked, my lord: why did she leave?"

"She wished to return to her home where she would not be whipped or accused of theft!" Robert flung at him.

"I know nothing of the former, my lord, but as the Earl's secretary —"

"Spymaster," Robert spat.

Sawcliffe smiled. "Indeed, my lord, I am retained to protect my Earl's interests both here —" he waved towards the window — "and abroad, and as such suggest the box should be searched. The girl also."

"You go too far!"

"I go as far as I think wise, and wisdom, in these troubled times, is in short supply. Although perhaps innocent herself, she might be bearing papers for … another?"

Robert could hardly prevent his disdain. "You would have the Earl believe Isobel Fenton an *espiouress*?"

Sawcliffe inclined his head in a gesture of solicitude. "I repeat only what I know, and I know that Mistress Fenton has lately received a letter from Thomas Lacey —"

The Earl's closed fist came down on the table. "Out!"

The low murmur in the room came to an abrupt halt, and all faces pivoted towards him.

Sawcliffe raised neatly arched brows. "My lord…"

"All of you. Out. *Now*. Robert, bring Mistress Fenton in."

Waiting outside the council chamber while the constable went inside to speak to the Earl, Isobel began to understand how criminals must have felt as her father dispensed the king's justice at Quarter Sessions. The casket had been taken from her, and her empty hands twisted jerkily. She caught the guard looking at them and retrieved her beads from inside their purse, trying to focus on her Ave.

"*Ave Maria gracia plena aconite, aquilegia, dominus tecum benedictus betany, bay, borage tu in mulieribus camomile, cinnamon, clove et benedictus frutas dittany, dill, ventures tui ihesu. Amen.*" Grasping a jet gaud, she started again. "*Ave Maria* —"

She heard a raised voice from inside the room that she recognised as the Earl's, then the door opened and the constable came out straight-faced and empty-handed. He spoke quietly to the guard, cast a sideways frown at Isobel, and disappeared down the curving stair. She clutched her beads. "*Ave Maria gracia plena* —"

The door flew open again, and she stepped back as half a dozen men herded from the chamber buzzing with whispered comments and hooded glances. All except one. Nicolas Sawcliffe followed a few paces behind the others. Seeing Isobel, he stopped, inclined his head towards her, and, with his ever-present smile that left her cold, his eyes moved to her fractious hands then back to her taut face. She stuffed her beads in her purse, and he smiled again and moved on. Moments later, while her heart was still popping with fright, Robert Langton appeared.

The contents of the casket lay jumbled on the table in front of the Earl. He had barely looked at them since tipping them out and had returned to his sightless reverie. He came to as the door opened. Now Isobel Fenton stood before him, drawn and sleepless, fidgeting. She looked young, vulnerable. "Stand still!" he barked and then regretted it as she flinched. "You left without permission."

It sounded more like a complaint to his ears, rather than a matter of discipline, and it irritated him. He considered following up with a question about why she had left, but he already knew the answer. Instead, methodically stroking the scar on his top lip, he contemplated her. "You have a letter." Startled, Isobel looked up for the first time. She didn't deny it, he noted. "Give it to me."

He held out his hand and she handed it to him. He felt the vibration of her fear as their hands briefly touched. Or was it guilt? Or hate? He read the letter, checked the broken seal, then gave it to his brother. Robert's brow raised as he read it. He handed it back.

"And you believed this?" the Earl asked Isobel, holding the letter up as an accusation.

Her forehead puckered. "Yes, my lord," she ventured uncertainly.

"Why, in Saint John's name, would Thomas Lacey write to you because your *servant* is ill?"

Her hand fumbled at her side.

"Well?"

"I thought…" she mumbled.

"Speak up!"

"I … I thought he might miss me, and this was his way of … of … showing me."

"I doubt he knows such subtlety," the Earl growled. "He knew you would return, but I did not take you for a fool to do so." He threw the letter on the table. "This is treason."

Her mouth dropped open in horror, and all remaining colour fled from her face.

His brother uttered a grunt of protest. "Foolishness, perhaps, but not treason! She did not know."

"Did she not? Do you see this?" The Earl held up the letter with the red seal like blood, staining the bottom edge. Isobel nodded. "Did you not think to ask why Thomas Lacey uses his father's seal?"

He watched her think back to the harried moments of the previous day. She shook her head.

"Henry Lacey is dead. Thomas Lacey has come into his inheritance and his uncle's title. He no longer needs my lordship, he wants a wife — a wife who will secure him the land south of the Humber and east of the Trent and, no doubt, the offices that go with it. Did you really think he would let you go once you returned to your land? He now has the men to command and the will to do so. He would have had you wed within a day of your foot touching the soil of your manor." She stood transfixed and colourless before him, and he relented a little. "As your overlord and while you are in your minority, any such move to secure your marriage against my express command is *rapere*. Unless —" he leaned towards her across the table — "it was with your consent."

She moistened dry lips, avoiding his eyes. He sat back heavily — it was all he needed to know. He had guessed the reason for her flight was less to do with Lacey and more his own behaviour the day before, and his anger was merely the pricking of his conscience. Had he sent her back as he intended, she would have walked into Thomas Lacey's arms, willing or not. This turn of events might prove beneficial after all.

"You will not answer this letter, and any other you receive from Thomas Lacey or anyone else you will bring directly to me. Do you understand?"

She nodded dumbly.

"Then speak of this to no one, and take heed of what I have said."

Robert waited until she had left, carrying her casket into which she had hastily gathered the contents under the Earl's remorseless eye. "There is no treason. She is guilty of no more than wanting to be free of this place and to return to the life she once knew."

"I know it well enough, but I wanted to make sure of what *she* knew." The Earl stretched his legs out in front of him and flexed his shoulders. "It makes clear our suspicion: Thomas Lacey is behind the disturbances on the Humber." The Earl's fingers tapped the letter. "There is no chance of keeping him close, not if his mind is fixed on treason."

With his foot, Robert hooked a stool towards the table and sat down. "The letter does not say so. He could not be convicted by it. The king has seen fit to return his uncle's title…"

"Against my counsel."

"…so His Grace must have some hope of his loyalty."

"Lacey has yet to show his hand openly. This —" he flipped the letter with his fingers — "is a conceit intended to deceive."

"Then Isobel Fenton is without fault and had no part in the deception."

The Earl looked at his brother. "Unknowing of Lacey's intent, perhaps, but without fault? When has woman ever been without fault since Eve beguiled Adam and sowed the seed of our downfall? When is any woman truly innocent? They deceive us all, Rob; knowingly or unwittingly, they are a trap into which we must fall."

Robert's dark eyebrows rose. "What has she ever done to deserve your spleen?"

The Earl upended the eating knife with which he had been playing, letting it slide through his fingers to be turned about on its jasper handle in a repeated motion of tail over tip. It had been their older brother's, and before that, their father's — the gift of a former king in gilded times. Now he watched the light reflect from the gold blade as he answered. "Spleen? I did not say I hated her. Nor have you said why you jump so readily to her defence."

"She reminds me of her mother."

The knife stopped point down, the Earl's hand still. "And why should *that* be of any consequence to *you*?"

Robert contemplated his boots. "In the midst of her own suffering, Lady Fenton showed kindness to a boy fresh from the slaughter of his first battle. I have not forgotten the generosity of her spirit and see it in her daughter also. She is very like her mother." He paused as he looked up. "You must remember Lady Fenton, brother? You were there."

The Earl's face froze. "I remember nothing of that time other than the betrayal of our father. I think of nothing more than seeing him on his knees in the mire and guts of other men and the cleaving of his skull as he cried for mercy. He had his beads in his hand, Rob, his *beads* — and Ralph Lacey cut him down." The Earl thrust his fist into his hand and screwed it hard, the prominent ring scoring redly into his palm as his normal self-possession threatened to implode. He breathed out, slowly. "That is what I remember — what *I* choose to remember."

"We lost much at Sandal, I know that all too well, and you never cease to remind me; but God saw fit to give us victory at Towton."

The Earl took in his brother's serious face. "Did He? We won the battle, but I wonder sometimes whether our family was visited by God's wrath at Sandal, and thence after — Towton, too."

"Why?"

"For our sins, Rob."

"Sins of omission — or commission?"

"Both."

The light wind of the morning had strengthened, gasping and sighing at the leaded casements. Robert went over to the windows and held his hand to the mullions where the wind squeezed through the fractured stone. "I do not ask what sins you have committed that you should believe there is no hope of redemption. For my part, a woman showed me that mercy lay at the heart of war. It is a lesson I have never forgotten; it is what *I* choose to remember." He swung around to face his brother. "On the same day Ralph Lacey took our father's life, Geoffrey Fenton would have given his to save him. When you deal with his daughter, remember *that*."

"You lecture *me* on duty? Fenton was well rewarded for his loyalty — more than you will ever know." The Earl laughed without humour. "With your wife dead these past months and all the children she bore you with her, how can you not believe that you are being punished for your transgressions? Is your life so blameless?"

Hurt momentarily creased Robert's face. "Is yours so full of sin?"

The Earl looked away. Sin? So much so, he thought, that he had cut out his heart and turned his face from the mirror of his soul. When had he last made confession and meant it? He slid the knife into its decorated sheath. "I think we will keep Yule here. His Grace will wish me to attend Court, but I shall beg his indulgence and plead the unquiet of the region, and he will relent readily enough. Elizabeth will be wed by then. What have you a mind to do?"

Robert took moments to answer. "I have no heart for festivities at Court."

"Then you will stay here?"

"I'll stay."

Isobel carefully folded crumpled squares of cloth and placed them with the other items in her casket. She dragged her hennin from her head and discarded it beside her on the pallet. She felt like a fool. The Earl had said as much, and now that she ran through the letter in her mind, she could see the truth behind his words. That she had been prepared to offer herself to Thomas in marriage to secure her freedom was one thing; to be abducted and forced into it, quite another. Foolishness, yes, but treason? What had Robert Langton referred to when he said she didn't know? Didn't know what?

Soft-soled feet tapped rapidly across the floor outside the room, then Cecily appeared in a flurry of limbs and threw herself at Isobel. She smelled of washed hair and clean linen, and she brought with her the fresh scent of freedom.

Isobel hugged her. "Where have you been?"

"Meg had to go to Maman, so Alice took Nan for a walk, and I went too." She wiggled around and sat on the edge of the pallet, swinging her legs. "Where were you? Nan missed you."

"Did she?" Isobel smiled at the little girl's upturned face, rumpled in a frown. "Your father the Earl spoke with me."

"He talked with Nan yestermorn."

"And did Nan talk to him?"

"Yes. And he gave me this." Cecily thrust out a hand in which she held a shiny groat. "Nan likes him. He made her laugh, and he said she is a good poppet. And he asked Nan if she likes you, and I said that she did, and he said 'why?' and Nan said, 'cos you don't shout at her or pinch her."

"And what did your father say to that?" Isobel asked quietly.

Cecily hopped off the bed. "He didn't say anything." Pulling her skirts over her head, she ran out of the room squeaking like a mouse.

CHAPTER SIXTEEN

Margaret flopped pale and wan on her bed. Isobel took the heated stone wrapped in cushioning wool from Alice and laid it by the girl's stomach. "The pain will pass soon; this will ease it. Did you take the powders I made for you?"

Margaret gave a weak nod. "Maman said I must tell her when my courses run and for how long. She seemed pleased that they have begun. I am *not*." She winced as a wave of cramps wore at her and pulled the stone tighter to her stomach.

Isobel smoothed the hair sticking damply to her forehead. "I will see if I can get some wine for you. A little mixed with honey and poppy will help you sleep."

"I wanted to see the duke when he arrives," Margaret moaned into her pillow. "Bess has been going on about him, and she will get to dine with him, and I will be stuck *here*." She thumped the pillow, making it sigh under her fist.

"I did not know you wanted to see His Grace, my lady. I thought you wanted the peaceful life of a convent, not the splendour of your father's court."

Margaret raised her tacky face. "I do want to be a nun, but I would like to have been asked to dine. It is not fair. And I have a spot." She prodded the offending lump, scowling.

"Why not dress as if you were to attend like Lady Elizabeth? Wear your best gown, and I will bind your hair in ribbons and make an ointment for your skin. Then you can watch from the gallery as I used to do when my parents had guests. Sometimes they spied me there and bade me join them."

"Like a servant?" Margaret grumbled. "All right, but only if you come with me, then I'll not feel such a fool as were I seen alone. If only my stupid stomach would not hurt so."

"She'll need more than a wine potion come Whitsuntide," Joan remarked with one of her knowing looks when she and Isobel were out of earshot. "Jon said he heard that a match with Lord Raseby is already agreed upon, and you know what they say about *him*."

Isobel had heard the rumours, but that wouldn't stop Joan from telling her anyway. She inspected the hem of her best gown sent recently from home. It had snagged on a rose thorn in her garden when she had slipped out last Yule to check that John had remembered to protect the lilies from frost with straw. She had hidden it from Buena's sharp eyes that could scold better than any tongue.

Joan peered over her shoulder. "That's a right fine gown though not as fit as it might be for Court. Still, that rose pink is fair enough with the silver worked through it. What are they? Gillyflowers? Ee, but you and your flowers; I don't rightly know what goes on in that head of yours. Mind, you should give it to Alice to mend that tear. As to Raseby, he's been through two wives already — fair worn them out, he has, if you know what I mean. But he has no sons for it, and age hasn't slowed him down. If merciful Mary be on her side, Lady Margaret might see him out, but I don't fancy her chances of it, he's built like an ox. Took on three men at once in battle last summer at Edgecote and barely raised sweat."

The thought sickened Isobel. "She will be but fifteen winters!"

"And not a moment too soon, if you ask me. The countess can't wait to be rid of her — thought she'd never find anyone to take her on. It's not so bad," Joan added philosophically. "She'll have a large household, fine estates, and with a bit of luck she'll be with child soon enough, and her husband will sport himself with a mistress." She hoisted her breasts into a forward-facing position. "Now, if my Jon ever did *that*, I'd make dice out of his numbles, make no mistake. Not that I'd give him reason to, mind; I'll keep him busy, I will." She winked.

Consideration of Margaret's marriage and her own stateless position occupied Isobel during mass, so she didn't see Robert Langton watching her until the chapel was almost empty. He waited for her outside the ornate arch and sent Martin ahead.

"I did not expect to see you here, Mistress Fenton," he greeted her as she passed him, one of the last to appear through the open door. She joined him in the shadows which made the cool wind cold. "I thought you would accompany my nieces to the family oratory now that you have charge of them."

She remembered to curtsy this time. He bowed in return, and she detected the humorous glint she had once seen so long ago when they had first met in her garden.

"The countess wishes me to conduct my devotions in the castle chapel, my lord," Isobel said carefully, "and in this, I am content to do my lady's will."

"Hmm, are you indeed?"

Isobel found it hard not to return his smile as he raised an eyebrow in a droll curve, and she lost a little of her shyness.

"In truth," he said, taking on a conspiratorial tone, "I, too, find the castle chapel more pleasing of late, but it is more to do with who attends than who does not."

She felt the beating of wings inside her, rapid and tenuous. This time she didn't look away when colour rose to flush her skin; in meeting his eyes, she returned his smile. But she had nothing to say that sounded reasonable and would make him stay; no witticism, no clever remark, nothing that he might have come to expect from a woman of rank. She felt young and ignorant, ungainly and foolish. Where before she had not given it a second thought, now she sought his approval. Yet he showed no sign of wishing to leave.

"I ... I must attend my ladies..." Isobel ventured half-heartedly, feeling the drag of duty despite her urge to stay with him.

His smile wavered. "Will you not walk with me a while? I would have your company. I have been too much in my own of late. My nieces will wait; send your servant to attend them. Spend this little time with me before I leave."

Her nascent hope withered. "You are going, my lord?"

"On the morrow. I join the Duke of Gloucester when he arrives later today. His Grace bids me attend Court at Westminster."

"How long will you be gone?" He must think her too eager. She squirmed inside. Several people turned curious faces towards them. She imagined their comments.

"I do not know," he said. "Does it matter?"

She wanted to say "yes" but instead said, "I am friendless here."

"You have a friend in me when you have need, and my brother will always ensure your protection."

Her reply was made sharper by her disappointment. "I think not!" He looked puzzled and she qualified it with, "The Earl has greater concerns."

"He always keeps his word," he insisted. He must have sensed the regret oozing out of her like mud. "We cannot talk here; come out of the wind." He motioned the way with his gloved hand but, when she didn't move, placed it on her slender forearm that shook a little at his touch. "Come," he encouraged, "let us find somewhere warmer and with fewer ears intent on hearing our business."

Isobel followed the direction of his gaze and saw Nicolas Sawcliffe a pole's length away facing them. He was listening to one of the clerks, but every now and again he raised his eyes to look at them. She needed no further inducement.

"I do not like that man," she muttered half to herself, trying to keep up with Robert Langton's long stride as they crossed the bailey towards the great hall. He slowed to match her shorter pace.

"It is as well to mind yourself around him. He has ears and eyes keen to seek out the business of others and make it his own."

"Why does the Earl trust him?"

Lord Langton stopped short. "Trust? He does not trust him, but he needs the information he supplies. My brother no more trusts him than one of his own dogs. Even the most loyal hound can bite its master. There," he laughed, "do not look so worried; you have nothing to hide and therefore nothing to fear."

They reached the entrance to the great hall, where preparations were being made for the duke's arrival. Servants swarmed like blue and yellow insects. Robert Langton guided Isobel past the trestles on the dais and behind the canopy under which the Earl and countess sat on formal occasions. Here an arras tapestry of hunting dogs and noble lovers hung across the length of the back wall. Lifting one end, he opened a door hidden behind it and let Isobel go first.

"I did not know this was here!" she exclaimed as he showed her through a small chamber and out into the sunshine of a wall-enclosed garden.

"Few do," he said. "This is a private court meant only for the family. You see," he said, looking around at the blank-faced stone, "it is not overlooked."

She felt suddenly conscious of being alone with him but accepted the bench he offered her. He sat at the other end, far enough to be respectful, but close enough for her to imagine she felt the warmth of his thigh. She saw the movement of his chest beneath his doublet and the stirring of the fur that lined the edge of his gown. He had only to reach out and take this hope that grew in her.

"When I first spoke with you in your garden, you did not have these." He gently placed the tips of two fingers to the creases between her eyes, and she felt the lines smooth under his touch. "And you laughed more. Where is that girl with fingers stained as green as her garden?"

She shook her head, smiling. "I left her behind in my manor. I know not whether she is still there." She tipped her face towards him. "And you, my lord? Where is your happiness?"

"I buried it with my wife," he said shortly. "Change comes unlooked for and unwelcome, stealing our contentment."

"If it is stolen it can be reclaimed," Isobel stated sombrely. "It is not dead."

He threw back his head and, to her relief, laughed. "That is true enough. Well said, little columbine." And then, as if he couldn't quite believe it himself, "I will miss your unguarded wisdom. There is little of that at Court; the place has a way of corrupting innocence. Promise me one thing," he said after a moment when neither spoke, "that I will still find Isobel Fenton unchanged when I return."

Her heart stumbled over itself, steadied, slowed. "I'll still be here." Yes, she would, waiting while he went to London with the king's brother. She would be unchanged, but would he? And suddenly, out of nowhere, she found herself inexplicably envious of the men he would meet and the women he would talk to, because they would have his time and she would have none.

"Something ails you?" he said when she looked away consumed with fear that she might lose something she hardly knew she had, and that he would leave not knowing, and in not knowing, find another.

She shook her head. "I am well." Then, more boldly than she felt and in a rush, "May God speed you safely back again, my lord." And if her words didn't make her meaning clear, her eyes did.

Richard, Duke of Gloucester dismounted without waiting for a groom, landing surefooted despite long hours in the saddle that made his back ache. He had travelled light and swift, and his small household retinue — made up of practised knights, men-at-arms, and those newly sworn to his service — had been put through their paces to keep up with him. The Earl had sent out an escort of liveried men once he had learned of Gloucester's imminent arrival, and he now bent his knee before him in a show of deference as, beside him, his wife swept the ground in a curtsy worthy of the king.

Gloucester threw his reins to the waiting boy. "Well met, my lord Earl. Lady Felice, I thank you for your hospitality."

The Earl straightened. "Your Grace is welcome to what little we can offer."

Given the wealth worn on the Earl's back and the handsome jewelled collar that adorned his countess' neck, that must be considerable, Gloucester thought, but returned the courtesy with a nod of his head. The countess, still as beautiful as a frozen lake and as featureless, offered a sugared smile.

"If Your Grace will honour us with your presence, we are about to dine."

The young man groaned inwardly. The hours had been long since he had broken his fast before dawn, and he could happily have devoured a flock of sheep had they been offered to him, but formal dining meant ceremony, and ceremony meant delay. Yet he knew when his favour was being courted, as it seemed increasingly to be, and this earl had supported the king without deviation, and that was something Gloucester considered more important than the comfort of his stomach. Ignoring the grinding emptiness, he adopted the expression of benign attentiveness he reserved for court occasions. "Madam, the honour is mine."

In the chamber set aside for him, Gloucester eased his shoulders, rotating them until some of the stiffness abated. His esquire took the unbuckled sword and laid it on the table then turned back to help with the heavy doublet quilted against the cold. Hunger made Gloucester irascible, but at least the fire in the guest chamber had been lit well in advance, and the deep basin of scented water was hot enough to wash away the accumulated grime of the journey. Fresh linen, warmed before the fire, made him feel human again, but he regretted not being shaved that morning as unaccustomed stubble roughened his chin. There was no time now; it would have to wait. He looked up as his esquire caught his eye.

"Lord Langton, Your Grace."

"I thought Your Grace might be in need of refreshment before he dines." Robert Langton lifted the corner of the linen napkin covering the tray borne by his servant.

Gloucester viewed the loaded dishes. "I am indebted to you, my lord; you know my mind."

"I know what it is to travel all morning on an empty stomach, Your Grace. A man might feast on ceremony, but it cannot fill his stomach."

Ravenous, Gloucester selected a roll of beef encased in pastry in one hand, a crown of stuffed capon in the other. "Will you join me, my lord?"

"I ate well enough this morning and not as early as Your Grace."

"I do not refer to your stomach, my lord. Have you considered my offer? Will you join me?"

Robert Langton kneeled. "If Your Grace will accept my fealty, in the name of God and in the presence of all His saints, I swear to uphold it."

"I accept it right gladly, my lord, and hold you to it, and shall be your good lord in all things, as you shall serve me in all matters pertaining to that good lordship. I have the papers drawn up and waiting."

"Your Grace knew I would serve?" Robert asked.

Gloucester examined him long and hard before answering. "I did not know, my lord, I merely hoped," he said, and grinned.

"Quickly, my lady!" Isobel held out her hand, and together she and Margaret ran the length of the mural hall, dodging servants in their ceremonial best, and up the steps to the gallery overlooking the great hall where musicians were already tuning their instruments. Out of breath, they leaned against the gallery wall, hidden by the hangings either side of it and trying not to giggle at their ridiculous subterfuge and the long faces of the men near them.

Margaret peeped around the yellow and blue, chevron-edged hanging. "They haven't arrived yet, but my uncle is there. I like what he is wearing."

Isobel joined her. "Where?" She craned her neck and saw Robert Langton among a group of men she didn't recognise, the rich blue of the brocade he wore made bright with intricate patterns of silver. He wasn't so very far away, and she wanted him to look up and see her and perhaps smile the way he had done early that morning when they had been alone.

"He looks very lordly," Margaret observed. "Do you not think so?" She nudged Isobel in the ribs when she failed to answer.

"Yes," Isobel said quietly and with an unexpected longing that sprang from deep inside, "he is." Too much so, perhaps. As Lady La Roche had frequently pointed out, Isobel was of little station. Had she been more, she would be down there with him, not up here hiding like a servant or a child. As if to confirm it, the musicians started up a fanfare next to them.

Covering her ears, Margaret screwed up her face at the blare, and Isobel pulled her back out of sight, laughing. When they dared look again, the Duke of Gloucester occupied the place of honour on the dais, the Earl and countess sitting next to him.

Margaret huffed loudly. "That's not fair! Bess is sitting at the lord's table, and I am not even allowed to dine in hall." She pouted spectacularly, and Isobel had to hush her despite the noise of the instruments that deafened the air around them, as the Master of Music threw disapproving looks in their direction. "But it is *not*," Margaret insisted, her arms crossed over her thin chest. "Bess should not be there at all. She is betrothed, but all she talks about is His Grace and how she would rather wed him. She cares little that she is to be married to another; she loves the duke. *And* Lord Dalton gave her that pretty palfrey," she added as if that was the final straw.

Isobel peered around the hanging. Sure enough, Lady Elizabeth spent much of the time gazing at Gloucester, who remained assiduously unaware of her attention. Isobel smiled to herself, and then remembered that she might be in much the same situation had Robert Langton not indicated otherwise, and then where would she be? With neither hope of his love nor promise of marriage to Thomas, she thought, and casting eyes at a man who remained oblivious seemed an empty, hollow life, devoid of joy.

At least Elizabeth had a chance of happiness with a husband who would adore her. Margaret, on the other hand; what did she have to look forward to? Was she aware of what was planned for her? Isobel thought not. "My lady," she whispered, her mouth close to her ear, "we must go."

"A little longer," Margaret begged, as the chaplain made ready to say prayers and the musicians stopped playing. They watched as the assembly bowed their heads, Gloucester lithe and graceful, the Earl handsome in red and gold, his countess resplendently aloof. Robert Langton didn't look down at all. Instead, something had caught his eye, and he glanced up towards the gallery. Isobel's heart sang as she met his eyes and he smiled directly at her.

A sudden movement and an explosion of sound behind her broke the spell as one of the musicians simultaneously sneezed and dropped his instrument into the silence of the hall. As one, the diners swivelled where they sat and stared towards the gallery. The chaplain ceased his prayers and the hush deepened. Appalled, Isobel curtsied for want of anything better to do, grasped Margaret's hand as she stood immobilised with horror, and pulled her along after her, accompanied by the lasting image of the duke's nonplussed look and the countess's frozen glare.

If the incident in the great hall had caused displeasure, Gloucester did not mention it. Rather, when the Earl alluded to the frivolity of women, Gloucester responded by praising God for the levity of maids in such lean times and hoped that they would escape punishment. Now, with all formalities satisfied, the Earl had invited Gloucester to retire to the privacy of the council chamber out of the eye of the world, accompanied by his brother and his dogs. He had welcomed the news that Robert had tendered an oath of fealty to the duke. The lad might not yet have reached his majority, but he was fast making his mark, and the king appeared to have a degree of faith in him. There was something he wished to bring before Gloucester. He had thought long and hard on the matter, but his brother's decision had tipped the balance: Robert was a good judge of character.

One of his best dogs, a young bitch with a coat shining like blued steel, placed an elegant paw on the duke's foot, begging for attention. He stroked her head. "I trust the dog pup is proving satisfactory, Your Grace?"

"He grows apace, my lord, and gives little thought to the dignity of my station nor the depth of my purse. He has been found in the kitchens once too often and chewed his way through my noble dam's gown as she slept." Gloucester smiled ruefully. "My mother has a new gown out of it and Hector a chain of steel to keep him from wandering. He is a fine gift indeed."

"He will be done with teething before long, Your Grace, then it will not be women's skirts he is after. Keep him separate, and give him an older bitch to mount until he knows what is expected of him. 'Hector' is a fitting appellation; let us hope he lives up to his valiant namesake." The Earl raised his cup in salute.

"I confess," Gloucester said, refusing a second cup of wine, "that I did not name him." He paused. "I believe Geoffrey Fenton's daughter is in your charge?"

Robert Langton looked up at the mention of her name and glanced at his brother. The Earl slowly lowered the cup he had brought to his lips without tasting the wine. How in St George's name did Gloucester know what he wanted to speak with him about? Had Robert already mentioned her? He thought not; his brother was clearly as interested in where this was going as he was.

"She is, Your Grace."

"The king will be relieved to know that the lands south of the Humber are secure. Not all manors in the region can be relied upon. There are some, recently acquired, where loyalties might be ... confused."

Ah, so Gloucester suspected Lacey. What was more, his own conversation with the king had borne fruit after all, which was gratifying at least. Gloucester surveyed him with shrewd eyes, waiting. "That is so, Your Grace."

"It would be as well that we can be certain of which way the stone will fall when it is cast. And some have yet to be thrown. Isobel Fenton is fair enough, but she is made comelier by her inheritance. Has a match been settled on her yet?"

"No..." The Earl hesitated. "Your Grace, the Lacey cub has been disappointed of that ambition, but I have reason to believe he harbours it yet."

Beside him, Robert shifted uneasily. Lacing his fingers together, Gloucester contemplated the brothers. Finally, he said, "Do you fish, my lords?"

Robert shook his head, and the Earl answered, "No, Your Grace."

"I prefer hawking, but the king is fond of fishing. His Grace especially enjoys seeking out pike. It is a ravening creature and owes allegiance to none other than itself. It likes to work dark waters where it waits until some hapless fish or duckling passes, when it will take what it wants without mercy." Gloucester paused. "The king, my lords, seeks to rule the waters of his realm and bring peace to their depths so other fish might benefit to the common weal. He finds a fair lure is most effective when the line is kept fast in the hand. He knows where the fish is at all times, and it can be played then, and landed at his leisure." He levelled his gaze with the Earl's. "Isobel Fenton has pleasing eyes, does she not? Keep her safe, my lord."

CHAPTER SEVENTEEN

Isobel had hardly slept, but she craved to see the dawn. Thoughts had chivvied late into the night, and her blood hummed. Impatient to begin the day, she woke Alice and sent for hot water, and had bathed before either child lifted their head from the pillow.

The shutters opened on a deep frost. Sun had shattered the night and now glanced off the silk-white land.

"Why must we hurry?" Margaret moaned as she hid her eyes from the day.

"Because there is not much time if you wish to bid your uncle farewell, my lady," Isobel answered brightly.

"I did a pee," Cecily announced proudly, returning from the privy.

Isobel patted her head. "Well done. Wash your hands. Are you coming to say goodbye?"

"Can Nan come too? And Nan's ball?"

"Of course; your uncle will expect to see them."

Cecily beamed. "I like him."

Isobel glowed. "So do I. Now," she said briskly as she caught Margaret's curious stare, "what will you both wear?"

"I would rather be abed." Yawning, Margaret leaned against Isobel. "And it is *cold*. Why did we have to come to bid farewell? We do not for our father."

Isobel squeezed the girl's chilly hand and thought she should have remembered gloves. "You do not wish him to leave without knowing your affection, do you?"

"We don't for our father," Margaret repeated. "And why do you have that gown on again? It's not a feast day." She groaned. "What is Bess doing here? And why is she dressed like *that*?"

Elizabeth Langton looked dazzling in a vivid gown enriched with gold, her elaborate coif edged with pearls, and a collar of stones that would befit a duchess.

"That is her Court gown!" Margaret cried. "And that our mother's jewel! She looks such a wagtail —"

"Meg!" Isobel exclaimed. "Where did you hear of such a word?"

"Joan said the queen looks like a wagtail—"

"Shhh!" Isobel cast around to make sure no one had overheard them. "Never, *never* use that word, my lady, especially about Her Grace. Joan should know better."

Margaret opened her mouth to ask why, but Cecily jerked Isobel's arm half out of its socket as she began jumping up and down, squealing, "I want to see the horsies!" and saving Isobel the trouble.

The bailey was filling with people, but neither Gloucester nor Robert had yet appeared. Cecily's bouncing was becoming unbearable. Isobel gave up searching the faces of the men and relented. Picking Cecily up, she took her across the slippery cobbles to where the horses stood breathing fire into the icy air.

"Which one is your uncle's?"

Cecily pointed to a bay stallion, its trappings of dark blue looking rather plain next to the duke's mount. Isobel gazed at Robert's horse with its gleaming coat and liquid brown eyes and loved it because it was his. She reached out and gently stroked its long muzzle over the nose straps of black leather, silently urging it to carry its master safely wherever he must go.

"Horsey!" Without warning, Cecily thrust Nan into the horse's face, and it shied away, the stable lad hanging onto the reins as it backed into the duke's horse, sending the rest of the mounts skittering on their leads. Slipping on stone, Isobel swung Cecily out of the way as the animal's head came perilously close to the child. Ripples of anxiety ran through the other horses, curses from the stable hands, curt commands from the Master of Horse.

"Steady, steady." A gloved hand grabbed the bit while the other came between the horse and Isobel's startled face. "Step away," Robert instructed, then spoke soothingly until his horse gentled and the lad had him under control.

"Your pardon," Isobel began, when he turned to her. "I just ... I mean ... Cecily wanted to see and I ... I wanted to say..." Whatever it was, her words were swallowed by a swell of voices from behind them. Robert bowed, and Isobel, still holding Cecily, managed to curtsy as Gloucester, accompanied by the Earl and countess and closely shadowed by Elizabeth, crossed towards them.

"Mistress Fenton." Gloucester came to a standstill in front of her, riding gloves in one hand. "I know not whether it is divine judgment visited upon me," he said with a glint of humour, "but it seems that whenever I am in this place, I am confronted by animals and maids intent on disorder."

"Forgive me, Your Grace, I meant no harm."

"Then Heaven be merciful when you do mean it, mistress. Indeed, I shall request that you are placed at the forefront of His Grace's army, and we shall defeat our enemy without striking a blow. You are enough to disarm a man."

Regarding Gloucester with round eyes, Cecily, who had been quiet until this moment, suddenly extended her hand in which she held her harlequin ball. "Piggies," she announced, making little snuffling noises and wrinkling her nose at the duke. "Nan likes the piggies." And, shaking the ball, she filled the emptiness with the clear peal of its bell.

Felice Langton was seething. "That girl humiliates us before His Grace," she said to the Earl once they had bidden Gloucester farewell and retreated to her private chambers in a pretence of unity that fooled no one, themselves least of all. This was the first opportunity that had presented itself to vent the frustration she had harboured ever since her daughter and the Fenton girl had intruded upon them so unashamedly the day before. "You insisted on retaining her against my wishes, and this is the result of your stubbornness. I will have her whipped."

"You will do nothing of the sort, madam. I will not have you taking out your spite on Isobel Fenton. His Grace chose not to be offended by it, and nor should you."

"You are grown soft, my lord," she snorted.

"And you too hard."

Feeling the barb, she turned her back on him before he saw its effect. What did she expect after a lifetime of marriage to a man who did not know how to love or else had forgotten? She thought back to their early years together but found she could not recall a time when she had felt accepted by him. He had been diligent as a husband — more than many — and their marriage bed had been fruitful, but love? She had spent so long trying to please him, wasted years when she might have found happiness elsewhere, before she concluded that the fault did not lay at her own feet. She might not have his love, but she had his name, bore his children, and she would demand his respect.

"I noticed your brother this morning," she began, "when he was speaking with the Fenton girl."

"What of it?"

"Have you not noted? He seems less grieved of late. I think he must be beyond the worst of his mourning."

He peeled off his gloves and flexed cold fingers. "My brother's welfare is none of your concern. You hardly showed sisterly affection when he was married; why do so now?"

"He went against your wishes when he married Ann, and I only desired to support you."

"You made your dislike of his wife clear enough, Felice, so do not dress it as spousal loyalty."

She inclined her head, exposing her long neck in a graceful curve, and saw his hand twitch in response. "I am at fault, and you are right to reprimand me, my lord." She heard his breath halt and redoubled her charm. "I was not in a position to be of service to your brother before, but now, being so lately at Court and favoured by Her Grace…" She leaned a little closer, her rose-scented skin young and taut again on the curve of her neck. "The queen has many kin who seek good matches, and it would bring favour on our house." She felt his breath stir her silk veil. She turned her head, bringing her mouth close to his as he bent towards her, and looked at him. He held her glance for a moment, then, straightening abruptly, drew away.

"Do not meddle in my affairs, Felice," he said gruffly. "My brother would not thank you for a match with the queen's kin, and neither would I."

The Earl made his way back to his tower feeling oddly out of sorts. Felice had the annoying ability to stir his blood despite himself, but she left him cold. Had he been as young as Gloucester and away from home, he would have had a girl waiting to warm his bed. And he had once, he reflected sombrely, until duty and circumstance dictated otherwise. He kept his pleasures away from his own roost, unlike the king. He could have done with a girl now. His thoughts drifted, unbidden, to Isobel Fenton, and the swiftest smile that had warmed her eyes as she bade farewell to his brother.

"*Louys!*"

His stocky esquire, dark tight curls like his French mother, thick set like his Worcestershire father, appeared, panting a little. Sweat filmed his swarthy skin.

"Have you been in the practice yards?"

"Yes, my lord."

"Get yourself cleaned up and send for my horse and falconer. I will ride out." And perhaps, he thought, put all notions of soft thighs and welcoming eyes to bed after a day spent in the company of a merciless hawk and a hard saddle.

Isobel spent her day waiting to be summoned by the countess. She could be in no doubt that she had sunk even lower in the woman's favour, if that were possible, and she had not intended to make an enemy of Elizabeth, either. She couldn't help it if Gloucester had laughed or considered her replies amusing. For her part, she found his dry wit appealing and his presence beguiling. He had a way of making her feel that her opinion mattered, and she had been surprised at first that he had remembered her name. He had swung easily into the saddle, leaving her standing next to Robert, and she thought she had caught the faintest lift of his brow as he looked down at them, before he pulled his horse's head around and headed for the gatehouse. That left seconds for Robert to swiftly bend close and mirror her own thoughts as he murmured, "Keep safe, little dove, and may God guard your rest," before his lips brushed the top of Cecily's head and, cleanly mounting his horse, he had left her standing there. Then, with regret, she had turned to face the countess.

"Margaret, take Cecily inside *now*. You..." she stabbed at Isobel without raising her voice or her finger, "will wait in your chamber until you are summoned." Swinging around in a flow of skirts, she took her eldest daughter by the elbow and pulled her along beside her. "What do you think you look like?" she hissed. "Go straight to your room and change. And return my jewel immediately. You can wear the one Lord Dalton gave you and show a little of the eagerness you reserve for His Grace. You will bring shame on this house."

The bailey had all but emptied of horses and men, and only a few lads from the stables were left to collect steaming horse excrement with short wooden paddles. The Earl hadn't moved since he had bidden Gloucester safe conduct and clapped his younger brother on the back in farewell. Isobel wondered what he was waiting for. She ventured to look at him and found him considering her. Then he turned smartly on his heel and walked purposefully towards the hall.

It had been worth it, she thought, remembering the way Robert had looked as he bent to kiss Cecily's soft curls. The kiss, planted so gently on his niece's head, she imagined had been meant for her.

The Earl ran a finger rhythmically across his top lip, feeling the stubble scratch. The day spent in the saddle had given him time to think, and he found some semblance of peace in the open undulating space of his estates, where the hollow-hooved drumming of his horse across the frozen ground drowned out the darker debates that played on his mind. He had paid little heed to the cavorting of his hawk until the bird refused to come to the lure, and the Earl was reminded of Gloucester's words of the previous day. It was to this that he now turned his mind.

Gloucester was sharper than his seventeen years gave credit. He had lived in the eye of the storm that raged about the throne since his birth and had spent formative years in the Earl of Warwick's household. Now Warwick toyed with Gloucester's older brother, George Clarence, but the Earl wondered whether his old friend had missed a more potent plaything in the youngest duke. Or perhaps he had already tried and found the boy less malleable than he had hoped. Three years Gloucester's senior, Clarence might be brashly confident, but he threatened to outgrow the king's shadow and fly too close to the sun. He lacked his younger brother's sound judgement, and his ambition made him insincere and as fickle as a whore.

A log threatened to tumble from the fire, and the Earl shoved it back with his foot. He settled into his chair again. Despite his youth, Gloucester seemed to know what he was about. He appeared to be growing into his boots with a grim determination that echoed the Earl's own resolve. The king recognised it, and valued that loyalty as much as the Earl esteemed Robert's, for where would they all be if loyalty was like oil on water? And who would be the one to place the lighted taper to its surface and watch the world be consumed by fire? Not the likes of Lacey, that was for sure. He had not the wit. But Warwick?

He pushed himself out of the chair and went to the aumbry on the other side of the room. Each of the four heavily coffered panels held an intricately carved shield in relief — one for each of his grandparents. It had stood there for as long as he could remember, the vivid colours slowly fading with age.

He fingered the score marks of a tiny rough shield crudely carved below one of the panels. His father had beaten him for putting it there, but the childish image had survived long after his father had been killed. The Earl wished his own son had lived long enough to have made his mark. "Louys…" The Earl opened the aumbry door and found what he was looking for.

"My lord?"

"Have Master Sawcliffe fetched. I wish to dictate a letter." He unfolded the parchment with the broken seal dangling, read a few lines. "And, Louys…" The young man halted at the door. "I am sharp-set tonight; send down to the kitchens."

"What do you desire, my lord?"

The Earl was absorbed by the contents of the message, pulling at his top lip as he read. His esquire knew better than to press for an answer and waited patiently. Without looking up, the Earl waved a vague hand. "I care not."

Louys bowed and left the room.

"Wait!"

The lad reappeared, red-faced.

"Do not disturb Master Secretary, bring Mistress Fenton here instead."

"Mistress Fenton, my lord?"

"That is what I said. Go to it."

Isobel had almost given up waiting. She sat by the fire long after Joan had started her snoring from the pallet chamber and had let the last taper burn down until only the light from the hearth lit the room. She watched the low flames illuminating the blue and yellow chevrons that sawed across the wall and the cheerful stars that filled the space between the zigzags and the floor. She could not say what she waited for, only that she did not want to go to bed just to wake to another day filled with anxiety. Already she missed Robert. She had not recognised the empty feeling inside until she tried eating to ease it and found that food had no impact on the raw sensation lodged around her stomach. The castle seemed empty without him, as if merely by being within its walls he had filled it with his steady presence. As the day grew old, she grew weary with it until, by nightfall, she felt its oppression.

Retrieving her mother's casket, Isobel washed behind the screen so as not to awaken Joan's curiosity. She had endured the woman's snooping most of the day until she had finally snapped back and then spent the rest of it on the receiving end of Joan's sullen silence.

She finished cleaning her teeth with a birch twig, polished them with powder of sage, and rinsed her mouth. She banked up the fire with blocks of peat and left it to smoulder.

Barely had she drifted into sleep when a subdued tap on the door in the outer chamber roused her. She waited until she heard it again, louder this time, and, wrapping her mantle around her shoulders, went to open the door.

Holding a horn lantern, a youth with hair made of charcoal coils peered at her. "Mistress Fenton?"

She nodded.

"My lord wishes you to attend him."

She recognised him then as one of the Earl's esquires. "Now?"

"Yes." He looked embarrassed. "If it please you."

It didn't, but did she have any choice? "Why?" she asked anyway.

He shrugged. "My lord commands it."

The vacant sensation that had dogged her all day became filled with ants. She might lock the door and refuse to leave the room, but she knew it to be pointless. "Wait," she said, and went to dress.

The decision made, the Earl's mood was more buoyant by the time Isobel Fenton was shown into his private chamber. He noted the quick glance as she took in the writing slope at one side, her frown at the table covered with food, and then she looked down at her clenched hands and would not meet his eyes.

"I expect you wonder why I have asked you here?" he began. Still she stared at her white knuckles. "I have a service I would ask of you. A letter," he clarified when she didn't answer, "in your own hand."

"A letter, my lord?"

"You can write, can you not?"

She nodded.

He wanted more cooperation than this or it would show in the stiffness of her writing. She shivered, although the room felt warm enough to him. "Have you supped?" he asked and, when she confirmed otherwise, said, "Sit. Pray, eat." He indicated a chair banked with deep cushions, and she did so with reluctance. The Earl took up his chair opposite and waited until she had washed her hands in the bowl his groom held, before resuming eating himself.

The groom offered segments of tiny birds dressed in saffron cream. She refused. He tried again, this time with flakes of white fish, fresh from the sea, bedded on glossy dried fruit steeped in honey and studded with golden pine nuts. She shook her head. Thwarted, he attempted to pour wine, but she swiftly covered the gilded glass. The Earl frowned, and with a jerk of his head dismissed the man to the far side of the room.

"I have these sent from my estates in Portugal." He picked up a silver dish. "They are picked from the tree as the sun sets and packed into jars of sweet wine and spices." The girl looked at the little fruit the size of a small pear, but fat like a raindrop and red-brown. A heady aroma of cinnamon and aniseed rose from the dish. "Do you know what they are?"

"No, my lord."

"Figs. The king is particularly fond of these. Try one." He speared a single fruit with a gold knife and placed it on a small dish in front of her.

She contemplated the fig. "My lord, I have no knife."

He waved the groom back. "Use mine." He wiped the blade with care and proffered it pommel first. The weighted handle of blood-red jasper mounted in elaborate gold would feel cool to her touch. He watched as its blade sank through the yielding flesh of the fruit, spilling black seed onto the silver dish. She tested a fragment; then another, and he imagined her feeling the gritty texture between her teeth.

"Why are they picked at sunset?" she asked.

"They say the sun is trapped within the skin and the fruit is sweetest then. Would you agree?"

The notion seemed to intrigue her. "Are the trees grown against a wall like they say peaches should be, and do they take the frost? Can they be stored like apples, or must they be preserved like cherries?"

"I care not how they are grown or stored," he said, exasperated. "I am not a gardener." He regretted his lack of patience as her face fell, and she withdrew inside herself like the sun going in. "But these…" he said, holding up a hard-skinned fruit glowing the colour of rubies in the candlelight, "grow wild where they are sheltered from the sea, and in the gardens of the villages and towns where they are valued above all other fruit." He gave it to her, amused by her almost childlike fascination.

"Pomegranate," she said, awed by its perfection, turning it over and over in her hands and inspecting every aspect of its sun-polished skin.

"You have seen one before?"

"I have read of them and seen their likeness in the margins of books. And my servant..." She stopped. "And they have been described to me." She raised it to her nose. "It has no scent," she said, surprised.

He held out his hand, and she gave it back to him, but reluctantly, as if returning a favourite toy. He took a steel-bladed knife from beside his plate, still wet with the blood of a fig, and placed the tip against the hard skin. Without mercy, he shattered the fruit, sending drops of garnet across the embroidered cloth. If she mourned the loss of something so perfect, it was quickly overtaken by inquisitiveness at the jewels contained inside.

The Earl spooned glistening seeds onto her plate, then sat back, watching for her reaction. "Well?" he queried, as she took a few in her mouth, testing them with a thoughtful expression that made him warm despite himself. The surface of each seed swam in fragrant juice.

"Well?" he asked again.

She swallowed. "It is sweet, my lord, but bitter also."

His mouth slanted into a smile, and his eyes focused on her lips. He leaned forward and drew his thumb from the corner of her mouth in a slow upward movement. She flinched from him. "So I see," he said, softly, and licked the juice from his thumb.

He suddenly became businesslike and, standing, beckoned her. She kept her distance but followed him to the other side of the room where the writing slope stood on its stand.

"Leave us," he said over the girl's head, disregarding her nervous glances as the groom left. "Be seated," he instructed, pulling out the raised stool for her and waiting until she settled. He took a piece of paper and laid it in front of her. "Does Thomas Lacey know your hand?"

"Thomas, my lord? I … yes. I have written to him before."

"Start with the greeting you have formerly used: 'Right trusty and well-beloved…' or some such."

She took up the honed quill he offered her and the ink in its stubby pot. 'Thomas,' she wrote, labouring under the Earl's watchful eye as he charted every letter formed with intense concentration.

He frowned. "Is that what you write? Nothing more?" She gave a shake of her head, and he wondered at the informality of the young. "Hmm, well, continue thus: 'I greet you most cordially…'" He waited until she had written the line, pacing behind her as she did so and holding the letter she had received from Lacey in his hand. "'… and wish unto you, health and good weal in all things. In so much as it pleases me to do your will…'"

She looked up. "My lord?"

"What is it? Do I speak too fast for you?"

She shook her head. "Is this letter to be from me?"

"It is."

"These are not the form of words I would use, and if Thomas —"

"What would you say?" he asked, interrupting her a shade brusquely.

259

"I ... I would merely thank him for his letter and hope that mine own finds him well."

"Make it so." He wished he had been blessed with greater patience as her words flowed slowly but evenly onto the cream surface. She gave it her total concentration, and the tip of her tongue found its way to the corner of her top lip as she wrote. He watched for a moment, then looked away.

"Finished?" he asked, then continued almost immediately. "'I am beholden to you that you made such good offices to me in the affairs of my estate and my people.'" As her head bent towards the page, a wisp of hair at the nape of her neck escaped the confines of her headdress. She did not pluck her hairline like the fashionable women did at the king's court or his own. The coil of amber smoke held him spellbound, and he wanted to reach out and wind it around his finger and feel its softness, to slide his hand down the slope of her neck.

She twisted around, and he found her looking at him warily. He cleared his throat. "'Inasmuch as I have no kin, I shall make my suit and look to you for friendship and would that your good lordship held sway over mine...'" He paused as Isobel placed the quill down carefully. "Why have you stopped?"

"What is it you would have me say, my lord?"

"It is not for you to know my will in this. Continue." She did not comply. "Do as you are bidden," he said with a hint of threat.

"My lord, I cannot write what I do not know. If I am to put my name to it, tell me your intention, and I will do my best to serve you in words that convey your message."

He snatched the quill and thrust it towards her. "I will not debate with you. Write!" She made no move to take it. "God's teeth, you madden me. Take it!"

"Thomas will know your words are not mine," she insisted.

Slowly, he lowered his hand. Then, seizing the paper from in front of her, he marched to the fire and rammed it between two burning logs. From the cabinet, he took a clean piece and, placing it before her, proffered the quill. "Take it and use your own form of words."

"What will you have me write?"

A shutter rattled in the wind. The Earl went to the deep window embrasure and reached to the iron bar. "You are to say that you were glad to receive his letter and that you soon expect to return to your manor. Speak of love, if it please you. Flatter him —"

"You wish me to deceive him?"

His hand stilled. "Yes. As he would others." The iron bar fell back against the stone dressings, filling the brief silence with sound. "Let him believe there is promise of marriage." He swung the shutter from the black-faced window, and the cold light of the moon illuminated his upturned face, silvering his dark hair.

"*Is* there, my lord?"

He looked back over his shoulder, his face thrown into shadow. "No."

Isobel stared at the blank paper in front of her. For moments, it seemed as if she would refuse to cooperate, but she dipped the quill into the ink and with even letters wrote, '*Thomas…*'

The raw air cooled his face as he listened to the scratch of the quill as Isobel scribed the words to lure Thomas Lacey into false hope, much as Ralph Lacey had done to his father before delivering his final blow. A part of him regretted involving the girl, but there was more at stake than his sensibilities, or hers, and she was as much a part of the problem as the solution, whether she realised it or not.

He became aware that the movement of the quill had ceased. "Have you finished?" he called from the window. She continued to sit with her head bent and her back to him without answering. "Well?"

She rose and crossed the room and handed him the letter without raising her head. He read the contents, smiled grimly to himself, and only then noticed the damp marks on her cheeks. "What in the name of Mary are you crying for?"

She scrubbed fiercely at her eyes. "May I leave now?"

Why did everything have to be a battle with this girl? "You may not. Answer the question." She stared at his feet. "And look at me when I speak to you!"

She lifted her face, and her eyes gleamed in the subtle moonlight. "My father would be ashamed of such deception," she stated.

He felt her criticism like a blow and in a rush of blood raised his hand to strike the accusation from her eyes. She did not flinch. He read her challenge and rose to it, in that instant registering with a surge her look changing from defiance to fear.

She had half turned from him when he reached out and caught her wrist. In panic, she tried to writhe from his grasp, but he held her fast, feeling soft flesh twist under his fingers, both confused and frustrated by her fear and angry that he had somehow been the cause of it.

"I have not given you permission to leave," he said, feeling her wrist bruise in his grip.

She lashed out with her free hand, fingers arched in defence, wild as an animal but futile against his superior strength. He caught her hand before her nails could rend his face, his blood burning. "You will hurt yourself ... stop struggling!" He swore as she again tried to wrench away, pinning her hands, feeling her body stiff with fury against his own. And, on contact, his anger softened; became something else — a memory. He let go.

She remained immobile, a hind ready to flee. He made no other movement but held out his hand to her. She looked at it, shook her head, and backed away.

"Isobel," he said, and then simply, "Come."

PART FOUR

CHAPTER EIGHTEEN

Isobel waited until the Earl's breathing evened and deepened before she attempted to move. His arm lay heavily across her, and his muscled thigh pinned her leg beneath his. Trapped between his body and the deep mattress, she felt suffocated but dared not wake him. In the coffered panels above her head painted images floated indistinctly in the dark.

Isobel inched from under him and gradually distanced herself from the weight of his body. He stirred, murmured in his sleep, and turned his head away.

The last of the fire cast a dull glow against the wall, but the room was cold. Isobel slipped on the edge of the dais, grabbed the bed hanging, and found her footing. The Earl slept on. She searched blindly for the shoe that had been knocked off in the struggle but found nothing but the hard surface of the floor and the warm silk of the drowsing dog. It sighed and she jumped. Shoeless, Isobel fled the room and down the stairs of the sleeping tower.

Nothing had changed since she had left the girls. Peat still smouldered in the hearth, scenting the air, and from the pallet room Joan's fat snores rolled.

The remains of the water slopped in her bowl. Shaking, Isobel peeled the hose from her legs, pulled her gown from the shoulders, then her kirtle. Icy water soothed the burning between her legs. With increasingly frantic movements, she scrubbed at the sticky residue until all remnants of his seed had been washed away and her abraded skin retained no memory of his abuse.

Then she dragged her gown around her and, shivering, slumped against the wall in the dark. Her wrist ached, her thighs bruised where he had forced her legs apart, and her lips stung from the pressure of his hand across her mouth, but she felt none of it.

She felt old. Soon the darkness would give way to dawn, and all that she had known would be diminished by this single act. Would anyone know? Could they see? Did they care? Like Eve, her shame condemned her in the eyes of the world. She was glad her father was dead. She was glad he was no longer alive to see her dishonour. She choked on the lump of emotion, clasped her hands over her mouth to keep from waking the children, and shook.

Thin dawn bled through the shutters, and Cecily stirred. Chilled through, Isobel gathered her clothes. As she reached for her smock, she spotted a dark mark glaring accusingly from the hem. Blood. Her blood. Seizing the smock, she ripped the hem free, went to the hearth, and, making a hole between the peat turves, fed it in with the poker until it no longer resisted the heat, and the evidence became consumed by flame.

She could hear dogs barking in the Earl's kennels, and the light outside the window was stronger now. She quickly dressed. She had undone her scuffed braid and was combing it out when Joan appeared at the entrance to the pallet room, yawning.

"You're up early." She lifted her arm and sniffed her armpit. "What were you about? I took a piss, and you weren't abed."

Isobel braided her hair, feeling her wrist twinge.

Joan wandered over to the fire. "It's cold enough to freeze ice." When Isobel still didn't respond, she shrugged and called to one of the maids who was supervising a sleepy Cecily towards the privy. "Have more wood fetched when she's done.

My lady here will be wanting the girls washed, no doubt." When Isobel failed to rise to the jibe, Joan stabbed at the peat, muttering to herself. She stopped suddenly. "What's this then?"

Isobel turned to see her prodding something in the hearth. "Leave it!" she said, but Joan had already extracted a fragment of singed cloth and held it suspended on the poker, squinting at it in the nether light.

Isobel snatched the strip from the poker and thrust it back into the fire. "It is nothing, let it burn."

Joan stared at Isobel's chest. "What've you got there?" And, before Isobel could react, she jabbed at her collarbone. Isobel yelped and brushed her hand aside. Joan's mouth pulled down. "Looks nasty if you ask me."

Isobel yanked the shoulder of her gown over the area, feeling the tender point as the fabric brushed against it. "I must have slipped," she mumbled, recalling the stab of her father's seal as the Earl crushed it into her flesh with the weight of his body, a pain among so many others she had hardly been able to distinguish between them. She cowered from the memory.

Joan sucked her teeth and tutted. "Oh, aye?" Narrowing her eyes, she looked at Isobel properly for the first time that morning. "Whatever you say."

The Earl awoke from a laboured sleep to a sound he could not define. Lying at an awkward angle and still partly clothed, it took him moments before he located his position on the mattress and the reason for it. He lay until the sound of tearing from beneath the bed shook him fully awake, and he rolled to his feet as the vestiges of his dream fell from him. At his movement, the noise stopped, and the lilac muzzle of his favourite dog pushed out from the draped covers with the remains of something in her jaws.

"Here, Chou." He held his hand out to the dog. "Leave it." He removed the object, wet with drool, and held it up to the thin light. Shredded blue leather. A woman's shoe. Beyond redemption. He dropped it like a hot ember and, wiping his hand on his shirt, took in the state of the bed and the dark evidence staining it. Taking a vicious punch at the crumpled linen, he swore out loud.

"My lord?"

He turned to find the startled face of his groom looking at him. He fingered the stubble roughening his jaw. "Is my bathing water ready?"

"It is, my lord."

"Get this cleaned up, then send for my messenger."

The water was hot — too hot — but it left his skin scoured and drove away some of the demons of the previous night. He was holding out his arms to receive his tawny velvet houppelande when the messenger arrived. The Earl waved the groom away. "Do you know the lands east of Barton?"

"Well enough, my lord."

"I want you to bear a message to Lord Lacey — Thomas Lacey. If any ask, say it is from Mistress Fenton, understand?"

The man nodded.

The Earl went to his aumbry and unlocked it. "Go in haste and without badge or identification." He reached inside, withdrew the letter, and, for the second time that morning, uttered an oath. The unsealed letter hung open in his hand. "Wait on my order," he said curtly to the man, then to his young page, "Go to Mistress Fenton and fetch the seal she wears about her neck. Now!" he snapped when the boy glanced enquiringly at the unsealed letter in his lord's hand.

*

Isobel had spent so long on her knees after the final prayers of morning devotions that they were now numb, and she had lost count of the hour. She shifted to her feet, bowed to the altar behind the rood screen, and crossed herself.

Reluctantly, she left the scented sanctuary of the chapel. Her movements made clumsy by the chafing of her thighs, she made a conscious effort to correct her gait. Sometime during the night, low cloud had brought the threat of snow, and now Isobel stood at the door to the chapel as the first few flakes began to fall. The girls would be thrilled. Cecily would start begging to be allowed to chase the wind-blown scraps the moment Isobel stepped inside the room, and Margaret would hardly be able to contain her excitement. But the thought of their simple pleasure repulsed her, until she realised that it was their unmarked innocence from which she recoiled, and resentment against their father filled its place instead. She hugged her cloak around her and stared miserably at the leaden sky and wondered whether she would ever be able to enjoy snow again.

There was little point standing there getting colder by the minute. She had tried to leave the castle once before; now, after this, the Earl would have little reason to keep her there. She was spoiled, like the girls who tumbled in the copses on Midsummer Night, and Thomas would have no use for her. Isobel turned her face upwards to catch the quickening flakes against her skin. At Beaumancote, on the banks above the river, the eastern wind would make waves of snow amongst the sedge and rim the golden heads with white. She would be there before the first heavy fall of the winter. He *must* let her go.

"Where have you been?" Joan groused as Isobel unwound her cloak from her shoulders. "I've had nothing but numbleheaded wenches to help all morning, and what am I to do with her, might I ask?" She scowled at Cecily who was running around in circles whooping. "And he's been waiting nigh on the hour, and he were in a hurry straight off." She jerked a thumb towards the corner of the room where a young boy in livery watched Cecily's antics with baffled disdain. "The Earl'll not be best pleased, I'll warrant."

At the sight of the griffin, Isobel shrank back. Scooping up her cloak, she headed back to the door.

"Here, and where do you think you're going now?" Joan called out.

Isobel quickened her pace at the sound of feet hastening after her.

"Mistress!" The Earl's page caught up with her. "My lord commands you," he said with a degree of self-importance beyond his years or stature, "to give up your seal."

Isobel enclosed her father's seal in her fist. "Why?"

"My lord commands it," he repeated.

She felt a trickle of anger at the adolescent arrogance and towards the Earl that he would demand something more of her after all he had taken. "No," she said flatly, and turned her back on him and would have walked away, but the page took hold of her sleeve.

"You must!" he insisted, a little of his superiority slipping. "I cannot go back without it!"

She might once have been persuaded by the boy's scared face, but the thought of giving the Earl anything he wanted far outweighed her fear of him, or any sense of charity towards his page who demonstrated the same haughty disregard for her station and her sex.

She jerked her sleeve free of his hand. "Tell my lord," she said bitterly, "if he wants it, he will have to take it," and she swung about, stalked back to the girls' chamber, and shut the door on the boy's open-mouthed face.

"She said *what?*" The Earl's features clouded as, stuttering, the page began to repeat Isobel's answer word for word. "Enough! Get out." Leaning his knuckles on the table, the Earl counted slowly to ten. The letter — impotent without its seal — lay in front of him. Swinging about, he marched past the bored messenger still waiting for orders outside his chamber, down the stairs of the great tower, and towards the apartments occupied by his wife and daughters.

She had been waiting for him. While his daughters' attendants scurried into startled curtsies, Isobel Fenton rose slowly from by the window and stood facing him with her face averted, bleach-lipped and mute.

Cecily danced up to him, singing, "It's snowing, it's snowing," swirling around her father like a snowstorm until Margaret ushered her away, wide-eyed and watchful. The Earl took in Isobel's stance, her hand gripping the ribboned seal around her neck, the intense interest of the attendants and of his own older daughter. "Come," he said for the second time and didn't wait to see whether she followed him or not.

Snow settled in the creases of the stone mullions outside his window, blown by a strengthening wind. He waited until he heard the door to his chamber close behind the last of his servants before he spoke. "You will not defy me again." He turned without warning, and Isobel dropped her gaze, but not before he had seen the burning resentment in it. He held out his hand. "Your father's seal — give it to me."

Lock-jawed and silent, she showed no sign of compliance. He moved towards her. "Do not make me take it by force." Her eyes flashed to his, defiant, intransigent, then slowly she removed the ribbon from around her neck and placed the seal on the table next to several coins. He picked it up, polished the head against his sleeve, and examined the engraved face.

She watched as he melted resinous wax in the candle's flame and let it fall in red blobs on the sealing ribbon. Then, taking her father's matrix, he pressed its face into the molten wax until it set in glossy bulges around it. He checked the imprint, and, satisfied, handed the seal back to her. "It is done."

Isobel placed the ribbon around her neck. "It was not yours to take," she said quietly.

The Earl overlooked her lack of courtesy. "You have it back. You may go." He strode to the door and, flinging it open, hailed the messenger. "Take this. You have my instruction," he said, giving him a coin and the letter. "By this lady's hand."

The messenger glanced beyond the Earl's shoulder to where Isobel still stood. "Aye, my lord," he said, and left.

The Earl closed the door once more. He was surprised Isobel was still there. "What is it? I told you, you can go."

"I wish to leave."

Irritated, he looked at her. "That is what I said. Go!" The candle gutted in the draught from the window. Pinching the wick between thumb and forefinger, he snuffed the life from the flame. He wiped residual soot from his fingers.

"I wish to return to my manor."

He looked up. "Have you understood nothing about your situation? You cannot return."

"I understand, my lord. I also understand that Thomas Lacey will have no use for me, now that…" She halted and looked away. "It was not yours to take," she repeated, pinching her lips together in an effort to control herself.

"None else know of it. There is no need for shame."

"*I* know it," she almost shouted. "*God* knows it. I cannot hide my shame from *Him*!"

"Lower your voice. You have no family to take injury. The knowledge of this is your own, as is the shame, if you wish to take it. The choice is yours. As for the damage to your shoe, I will make reparation for it. Here…" From the scattering of coins on the table, he selected one and held it out to her. "Take it," he insisted. "That will pay for a dozen pairs." When she didn't move, he took her hand and pressed the coin into her palm. "The debt is paid; there is no more to it."

She looked first at the silver disc in her hand and then at the Earl. With deliberate slowness, she tilted her hand until it became a slope, and the coin dropped with a resolute *tang* onto the floor by his foot. She then turned and walked from the room.

Still steaming, Isobel returned to the nursery; no sooner had she passed the threshold than Joan accosted her. She was alone. "What did the Earl want?" she demanded, arms crossed on her chest, barring Isobel's way.

"It is not for me to tell you the Earl's business, nor for you to ask," Isobel retorted.

Joan didn't budge. "It is my business when it affects me. What were you about last night when you should have been abed?" When Isobel failed to reply, she prodded her in the chest. "You'll not be so mighty if the countess hears of it. Who is he? Don't think I don't know what you've been up to."

Isobel looked down at the jabbing finger, then at the woman's face. "Take. Your. Hand. Off. Me."

Joan sneered, but she backed away, and instead fished inside the purse hanging at her waist from which she took a fold of coarse wool. Wrapped inside was a strip of charred cloth with a band of interwoven green and yellow stitches along the hem. "What cause did you have to be burning this, then?" She dangled it from between two fingers. Isobel tried to snatch it, but Joan drew her hand out of reach. "Not so fast. My lady will be wanting to make it her business, and I'll make it mine to tell her."

"Tell her what?"

Joan folded the cloth and replaced it in the purse. She patted it fondly like a dog. "Never you mind; it'll keep. Like as not you'll want me sweet, so you'll not take ill to me borrowing your ribbon when I ask for it, or anything else that comes to mind."

"I'll not give you anything."

"You can find something else to dangle your fine seal. The countess has taken against you from what I hear, and she'll be eager to believe aught I tell her, mark me."

Isobel yanked the ribbon over her head, undid the knot, and slipped the seal from the silk. She deposited it into the woman's waiting hand. "I have no need of it. Take it and keep your lies to yourself." Isobel instantly regretted her action. She might as well have told Joan what had happened the previous night since she had confirmed her suspicions by acceding to her demands. *Fool*, she chastised herself silently as Joan gloated over her win. *Stupid, stupid fool.*

"There now," Joan crowed, running the length through her fingers, "that weren't so hard, was it?"

Girlish high voices, excitedly gabbling, came from somewhere beyond the room, and Joan rolled the ribbon into a crude bundle and stuffed it out of sight between her breasts as the door opened.

Cecily tumbled in with Alice in tow, rose-cheeked and puffing. "I catched the ball, I catched the ball," she sang, bouncing up to Isobel. "And I made this for you," she declared proudly, holding out her hot, pink hand in which an irregular ball of ice dripped. "Nan wanted one, but I said she must be growed up like Is'bel, and she looked like this…" Cecily made a grumpy face, then beamed.

Isobel kneeled in front of her and took the ice ball from the child's hand. She felt weary, as if she had forgotten what childhood had been like, and now that she had been forced into an unfamiliar world, she saw everything through tarnished eyes, and this child, bright as sunshine, made everything dull in comparison. "Thank you," she whispered.

Joan hustled past. "Eh, I don't know what you think you're about, my lady, but that thing is making a mess of the floor. What sort of gift is it that doesn't last, I ask you?"

"Some things are not meant to last," Isobel said quietly, "and are no less cherished for it." She smiled at Cecily's eager face. "Let us put it out on the window ledge to keep cold, my lady. We can see it then, and when it disappears, we will know that it tired of being a gift and ran away and found freedom with its friends."

Cecily took the slippery ball and skipped over to the window. Alice held her while she carefully placed the ice on the gathered snow.

"You should tell her it is going to melt and be done with it," Joan said.

"Why? What purpose would that serve?"

"It'd teach her a lesson she'll learn soon enough: there's nothing fair in this life and none to look out for ye except yourself." She gave a knowing tap to her breast to illustrate. "That'll be Lady Margaret back from seeing the countess now. Wonder what she has to say for herself?"

CHAPTER NINETEEN

Days passed and the nursery was thrown into a heightened state of excitement which helped distract Isobel from the nagging memory of that night.

"I have a spot," Margaret wailed. "It is my first feast day at my father's court, and I look like I have pox!" She pouted at the mirror. "Lord Raseby will be there, and I look like this! He won't wish to marry me; I look like a little girl. Why can I not be like Bess?" She breathed in shallowly, sticking her flat chest out as far as she could, and then exhaled, her shoulders sagging back to their accustomed bow.

Joan fussed around her. "Lord Raseby isn't marrying you for your looks, my lady. Stay still or I'll not get your brow plucked, and as like as not it will be all askew."

"*And* I will look like a plucked fowl," Margaret said, despairing. She held her mirror at an angle to see behind her. "Isobel, make me a salve. I do not want to look like a spotty chicken for St Catherine's feast. Can you not do this? Joan is so clumsy." She twisted on her stool. "Why are you not readying yourself? Alice can prepare my gown."

Isobel examined the tuck on the almost transparent veil for Margaret's hair, smoothing it with her hand. "I am not attending the feast, my lady."

Margaret knocked Joan's hand out of the way. "Why not? You have to. All unwed maids of any station attend. It is expected. Anyway," she added with an uncustomary simper Isobel didn't like, "you can pray to St Catherine to find you a husband."

"Stay still, my lady." Joan tipped the girl's head forward, exposing her hairline. "It'll take more than the blessed St Catherine to find *her* a husband."

"Why? Isobel is not yet old, and she is fair enough, and St Catherine has found *me* a match."

"Your noble *father* found you a match, my lady. And St Catherine only blesses virgins with a husband," Joan added under her breath.

"Isobel cannot help it if her father died. Now that I am to have my own household, I will have Isobel attend me, and I will find her a husband."

Cecily had been solemnly watching proceedings and preparing Nan's attire for the feast. Now she slithered off her stool. "And me, and me. I want a husband, too."

Margaret gave her a condescending pat. "You are only a child; you have to wait until you are grown. Ow, that *hurts*! Isobel, make me a salve!"

"You don't need none of that witch's muck, I have what you need." Joan went to the window. Leaning out, she retrieved the ice ball still sitting on the ledge. "Here, this'll make it right, and none'll know the difference."

"That's cold!" Margaret complained as freezing water trickled down her neck.

Eyes wide, Cecily pulled at Joan's arm. "That's Is'bel's. Meg, Meg, that's Is'bel's. Give it back!" She tugged harder.

"Cecily, stop it!" Margaret snapped. "Nobody cares about a silly ball of ice."

Cecily's lip wobbled and her eyes filled, but she ceased tugging and went to sit by herself in the corner.

Isobel found Nan abandoned on the stool and, kneeling next to the little girl, placed the doll in her arms and soothed her hair. She wanted to hold her, to tell her not to cry, but inside she had shrunken to a dot and no matter how she searched, she could not locate a spark of compassion with which she could comfort the child. From over by the fire where she still examined her reflection in the mirror, Margaret called, "Isobel, you are to get ready; I command it."

Seeing the two sisters, one preening, one crying, Isobel couldn't decide for whom she felt more sorry.

Expectation burgeoned among the waiting court, rustling like a strengthening wind through autumn trees. Isobel hung back. In front of her, at the entrance to the great hall, Margaret stood on tiptoes, her plucked brow and elaborate headdress making her look too old for her child's body. In a few short weeks, young Meg had become Lady Margaret, a fruit just short of ripeness waiting to be plucked. Isobel compressed her lips and composed her features.

"I cannot see him. I know I have met him before when I was a child, but I cannot remember what he looks like." Margaret looked over her shoulder. "Don't stand there where you cannot see, Isobel. Come here and help me find him. You are very sour this day, and where is your ribbon? You look quite plain without it. Maman gave me this beautiful necklet to celebrate my betrothal." She showed Isobel the lozenge-shaped, silver-gilt pendant, adorned with pearls and a blue stone, which hung from a red ribbon. She had never shown any interest in jewels before.

At the far end of the great hall, partly masked by a constant flow of bodies to and from the kitchens, Isobel could just make out Joan's full figure next to Jon's skinny form. She was showing him something and every now and then looked in her direction and sniggered. "I misplaced it, my lady," Isobel said, but Margaret wasn't listening.

"Here they are at *last*!" she exclaimed, looking towards the dais. "Maman is so fair, is she not? Like Our Blessed Virgin Lady in that blue gown. And Bess is wearing the dress Lord Dalton gave her — Maman must have told her to … oh, and look at my *father*…!" It was the last thing Isobel wanted to do. "Look, Isobel, *look*! He could be the *king*!"

Isobel looked. The Earl was indeed majestic in vibrant grayne-red and cloth of gold woven in the form of pomegranates, and the heavy collar of gold and enamelled caranets would have looked equally at home around the neck of the king. But it was not what she saw. She felt his thumb on her lips, his breath against her neck, and she sickened at the memory. As the Earl's gaze swept over the assembled crowd, she drew back further out of sight.

"All these people are here for me! Bess didn't have so many guests at *her* betrothal feast. Is that Lord Raseby? I cannot see him clearly. What does he look like, Isobel? Is he handsome? I am so nervous, look, I'm shaking." Margaret held out her hands in front of her, quivering and pale like a new beech leaf. "My father beckons," she hissed. "Wait upon me!" She straightened her shoulders, adopting a look of demure superiority she had been practising in front of the mirror, and stepped forward.

As Margaret walked in stately procession towards her waiting parents, she seemed to grow into her own importance at the acknowledgement of the lords and their ladies, some smiling as the girl passed, others curious. Following at a respectful distance, Isobel wondered if this is how she had appeared when she had been presented to her father's guests: small, insignificant, and slightly ridiculous. She concentrated on matching Margaret's short steps. As they neared the dais, Isobel heard a sudden gasp.

"That cannot be him!" Margaret whispered as her step faltered. "He's so *old*!"

"Little cousin!" Raseby bent to greet her, his beefy hands enveloping her scrawny arms as he kissed her on both cheeks.

Isobel saw the look of triumphant relief on the countess's face. She looked away and caught instead the Earl's grey eyes, watching. She held his stare for a long moment, then deliberately, consciously averted her gaze and returned to the trestle at the other end of the hall where she belonged.

Protocol observed, gifts exchanged, the blessing made, Margaret was led to the canopied dais where she sat with her parents and sister and the man to whom she would be married in a few short months. She didn't touch her food; she barely smiled. Occasionally she darted looks towards Isobel and Joan near the end of the long trestle at right angles to the dais, but most of the time she looked at the white linen tablecloth with red embroidered griffins, as food and wine passed before her, untouched.

Apart from a few pleasantries, Lord Raseby ate heartily and appeared to be recounting some battle, judging by the execution of the ornate pie in front of him. He thrust his eating knife into its heart and rotated it with an upward jerk. He laughed. Margaret looked as if she were about to cry, but the Earl, listening to the account without comment, ceased stroking his top lip and, taking up his cup, drank.

The countess said something at which Raseby roared, and she smiled appropriately. There the Earl sat, seemingly indifferent to the life to which he condemned his daughter. Isobel noted the girl's scared face and remembered her own fear.

Joan nudged her out of her reverie. "What are you gawking at? That'll be the closest you'll ever get to feasting on their food, no point wishing it were otherwise. This'll do me. Are you eating that?" She pointed at the untouched trencher with her knife, earning a reproving look from one of the countess's women nearby. "She needn't be so high with me," Joan said, ignoring the woman's frown and turning her back to her. "In my family you get nowt and starve unless you take it yourself, and this far down the table, who's going to notice that matters, eh?" She slid Isobel's food from in front of her and tucked in. "What do you think of Raseby? He'll give Meg something to think about on their wedding night, make no mistake." She took a slug of ale, belched. "You'll be knowing a bit about that now, won't you?" she slipped in, sly. "Is he here? Did he say he'd wed you?"

"Be quiet!" Isobel flashed. "Keep your jangling tongue to yourself. You chatter like a crow and know nothing of worth."

Joan stopped mangling her food and her eyes became slits. "I know nothing, do I? I know enough to make things mighty uncomfortable for you. I see you're not wearing those fancy shoes. They would look a treat on me, they would, so I was telling Jon."

Isobel ground her teeth. "You will have nothing more from me."

Joan wiped her mouth on her sleeve. "Oh, aye, we'll see about that."

The Earl had spent long enough listening to Raseby recount tales of his battle scars. He would be glad to have him guard his back in a melee, and his power base along the Welsh Marches and his manors bordering his own lands brought a welcome ally in the West Country. As a son-in-law he would have his undoubted uses, but as a table guest, his appeal was limited. He cast a look at his daughter's ashen face, at his wife's callous indifference, and then at the girl whose contempt had burdened his thoughts these last few days. They all depended on him one way or another, and one way or another, he had failed them all. He stood abruptly, cutting through the flow of martial narrative, bowed his head to his guest, and left the room to a stunned hush.

Leaving the suffocating confines of the castle, he had no intention other than to find space and air in which to be alone, and found himself treading the paths towards the wilderness of the old pleasance. Snow had thinned and refrozen to an icy crust that shattered beneath his feet, and all else was numbed but for the river in the distance and its incessant chunter. He steered a course away from it.

Crowned in snow, the apple tree stood alone. Although the sun had yet to set behind broken cloud, no one had cause to be there. Drawn under the arc of the canopy, it took the Earl moments before he could face what greeted him. Eve wound her scaled way in strangulating coils about the trunk, her breasts a lure, her glass eyes, death. How many times had he contemplated her over the years, and how often had she stared back, remorseless? He traced the swelling form, felt the hardened nipples beneath his fingers, closed his eyes as he felt hers scour him, then covered her face with his hand, smothering her leer, obscuring her sight. He leaned his head against her, trying to erase the image from his memory. Failed.

With a low moan, he brought his head against her, hard — once, twice, thrice — until he felt his skin tear. The river mocked his back. Cursing, he pushed himself away from the trunk and, sliding on the uneven ground, headed towards the naked arbour.

He could not tell how long he had been there nor why he looked up. The sky had darkened at the edges, leaving a strip of light nearing the horizon to gild his face. One hand on his dagger, he shielded his eyes with the other. A sound, so slight it might have been a whisper of the river. And again, but clearer this time. Singing.

He stood cautiously. It came from the tree — clear, distinct — melodic. He stumbled into the light. He found his voice. "I hear you." The singing stopped. He halted, his pulse bursting in his veins. "Wait!" he called, desperate to hear her voice again. From somewhere nearby, a robin scolded.

The Earl approached the tree carefully now, his footsteps breaking the peace of the garden, almost expecting the serpent to uncoil before his eyes and call to him — words of silk, searing fire. He had almost reached the tree when movement behind it broke the spell. Stepping swiftly to one side, the Earl drew his dagger.

"God's teeth, what are you doing here? I could have killed you!"

Isobel Fenton stared at him like a frightened rabbit, and he lowered his dagger and replaced it in its jewelled sheath.

"Do not look at me like that, I'll not harm you." Still she said nothing and, irritated, he added, "You should not be here alone; it is not safe." He saw the look flash across her face that damned his choice of words. He steadied his temper and his voice. "Go inside; it is nearly dark," and when she did not move, "It is cold out here."

Her gaze flicked to his brow. He touched his scalp and felt crusted blood among his thick hair. He looked at the smear of fresh blood on his fingers and grunted. "It is nothing. What are you doing here? You should be at my daughter's betrothal feast."

"My lord, I have no appetite for it."

"That is not for you to decide." He curbed his tone. "Why did you come to this place?"

"I came … I come … to talk to my mother."

Unwittingly, his eyes cast in the direction of the snake, then focused on Isobel again. "You are either fanciful or bewitched."

"No, my lord, I am neither. This is where I can remember my mother — in a garden among living things with the plants she loved to grow."

"This place is dead," he stated.

"But it is *not*," she said with a rush of warmth. "There is so much beauty here. How can you not see that?" Her words trailed to a close under his scrutiny.

He tried to see what she saw but only made out contorted stems and life curtailed by winter. "I see nothing," he said finally. "It is dark, and you are cold. Fetch your casket and attend me."

Isobel hugged her casket, avoiding the questioning glances of the Earl's grooms as she waited outside his chambers. Her feet were frozen, her hands barely warm, but neither compared with the ball of ice filling her gut that made her want to retch. The fear that had once been unknown had now been realised, but knowing it didn't make it less. That vague threat she had grown accustomed to with strangers, from which, she now realised, her parents had sought to protect her, had a name and a face, and he waited beyond the oak door that represented nothing but air between them.

The door opened without warning. A groom of the bedchamber gave a cursory bow and stepped back to allow her in. The room was warmer than the stair outside, and spiced hypocras scented the air. The Earl, legs outstretched before the fire, had divested himself of the richly decorated gown and now simply wore a white linen shirt and a long, loose-fitting robe lined with fur. He looked up as she came in and raised a wine beaker.

"Mistress Fenton, you can see I am in need of your physic." Only then did she see the fresh-patched blood anointing the Earl's collar. He indicated the table next to him. "Place your casket there. What else do you need?" He crooked a finger to his waiting page.

"Water. Fresh-boiled and clean, my lord. The bowl must be scoured."

There was nothing to fill the awkward silence, so Isobel began to assemble the few things she needed, grateful when the boy returned with a bowl and ewer. She dipped a linen swab into the water and soaked the narrow wound, made almost invisible by his dark hair. He winced.

"It is nothing, my lord. The scalp bleeds freely at the merest scratch."

"But the water is hot." He sucked his teeth. "That is the second time you have reprimanded me for bleeding like a girl." His shirt exposed his forearm and the scar from the stag's antler that decorated it.

She concentrated on dissolving the dried blood in his hair until the wound stood free of it. "I did not reprimand you, my lord, I made an observation."

"There, you have done so again. Why does it always feel as if you rebuke me?"

She shook her head, confused.

"If not with words, with a look; if not with a look, your silence."

Isobel dampened honey with three drops of lavender and one of oil of clove. "You do not wear the shoes I sent you. Did they not please you?"

He noted her furtive glance towards his groom. "Alun, you may go. You, too," he said to his page when the boy made no move to leave. Isobel wanted to go with them, and she quickly spread the salve on the graze. "Sweet Jesu, that stings!" He grabbed her wrist as she went to wipe the residue. She cringed and he let go, and she stood nursing her arm. "Let me see that. I did not hurt you."

She hesitated, then, inching up her sleeve, revealed the blueblack bruises on her fair skin.

He slumped back in his chair. "I did not intend to injure you, Isobel." He threw a look at her, but she had her face turned from him, and only her profile was lit by the fire. "It is as it is," he stated. "There is nothing I can do. The past cannot be undone," he said almost to himself.

She broke her silence. "My lord, you can let me go home."

He stood abruptly. "No."

"But Thomas will have no use for me now that I am … spoiled."

The Earl grimaced. "Do you think he cares? Your chastity is of little interest to Thomas Lacey. Your lands, on the other hand, would make a virgin out of a whore in his eyes."

"I … I thought that was why you…" she trailed off.

"What? You believe I intended to put you beyond his reach or his interest by *bedding* you?" He nodded slowly. "Ah, I see that you do. No, I am not that calculating." He ran his thumb along his eyebrow. "I sometimes wish I could temper my humours more effectively. In your case, I find that … difficult." He gave a rare smile that disappeared just as quickly.

"I have no intention of sending you back to your manor, or anywhere else for that matter."

"Until I marry. You said that you would find me a husband, someone — anyone — other than Thomas. You said —"

"Did I?" He frowned. "Perhaps I did. That was then. Things have changed, and I am not inclined to let you go."

"You cannot keep me here! My lord, I have done nothing wrong; am I to be kept prisoner?"

"*Prisoner*? Is that how you see it?" He waved a hand at the room. "You are safe here. I can protect you."

She held up her wrist. "Is this *protecting* me, my lord? Is this keeping me *safe*? I will petition the king —"

He gave a gruff laugh. "His Grace has greater matters to occupy him than the affairs of a girl. He is only too pleased to have you secure."

"And what of my lands, my people? I know them better than any; who will protect *them*?"

"Is your father's steward not to be trusted?"

She recalled Arthur Moynes's earnest face. "He is," she answered, uncertainly.

"I will ensure the security of your manors and your servants." He read her misgiving. "Do you not trust *my* good lordship?" Isobel thought she saw the twist of a smile as he turned away and doubted he expected a reply. "You enjoy a position in my household many girls in your situation would covet."

"*My* situation, my lord?"

"Yes, Isobel, *your* situation. Without family to protect you, who else will keep the wolf from your door?"

"The king."

"And who do you think protects him?"

Isobel recalled the lesson her father had taught her as they watched the grains of earth dancing attendance in the water of her bowl, until finally settling in degrees of magnitude in the bottom. Where did that leave the Earl in relation to the king, and where, for that matter, did it leave her? Probably the smallest speck of soil surmounted by all the rest, she thought glumly, if these past months were anything to go by.

The Earl was studying the line of his ancestors stretching towards the ceiling and appeared to have forgotten her. Quietly picking up the casket, Isobel started towards the door.

"Do you find my company so displeasing?"

She had nothing to say to that.

"I see that you do. Perhaps had circumstances been different…" She saw a swift look of regret. He moved closer. "I wish you to bide with me a while."

Swallowing, Isobel checked over her shoulder. "My lord, I must attend my ladies."

The Earl removed the casket from her arms and placed it on the table. "You will bide with me," he said flatly. He picked up his empty beaker and held it out to her. "Can you make hypocras?" She jerked a nod. "Make me hypocras, Isobel."

CHAPTER TWENTY

The Earl summoned Isobel again the following evening.

"Off to see your sweetheart?" Joan stopped Isobel at the door in an attempt at light-hearted pleasantry that fooled no one, and Isobel wanted to tell her to mind her own business, but instead answered truthfully.

"No."

"Oh, aye, so you'll be back afore long, then?"

Isobel didn't meet Joan's eyes but tried to get around her bulk laying siege to the doorway.

"Lady Cecily will be wanting her song sung, and Lady Margaret will ask where you are."

"I will be where I am commanded, and you will be here with my ladies, as your duty instructs."

"Only…" Joan lowered her voice, "I had a mind to see my Jon, and what with you abroad in the castle when you shouldn't be, like…"

"You will do your duty," Isobel repeated, pushing past her into the passage beyond, "and I will do mine."

The countess's expression didn't change, and Joan wondered whether she hadn't made herself plain.

"In the fireplace, my lady, with blood on it. I thought it my duty to tell you without delay, my lady." Again, Joan held out the stained and charred scrap, but the countess barely looked at it. "She's been acting strange of late, creeping around all times and not with a word said to any." She paused. "She's been gone now these last hours," she added for good measure.

The countess's mouth cracked open enough to let out a curt, "You may go," leaving Joan unsure whether her disclosure had reaped the desired effect or not. The countess brushed her sleeve free of an almost invisible speck of linen ash, and Joan felt herself dismissed. She left the fabric on the table by the basin of jasmine-scented hand water, bobbed low, then left the room, disappointed.

Felice Langton waited until Joan was beyond earshot before calling to one of her ladies. "Fetch Master Sawcliffe," she said, and watched the woman hurry away. Felice could not say she liked her daughters' attendants — any of them — but the doughy, waggle-tongued girl with probing eyes had uses other than serving the girls. This information might be just what she needed to regain control, and Joan would be rewarded — enough to keep her keen, but not so much she might be tempted to ask for more.

Placing the tips of her fingers together, Felice gathered her thoughts as she waited in perfect repose. At this late hour, even Sawcliffe would need his rest. Briefly, she wondered whether her husband had him spy on her, and then dismissed the idea as far-fetched. To do so would mean he would need to consider her at all, and she to give him a reason to suspect her, and both were too artful for that. She did not care whose company Isobel Fenton sought, it was irrelevant, but it played to her twin abhorrence of whoring and this girl, plucked from obscurity, who pricked her consciousness every time she saw her. At this time of night, undistracted by his estate and the king's business, her husband would be alone now, reflective — perhaps receptive. She resolved not to wait for Sawcliffe after all and beckoned to her ladies.

Felice could smell the river in the chill clinging to the stone passages, but the rose combed into her hair scented the air in snatches, and the fur-lined mantle — donned to keep servants' eyes ignorant of what lay beneath — insulated her from the cold. Something like a thrill quickened her step, an almost clandestine arousal, quashed as soon as she recognised it and refashioned into spite.

Her husband's square-headed groom stood outside the chamber door. He must have been dismissed for the night, which boded well. Alun bowed his head when he saw her approach, hardly containing his surprise, and she waved him aside. He shuffled awkwardly but continued to block her way. "My lord has retired, my lady."

As she had hoped. Again, the shiver of anticipation warming her face, swelling her lips. "Stand aside."

Alun didn't budge. "He is not to be disturbed."

Felice's face froze into a mask of displeasure, and he took a step back against the door. "Get out of my way."

"My lord said —"

She could crack bones with a glance. "Insolent knave! Move or I will have you whipped."

Mumbling an apology, Alun opened the door, backed through it, and swiftly shut it in her face. He reappeared moments later. "My lord will see you now, my lady," and he stepped to one side as she swept past, leaving her indignation to cool his flaming face.

Tousled, the Earl had evidently been awoken and had thrown his gown in an untidy swathe around his shoulders. For all of that, he greeted her civilly enough and she forgot her anger at the sight of him.

"What is it?" he asked.

She pushed the nosing dog out of her way with her knee and moved closer. "I wish to speak with you." Her loosened fair hair escaped the mantle, releasing floral scents.

He tapped impatiently. "Could it not have waited until morning?"

She lowered her eyes and turned slightly, her mantle gaping and exposing a shoulder to the soft light from the pricket. "It is important, and I need your guidance."

The Earl frowned. "There is nothing that cannot bide. I will speak with you in the morning." He indicated the door with his hand. His gown shifted, and he secured it before it fell open.

"You have hurt your head," she said, reaching out to him. "Let me tend you."

He drew back. "It is nothing. Go to bed, Felice."

She detected something different about him tonight: a pulsating energy, the note of his voice enriched, deep, heavy, once reserved for their moments of intimacy before the winter in their marriage had set in. He seemed eager to be rid of her, too eager for sleep. She looked around the room. A decorated glass, half full, sat next to his wine cup. No man she had ever known left his wine unfinished. He stood conspicuously in front of the bed, the hangings partly drawn. She craned her head past him and thought she saw linen on the bed rumpled and unruly.

"You are not alone? You have brought a girl to your bed," she accused. "Who is it? That wanton from York?"

"It does not concern you," he said gruffly.

Her voice rose. "You've broken your oath! No women, my lord, not in this castle, not while I live." She attempted to get past him and the dog, frazzled by her agitation, pawed at her mantle. He held her back.

"Leave, Felice. Now."

Her movements were adding to the dog's frenzy, and it leaped about her, its sharp barks splitting the air.

"Get the animal off me!" She aimed a vicious kick at the dog, and it yelped as her foot caught its leg. The Earl swore and threw out his arm to protect the animal as she drew back to strike again, but Felice ducked beneath it and flung back the hangings.

"Get that *whore* out of here!" Felice spat when she regained her voice, pointing at Isobel cowering beneath the sheets with her hands covering her face.

"Felice —"

"You shame me under my own roof. You bring dishonour to us all and we will be made a mockery at Court. The queen will want nothing to do with this family."

"There was a time when you did not care what Her Grace thought. She knows better than to criticise her husband and when to look away. You could follow her lead."

"As you do the king's?"

"Jesu, madam, you have said your say. She stays. That is enough."

"Enough?" The countess spun around, pointing an accusing finger in Isobel's direction. "I will not forget this. Do not, for one moment, believe I will let it lie." She directed one last, withering look at Isobel and left, leaving the door swinging open for a startled Alun to shut.

Her face still burning, Isobel donned her smock and bent to find her shoes.

"What do you think you are doing?"

She straightened, shoes in one hand. "I cannot stay."

"I did not give you leave to go."

"But … my lady —"

"Is not your lord." The Earl joined her by the side of the bed, taking the shoes from her hand and dropping them to the floor. He bent to kiss her, but she turned her head away. He pulled her chin around, forcing her to look into his grey eyes made darker by the low light. "I do not like my pleasures interrupted, Isobel. I do what I desire, and in the realm of this castle, I am king. Now, take off your smock, we will resume.

By the time Isobel made her way back to the nursery, the dank wind of the night before had melted the snow and made all dreary. If she harboured any expectations she might return to a semblance of normality, it was a false hope.

Alice was helping Cecily into her smock. She looked up as Isobel slid into the room, and her expression changed. Cecily squeaked and wriggled free as Isobel put out her arms to her, but Alice pulled the little girl back, darting a look towards the pallet room where muffled voices crowed. Without a word, Isobel crossed the room. Joan and her servant were bent over something on the small table. Isobel caught sight of the carved cream of her casket. "What are you doing? Leave that alone, it's mine!" She then saw her clothes scattered on her pallet, her few possessions ravaged.

Joan faced her, a mirror in her hand. "Look who's turned up like dirty linen. Well, you'll not wash it in *these* chambers, not now you won't. The countess orders you gone from here. You're not to see or speak with the girls. Unclean you are, not fit. Thought you could win favours with the Earl, did you? You should be ashamed. I warned you, I did. I said what comes of getting caught. Like as not my lady will have you whipped naked in the servants' hall and driven through the streets like a common harlot. You know what they make whores wear around here, don't you? A striped hood, that's what. The only place you'll be welcome is in a brothel."

"Give that to me." Isobel pushed between the women, snatching her mother's mirror from Joan and closing the lid of the casket.

Joan pushed her away before Isobel had a chance to pick it up. "Don't think you're taking that," she leered. "The countess said you are to leave with nothing. I have been given charge of the nursery now, and when the skinny wench out there is wedded, I'll have that Devil's brat right here…" She tapped the palm of her hand. "And do you know what's the first thing I'll do?" She waited for effect. "I'll burn that poppet of hers. In the fire. And make her watch. And if she cries, I'll pinch her till she stops —"

Surprise barely had time to register on Joan's face as Isobel's fist made contact with her nose and she reeled backwards against the embrasure.

"Don't you touch her! Don't you dare hurt her!" Isobel yelled.

Stunned, Joan put a hand to her bloodied nose. Recovering, she punched out heavily, grazing Isobel's ribs, then went for her eyes with her nails. Quicker on her feet and still blind with rage, Isobel dodged to one side, grabbing Joan's wrists and shoving her backwards against the pallet. Running from the room shrieking for the guards, her servant didn't see Joan lash out again, ripping Isobel's dress at the neck as she tried to rend her skin and, using her body weight, forcing the slighter girl against the wall.

"Thought you could better me, did you, you skulking whore?" Joan panted into Isobel's face. "Thought you would lay with the Earl and play the fine lady? You haven't the wit. Want to know what happened to the last girl my lady suspected? Had her taken to Rose Street when foreign mercenaries were stationed there and left at dusk. Found the next morning floating in the mill race — and not a pretty sight, by all accounts. And what made me laugh for days — the wench had done nothing more than *look* at the Earl."

Heavy footsteps sounded outside the room, and Joan suddenly released Isobel and collapsed in the corner, holding her hand to her face. "She attacked me!" She waved a shaking finger in Isobel's direction as two guards burst into the room. "I did nothing, but the witch attacked me!" She held out her reddened hand as evidence.

One of the guards, taking Isobel by the arm, started to drag her from the room.

"Stop! Let go." Isobel tried to prise his fingers from her arm. "Wait!"

"You can explain yer sen to t'constable. There'll be no fighting in t'castle." He pushed her roughly in front of him.

Alice held Cecily in her arms, the child's thumb lodged in her mouth, round-eyed and frightened. Beside them, Margaret stood stiffly, her shoulders rigid, her thin face tight. As Isobel stumbled past, Margaret followed her with cold eyes.

"Meg!" Isobel called out. "Protect Cecily. Look after her."

"I am Lady Margaret Langton to you," Margaret replied, and slowly, deliberately, turned her head.

The last thing Isobel saw as she was hauled from the room was Joan's triumphant sneer, as she made a pinching movement with thumb and forefinger behind Cecily's trembling back.

"Where is she now?" the Earl asked as the constable bent close to relay his message. "Is she injured?"

He stared at the map spread on the table in front of him as the castles and manors, rivers and woods under his lordship merged and swam until he found himself focusing on the lands around the Humber and the fortified manor of Beaumancote. He was deluding himself, he thought grimly, if he believed his wife exaggerated her intentions, but that she had moved so swiftly against the girl bore witness to the depth of her spleen. He did not doubt she would carry out her threat to have Isobel Fenton publicly beaten and driven through the streets as a whore, but she was mistaken if she thought he would stand by and let her. In bedding the girl, he thought he would have sated his curiosity and erased her from his mind, but she possessed him in a way he had never believed possible, slipping under his skin and warming him like the sun after a cloudy day.

He lifted his face to the beamed sky of his council chamber and felt her warmth. A small cough next to his elbow reminded him that his constable waited for instruction. The Earl focused again. "I charge her safety to you until I decide what to do with her."

"She is not to be punished for her disorder, my lord?"

"You have your orders."

Isobel stood in the middle of the bare room, shivering. Other than a stained pallet along one side of a plain-washed wall, the only other source of comfort was a blackened hearth. No fire warmed it and no fuel lay in waiting. She wrapped her arms about herself to keep warm, regretting it as her ribs ached, and went instead to a window letting in a narrow strip of light.

High above the river, she could just make out the bark of a dog and the curse of a man, but the only scent of it came down the chimney tainted by soot. The chamber had been added to the top floor of the tower to house some of the castle ordnance, and racks of crossbows lined the walls and barrels the stone floor. Now it was to accommodate the Earl's mistress. The air smelled of oil and rust and iron, and her stomach churned. Some part of her would have preferred a whipping, and even humiliation in front of strangers might have been better than *this*.

She looked for something to sit on, lifting the corner of the pallet sprouting straw from crude seams and letting it fall back damply, dislodging clouds of dust. Wiping her hands on her skirts, she turned around and nearly screamed. A woman, widow-coiffed and skin creased like linen, hovered behind her, watching with faded blue eyes. Her fingers — knuckles swollen and disfigured — repeatedly worked a bead at the end of a short paternoster worn about her neck.

"I know who you are," she said, spinning the bead. Isobel thought she would continue, but she didn't, nor did she introduce herself.

"You do?" Isobel asked, tentatively.

"My son will come," the woman said. "He is a good boy, dutiful." She seemed to expect Isobel to say something.

"Yes?" Isobel ventured, not sure what else to reply.

"I know who you are," she said again, and her look became almost wistful, shedding the years worn into her face. She reached out and stroked Isobel's cheek before she could pull away. "You are very young, like my boy. I was young once." And she touched her own softly downed cheek and smiled, revealing teeth once white, now cracked and stained.

Something about her reminded Isobel of Buena, but the memory of her servant brought her crashing back to reality. "Tell me who you are," she said more assertively.

The woman became rather less reflective and more puzzled. "I am come to serve you, my lady. Were you not told?"

Isobel thought she might have been, but in the last few hours so much had been said that she had lost half of it in the confusion. Already missing Alice's level-headed simplicity, she shook her head. The woman raised a brow long since plucked clean of any expression, like Nan. "I am Ursula Bere. Perhaps my lord mentioned me?"

Isobel shook her head again, and Ursula looked a little crestfallen.

Isobel gestured around the room. "There is nowhere for you to sleep. I can retain you, but no one will wish to be associated with you, not now, not after…" She trailed off, not sure how to encapsulate her present situation.

Placing a knobbled hand on Isobel's arm, Ursula peered into her face. "No one has spoken to me for years. They think I am feeble-minded, and perhaps they are right. I am nothing. I am no one. I do not exist. There —" her fingers fluttered above her head — "I am…" she caught air in her hand like a moth and, turning it over, opened her fingers and blew gently across her empty palm — "invisible." She smiled. "As for sleep, I close my eyes. It is enough." She looked around as a lively ticking of claws on stone preceded a greyhound bearing the silver collar of its master. It careered into the chamber, thrusting its muzzle into Isobel's hand.

"Chouchou!" Isobel wrapped her arms around the dog's neck, welcoming the warmth, the unconditional acceptance, and realised how much she already missed the children.

"Isobel."

She jerked away from the dog and stood clumsily. She had not heard the Earl enter. He appeared incongruous in gold-figured velvet in such austere surroundings as he examined the chamber, lips pressed together, then brought his gaze back to her drawn face and unkempt hair.

"Your gown is torn."

Isobel pulled the ripped fabric together. It sagged apart again. "I will mend it, my lord."

"You have others; have them fetched."

"No. I mean, I did, my lord, but my lady gave them … that is, I do not have them now." At the mention of the countess, the Earl's face hardened. His hand, resting on the decorated pommel of his dagger, twitched. Isobel swallowed. "My lord … my casket —"

"I will expect you in my privy chamber later. You will sup with me." The dog had been nosing around the pallet, and the Earl snapped his fingers. "Chou, leave it!" She trotted to her master. "Do not keep me waiting," he said to Isobel, and left her standing there feeling like one of his less favoured hounds.

"You see?" Ursula trilled from beside the window where she had spent the entire exchange looking fixedly at the Earl. "Invisible."

Isobel viewed the torn fabric in despair. Ursula had brought her own few possessions in a small chest and placed it in a corner of the room. From the neatly stacked contents, she found a carefully folded cloak of some age, and this Isobel now wore over her kirtle and smock to keep out the cold. She blew on her fingers to warm them and tried stitching again. In the low light, the needle pricked her finger, slipped, and fell to the floor. She hunted for it without much hope in the dusty cracks between close-set flags. Even with her gnarled hands, Ursula could have made a better job of it, and Isobel regretted having refused her offer of help.

Ursula hovered nearby. "My lady, let me finish the sewing."

It took a moment for it to sink in. "What did you call me?"

Ursula took the dress from Isobel, settled on the chest, and started unpicking Isobel's clumsy attempt. "My lady?"

"Why do you call me that? No one has given me that courtesy since I came here."

The woman continued working using small, neat movements despite her twisted hands. "You are my Earl's lady," she answered simply, and began humming to herself as she sewed.

Wrapping the cloak tightly around her neck, Isobel rose from the pallet and stretched her cold bones. She ached where Joan's knee and fists had made contact, and her thighs still chafed a little from the previous night. She stood on tiptoes, craning to see out of the windows set just above her head height, but all she could make out was a square of milky sky and the top of what might be a stone parapet.

She gave up and wandered over to one of the many barrels. Using a metal bar, she wrenched off a lid and was immediately met with the tang of greased iron crossbow bolts waiting in readiness. She replaced the lid. She felt sore and grimy in this bleak, bare room decorated with implements of war, and with a woman who was a stranger to her in more ways than one.

Nothing convinced her that Fortune was about to turn the Wheel.

CHAPTER TWENTY-ONE

Woken as the dog stirred beneath the bed at dawn, Isobel slipped from the sleeping Earl and, taking a single taper to light her way, crept back up the stairs to her own chamber without waking him. Unwashed, she yearned to bathe and scolded herself for not asking him to have her things returned. He had been taciturn all evening, his questions pointed, his answers short, and she had not dared raise the issue of her belongings.

She unlatched the door and stopped: the room had been transformed. A bedstead stood laden with linen and hung with thick curtains and, beside a fire still glowing in the hearth packed with fuel, a chair with cushions. A coffer, large enough to provide a seat, sat at the end of the bed while, on a small table beneath one of the windows, lay her mirror, comb and casket. With a small gasp, Isobel ran her hands over the intricate surface, then opened it. The lid fell back unevenly on hinges bent by ungentle hands.

"It can be mended," a voice said behind her.

"How did you do all this?" Isobel asked, taking in the room, her things, her precious casket.

Ursula blinked slowly like a cat. "I have done nothing. My lord —"

"He did *this*?" Isobel interrupted, incredulous, then under her breath as she breathed in the scent of camphor wood lining the box, "I did not think there was any kindness in him."

Ursula touched the beads at her neck uncertainly. "My lord was not always so harsh."

Isobel felt her mouth twist. "I have known no other side of him."

"You are very young," Ursula reminded her, although God only knew Isobel did not feel it at the moment. "When I first came to the castle, he was younger than you are now." She closed her eyes, lilac-lidded and translucent in the dawn light, trembling with distant memories.

"How long have you been here?"

"A long time, but not forever." She opened them again. "I served the Dowager Countess; I dressed her hair, perfumed her clothes. She held me her favourite." She extended her hands in front of her and they shook a little. A small ring of gold pinched the flesh of one finger above its joint. "He was young then, and the world more innocent. We were often at Court before all turned sour and the old king lost his wits. Do you remember how he danced at the Feast of St Nicholas?"

"Who?"

But Ursula was waving her arms to and fro in a swaying motion, caught up in a slow dance, humming the same tune she had before.

"Saw who dance?" Isobel tried again. "I was not there."

Ursula stopped singing. "It is the Feast of St Nicholas, and I will dress your hair, my lady, and lay out your clothes." She picked up the ewer from beside a copper basin with enamelled fish swimming around the sides. "Will you be pleased to bathe now?"

Without the girls to care for, by mid-morning Isobel was at a loss. She had allowed herself to be primped and primed and her hairline tidied despite her protestations. She had sorted the contents of her casket, noted the missing items, and made a list for their replacement. Ursula had been sent to find the best source of spices as she seemed to know every inch of the castle and town and delighted in being given the task. But now, still early, Isobel had nothing left to do.

Filled with furniture and boxes and barrels, the room felt cramped and stuffy, and its proximity to the Earl's own chamber was a constant reminder of his expectation. Isobel flopped into the chair and rubbed at her sore hairline, feeling like a new-plucked fowl. She restlessly rose, and paced to the table to pick up the mirror. Her uneven reflection looked as it ever did, if more groomed, but the eyes that stared back at her belonged to someone else; older, wary, and she replaced the mirror with a thump that shook the table.

Sweeping her cloak around her shoulders, Isobel intended seeking solitude in the wild garden, but instead found herself automatically making for the countess's apartments.

Outside the girls' chamber she tucked herself unobserved into a nook where a window had been let through the depth of the wall and trained her ears to the sounds beyond the door. Indistinct voices slowly materialised into recognisable cadences: Margaret bemoaning her skin and Alice saying something soothing in reply, and Cecily singing in a jerky little voice as if skipping around the room. They sounded content.

Isobel slouched back against the wall, deflated. What had she expected? Did she really think she had made so much difference to their lives that her absence would be noticed? She missed them more than they did her, and Joan's threats had been just that. Isobel's throat tightened and, before the tightness erupted into tears, she pushed herself away from the wall. Deep voices travelled the length of the passage towards her, and she hurried, head averted, to pass them.

"Isobel! What are you doing out here loitering like a thief? I came to find you." His stained travelling cloak over one arm, Robert Langton grinned down at her.

Isobel's heart stumbled. She managed a curtsy, started to say something resembling a greeting, but stuttered to a halt and looked down at his mud-spattered riding boots rather than face him.

"What is it? You have become as pale as one of your lilies."

"I … I did not think … I did not expect to see you, my lord."

"I wanted to surprise you, and it seems I have done so. Martin…" From a rain-mottled leather document bag he took several small parcels, then handed the bag back to his esquire. "Take this to my lord Earl, and see it delivered to his hand only." He waited until the young man was out of earshot. "I thought you would be pleased to see me."

"I am!" she exclaimed.

"You do not seem it." His smile faded. "What is it? You look different." He reached for her hand, but she drew away and sensed his disappointment. He stood back. "Perhaps I should have warned you of my return after all," he remarked, and when she didn't reply, added, "I came to give my nieces *petits cadeaux de la fête Saint Nicolas* and to see Meg after her betrothal. The last time I saw her she wished to enter the convent." He frowned. "It seems that more than one person has changed since I have been away."

Isobel wanted to tell him that she hadn't changed, that change had been imposed upon her, but she bit her lip and held back.

"Well, in that case you had better take me to them; perhaps they will be glad to see me."

"They have missed you, my lord." *As have I*, she thought, miserably. "My ladies are in their chambers."

"Lead on," he said, standing back for her.

Isobel shook her head, once. "I cannot."

"Why not? You have other duties to detain you?" She threw him a look. "Isobel? And where is your ribbon — your seal —"

"Robert!" They both turned at the sound of the Earl's voice, and Isobel shrank back as he strode swiftly towards them. "I thank God for your safe return. I did not expect you this side of Yule. When did you receive these?" He held up a clutch of letters.

Robert returned his embrace. "Two days ago. I brought them myself rather than entrust them to another."

The Earl nodded. "And rightly so. Is anyone else aware of their existence?" He then noticed Isobel hunched to one side. "Isobel, go to your chamber. I will summon you when I am ready."

Robert looked first at his brother, then at Isobel's wan face, and in the split moment it took for him to understand the situation, disappointment chased shock, became disgust, and Isobel's remaining hope imploded. Tucking a slim package he had been holding into the breast of his doublet, he looked away, his eyes stone.

Isobel ran across the bailey to the great stairs of the tower pursued by his censure and the enquiring glances of those she passed. The guards let her by without hindrance into the tower basement and up the narrow stairs within the walls to the Earl's council chamber. She crossed it without stopping, accessing the next flight of stairs past his privy chamber and up to her eaved room. Throwing herself on the bed and burying her face in the bolster, she gasped in short, sharp, silent bursts that hurt her chest. Why couldn't he have come back sooner? Why now? A week would have made all the difference.

Would it? Would Robert have opposed his brother in *any* way? She rolled over and sat up. What did she know of him other than from the few short times they had chanced to meet? Had he, at any time, expressed a desire to court her, or was his interest mere courtesy? And what had she to offer a man of his estate anyway, except her love, unless... *You fool!* she cursed herself. *You addle-witted imbecile.* What did any man want when it was his for the taking and without needing to pay the price of marriage for it? Buena's dancing fingers had been a just warning, but what could she do against such a rout? What recompense was there that could address such an act? Even had Robert been aware of his brother's intention, could he have done anything to prevent it? Would he? Isobel wasn't his kin, and he owed her no obligation. Who would act as her protector if her own lord violated his responsibilities?

Sobered by the thought, Isobel swung her legs to the edge of the bed and took in her room with a single sweep. That small act of kindness in restoring her things to her had been no more than a salve for the Earl's conscience, she thought sourly. Was she so cheaply bought? She regarded her mother's precious milk-white casket and, with a twist of guilt, felt thankful that she was no longer alive to witness her daughter's seedy descent.

She looked up as Ursula let herself into the room carrying a small basket in which lay slender bundles of cloth and a larger round object from which a meaty smell rose. Spice enriched the air as she placed the basket down.

Isobel welcomed the distraction. "You have been gone a long time," she said, unwrapping the first bundle, revealing aromatic sticks of cinnamon. "Did you get everything on the list?"

"My lady has been crying," Ursula observed.

Isobel felt more annoyed with herself for letting it show than at Ursula for noticing it. "It is nothing. Did you get all I asked for?"

"There was none to be bought so close to Christmastide."

"Then where did you get these?" Isobel picked up the next package with the crudely faceted red-brown grains of paradise. Ursula put the purse Isobel had given her on the table by the basket. It chinked replete. She smiled vacantly.

"I said that they were for my lord's lady."

Isobel looked at her aghast. "You are *never* to say that again, do you hear me? I will pay for my spices. I will pay for anything I need. I am not his 'lady', I am Isobel Fenton of Beaumancote and I belong to no one."

Ursula gave a rapid series of blinks, and then a slow smile passed over her chalk face. Putting a finger to her lips, she whispered, "I understand, my lady, I will say nothing," and she tapped her finger against her lips to seal them.

Isobel hardly knew whether to laugh at the woman's idiocy or cry with frustration; either way, the whole castle seemed to know her business, rendering Ursula's silence moot.

Isobel said in resignation, "Have you dined yet?"

Ursula lifted the large, wrapped object from the basket. "I brought this pie for your dinner. Pork pie with honey and spiced fruit, fresh made. I paid for it," she added before Isobel could ask.

"You are certain of this?" the Earl asked his brother.

Robert waved towards the letters on the table between them. "As you can see."

The Earl grunted. "These in themselves say nothing. It is what is *not* written that concerns me, and the very fact they were written at all."

"Has Lacey replied to the girl's letter?" Robert couldn't bring himself to say her name, which the Earl noted.

"No."

Robert paced to the window. "What game is he playing? Warwick courts him, and we have offered him a lure he was only too eager to seek before." He stopped. "Is he aware you have taken the girl as your mistress?"

The Earl looked up at the change in his brother's tone. He had never considered him prudish before. "Not that I know. It has been but a week and less since it was made known. Unless Felice sent heralds to announce the fact."

"You will not be able to keep the knowledge of it from him for long; he might consider the girl ... spoiled."

"And lose the chance of getting her land? I think not. I doubt he has that much honour. He would wed a whore happily enough if it gained him a manor."

"Is that what she is to you? A whore?"

"Did I say so? Sweet Jesu! What makes you so ill-humoured of late? Here, drink this." The Earl held out Robert's cup of ale. "I'll ask Isobel to make you a potion to temper your choler."

Robert regarded the cup, then took it and sat back down. "So, Lacey..."

"...is playing both sides," the Earl said, rotating his own beaker in his hands. "He is waiting to see which way the Wheel turns to ensure he lands on top. He will back neither side until it is clear who will win, and then —" he flicked the beaker with his finger, making the silver ting — "he will be the loyal dog that mounts the winning bitch."

"And what sort of bastard will that breed?" Robert muttered into the depths of his ale.

"What indeed?" the Earl remarked mildly. "That sort of loyalty is easily bought…"

"…and as soon lost," Robert finished. "The king does not see it."

"He *chooses* not to see it; there is a difference. He still has hopes that Warwick will come to heel and bring Clarence with him. Lacey does not overly concern the king, for as yet he has no bite in him. Lacey must be kept toothless, and we will pull his teeth if need be. His lack of affinity makes him a runt of the litter, and without the means to buy loyalty, he will do no more than yap."

"His Grace is not so sure."

"Gloucester is still a boy —"

"Whom you were keen for me to serve," Robert reminded him. "He might not have his brother's years, but he is no fool and knows how to govern himself. He shows sound judgment and an even hand, and rewards loyalty well. I dare say he will make his mark."

"Thank God we do not have another Clarence. With the Lord of Misrule abroad I would not have a brother like that at my back on a dark night. I would never know which way he was facing until dawn, and by then it might be too late." The Earl raised his cup. "May God grant the King's Grace foresight, and the wisdom to use it. To our king — and to those whom loyalty doth bind."

"Amen to that," said his brother, with feeling.

CHAPTER TWENTY-TWO

Like a hive on the first warm morning in spring, the castle buzzed with expectancy as Christmas approached. The great hall greened with garlands of ivy and holly and, from the chapel, choristers hung votive chants on the air. The first of the visiting players arrived, trundling wagons across the cobbles of the bailey where they set up makeshift stages on which to practise their seasonal frivolity.

Life continued all around Isobel but, isolated like a rock in the middle of a stream, she played no part in it. Avoiding the halls and galleries, she only ventured from her room when she could be certain of remaining unseen, sliding into the chapel at the back, or slipping into the wild garden at dawn to be alone. There, except for an occasional servant on the back stairs, or a gardener securing straw and sacking over the frost-tender plants, Isobel had the wilderness to herself.

The week following his arrival, Isobel saw little of Robert Langton. The memory of his sudden chill curdled her inside until she was no longer certain what she had seen or what was the legacy of her imagination. Once, on a day when the rain stopped long enough to allow the sun through, she had heard his voice from the fair court and furtively crept to the window to see Cecily riding his back with a whip of ivy and Margaret calling instructions from the side. Her skirts flying, he swung his niece over his head with her squealing like a piglet, and he had thrown his head back and laughed. Ribbons of resentment, of longing, of *envy* ran through Isobel, so powerful, so damning, she clasped her hand over her mouth to prevent it escaping. Her movement must have caught his eye, because he halted the game, the child suspended upside down, and his smile froze. Then Cecily wriggled and kicked, and he let her down, and Isobel began to breathe again.

On the second occasion, if she had been in any doubt as to how he now viewed her, she was left with none. Ursula came into the room in a flurry, her normal docility ignited. "My lady, see, they are come! They make such revels! Come! Come!" Removing the pestle from Isobel's hand, she hurried her from the room, along the passageway, and down the stair to the bailey, where people jostling for a place already gathered on stone slippery with recent rain. There were as many people here as she had seen at the market in Lincoln, numbers swollen with guests and their servants arriving for the winter feasts. Strident shawms and tabors set to with upbeat timbres.

"See how they process!" Ursula exclaimed, clapping her hands in delight and laughing like a child. Smaller by inches and craning as far as her neck would allow, Isobel jumped up and down to see beyond the shoulders of those crowding in front of her, as multicoloured balls and sticks of flame appeared for vibrant seconds over the heads of the onlookers.

"Are they jongleurs?"

"The town waites are with them — they have new livery — can you not see, my lady?"

Isobel caught flashes of blue and yellow, as bright as the blaring of the shawms. "No, I'm too short."

Ursula took hold of Isobel's hand and began pulling her into the mass. "Make way! Make way for my lady."

"Ursula, no!" Isobel said, horrified as she became engulfed by the press of bodies in damp wool tunics smelling of wet dog and sour armpits. "I do not wish to be seen."

She tried to disengage her hand, but Ursula parted people in waves which converged behind them like the Red Sea until their retreat was barred and she had no option but to push forward to find clear air. From behind the broad back of a dun-furred merchant, she came as near to the front as she dared.

Flipping and tumbling, jongleurs passed in front of the cheering crowd that had gathered in a wide line either side to watch them, followed by jugglers and stilt walkers, and accompanied by musicians from the town and minstrels from the castle. Isobel became a girl again, watching the players perform for her father and mother in the great hall of her home, surrounded by vibrant music and the smell of smoke from the hearths.

Too soon they passed, taking her memory with them, and the drab sky replaced the light and colour. Only then did she realise that heads were bowing as the countess crossed the bailey with her daughters and, with them, Robert. She ducked her head rapidly, hoping the merchant blocked her from their view.

"Is'bel!" a high voice called, and Cecily tumbled from between the heavily brocaded gowns of her family, barging past the merchant and into Isobel's startled arms. "Where have you been?" she demanded, as Isobel's face flared vermilion. "Nan is cross with you. You must come back *now*." She shook a stubby finger.

With a single word from the countess, Alice was despatched to fetch the child, but Cecily refused to budge.

"*Please*, my lady," Alice begged.

Cecily crossed her arms and planted both feet squarely with a look that would have felled Goliath. "Nan wants Is'bel."

"I cannot come with you," Isobel said quietly as the countess drew level with them. "Go with Alice. Your lady mother is waiting, quick!" She gave her a gentle push in her mother's direction, but Cecily clung to Isobel's skirts.

"I don't care, I don't want to go to *her*, I want Is'bel!"

By now the group of onlookers had begun to drift away, leaving Isobel conspicuously alone; but those remaining were showing a greater degree of interest. "Be brave," she whispered into the child's thick curls, and placed Cecily, still protesting, into Alice's arms.

"Why do you let her stay, Maman?" Lady Elizabeth asked in a hushed voice that carried audibly within the walled confines. "Lord Dalton says she should be sent to the stew."

"Quiet, Elizabeth!" Isobel didn't hear the rest of the countess's reply as they moved away, but it was not the countess's venom that stung Isobel, rather it was the air of indifference from Robert Langton as he passed her that branded itself on her mind.

The day had been longer than anticipated, and the Earl looked forward to an evening alone with his mistress. He had returned late from Leicester but still presided over the festivities as required, despite his wife's waspish demeanour. Once he might have enjoyed the antics displayed for his pleasure; now, however, he found his palate jaded by too many years spent at the Royal Court: the tumbling men were predictable, their jollity false.

Felice behaved appropriately enough, he gave her that, and he could find no fault in the role she played. Even when she leaned towards him and, placing her long-fingered hand on his in a gesture of mutuality, whispered, "Have your whore removed from this castle, my lord," she had smiled, and none would have known of it but he. Robert, on the other hand, on whom he could normally rely for sound company and lively wit, had been distant all evening. He had made his excuses and retired to his chamber early, and it was to his own that the Earl now headed, glad to be away from them all.

"Eat, Isobel." The Earl watched her pick up a fragment of pike and then put it down without tasting it. "Are you not hungry?"

She shook her head.

"Perhaps I should not have sent you the sweetmeats; they have stolen your appetite." He waited for a response. He was getting used to her silences and did not let them gall him as they once did. "A little wine will help. Spice it well."

"I have no douce powder."

"No matter. It is best freshly made and with red wine, not white."

"And no grain of paradise, my lord, and little nutmeg."

"There is all that you need by the fire. Come." He waited for her to join him by the fire and sat down. Resting his head against the carved back of his chair, he watched her self-conscious movements. She set his heavy cup on the hearth and the flagon on a trivet by the fire to warm and picked up the spice grater. "Did you do this for your father?" he asked.

"Yes, my lord."

"And did your mother instruct you?"

She clenched the whole nutmeg between her thumb and fingers, the air filling with the fragrant woody scent of it as she drew it across the grater. "Yes."

Light from the fire blushed warmth against her skin, deepening the cleft between her breasts, gilding the curve of her eyelashes. He wanted her to tilt her face towards him, to reward him with her smile. If he could turn back the tides of time, he would have wooed her, won her with kisses and promises. But time had eroded his patience and cast its own long shadow, and he had been as much in its grasp when he first took her, as she had been in his. It changed nothing.

"You will have everything you need, Isobel," he said quietly.

She yelped as her fingers slipped, her skin catching on the metal teeth, sending the nutmeg rolling under his chair.

"Show me," he commanded, holding out his hand. She continued to kneel before the fire, head bent over her hand. "Show me," he said again, dropping to his knees next to her and taking her hand in his. "You seem," he said, holding her fingers to the firelight, "in need of physic." Her tagged finger glistened with blood, and he lifted it to his mouth, feeling her desire to pull away from him running in tremors down her arms. "You taste of honey and spice." His voice dropped. "Do I frighten you? I do not wish you to be frightened of me."

He pressed his thumb into the cup of her hand, opening her fingers like the petals of a flower, and kissed her palm, breathing in her scent. She tried to tug her hand away, but he held it firmly, now bringing his mouth to her neck, following the taut tendons to her collarbone as they flinched at his touch. Salt sweat glazed her skin, her pulse like a tambour beneath his lips.

Reaching behind with her free hand, she grabbed the first thing she came to, swinging it around with all her force.

"No!" He intercepted the wine cup within inches of his head. "Do not fight me," he warned, prising the cup from her fingers. Then, as if puzzled, "Why do you fight me?"

She glared back at him with a mixture of alarm and antipathy, and he wanted to extinguish that hate, quench the fire of her hostility. He lowered the cup and released her. "Once — a long time ago — I shared wine with another from this," he said, turning the handsome fluted beaker in his hand. He retrieved the nutmeg and held out the cup. "Continue."

Isobel finished grating nutmeg, selected the cardamom, clove, ginger, and cinnamon. She added grains of paradise and galingale, grinding and combining the ingredients. The Earl did not try to engage her further in conversation, but the weight of it hung between them as tangible as smoke. She strained the fragrant wine into the cup, then held it out to him wordlessly and without meeting his eyes. He pressed it back into her hands. "Drink," he said.

"I have not poisoned it, my lord!"

A rare smile turned the corner of his mouth. "I did not think you had. Drink. Share it with me."

Reluctantly, Isobel took the vessel, sipped once, then handed it back.

"More," he insisted.

She drank again.

The Earl lifted the cup and drank, the muscles of his throat pulsing strongly. He wiped his top lip with his forefinger and bent towards her. "Do you see these?" He tapped the painted images. "Do you know what they represent?" She shook her head. "They are an allegory from *Roman de la Rose*. You have heard of it? No? As *The Romaunt of the Rose*, perhaps?"

Isobel flushed. "My mother forbade it mentioned."

He was surprised. "Did she? Her father had a fair copy of the *Roman*, a gift, if I remember, from a Burgundian after the battle at Cravant. It is more eloquent in the language of its birth."

"She did not say, and I never met my grandfather."

"No, he must have died before you were born. I did not know him well." He considered her for a moment. "Finish the wine."

"I have had enough, my lord."

He pressed it into her hand. "Finish it, Isobel."

She did as bidden.

Taking the cup before it slipped from her hand, the Earl cushioned it in his. "This was made as a loving cup." With the tip of his finger, he traced the twining stems and outlined white petals. "The rose is the flower of virtue men desire and their thorns all that stand in the way of the love that Nature, as God's intercessor, decrees. Do you understand, Isobel?"

She shook her head and put a hand on her brow as if to steady herself from the potent effects of the wine.

"Man cannot help but interfere with Nature, but Man's construct falls short of perfection and tarnishes all that he touches. But Reason would have us believe otherwise. Man is all Reason. Reason kills love." He sighed. "And where would you be but for Reason, Isobel Fenton?" He cupped her chin and brought her face around towards his. "Dreaming in your garden, or wed to Thomas Lacey? That is something at least from which I have saved you. Perhaps one day you will thank me for it."

She twitched her head free of his hand, scowling.

"Or perhaps not," he amended. He held out his hand to her. "Help me disrobe; this collar makes my neck ache if I wear it too long. Here…" He lifted it from his shoulders and placed it over her head. The heavy gold links, separated by caranets of enamelled flaming roses and a central motif of his own noble house, rode the ledge of her breasts unevenly, and he adjusted the collar so it sat in a uniform curve. He rested his hand against the warm skin of her neck. "This jewel was the gift of the king; it looks well on you." He bent to kiss her, but she made to remove the collar. "Let it stay," he insisted.

"I should not wear it, my lord."

He kissed the length of her collarbone, easing the dress over her shoulder and exposing her neck to his mouth. "Why not?" he asked, untucking his belt with one hand and releasing it to the floor.

"It is not meet that I wear the king's gift."

"I will decide what you wear, and it pleases me to see you in this. You look like a countess."

"Let me go, my lord," she pleaded, her voice stretched thin as she pushed against the wall of his chest that yielded no further than the depth of the deep brocade.

"Do not fight me, Isobel, this is not a battle you can win." With a hint of regret, he said, "It is too late for that."

The bed hangings swayed to the Earl's steady rhythm, and each motion pressed the jewelled discs into Isobel's skin. It wouldn't be long now; she recognised the signs of his building tension in the muscled traction of his jaw and the intense focus of his gaze. She could not look at him. She closed her eyes.

"*Ave Maria gracia plena dominus…*"

"What are you doing?" he breathed heavily against her neck, his movement increasing.

"…*tecum benedicta tu* —"

"Stop it," he said, urgency thickening his voice. "Look at me, Isobel."

She opened her eyes but fixed them on the painted tester of the bed above her rocking to his thrusts, anywhere but at his face inches from hers.

"Look at *me*," he commanded, his breath shallower now, building.

She turned her eyes — angry blue-green pools flooded with liquid hate — and through clenched teeth recited, "…*in mulieribus et benedictus fructus ventris tui ihesu…*"

He clamped his hand over her mouth. Feeling the pad of his thumb against her teeth, Isobel bit deep, tasting blood. He drove hard, once, and collapsed, breathing heavily.

"*Amen*," she finished.

He rolled from her and onto his back and sucked at the punctured pad of his hand. "Why?" he asked, when he had recovered enough to speak. "Why do you fight me?"

"Who am I?"

"What in Jesu's name are you talking about?" The light from the pricket wavered as he turned onto his side to look at her. "What do you mean?"

Almost absent-mindedly, she fingered the flowered collar. "Today, my lady would not look at me, and I heard her refer to me as 'it'."

He grunted and lay back again, folding his hands behind his head. "She has a spiteful tongue; it is of no matter."

"When I came here, I was Isobel Fenton, daughter of Sir Geoffrey Fenton, granddaughter of an earl. My servants called me 'my lady', and I was promised in marriage to a man who would give me his name, a title, and a place at his table. Now I am 'it'. I am no one. I am invisible."

The Earl brought his arm down with a thump. "This is fanciful nonsense —"

"Is it?" She sat up, the great chain bouncing weightily against her. "This is who you are," she said, lifting the central caranet with his coat of arms in vibrant enamels out to him as evidence. "All who know you call you 'my gracious lord' and bow and do you courtesy."

"You are a woman —"

"I am *nothing*! I have no place in society. I am no man's daughter, sister, wife, *mother*... What I had — my estates, my servants, my ... my *virtue* — you have taken from me, and I am left with nothing. I am not allowed to speak to Cecily, and Margaret will not even look in my direction. Lord Raseby once said that he wished me to meet his daughters, yet only yesterday he pretended not to see me and crossed the bailey to avoid me." She gathered breath. "I thought, when I came here, that I had lost everything that was ever dear to me, but I was wrong, so wrong, because I still had my father's name and my pride. Now I cannot even think of my parents without shame."

He grasped her wrist, holding her within his iron hand. "Do not think that because you —"

"What, my lord, will you tell me what to *think*, as well as what to say and do and wear?"

He let go.

"Will you keep me from sight when noble guests arrive, bringing me out at night to serve your *bed*?"

"You are my mistress."

"And what is that but an unpaid *whore*." She controlled herself and let her voice drop. "And when you tire of me," she said, "what will you do with me then? Will you let me go home? Will I have a home to go back to, or will it have passed into another's hands as I seem to have done?"

A rigid line set up in his shoulders, and she wondered whether she had gone too far. She waited for his backlash, but instead he replied evenly, "I have not taken your estates. You could not have managed them yourself, and the choice of husband your father made for you was ill-advised. I said that I would oversee your manors in place of your father, and I have done so."

"But I *haven't*," she said bitterly. "They are *my* people, and I have a duty to them as much as you do to yours. While you play the good lord here, who presides at festivities at Beaumancote? Who will crown the King of Misrule and wash the feet of my servants as my father did before me? They wear my colours, but will they do so if they know in what circumstance I live here? Will they also wear my *shame*?"

"Do you hate me so much?" he asked in a low voice.

She looked at him, startled by her own outburst and his insight. Clasping the linen to her nakedness, she retreated into silence.

"You better go to your room," he said, pulling the covers back and handing over her smock.

Lifting the gold collar from around her neck, she laid it on the bed next to him and, gathering the rest of her clothes, let herself out of his chamber.

Surprised to see Isobel return so soon, Ursula roused herself from the stool. She took Isobel's clothes and, wrapping her in a soft mantle, left her by the fire while she took the ewer from its trivet, poured warmed water into the copper basin, and laid clean washcloths next to it.

Ursula touched her fingers to her own chest. "My Earl is displeased with my lady?"

Isobel looked down and saw faint imprints across her breasts where the collar had lain. She shook her head. "Perhaps, but he did not do this."

"My lady is displeased with me?"

"No. Why, should I be?"

Ursula played with her beads. "My lady was upset yestermorn. My lady would not speak to me."

"Oh. No, Ursula, it is not you. I am not upset because of anything you have done."

"Perhaps it was my lady…?" Ursula fished, uncertainly.

As much as Isobel would like to have held the countess responsible, a part of her— the bit which paid heed to caution and level-headed justice — could not find it in her to do so. "The countess is within her rights; my presence wounds her. I cannot blame her for hating me."

"She will not forgive you," Ursula cautioned. "She never forgives those who offend her."

"What do you mean?"

Ursula started rocking back and forth, twirling her bead with vexed fingers. "I may never speak of it."

"Ursula, what is it? Tell me. Did you cause the countess offence?" Ursula's eyes swivelled. "What did you do?"

"My Earl … I must not say…" She raised a finger to her lips.

"You were his *mistress*?" Ursula must be ten years older than the Earl, if a day, and if he was old at nigh on thirty-five winters, she was *ancient*.

"I comforted him. In the days before his marriage. So handsome, so sad. She must never be mentioned … never, never…" Her head swayed from side to side.

"Who mustn't — the countess? What happened? I thought that the countess would not allow the Earl to keep a mistress at the castle? Why are you here?"

"My lady was very angry and wanted me punished, but my Earl gave me a dowry and found me a match — a merchant from Hull, not a gentleman. George was a good husband, kind. He gave me my son, a strong boy. When my husband died, his nephew took the property and left me with nothing. No land, no land…" Ursula sang softly. "My Earl heard of my distress and let me live here until my son comes for me. My beautiful boy."

"What is your son's name?" Isobel asked gently.

"Edwin." Ursula gave a wistful smile. "He is a little younger than you. He will be apprenticed now." She began cooing and rocking, and her hands played with the beads at her neck, twisting, pulling. "I will be sent from here… I will be beaten. My son must come. Where is my boy? Where is he?"

Isobel looked with pity on the woman muttering and moaning incoherently and wondered if that was what would become of her one day once the Earl had tired of her — or the countess held sway.

CHAPTER TWENTY-THREE

It had been some time since Robert Langton had an appetite for the chase. Even had he not still been in mourning, he was kept occupied with other, weightier, considerations that hung heavily on his time, Isobel Fenton not the least. He slammed his heel into his boot, secured the buckle, and stood to receive his hunting belt with the serrated boar knife from Martin, his esquire. He had thought better of her — if not his brother — and perhaps that explained the depth of his reaction.

He rammed his arm through the sleeve of his quilted jack, and his finger caught the lining and bent. He swore savagely, and Martin backed off, but his wrath was directed inwards. Whom was he trying to fool? Himself, obviously. Still bound in its protective slip of leather, the gift he had so carefully chosen lay on the aumbry where he had tossed it on his return from seeing his nieces. It looked as he felt: unwanted, disregarded, chewed up and spat out like gristle.

Had he made his interest clearer before he went away, would it have made any difference? Would she have waited for him? Could he blame the girl if, plied with his brother's undoubted charm, she had succumbed? After all, he had offered her nothing in the way of a promise, though what she thought she might gain from her lover in the long term he could only hazard a guess. Perhaps she had been innocent in the seduction?

He took his felted hunting cap from Martin's hand and crammed it on his head as he strode from the room with the lad hurrying to keep up. Perhaps he was deluding himself. And, while he was in the mood for self-interrogation, had he even realised how he felt about her?

Waiting in the bailey were the esquires and servants of the Earl's guests and their wives, and he hoped that his brother's annual Yuletide boar hunt might return his humours to their relative balance. Grim-faced and pulling on his gloves, he greeted his brother with a nod. He noted the Earl sported vibrant greens, whereas he wore plain greys, and wondered whether it was in consideration of his dead wife or a reflection of his state of mind. Either way, he pitied the boar that might find itself in his sights.

Robert had rejected the caparisons bearing his arms in favour of the leather bards attached to his horse's belly and chest to ward off tusks and brier, and he now ran his hands over them, checking they were secure. Keyed by the atmosphere of heated expectancy, the animal's hooves struck the flags, and Robert soothed the mare as he adjusted the straps. He flung himself into the saddle without waiting to be helped. "What are we waiting for?" he muttered under his breath.

"My lord..." Martin indicated with his head the dark-robed figure of Nicolas Sawcliffe scurrying down the steps towards the Earl, who was already mounted and making ready to leave. He spoke rapidly and handed something to him. The Earl glanced at the item, then slipped it inside the breast of his tunic. Raising a gloved hand, he signalled to the Master of Hounds waiting by the inner gate, and the company moved in a varicoloured mass of men, women, horse, and dog, carrying their noise with them. Robert caught his brother's eye, waiting until the last of the mounted guests had passed before pulling his horse's head around and joining him in the weak winter sun.

"I did not think you would be riding with us this morning," the Earl remarked. "I have seen little of you these past days." He clicked his tongue, and his horse, eager to be off, skittered forward.

Robert caught up as the Earl brought his horse under control. "And I thought you would be too busily engaged in other pursuits to take time to hunt."

"Do I detect your disapproval?"

"I was surprised, that's all."

"By my choice of mistress?"

"That your wife would tolerate her under the same roof. I note that Felice rides out today."

They passed under the arch of the gatehouse and crossed the moat to be met by the baying of scent hounds tugging at their leads on the other side. Surrounded by the wives of their guests, Felice held court with Elizabeth on her bedecked palfrey, with Dalton looking as if he wanted to be on it with her. On her own horse and to one side, Margaret huddled into her furs, looking insignificant.

"Felice makes a point of it for Dalton's benefit and because she knows it irritates me. The women will only go as far as the ford. They will dine there and watch their entertainments while we ride on."

"I am surprised you have not included Mistress Fenton in the hunt," Robert said caustically.

The Earl lifted his brow. "I almost did," he replied. "When we are beyond the ford and women's ears, I have something to discuss with you."

"Oh?"

He tapped his chest at whatever lay concealed there. "Later," the Earl said, spurring his horse into a trot.

Despite the early hour, the town's inhabitants gathered in doorways and hung from windows to watch their earl and countess pass through the streets of the town. This was a well-attended tradition, made more popular by the rarity of the spectacle, for the Earl kept his woods — stocked with boar — jealously guarded.

By the market cross, the company halted while mass was said and the hunt blessed. The Earl received the customary Yuletide homage of a hogshead of wine from the citizens, and in return pledged his good lordship for the following year and the gift of meat from the day's hunt for the poor. This ritual, solemnised by convention, he and his brothers had watched their father perform in the years before his death. Passed from father to son in perpetual bondage between the lord and his people, at what cost would it be broken? This unity that represented the relationship between Christ and his people, the obligation of lord to his king, vassal to his lord, the bond between father and son. Or brother and brother.

This time last year Robert and his wife had looked forward to the birth of their child as they celebrated the coming of the Saviour in their own home. Now his wife and child lay rotting in their stone-cold tomb, his great hall bereft of its lord and devoid of cheer. So he had returned to the home of his childhood. Had he hoped that he might find some comfort here? He looked at the faces of his kin: his brother, lordly and attentive to his duty; his countess, playing the role of dutiful wife; Elizabeth, on the eve of a well-made marriage, and Margaret, neither betwixt nor between, but soon to be wedded to an ox.

Who could guess what the next year would bring? If any of them foretold the future, would they wish to face it? Divine it as they might from the conjunction of the stars, only God knew what lay ahead, and He would not tell. Each one of these people here, whether lord or merchant, master or apprentice, made plans, but what was the point if, on the turn of the Wheel, all hopes were made futile? His brother had placed his future in the hands of a child and seen it drowned in a moment of neglect, and he had fared no better. Masses were said and candles lit for the boy's soul, but in the years since his son's death, the Earl had not spoken about him once.

Gifts made, pledges undertaken, the hunt moved on. Sun graced the roofs, and the clearing sky brightened, bringing a cooling wind from the east. From the town gate and across the fields, the hunt picked up speed.

Recent rain had left the ground mired and the ford swollen, but beyond the trodden trackway, virgin ground lay firm under hoof. Robert urged his horse towards the thickets where the shaggy-coated scent-hounds bayed. Entering the undergrowth, his vision broken by trees, he followed the song of the dogs' pursuit as horsemen converged on an area to the west. He searched for his brother and saw him yards away. As Robert brought his horse about to join him it reared, almost throwing him, as a dark bulk crashed through the stems and hurtled past.

"*Rob*!" the Earl called.

"I see it," he yelled and, steadying his horse, set after it, ducking the branches whipping his face and leaving the sounds of the pack behind. Side by side he rode with his brother in relentless pursuit until the boar zagged sideways and under the hooves of the Earl's horse. Two strong-limbed alaunts emerged barking from the ambush of a hidden dip, and the Earl wheeled around.

"It's mine! *Spear*!" he bellowed, catching the boar spear flung to him by the huntsman and, digging his spurs into the flanks of his horse, riding after it as it darted towards the heart of the wood.

Between the trees, Robert saw his brother draw back his arm to strike, but lost sight of him at a rise in the ground. Breaching the crown, he saw that the Earl had been forced around the limbs of a fallen beech, and taking advantage of the unexpected lull, the boar doubled back and now made its way up the rise towards him. "*Here!*" But it was too late to take the offered spear. The boar thundered towards him and, without a moment's hesitation, Robert threw himself from his saddle onto the animal as it passed him, falling awkwardly but momentarily knocking it off balance. Heaving to free itself, the boar's head whipped around, curved tusks carving air, snorting. As the Earl flung himself from his horse readying the spear, Robert managed to align his dagger and, with an upward thrust, drove the blade into the animal's throat. It kicked wildly for a few seconds, then lay still.

"Clean kill," the Earl remarked, panting, leaning on the spear and surveying his brother's blood-specked face and blazing eyes. "Did it get you?"

Breathless, Robert shook his head. He tugged to free his dagger, wiped it on the boar's greasy fur, and inspected the blade. "I thought you had it cornered back there," he said, replacing the blade in its sheath. The Earl's prized French griffons had caught up and were baying wildly for blood. The Earl shoved them away.

"So did I," he said, collapsing beside Robert and scrutinising the carcass. He whacked the coarse black fur of the hefty shoulders. "Not a bad day's work for a boy; you have earned your keep. I might even let you sit with me at supper if you promise not to wipe your nose on the tablecloth."

"And I might refrain from splitting your guts for the dogs," Robert returned, dryly.

The Earl grinned. "Jesu, remind me to keep on your good side." He checked they could not be overheard. "While we are alone, I received this at first light. Sawcliffe intercepted it." Taking off his glove, he pulled the letter from inside his hunting jack and held it out.

Robert inspected the seal, took off his own blood-soaked gloves, and unfolded the paper. He read swiftly. "What makes Lacey think she will return?" He handed the letter back, and the Earl tucked it inside his clothes.

"She might have written a missive to give him the impression."

"Ah."

The ground beneath their backsides was cold and wet. The Earl shifted to a dryer patch of leaves. "I want you to escort Isobel back to Beaumancote."

"What! When?"

"After Lacey receives a reply from her, but before the turning of the year."

"No."

"Robert, this needs to be undertaken by someone I can trust absolutely."

"Then take her yourself."

"Hens' teeth! What demon's spat on your back? I'd get more cooperation from this hog." He nudged the beast with his elbow. "Escort Isobel Fenton to her manor, and I will ensure you are back here feasting before Epiphany. We will make it known she is to return — draw Lacey out of his rat-hole and drown him in his own guile."

"What makes you think he will be interested in her *now*?" Robert made to shove to his feet, but the Earl gripped his arm.

"You have made your thoughts very clear. If you will not see this as a request, I'll make it a command."

"When I swore allegiance to the Duke of Gloucester, you lost the right to command me."

"I am your brother and head of our family. It is your duty…" He stopped as Robert stared at the hand gripping his sleeve. He thrust it inside his glove and out of sight.

"What happened to your hand?"

"Nothing. One of the dogs…" The Earl gave a dismissive shrug and climbed to his feet.

Robert followed suit. "That is no dog bite; I am not a complete fool."

His brother waved to a handler to take the alaunts and griffons, whining for blood. "Cecily, then. We'd better have this animal unmade before the dogs decide to turn on their masters." He nodded to the waiting men and turned to fetch his horse standing nearby, fretful and wary of the hounds.

Robert trod the mauled undergrowth after him. "And it is too big to be the bite of a child. Do not tell me it was Felice? You barely speak to one another, let alone frequent her bedchamber, and the wound has not festered enough to be of her making. I am in no mood for guessing games; what are you not telling me?"

"There is nothing to tell." The Earl gathered the reins in one hand and righted the skewed stirrup, readying to mount.

Robert felt the sweat around his collar chill. "*Isobel* bit you?"

"I did not say so."

"Nor do you deny it." Robert felt a slew of disappointment. It might be expected in a brothel, but from the daughter of Geoffrey Fenton? Why not? Even harlots had fathers. "Your games are your own business," he said, acidly. Then, as an afterthought, "Why did she bite you?"

"What matter is it to you?" The Earl put his foot into the stirrup, but Robert took the reins from his hand.

"Did you force her?" He might have missed the muscle work in the Earl's jaw had he been looking the other way, but Robert had known his brother for too many years to mistake the telltale signs. "You *forced* her? What did you think you were doing!" Astonishment gave way to anger. "Do not turn your back on me!" He slapped the horse's rump, and it startled a few steps out of reach.

His brother turned darkened eyes on him. "It is done; leave it."

"What do you think you were doing? You have the choice of women without forcing a girl. In God's name, you took an oath to her father to protect her; is this how you repay him?"

"You do not understand..."

"Of all the men..." Robert interrupted. "Of all the men I know, you are the last I would have suspected of resorting to *rape*." His face twisted.

"It is not how it seems."

"*Seems*? You mean she gave you signs you mistook for consent, is that it?"

"No."

"Is that why you want her taken back to Beaumancote, as a salve to your conscience? And what then — you arrange for some poor milksop to marry her in haste in case she carries your bastard child as evidence of your infidelity?"

"You must understand, Rob," the Earl repeated, "I cannot let her go. You are to bring her back when Lacey has made his move."

"You are right," Robert said, "I do not understand."

The Earl's fingers dug into Robert's arm, preventing him from leaving. "You must believe I did not set out to wrong her, but now that I have, I will not … I cannot … let her go. I cannot turn back time. If I could … if I could have chosen a different path…" His voice thickened, and Robert had the impression that his brother was not referring to Isobel Fenton. "I tried to send her back once before, but she has unseated me."

Robert gave him a sharp look, but saw no hint of irony, only a sincere attempt to explain himself. "Then you have asked forgiveness?"

"She has no kin to whom I can make amends."

"I meant, have you asked forgiveness of *her*? She has no family, as you so rightly said. It is not her *kin* you have offended. You are her lord, and you can hardly ask it of yourself, although God knows you have much to confess." From nearby, the whining of the hounds gave way to the rending of guts and the iron smell of hot blood as the dogs were fed their spoils of war.

The Earl watched their frenzied movements and then said, "More than you can know."

"Why?" Isobel viewed the Earl with suspicion.

"It pleases me to let you go. Did you not say you wished to visit your manor?"

"But I may not stay there?"

"No, you are to return here where you will be safe, once the festivities are over."

"I do not understand. I can go to Beaumancote over Yule because it pleases you, yet I cannot stay longer because it is not *safe*?"

The Earl tossed his gloves on the table. "You will be safe enough while my brother is with you, but he can be spared no longer than that." He undid his plain hunting belt, soiled with years of blood and grease, a belt that meant business, not for display.

"Lord Langton will accompany me? Why?"

"Does it matter why? I thought you would be glad enough of his company." She opened her mouth, but he intercepted her question with an irritable, "Because I can trust him above all others to undertake this task. Why do you have to question everything I say? It is enough that I tell you what is to be."

She ceased plucking at her thumb and raised her chin in the combative way he found both annoying and oddly alluring. "My father taught me to question men's motives."

The scented water in the basin slopped over the side as he roughly scrubbed at his hands and pared grime from beneath his neat nails. He inspected them, frowned, and repeated the process. "It is not needful for a woman to question her hus… her lord; only to do his will." She started to argue, but he held up a wet hand, the tawny stoned ring blinking in the winter light. "That is enough. You will write to your steward and tell him of your intention to visit this Christmastide. You have your father's seal?" He was grateful that she merely nodded and did not feel the need to debate it with him. He dried his hands. "Give it to me." He expected her to take it from around her neck, but instead she took her purse from her girdle.

"My lord, how many will need provisioning? Should I say Lord Langton will be with me?"

"Write that you will come with a small escort of merchants — perhaps less than half a score. There is no need to mention my brother." He deliberately avoided her sceptical gaze and held out his hand. "Your seal, Isobel."

She fished in her purse for her seal but brought out her chaplet instead. She handed it to him to hold and dug again. The jet and coral beads hung over the cliff of his palm. He held them for a moment more, the pilgrim's glass bead swaying and then, without comment, laid the beads gently, almost reverently, on the table next to the paper. His hand rested over them, then, flexing his fingers and seeing her scrutinise his face, he said brusquely, "Where is your ribbon?"

"I no longer have it, my lord."

"Hmm, well it is of no matter. Write. I wish to have this sent before noon." He sat in his chair by the table and waited while she scribed the letter to Arthur Moynes. Checking it, he supervised its sealing with her father's matrix, then he handed Isobel her chaplet and watched her place it in her purse. He appeared absorbed in some memory, and it wasn't until she grew tired of standing, lifting first one foot then another to ease her aching feet, that he noticed her waiting.

"Isobel, you must take care when you are away."

"I go only to my own manor, my lord."

"There are many dangers we cannot foresee. Do as my brother commands and come back safe to me." He lifted her hand to his lips, held it briefly to his cheek, then relinquished it. "Keep to your chamber tonight; you will need to be rested, and there is much to prepare before you leave in the morning. Go, now," he urged as if, should she linger, he would change his mind.

CHAPTER TWENTY-FOUR

Isobel hardly slept that night, waking at the slightest noise and lying there as she imagined riding into her own courtyard surrounded by the stone and brick walls that had protected her childhood, welcomed by her own household, her own dog. But every time she felt her weighted eyes drift towards sleep, it was not Buena she saw, but the Earl. Consequently, when roused before dawn, she shook her sleep-befuddled head, murmuring "Bayna?" before she saw Ursula's ghost eyes looking at her from the shroud of her face.

The palfrey she had been given to ride negotiated the frozen cart ruts leading from the town in the pale hour before dawn, and Isobel concentrated on staying in the saddle rather than attempting conversation with Robert, who rode in silence beside her. They had barely spoken two words to each other, and the air hung chill between them. Ever since she had learned he would be accompanying her to Beaumancote, Isobel had wondered what they would say to each other and now, riding together, it became painfully apparent — it would be nothing.

Turning in her saddle, she looked again at the small group of strays that straggled after her, ill-matched and ill-dressed, and she wondered, not for the first time, why the Earl had sent them with her. *Merchants*, he had said, impatient for her to be off, *on their way to Hull, wanting safety in numbers on an uncertain road*. They didn't look like merchants; most were lean-limbed and broad-shouldered, and the one who wasn't had limbs that stuck out like the branches of a tree from a solid, ungainly trunk.

They rode without talking and, once beyond the town, watchfully, warily. Itching to know, she threw a quick glance at Robert, but he stared studiously ahead of them and, fearing his scorn, she swallowed her curiosity. Instead, she tried to make out the road ahead, distinguished from the strips of field either side by ditches and banks of rough-turned earth and last year's stubbled crops not yet burned.

The lanterns had been doused as soon as enough daylight lit their way, but darkness still clung around the horses' hooves, and the brightening sky only served to throw the ground into shadow. She squinted ahead. She remembered little of this road which she had travelled only once before at the height of summer, and the trees on the rise ahead of them were but faint memories of what they had been when clothed in green.

Robert ordered two of the men to take the road in front, and she watched them ride confidently up the rise ahead and beyond sight. Curiosity burst from her. "Who are those men? They are not merchants, are they?"

Robert rode a few paces more before answering. "Is that what you were told? No, they are not merchants."

"Well, then, what?"

"Men of my brother's retinue, Mistress Fenton, sent to keep you *safe*." He ground out the last word, and Isobel felt his reproof. "And one of my own, such as he is." He stared straight ahead, not inviting further comment, but the peace of the new day now broken, Isobel pressed on.

"And why do you go abroad in such apparel? You might as well be a servant in drab. No one will know who you are like that."

"Why indeed," he replied, acerbic.

She sucked her cheeks, stinging from his rancour. "I did not ask for you to accompany me," she whipped at last. "I made it clear I do not need you."

He swung his horse around without answering and rode to the back of the small group. Isobel cursed her incontinent tongue, her blind stupidity. She heeled her horse into a trot, then, fuelled by anger at herself, at the Earl, at everybody, kicked harder.

Robert looked around at the sound of hooves beating the ground as Isobel's palfrey, scenting free rein, galloped to the crest of the hill. Swearing beneath his breath, he wheeled to follow her, his bigger horse hammering the frost-bound road in pursuit.

"Isobel, *stop!*"

She drove her palfrey into a thicket of trees through which the wan road wound. He spurred his horse, catching up with her as they emerged from the trees.

"Isobel, whoa…" He grabbed the palfrey's reins, bringing it to a breathless halt.

Panting, she yanked the reins from his hand. "This is none of my making, I did not want *any* of it!" Eyes wide, her hood fallen from her head and with hair combed by the flight of the horse, she glared at him.

"I know."

She scraped hair from her eyes. "I had no choice —"

"Isobel — I *know*." He brought his horse around to stand by hers. "My brother told me. These past days I have thought of little else."

Bewildered, she shook her head. "If you knew, then … then why would you not speak to me?"

"Because of his shame — and my own." Momentarily, he avoided her eyes. "I misjudged you; I thought you had gone with him willingly."

"No!" she exclaimed. "I wouldn't — couldn't." It was her turn to look away.

"I should have known better than to think ill of you. I ask your forgiveness." Removing his hat, he bowed his head, the rising sun bronzing his hair. She felt a welter of loneliness and regret, so long suppressed, and said nothing in case her voice gave her away. He looked up. "Isobel —"

"No, please," she swallowed. "My lord, there is nothing to forgive. The Earl has never said, never asked…" This time she had to control resentment as it seeped from her.

"He regrets it, Isobel." He might have gone on, but voices preceded the company as they emerged from the trees at a trot. "Stay close," he said simply as they waited for them to catch up. "We must make haste if we are to arrive by nightfall."

At the ferry, they stopped briefly to rest the horses, stretch their legs, and dine on bread and cheese. Every few minutes Isobel scanned the road ahead and checked the passage of the sun. Signalling to the men resting some yards away, Robert stood. "Your manor will be where you left it." He smiled and held out his gloved hand to her. "Had we the wings of Mercury we could not reach it any faster."

She took his hand, and he helped her to her feet.

"It seems as if the closer we are the farther we have to travel."

"It always felt that way when I returned home to my wife."

Isobel withdrew her hand. She brushed her cloak free of crumbs without further comment and made ready to mount her waiting horse. "Do you still miss her?" she asked suddenly.

"Yes," he said.

By the time they reached the stone cross marking the ancient boundary to her demesne, dusk fast encroached upon the light and Robert increasingly relied on Isobel's knowledge of the land to find their way. As they neared the woods, eager to be home, Isobel urged her horse forward through the deepening frost, the full face of the moon casting light through the naked branches of the trees, marking the path.

"Not so fast," Robert cautioned as she pulled ahead. "Keep close."

"Why? I know this land. The way is through here, past the dip where the carter lost a wheel last year in the dew pond, and up the slope towards our fields. This frost will help break the turves." She faced the dark as if she could see the new-turned soil.

"Wait. Listen." He threw up an arm, and the string of horses behind them halted as he cocked his head, his forehead furrowed in concentration. Hooves — perhaps a pair of horses — riding towards them. He waved two of the men forward, taking Isobel's palfrey by the halter.

"What is it?" she asked, but he frowned her to silence. As the riders neared, light glinted on bare metal as the waiting men drew swords concealed by their travelling cloaks.

"Who rides there?"

Harness chinked as the horses came into view and were drawn to a standstill on the narrow track.

"Earl's men," the foremost rider said shortly, bringing with him the smell of man and horse sweat as he levelled with Robert. "The way is clear, my lord, all the way past Stather and the ferry to Alkborough."

"Why would it not be?" Isobel asked as they continued through the trees.

"I swore an oath to my brother that I would see no harm comes to you, and I always keep my word," he replied, having failed to answer her question.

They cleared the woods into open land sugared with frost under the ethereal moon.

"I can smell the river!" Isobel exclaimed, forgetting all caution. "There's Beaumancote!" She didn't need to persuade her weary horse. Feeding off her excitement, it strained against the reins and broke into a gallop at the touch of her heel.

"Isobel!" Robert called after her, but she was making for the light of the brazier marking the gatehouse, hooves ringing on the frozen road. He spurred his horse after her.

Movement on the battlements signalled their arrival. They came to a standstill just short of the closed gates as torches flared above them. Isobel made out a half-dozen heads silhouetted by the light, the glint of armour. Deep-throated barking issued from somewhere beyond. The rest of the company joined them, their swords once again hidden, but the gates remained stubbornly closed. She opened her mouth to call, but one of the watchers hailed them first.

"State your name and business."

Robert answered before she could. "We come in goodwill in the name of your Earl and the king."

"Which one?" came the biting reply.

Isobel threw back her hood, craning upwards. "George, do you not know me?"

There came a shout and a burst of activity, and heavy bars rasped from their sockets. The gates swung open. "My lady," her sergeant-at-arms panted as he crossed the moat's narrow bridge to them, "I did not know you."

"It would concern me more if you had and still denied my way. Why the caution?"

George scanned the night behind them. "My lady, please, make haste."

They rode under the arch of the gatehouse into the courtyard, and the doors swung solidly behind them.

"You are expecting trouble?" Robert dismounted, helping Isobel down and steadying her until she found her feet, numbed as they were.

George peered dubiously at him in the dancing light of the lantern's flame, then at the men behind them. "Aye, we might be."

From the tower door, an object bolted towards them, nearly knocking Isobel off balance in its eagerness. "Alfred!" Standing on his hind legs, the dog put its paws on her shoulders, and she hugged him while he tried to lick her face, and she laughed. "Get down, you silly dog!"

"My lady!" She looked around to see Arthur Moynes, hastily belting his cote as he bowed to her.

"Well met!" She beamed on seeing him. "We have been on the road all day and would raise the dead for a bite to eat." Her smile hesitated. "What is it? Is something wrong? Where is everyone? Where's Buena?"

"My lady, we did not expect you…"

"Did you not receive my letter?"

"A letter? No, my lady, not since Michaelmas. We sent word to the Earl when we had trouble but have heard nothing."

"When was this?" Robert cut in.

Arthur squinted at him in the uncertain light. "My Lord Robert? Forgive me, my lord, I did not recognise you." He bowed. "You are most welcome. Pray, if it please you, come out of the cold, and I will explain."

He hurried them through the courtyard and into the great hall, where none of the household waited to welcome Isobel home. It felt as cold and bleak as it looked: no garlands hung behind the dais; no preparations made for the Christmas feast.

"Arthur, why isn't Buena here? Where is she?"

"She is abroad at present, my lady. I will send word to her. If it please you, my wife will be glad to serve in her stead until she returns."

Deflated, Isobel nodded and huddled into her cloak. Sensing her disappointment, Arthur's face creased into deep folds, then he gave orders to the servants appearing like mice around them. "I will have the fires lit and food prepared, but my own chamber is warm if you wish to take your ease a while."

The remains of supper lay on a small table before a good fire. It was quickly cleared and a further chair, softened with her own cushions, brought to the hearth. Isobel sank into the nearest one and peeled off her riding gloves, holding stiff, cold fingers to the fire. Now here at home, where she had imagined herself so many times since she had left it, she felt almost a stranger, hollow inside, a shrivelled nut in its shell.

Tail wagging furiously, Alfred nudged her hand with his wet nose. "Is that your bone?" she asked him softly, and he dropped the old beef bone and settled beside her as if she had never been away. She felt like crying and was grateful when she could distract herself by washing her hands in the bowl held for her by Arthur's wife.

"This must be strange for you," Robert observed, once they held cups of warm ale. "It will seem different in the morning when you have rested." He noted her lips quiver as she raised her cup to drink. She was saved from needing to reply by her steward's reappearance. He bowed again.

"Fires are lit in your solar and the guest chamber, my lady, and supper will be ready shortly. My wife waits your instruction."

"Are my men provisioned?" Robert asked.

"They are, my lord. If it please you, they will be quartered in the servants' hall. On the morrow, I will send out for commons and such foodstuffs as befits your lordship, if it can be had this close to Yuletide."

"No," Robert said quickly. "I do not want my presence here made known. Buy what is needed for my lady's comfort and entertainment, and make much of her return."

"And if any should ask of the strangers staying here?"

"Say we are merchants and their servants resting for a few days over Christmastide on your lady's charity, but no more, and instruct the household to say nothing other than that."

"My lady?"

Isobel nodded. "Do as Lord Langton instructs, Arthur."

Robert rose and stood with his back to the fire.

Isobel stifled a yawn, then another, and the corner of Robert's mouth lifted into a smile. "Will you not go to your chamber and sup there at your ease?"

"You are a guest in my house —"

"And will be tomorrow. Let your steward tend me, and take your rest while you may."

Robert had no such thoughts of bed once Isobel had withdrawn. "Tell me why you raised the alarm on our approach. What has happened here?" he asked Moynes. The steward gave a rapid look to where Isobel had been moments before, which Robert interpreted. "You may speak freely; I act on behalf of the Earl."

Arthur licked dry lips. "My lord, what entitlement has the Earl to act for my lady?"

"Entitlement? Sir Geoffrey gave her into the care of my brother on his death, you know this."

"But, my lord," Arthur persisted, "that was to be until my lady wed. The contract was not made. Has the Earl petitioned the king for her wardship? Or for the lands to be placed in feoffee until she is married, perhaps, and her estates settled on her husband?"

"Nothing has changed. The Earl acts as her lord in all things as before."

"If you will forgive me, my lord, but it is *not* as before. Sir Geoffrey had an understanding that Lady Isobel would wed with Thomas Lacey, and Lord Lacey has been disappointed of that ambition. My lady is without a husband to guide her, and we are left without protection."

"That is not so."

"Then why did no relief come when we sent to the Earl? We lost two men from the village and a boy from this house last All Souls, and there is none to keep peace and administer justice. Our people have been harried, crops burned, animals taken. A widow was ravished in her own home…"

Robert held up a finger, and Arthur stopped. "You say you have sent messages to my brother and received none in return?" Arthur gave a short nod of confirmation. "So, they have been intercepted," Robert said almost to himself. "The question is," he fixed on the steward, pinning him with his direct gaze, "by whom?"

Arthur Moynes's wife blithely chatted away as she helped Isobel from her travelling clothes and poured water in which she could bathe. There had hardly been time for the fire to take the edge off the chill, but the familiarity of the surroundings was enough to ease the knot in Isobel's stomach, and the food served on her table, with linen embroidered by her own mother, did the rest. The woman was full of gossip, and Isobel learned of the unrest that had plagued the village and threatened the manor.

"But who leads them?" she asked, when Mistress Moynes stopped for breath.

"None's owned to it, my lady. Since Sir Geoffrey's passing, God grant him peace," she crossed herself, "people have not been safe in their own beds. And since Widow Robbins was taken, men have not let their wives and daughters go about as they used to, even on market days, not without a servant, and even then, only if they be armed."

"The Earl said he would protect my lands," Isobel said indignantly.

"He might well, my lady, but he can't be all places at once, and without a lord attending to manor business, who's to say *yay* or *nay* when some varlet comes asking?"

"I would!" Isobel scrubbed the last of the journey from her feet and held them in front of her to be dried. "These are *my* lands and *my* people; it is my duty to protect them."

Mistress Moynes patted Isobel's feet dry and offered up her red embroidered slippers warmed by the hearth. "There now, I'm sure you would, my lady, and Sir Geoffrey would be proud to hear you say it."

Isobel baulked. "I mean what I say. I can govern my lands and order their protection as my father taught me."

The woman sat back on her heels, towel still in hand. "But not without a husband, my lady; none would follow your rule."

Isobel rose abruptly. "Why not? Wives oversee their estates when their husbands are absent; widows their own affairs. And the old queen commands men and *they* obey."

"But they do it in their husband's name, my lady, and men have more knowledge of these things than we do. Besides, they say the old queen is more man than woman and was bedded by Satan. Now if you were married —"

"But I am not. Nor like to be," Isobel added, a touch sourly.

Mistress Moynes waggled her head, making her chins wobble beneath her coif. "Now, now, Lord Thomas is not the only fish in the river. He can't be blamed for making a match elsewhere once he came into his inheritance, can he?" She wavered as she saw Isobel's expression. "My lady? Did you not know?"

Isobel sat down again with a thump, knocking the basin with her foot. "When?"

"This past fortnight, to a lady of some fortune and good birth. Her brother is close to the Duke of Clarence, and there will be advancement in it for Lord Thomas, I dare say. Did you not know?" she said again.

Why did it matter what Thomas did anymore? Those ties had been severed the moment the Earl had decided it, and no potion or prayer would remake that which was broken. Or was her sense of abandonment only heightened by his new wife's birth and her own shame? Probably, she thought, wearily, and wondered whether Robert knew, and if he knew, would he care? Should she tell him? He had probably retired to the guest chamber by now. It would present a chilly walk, and she had only just thawed after the ride. Had she the presence of mind, she would have ordered her father's chamber prepared for him as more fitting and closer to her own. She found herself looking at her bed as she tried to decide what to do, but the image conjured was unintentional, and she a sudden warmth flooded her skin. She was too tired to make any decisions. The only decision worth making at this time of night was whether to clean her teeth or if they too, like other concerns, should have to wait until morning.

CHAPTER TWENTY-FIVE

Something other than sunlight woke Isobel. It took a moment to realise where she was and another to ecognize the woman standing at the foot of the bed between the pated hangings.

"Bayna!" Painful joints and a tender backside didn't prevent Isobel from launching herself from her bed and feeling the blades of her servant's shoulders rise as she folded her arms around her and held her tight.

Eventually, Buena unhooked Isobel and stood back to examine her. Isobel did the same. Little about Buena had changed, but the hair modestly coiffed was greyer than it had been, and her skin sallower. For all of that, Buena's eyes were still as shrewd as ever, and Isobel found herself a child again beneath their stare.

Kneeling back, Isobel asked, "Where have you been? I missed you last night." Emerging from the comparative warmth of the hangings, she swung her legs over the edge of the bed and hopped onto the cold floor. Buena draped a mantle around Isobel's shoulders. "I didn't know where you were. I was worried about you."

Buena touched Isobel's cheek and gave a smile of regret, then, in a flurry of gestures, mimed. Following the story, Isobel's frown deepened. "You were at market and some boys threw stones at you? Why?"

Buena shrugged, then, indicating her face, pulled an imaginary hood over her head and made a scurrying motion with her fingers.

"You had to hide? And nobody stopped them? Who were these boys? They must be punished!"

Buena shrugged again, then continued to gesture.

"There is no law now that Fader is dead, is that what you mean? Has the king not made a new appointment to the Justice of the Peace?" Shaking her head, Buena confirmed the assumption. "When I return to the castle, I will tell the Earl — " Buena clapped her hands sharply and shook her head. "There *must* be order, Bayna. How can I keep quiet if you and my people cannot go about their business in safety? I couldn't bear knowing you lived in fear and there was nothing I could do about it." Isobel traced the stem of thread leading to an embroidered gillyflower on the yellow bed hanging. "The Earl will listen — I am sure of it." She shook herself from a moment of reverie and became briskly busy. "I will dress. I want to see my garden before breakfast and catch John slumbering in the shed."

Isobel ran down the path towards her garden with Alfred bounding along beside her breaking blades of frozen grass beneath his heavy paws. She reached the walls, paused, and quietly pushed the door open. She could hardly have expected to find it as she had left it, clothed in abundant green, but nor had she imagined the untarnished beauty of the fragile frost lying upon every white-brushed stem and branch.

Standing there motionless, she absorbed her sleeping garden, bathing in an unspoiled world devoid of the sin of knowledge that lay beyond its walls. Dipping her hand in the nook in the wall, she crossed herself and, revelling in the peace, took the path towards the arbour where it seemed a lifetime ago she had talked with Robert in the heat of a new day. John was nowhere to be seen but, had she found him there, she might have sent him away because there was nothing more to be done: the soil had been sifted to a fine tilth, plants pared and divided, sacking wound around the pots and urns. She could find no fault in it, and she felt ... surplus.

Alfred set up a furious barking by the gate. She swung around and stood on the tips of her toes to see beyond the trellised walls. For a second she didn't recognise the plain-coated man until he looked up, and she sang out in relief, "You found me!"

Robert located her, returning her unguarded welcome with a broad smile. "And where else would you be but in your garden, little dove, where we first met?"

Her smile dissolved. "I'm not that girl anymore."

He joined her. "Oh?"

She had not meant to say anything quite so dramatic, but it had spun out of her mouth before she could catch it and tame it with pleasantries. Now she had started, he waited for her to continue. "Everything here reminds me of how I have changed, because *it* hasn't."

He looked around them, his breath hanging in the air, then back at her. "Do you think you have changed so much? Do we alter because our circumstances are not what they were when we first met? Are we so fickle, Isobel?"

"I feel ... different. Do you not? Is it not disquieting to wake every day without knowing how it will end?"

He gave a short laugh. "I thank God that I wake at all." Then, seeing her anxious face, "Is it the changes you see around you that frighten you, or the differences you see in yourself?"

She couldn't give him an answer, but then nor did she have one for herself. He came nearer, enough to touch her if he leaned a little closer, but he kept his hands by his sides, and she wound hers into her thick skirts.

"Do not think you are any less Isobel Fenton because of what has happened to you over these past months. Not all change is for ill."

"How can you say that with your wife and child dead!" she exclaimed, regretting it instantly as pain visibly swept over him. "Forgive me!" she gasped, covering her face with her ungloved hands. "I did not mean… I never meant…" She felt her hands prised away and held within his own.

"I know, but it cannot alter the fact of their death. Their lives were not mine to keep. I have masses said for their souls and will have a chantry built to their memory, and pray my wife's time in purgatory is short because I can think of no great sin she has committed against God. That is all I can do, Isobel, the rest is beyond my control. I have to look to my own soul as you must look to yours. We do not know when we might be called to account for ourselves."

"And who will ensure masses will be said for *me*? My sins heap one on the other each time I…"

His loosed his grip and instead laid a calloused hand against her cold cheek, rough on smooth. "They are not of your making. I would have masses said for you, Isobel, but may it please God you will not be taken from this world before time, nor be punished for my brother's offences against you."

"And the Earl? Will you pray for him?"

He dropped his hand, and she felt the cold replace it. "He is my brother. For all the wrongs he has committed, I owe him loyalty."

"And your love?"

"Yes, that too. There is much that he carries — things you do not know; things he keeps even from me. Pray for him, Isobel. Forgive him."

She looked around her frozen world and found nothing inside her resembling the sun. "He has taken everything from me. I have nothing left to give."

"That is not so. You can forgive him. For your own soul's sake, you must find some pity for him."

She looked up into his earnest face, at his bluer than grey eyes, and saw in him the man that might have made her happy. "I cannot," she whispered.

The clack of the garden door alerted them to another's presence. Robert stepped away as Buena appeared, looking right and left until she spotted them. Her gaze stiffened.

"Is breakfast ready?" Isobel asked.

Buena nodded, and Isobel led Robert back through the garden, leaving unvoiced thoughts and unspoken desire behind them as the bell rang from the church tower.

"You are very quiet," Robert observed later.

Isobel kept her finger under the blurred word, trying to make out the individual letters. "I cannot read this."

"Let me try." She moved her finger out of the way so that he could read the section in the bailiff's manorial accounts.

"*Item. One dozen hides.*" He pushed the records closer to her. "Do you find your manor's affairs in order?"

She was not sure whether she detected a pointed cadence to his question but, at the quirk of his brow, smiled. "All is in order. The Earl said he would ensure the estates are well-run, and they have been," she conceded. "Arthur says the harvest was plentiful this year, despite the trouble since."

"Then why the silence?" He leaned closer so as not to be overheard. "Are you angry with me?"

"No, it isn't you. I heard last night that Thomas is married and he —"

"Why did you not say before?" he interrupted. "When did he wed, do you know?"

"But two weeks since, Mistress Moynes said, to a widow — Margery Cowdon of Newark, although her family is…" she searched for the name, "Blaise." She halted as his eyes flared at the mention of the name. "Why, does it matter?"

"Yes, it does." He tapped a finger against his lips in thought. "Blaise. Are you certain? This changes everything. Martin!" His esquire, dressed in the clothes of an apprentice and scratching his neck where the rough collar chafed, appeared.

"My lord?"

"I have letters to be sent in haste. Have a man well-versed in arms stand ready."

He pulled clean paper from under the pile of estate documents in front of Isobel, took up the quill, and opened the lid of the boiled leather ink box.

"To whom do you write?" Isobel asked.

"Shh, let me think." He smiled as he heard her *harrumph* of frustration but continued writing. Folding the letter and threading the ribbon, he removed his seal ring from his finger and found Isobel had already lit the taper ready for him to melt the wax. "My thanks," he said, then dropped blobs of wax onto the ribbon and sealed the paper. He then repeated the process with a second letter. He looked around to see Martin waiting with the tree-trunk of a man who had accompanied them on the journey. He handed the first of the letters to his esquire. "Martin, take this to the Earl without delay. You might be followed. Use any force necessary to accomplish your task. Do you understand?"

"Yes, my lord."

"And, Martin," he added as the young man took the letter, "exercise all caution; good esquires are hard to find."

Robert scribed a name on the second letter, blew sifted sand from its surface, and gave it to the other man. "Taylor, hand this to the Duke of Gloucester and none other. Wait until my esquire is beyond sight of the manor before you set out, and then take another road. Say nothing to anyone, and let no one see you leave."

Isobel waited until they were alone to question Robert further, having sent Buena on an errand. Only Alfred kept them company, and he lay stretched out by the hearth sound asleep. "Why did you not send one of my people; do you not trust them?"

"I do not know them, nor to whom they might have given their loyalty in these past months since your father died."

"They would not betray me!"

"Betray you? Perhaps not, but what can you offer them? Affinity? Advancement? Protection? These are not yours to give. My brother sought to keep these lands out of the hands of those who would use them against the king. While Thomas Lacey had any hope of marrying you, he had no cause to move against you and your people. Now that he has wed elsewhere, he will seek to extend his hand over your lands in whatever way he can, including buying the loyalty of those who served your father."

"So that is why I am here — to draw Thomas out? How stupid of me. I thought it was a moment of kindness."

"Do not judge my brother too harshly. His duty is to the king, but he also wants you safe."

"So I can continue in the exalted position of his mistress when I could have been a *wife*? My parents wanted me to marry Thomas Lacey, to have his title, to live here where I was born.

Who is the Earl to have rewritten my life so conclusively?" She pinched the skin of her hands, more frustrated than anxious.

"He is your lord. He makes the decisions by which others will judge him. This is not about your wishes, Isobel, about *your* life; this is about who sits on the throne and governs all our lives and lets us live in concord. Who do you think ensures you can tend your garden in peace, or your people their cotts? Who ensures fines are levied, foreign goods taxed so that fat English merchants, not French ones, can fill their bellies and those of their servants? I want a strong king on a strong throne so that you and your servants can live in safety, and if that means you are disappointed of a match with Thomas Lacey, then that is some small sacrifice to make for the common weal of this land." He slipped his fingers over hers, keen to impart his message. "My brother, Isobel, has put loyalty before his own happiness. Do you think he set out to take you from all this? Your father begged him to protect you if he died before you were married —"

She pulled her hand from beneath his. "Protect me? Hah!"

"Your father did not know then what my brother came to suspect — that Lacey could not be trusted to keep his oath. My family have borne the brunt of Lacey vengeance."

Isobel recalled the rolling head, Thomas's ashen face, and thought the Earl had exacted his revenge right enough.

As if Robert read her thoughts, he went on. "Lacey's wife — are you aware of whom her brother serves?"

"Mistress Moynes said he is in the Duke of Clarence's service."

"He is," Robert said grimly.

"But why is that such a bad thing? He is still the king's brother, just as you serve the Duke of Gloucester."

"Tell me, do you trust your dog not to bite you?"

"Alfred? Yes, of course."

"And what if you had a dog that bit you; would you trust it a second time?"

"I would be more cautious."

"And the third? I assure you that my brother does not give any of his dogs a chance to bite him a third time — not even twice. Once, he might view as an error in training, but twice, a fault in its temperament."

"But I thought the differences between the king and the Duke of Clarence were healed. Has the king not forgiven his brother for what happened in the summer and for marrying the Earl of Warwick's daughter without his permission?"

"There was little His Grace could do about it, and he has made the best of the situation, but the cause of the rift is far from healed. The queen's family, Isobel," he said when she shook her head, puzzled. "The king can only go so far to allay Warwick's grievances — and there are many — but he will not put aside his queen, and the queen's family lick Warwick's wounds with salt each time he comes to Court, or another office is granted to them, or an advantageous marriage made. And there are so *many* of them," he added, wryly. "Most of all, the king made his own match rather than the one negotiated by Warwick with Louis of France. In doing so, not only did Warwick lose face, but all the advantages that would have come to him had the French match been made."

"Surely that is in the past, and the Earl of Warwick would be well advised to make up with the queen's family?"

He answered her question with one of his own. "Until he has a son, who is the king's heir?"

"The Duke of Clarence, so there's all the more reason for peace between them."

"And to whom is Clarence married?"

"Warwick's daughter — Isabel."

"The queen already has two sons by her first marriage, and daughters by the king. It is only a matter of time before she gives the king an heir, and then where will Clarence and Warwick be?" He sat back and let her work it out for herself.

"You think the Duke of Clarence will turn a second time?" she asked slowly.

"Have you met him? He can be a bit of a tick sometimes, so bloated with his own sense of worth that he's likely to fall off the dog he's latched onto only to wonder where the next meal is coming from. I have the impression he wants more than he's been given, and the king has given him more than he deserves. He bleats about it loud enough to any who will listen. Warwick, though, is another matter altogether. If he were my dog, I'd muzzle him and keep him on a lead if there's any now strong enough to hold him."

"Why?"

"The king cannot afford to lose his support. Warwick holds much of the north right here…" He opened the palm of his hand and gripped the other until his knuckles whitened. "With Anjou waiting to take advantage of the least dissension, Warwick can play either side and still win. The question is, will he?"

"Will he?" By the hearth, Alfred grunted in his sleep, and Isobel tucked her toes into his warm fur.

"Warwick," Robert began, his voice low and the firelight illuminating his face, "is on one side only — his own. There was a time when our families fought together — yours as well, Isobel — and being kin stood for something. Now," he shook his head, "the same blood colours different rivers, and he who swam with one lord in the morning might swim with another by night."

"There," Isobel said, simply, "it is as I said before — change."

"And in that I agree you are right. When brothers cannot trust each other, what hope is there for the world?"

"My father said something similar. You serve the Duke of Gloucester, though, and you have not said where he stands."

"Have I not? Well, now," Robert sat back, lacing his fingers together and watching her, "you have met His Grace; what did you make of him?"

"I thought him..." she chewed her lower lip as she considered the question, staring at nothing in particular, "...clever, funny — and kind when he had no need to be."

"Ah, yes, Cecily's ball."

"I was rather thinking His Grace might have had *me* muzzled, since I managed to offend him twice."

He smiled at the image. "Gloucester is a fair judge and will have seen any fault in you as one of training, not of character. As for His Grace's own, he is someone I would trust. He keeps his word, unlike your Thomas —"

"He's not *my* Thomas," she butted in.

"No, he's not, nor ever was, I think," he said, viewing her with an astute eye. "This trouble in the village, around your manor, has arisen only recently."

She stopped wriggling her toes against Alfred's flank. "And you think Thomas might be behind it?"

"Maybe. And, if so, does he act in his own interest, or has his action been sanctioned by another?"

"The Duke of Clarence?"

"Perhaps. My brother refused Lacey an office because he did not trust him. I thought him mistaken, but now I am not so sure. If Lacey believes his future lies with Clarence, and Clarence turns against the king, it is manors like this —

strategically placed by a river, the head of a valley, or next to a port with a minor, a widow, or an heiress — that will be most vulnerable. Either way, you are not safe here. We will leave first thing in the morning."

"But I have only just returned home. I cannot leave my people so soon!"

"I am sorry, Isobel, but I cannot guarantee your safety."

"Because you promised your *brother* you would keep me so?" she retorted.

"Because I would never forgive myself if anything happened to you." His eyes held hers, dark except for the reflection of the firelight. He leaned across the table and took her hand again, and this time his thumb pushed under the edge of her cuff and stroked her wrist.

Her fingers pressed against his, and her lips parted, willing him to act. "Isobel, I want you to know —" He broke away as the door slammed open and Arthur appeared.

"My lord … my lady," he said, breathless, looking from one to the other, unsure whom to address first, "riders are approaching; Lord Lacey comes."

PART FIVE

CHAPTER TWENTY-SIX

Thomas Lacey didn't come alone. A woman's shrill voice preceded him into the great hall, accompanied by his laughed reply. They appeared at the door and stopped when they saw Isobel waiting by the fireplace, dwarfed by the room, and alone.

"Lord Thomas and Lady Lacey, my lady," Arthur announced.

Thomas pushed past him, looking around as if he expected to see someone else. "Isobel," he greeted her, extending his hand, "we came as soon as we heard the news of your return."

"Thomas," she replied coolly, "I did not expect to see you. You should not have taken the trouble in such cold weather."

"It was no trouble; we were on our way to our estates across the river," the woman answered, bringing eyes the colour of plum stones, and as hard, from surveying the hall to inspecting Isobel.

Isobel returned her look, noting the sumptuous clothes made for impressing, not travelling. She felt plain and unkempt by comparison. "Then I will not keep you from your journey."

"But now that we have taken the time," Thomas intercepted, unhooking his fur-lined cloak and letting it drop to the floor in front of Arthur, "we will bide a while. It has been months since we last met, and I have had some good fortune since then. Isobel, this is my wife, Lady Margery."

Isobel inclined her head; Margery Lacey did not, nor did Thomas return the introduction. Instead, he took possession of her father's chair by the fire, warming his hands and looking smug. Isobel waited until his wife sat down before sitting herself and giving instruction for hospitality to be served.

"I always liked this chair." Thomas patted the wooden arms and sat back, satisfied. "Yes, much has changed since we last met. Of course, now that I have my title and, with the addition of my wife's manors, am kept busy much of the time, I do not pass this way as often as I once did. I had forgotten how small this manor is and how inconvenient the location."

Isobel bristled. "I am gratified that, despite your great good fortune, you have seen fit to include a visit to Beaumancote on your lengthy sojourn around your estates."

Oblivious to her sarcasm, he waved an airy hand, his full sleeves wafting the scent of horse and river her way. "It pleases me to do so. Later, we will visit my brother-in-law… I expect you will have heard of my wife's brother — Edmund Blaise?"

Isobel frowned. "Blaise? There was a burgher named Blaise in Hull from whom my father used to purchase wine —"

"*Lord* Blaise," Thomas said, his reddening skin contrasting uncomfortably with the pea green of his houppelande. He adjusted his fashionable chaperon where it had slipped over one eye.

"The wine was *very* good," Isobel remarked, mildly.

"Lord Blaise has the favour of the king's brother, the Duke of Clarence," he continued, "and will rise even further in his service."

"Yes, I believe His Grace likes good wine —"

"He is not a *merchant*, Isobel," Thomas snapped. "You should show me more respect. I am not without influence, and I can make things easier for you, defend you, if I choose."

"I did not realise that I was in need of protection, Thomas," Isobel said evenly. "From whom would you seek to protect me?"

Realising he had overstepped the mark, Thomas shuffled his shoulders and rearranged the tail of the gaudy chaperon, his clothes reflecting expanding ambition. "Now that I am the king's Justice of the Peace for this area, it is within my influence…" He paused. "Did you not know?" he asked, as Isobel gripped the arms of her chair. "His Grace was pleased to confer the honour upon me. It seems I am trusted by the king to perform duties your father once held but which the Earl saw fit to withhold from me."

Margery Lacey had spent some time examining the contents of the hall from where she sat, and she now rattled a fingernail against the ale cup she held, testing the metal. "I see you are still unwed, Mistress Fenton."

Isobel, still reeling from Thomas's revelation, managed only to open her mouth before he responded. "Perhaps the Earl will find you an esquire who will turn a blind eye to your father's humble station in return for … this." Again, he indicated her entire world with a dismissive sweep of his hand. Considering his wife seemed to be rearranging Fenton arras and hangings in her mind, Isobel thought his candour overplayed.

"Perhaps I will keep my lands and not marry at all," she retorted. "But it is none of your affair, whatever I choose to do."

He smiled. "As if you have a choice in the matter."

Seething, Isobel wanted to wipe the smirk off his face, but she could think of nothing to say given that what he said was entirely correct.

"I see you still have this old cur," Thomas said, nudging Alfred's prostrate form with the toe of his boot. Alfred grunted and rolled over, emitting an odour of fire-warmed dog. "It's as ill-mannered as it is ill-bred. I thought it would have gone to his grave with its master."

Without warning, Isobel stood. "You have far to travel; I will not keep you from your journey."

Thomas rose more slowly, standing closer than she found comfortable. "As Justice, I have a responsibility to keep the peace. There have been disturbances in this area recently — bands of villains taking advantage of the lack of lordship. I do not want there to be an escalation, Isobel. I do not want to hear that you have had the misfortune to be waylaid by a rabble — you, or any of your people. That would be a shame." He raised a finger and drew the back of his nail down her cheek. "I would not wish to see anything happen to you, not after all the years we have known each other." He smiled as she jerked her head away. "By the way," he said, clicking his fingers for his cloak, "I understand you travelled with a group of men yesterday."

"Merchants. Journeying to Hull," she said, but a little too quickly.

"Merchants." Thomas nodded. "There is safety in numbers; a wise decision." He failed to say for whom, and Isobel had the distinct impression he suspected more than he was saying. Perhaps Robert was right, and someone in her household had sought a new master after all. She glanced at Arthur, but he maintained the meticulously blank expression he tended to reserve for people he patently disliked, and she was certain she knew where his loyalties still lay. He raised an eyebrow at her behind Thomas's back, and she felt her trust vindicated.

"My lord, this way." Arthur urged his departure and, before joining his wife waiting less than patiently by the door, Thomas bowed shallowly to Isobel.

"Mistress Fenton." On rising, his gaze fell on the dais and the painted screen that backed it. "Perhaps, when we meet again, your circumstances will have altered." He stared at the screen as if he could divine what lay behind it, before taking his suspicions and leaving Isobel and her manor to themselves.

"I think he suspected you were there."

Brushing his sleeves free of lime, Robert smiled without mirth. "He was fortunate there was so little room behind that screen that I could barely move, or I'd have made my presence known with my dagger in his stomach. I always wanted to know what a pike looks like gutted." His expression softened. "Do you regret not marrying him *now*?"

A cobweb clung to his shoulder and Isobel picked it from the wool. "No."

"However, besides braying of his good fortune in marrying that ferret of a wife, he made it clear you are not safe here, and now at least we know how he intends to go about his business."

"Do we?"

"Yes, we do; he will cloak misdeeds under the mantle of the law."

"Oh. Yes, of course."

"What is it?"

She raised her shoulders briefly. "Nothing. Only … we were friends once."

"I'm sorry, I forgot. That is something else that has changed, isn't it?" He touched her cheek swiftly, gently, as if unsure how she would react. He cleared his throat and became purposeful. "We must prepare to make a move as soon as I receive word. It is too late to leave today, but I want you out of here no later than tomorrow morn."

"My father improved the defences, and these walls are stout. Can we not stay?"

He must have detected the note of desperation that coloured her voice because he levelled his, speaking with an absolute certainty that she found difficult to counter. "Lacey means you ill, Isobel, and he intends to drive you from your lands. I have not the men to maintain these defences long enough if an attack is sustained. And there is at least one in your household who is not to be trusted, I am convinced of it. We can leave at dawn under cover of darkness when none will expect it."

"But we cannot leave unobserved. If we stay for the feasting, there will be so many people that we can slip away when no one will notice."

Robert looked at her, calculating the odds. Finally, he said, "Two days, then. In the meantime, I'll make what preparations I can for the protection of your people, although they are safer here with you gone. The Duke of Gloucester will inform the king of the unrest in the area, and I will ensure enough men are sent to secure your manors. Until then, my only concern is to take you to where I can warrant you will be kept from harm."

"Back to the castle," she stated, bleakly. "Did the Earl know this would happen if I came back here?"

"I do not believe my brother would have deliberately put you in jeopardy, Isobel; I would not have agreed to bring you if I did. Come," he smiled encouragement, "make preparations for the festivities as if you will be here to enjoy them. You are lady of this manor and I a merchant resting on your hospitality. I would that I had chosen a wealthier trade, and then I would not have to suffer this wool. It itches like fleas."

The freedom seemed all the more cruel for its brevity. Isobel ordered the household as she had done the previous

Christmas, when her father had been alive and all well, sending out to the farms and villages the customary invitations to share the feast, and hating the duplicity. When a lull afforded itself later in the day, she retreated to her solar with Buena and explained what she must do.

"If I had a choice, I would stay here with you and my people; but I have to go back. Rob… Lord Langton says it is safer for you all if I leave."

Buena narrowed her eyes at the mention of his name. She made two fingers dance and entwine, ending with a quirked eyebrow.

Isobel sighed; was there any point in denying it? "No, Bayna, I wish it were, but it is not Lord Robert." Isobel held her maid's eyes until they widened in understanding, swiftly followed by rage. She failed to see her hand until she felt it across her face. Isobel gasped, too surprised to be angry. "Why did you hit me?"

Buena had taken herself to the other side of the room, her arms curled over her head, and from inside the cave of her arms came a muffled grunting Isobel had never heard before. Shock gave way to concern.

Isobel approached her. "Bayna?"

The woman's shoulders shook to each guttural sound. In all the years Buena had been her maid, Isobel had never known her to cry. She placed a tentative hand on her back, but Buena spun round, eyes gleaming.

Isobel drew back. "It is not what you think; I did not go willingly."

Slowly, Buena straightened. Reaching for the ballock knife at her waist and taking it from its tooled red sheath, she picked up the nearest bolster and drove the blade into the heart of it, ripping upwards and scattering feathers in billows. She shook the cushion, threw it to the floor, and ground her heel in its face. She stood, glaring, re-sheathed the knife, and went to Isobel, crushing her to her bony chest.

Shaking, Isobel said, "I thought I would die of humiliation and, if I could have done, I might have taken a knife to him — or to me. All I could think about was what my mother would have said and the shame I have brought to my family."

Buena gave her an odd little look, then tapped Isobel's shoulder and gestured to the room, pulling her brow into a question.

"I have to return. Even if Thomas were no threat, the Earl will not let me go. Lord Robert is instructed to bring me back, and he will not go against his brother's wishes." She dropped her head, and Buena, placing her hands gently around Isobel's face, lifted it and held her with her own bronze orbs. Isobel smiled into them a little sheepishly. "Yes, I still like him; does it show? Ah, only to you, that is as well. If things were different, perhaps…" She trailed off into a bitter-sweet smile.

Buena studied her sombrely, then unhooked the dagger in its decorative sheath, and placed it in Isobel's hands.

Isobel pushed it away. "No, I cannot take it! My lady mother made a gift of it to you."

Buena clucked at the back of her throat, but Isobel insisted. "My mother gave it to you for your protection, Buena; you might need this more than I do. The Earl cannot take my honour again — what is done is done."

The first of the messengers returned the following afternoon, tagging onto a band of itinerant mummers hoping to enjoy generous Fenton hospitality and a warm hearth in return for entertainment on the eve of Christmas. Philip Taylor found Isobel and Robert in her father's privy chamber with Arthur, detailing measures to ensure the security of the estates. Robert took the stained leather bag from his outstretched hand and the message it contained. "Were you followed?"

"There was a man on the Lincoln road I thought had no business there, my lord, and another asking questions of a lad driving geese, so I took a byway to avoid trouble." He removed his plain felt cap, crushing it in his hands. "There is more…"

Robert waved him to continue. "Matters of security are as much the concern of this lady. Speak freely."

"My lord, on my return I took up with the mummering folk now lately come, and they were saying they don't rightly know what'll come of their entertainment on Fenton lands this time next year."

"Why not?" Isobel asked.

"On account that they don't know who'll be in possession of them, my lady."

"Meaning?" Robert pressed.

"There are rumours that these lands should have been made over to the new Lord Lacey on his father's death, and, begging your pardon, my lady, that they should never have been granted to Geoffrey Fenton in the first place."

Isobel started from her seat. "That is ridiculous! These were part of the estates given to my father as reward for his loyal service. These are Fenton lands now."

"Aye, my lady, but Sir Geoffrey left no heir —"

"*I* am his heir; my father knew the law better than anyone. The land and titles were not entailed to any other."

Robert intervened. "The point is not the legitimacy of the claim — that is for the king and the courts to decide — but who has the most to gain from spreading these rumours."

Isobel sat down in a flounce, seething. "Is that not obvious?"

"Yes, it is, but why now?" He struck the unopened letter against his thumb once, twice. "Taylor, go and find some food and rest, you'll be needed later. And for Jesu's sake, put aside your sword and hide that rondel; no merchant's servant I know goes about so obviously armed."

Taylor broke into a toothed grin and slid his dagger around his back and out of sight beneath his riding cape. He touched his fist to his forehead, gave a short bow, and left.

Robert broke the duke's seal and opened the letter, frowning and fingering his chin as he read. He looked up. "Master Moynes, what documents and charters are there kept here relating to the granting of these manors to Sir Geoffrey?"

"What there is will be kept in the strongroom, my lord."

"Bring them, and let none know of it. Then have the horses prepared for our departure as discussed."

"So soon?" Isobel queried when her steward had left them. "Tonight, and without waiting for word from your esquire?"

"His Grace urges us to return to the castle without delay." He handed her the letter and she read it quickly, pulling a face at the final remark. She gave it back. "Taylor's report confirms more than our suspicion. There is one question yet unanswered: Lacey might believe he has a claim to your lands, but what makes him think the king will honour it? Unless…"

"Unless he does not rely on the king to regain possession of it," she finished.

"But which king?" Pushing his chair back from the table, unsmiling, Robert remarked, "We have delayed too long. How soon can you be ready to leave?"

CHAPTER TWENTY-SEVEN

The Earl hadn't been paying attention to the cavorting of the jongleurs tumbling across the floor of his great hall until he became aware of a stippled orange ball hurtling through the air towards him. He caught it without thinking. Raising the hand in which he held the clove-stuck orange, he received the applause of his court, and tossed it to a lurid jongleur who bowed to the Earl without ceasing juggling multiple objects with ease. Laughter flowed around him, some of it genuine.

"Well caught, my lord; I did not think your mind was in it," Felice commented, accepting a posy of gilded roses from a tumbler with customary grace.

The Earl adopted the benign expression he was expected to wear at the antics playing out in front of his daughter and her new husband. "And where else would I be on Bess's wedding night, but here with my loving wife?"

"I thought you might be able to tell me that, my lord, since Raseby's girl has not taken her eyes off you all evening."

He followed the direction of his wife's gaze and found a pair of limpid brown eyes staring back from a not-uncomely face belonging to Richard Raseby's second eldest daughter. He thought his dogs more alluring. He adjusted his position. "I do not wish to argue with you, Felice. I did what you asked. Isobel Fenton will be gone for the duration of the festivities." He finished the last of his wine and looked to his page for a refill. The wine had taken the edge off the evening nicely, and he wasn't looking to re-sharpen it with his wife's tongue. That would not stop Felice from trying, though, he thought with resignation. "Your cup is empty," he remarked, ensuring it was filled. He winced at the blaring of shawms, but anything subtler would have been drowned out by the clamour of his guests.

"The wench might be gone from here, but not from your mind; she has possession of you..." Felice reined herself in as she saw his mouth tighten. "Bess has made a good match," she commented. "Dalton was a wise choice, my lord. That little infatuation with the Duke of Gloucester passed; Bess will make a dutiful wife."

"She looks happy enough," he agreed. "So she should. Dalton dotes on her. Look at him, he cannot take his eyes off her. Is she prepared for tonight?"

"Of course. She is rather too eager for modesty."

"Dalton will not mind that," he laughed into his cup, "and it will help secure him an heir." He downed the wine in a long draught, keeping half an eye on Raseby's girl, who was looking more appealing by the minute. Willing she might be, but he needed her father's goodwill more than he wanted her, and he looked away and saw Margaret clapping at the scene before them. It would be her turn soon enough. He shook the image of her wedding night from his mind rather than dwell on his choice of husband for her.

Conjurers presented Elizabeth with lilies. From the centre of their purity, they plucked an egg, breaking it into her hand and releasing a chick. Elizabeth squealed with delight and Dalton grinned, no doubt envisaging planting his seed into as fertile a flower. The thought of their tumbling warmed the Earl more than the wine, and he regretted agreeing to send Isobel away. He closed his eyes, imagining what she might be doing now, seeing her hair unfurl before him, feeling her skin against his.

"You are tired, my lord." He opened his eyes to find Felice — long-necked and softened by wine — stirring his blood despite himself. A raucous cheer echoed around the hall as

Dalton and his new wife were brought before him for his assent.

Rising a little unsteadily from his chair and descending the two steps of the dais, he kissed his son-in-law on both cheeks and his daughter on her forehead in blessing, and then watched them hustled by lewd-tongued youths and giggling attendants from the hall towards their bridal chamber. In a rush of memory, he recalled his own wedding night and then, in a deeper, darker echo redolent with pain, another.

At some point after St George had accepted the favour of a ribbon from his stubble-chinned lady, and before he pierced the heart of the dragon with his sword, Isobel had given up trying to follow the tortured plot, which had digressed from the theme of the year before. Instead, she applied a smile of beneficence while inwardly squirming with nerves. She had lost count of the number of times she had checked to see whether the agreed signal had been given, but Taylor, capped in red, stood as stolidly as he had before, and she writhed with impatience. She received the gifts of her servants and tenants and returned their small generosity with the largesse for which her father had been known. She accepted their thanks and best wishes, and the priest had blessed the evening's entertainment, before the garishly exuberant mummers launched into their robust parody.

Arthur kept close and watchful. At intervals, he ordered more ale be distributed and, by the time the dragon lay flailing on the floor in front of her to the crude delight of the audience, most wouldn't have noticed if she had disappeared. Still she waited, interrogating each face in the room as if she could fathom who, amongst them all, could betray her. The entertainment now complete, the dragon had been rolled to his feet and shawms, tabors, and a hurdy-gurdy set up strident melodies inviting people to dance.

"My lady." She twitched as Arthur touched her elbow; Taylor had removed his cap. Making her movements inconspicuous, Isobel eased from her chair, slipping behind the screen and through the door in the back of the hall obscured by it.

Changing quickly, she avoided Buena's eyes as she was helped into one of her servant's plain dresses, laces tightened over her breasts, and her hair coiffed. Finally, wordlessly embracing and tears pricking, she picked up the small bundle prepared for her, and left.

Robert waited by the stables, stamping his feet and blowing on gloveless hands. The courtyard had enough of a scattering of people to make Isobel's hooded presence go unremarked. He surveyed her. "You look suitably attired for the respectable wife of a merchant."

"And for an earl's mistress?"

He didn't reply but, bringing her hood further forward so that it obscured more of her face, briefly brushed her cheek with his fingers. The memory of his touch lingered long after he had turned to lead her to the horses, simply saddled and breathing fire into the still night air.

"Where is my horse?" she whispered, as one of his men, still dressed as a servant, brought a speckled rouncey of dubious stock for her to mount.

"It would be a little obvious if your palfrey was seen to be ridden out by a merchant's wife," he pointed out. "This will serve you well enough." He glanced over his shoulder as a tumble of revellers exited the great hall, shouting, and George with one of his men hurried over to curb their enthusiasm before it spilled over into a brawl. "Make haste," Robert said, helping her mount and then swinging into his own saddle.

Nudging his horse's flanks, he took advantage of the confusion to lead them under the gatehouse and into the night unremarked.

Isobel waited until they were beyond hearing and away from the light of the braziers silhouetting the castellations of her home. The waning moon ghosted towards the horizon, and only the lanterns, held by the men, marked their passage. Isobel caught up with Robert. "Are we going to Ferriby?"

"We're not — they are." At his signal, his men branched off on the road east to Barton, taking the lanterns with them and plunging the three remaining riders into darkness.

They watched the pinpoints of light trace an uneven passage down the road, then Robert swung his horse around to face west. "We'll leave the horses at Stather and take the ferry up the Trent. I sent Taylor ahead. Master Moynes says we should be able to pick up a horse at Crowle, and we can then take the road towards Tickhill. The roads might be watched, but I doubt the rivers will be. Take a care, the ground is treacherous, and without light we will be hard-pressed to find it."

"I know it well enough," Isobel said. "I can smell my way to the river and there is enough moonlight to find the path."

His teeth gleamed. "I forget you come from here."

"Yes," she said softly, feeling a sudden swell of pride, "this is my land." And with a surety she hoped was not misplaced, she led them along the high river cliff by the river Trent and down towards the village sitting on its banks.

Curfew had yet to be called, although the ferryman needed persuading to leave his ale and the warmth of the tavern. He smelled of river mud and permanently damp wool. "In need of the ferry, is ye?" He squinted at them in the yellowed light of his horn lantern. "And where'll you be goin' this Yule Eve, master? Your'n servant is tight wi' his words and I'll be needin' knowledge o'it before I'll carry ye."

Robert pressed a coin into the man's scabby hand. "Your duty does you justice…" He caught Isobel's slight frown and broadened his accent. "And rightly so. We travel to Crowle." The lantern was raised towards Isobel's face, and Robert pushed the man's arm away as she flinched from it. "Not so close, man; her head aches."

The ferryman lowered it. "Oh, aye, Crowle, is it? An' you'll be living there?"

"Yes —" Robert began, getting irritated.

"Nay," Isobel interjected, "at least not living there, but staying with my sister and her 'usband for Christmastide." She remembered to flatten her vowels enough to be plausible.

They reached the jetty where Taylor waited for them hunched to his ears in his cloak against the cold, and the ferryman, hooking the lantern on the pole at the bow of the boat, offered his roughened hand to Isobel. She stepped into the unsteady vessel. "I'll not be takin' anyone to Crowle, not this night nor none other. Eastoft is as far as I'll take 'ee, and Eastoft'll be a-ways to go. Cost a bit an' more, master, this being Yule Eve an' all. A fair bit more."

Robert sucked his cheeks and deposited a small bag in the upturned palm. The man felt the weight and emptied the contents into his hand, squinting in the low light. "I trust that will take us to Eastoft, unless you think it too much —"

"It'll do, master; it'll do." He tipped the coins back in the purse, secured it beneath his greasy cap, and pulled a well-worn hood over the lot. "Who'll that be yer stayin' with agin?" he asked Robert, who concentrated on getting in the boat without unsettling it or revealing the sword beneath his cloak.

Isobel answered, "Master Reed."

"Oh, aye? Is it now? Cast off, master, if ye will — aye, the stern rope. That'll be Reed the chandler, will it?" the ferryman asked as he cut the water with the heavy oars, heaving the boat towards midstream.

"Certainly not! It's *Master* Reed, the guildsman," she said quickly before Robert was pinned into an answer. His inquisitiveness seemingly satisfied at last, the ferryman concentrated on steering a course upstream, sending a shock of drops gleaming in the lantern light into the surge of dark water around them.

Hunkered down in the shallow bow, Taylor kept watch for movement up ahead on either side of the Trent, while Robert scoured the blank, black banks behind them. At one point, as they swung west onto the dyke connecting the Trent with the Don, Isobel thought she saw a light on the east bank, swiftly smothered, and the ferryman grumbled about "them poaching folk".

Poaching folk or not, Robert's relief was palpable as finally he helped Isobel ashore. A lone light burned on the jetty at Eastoft. Dawn was still some way off, and no one saw them climb stiff-limbed from the boat.

"He was too curious for comfort," Robert said when they were trudging up the slope away from the river with Taylor watching their backs.

Isobel breathed shallowly in the bitterly cold air. "My father had to ensure the proper use of the ferries; it was one of the offices he held. The man was doing as instructed."

"And who *is* Master Reed?"

"He supplies the finest linen this side of Hull, and he married again not long before my father died. The ferryman might know his wife, but he'll not be able to check whether she has a younger sister staying with them in the next few days, by which time we should be safely past Crowle, shouldn't we?"

"We should," he confirmed. "God willing we'll have you safe before long."

Scant buildings straddled the road through Eastoft, and the inn with its reeking stables stood towards the centre of it.

Robert sent Taylor ahead. He returned some time later. "The place looks secure enough to my eye, and there's a nag spare, if you'll have it, though it is a sorry creature and I daresay it'll cost more'n the price of ale."

"I daresay it will," Robert said, "but we have little choice until we make Crowle, and the sooner we are there, the happier I'll be. We are made more obvious by our very presence this Yule Day, yet obscurity is what we seek." He tested the hard ground with the toe of his boot. "At least the frost will make it easier to cross the moor. It should make it passable in places until we find a firmer road. We will head direct to Crowle. I doubt Lacey will have enough men to watch all paths between here and Thorne, but I want to cover as much ground as possible before we rest."

Stroking the pony's greying muzzle, Isobel nodded. "I'll keep up. I used to walk miles with Thom… when I was younger. Anyway, this poor thing will need carrying herself."

The pony from the inn could hardly be called one. She had seen too many years of scant grass and heavy loads. Tutting like a woman, Taylor had checked her shoes and mud-caked fetlocks in the dim dawn light. Still, she was the best available first thing on Christmas morning and would be better than nothing if it came to it. The pony looked as she felt — shabby, grimy — and had seen better days.

For all of that, Isobel turned her face, eyes shining in the light of the rising sun, towards the men. "Follow me," she said, and stepped out lightly across the frozen ground.

They made good progress along the narrow trackways that marked compacted ground. Taylor led the pony, and Robert and Isobel walked side by side, almost touching, but not quite.

"Not so fast," Robert warned, smiling nonetheless at her enthusiasm. "There are many miles to go yet."

But she wanted to run, she wanted to fly and spread her arms to embrace this new-found freedom. The whole sparkling world had expanded to encompass this one place in her heart where he had sown a grain of expectation. If she touched it, if she pressed her fingers to her breast through the thick layers of wool and linen, she could just detect the rapid beat of hope.

Keeping a watchful eye on Taylor's sturdy back, Robert sought her hand, and they walked together like this, content in each other's company.

They stopped mid-morning long enough to eat coarse bread and green cheese and to re-strap the wrappings on Isobel's shoes. By the time the sun neared its zenith, the soil was beginning to thaw, the crystalline world gradually turning brown and green and the rough-rutted ground giving way to mire. Oily water oozed at every step. Her hem soaked, Isobel slipped again before Robert could stop her. He hauled her wet-skirted to her feet.

"Ride a while," he insisted, "and keep a look out ahead."

Accepting defeat, she allowed herself to be helped onto the pony's dipped back, thankful to rest her legs.

The sun was dimmer now as if bathed in milk, and cloud clung like smoke on the horizon. Tiny birds ceased stripping the remaining seeds from the tall sedges lining the paths and fell silent. A head higher than the men, Isobel stood in the stirrups to look ahead.

"What can you see?" Robert asked.

"Scrub, mud, and marsh mostly, but that might be a building over there and perhaps a church tower. It must be Crowle."

"We can rest up there. Where there's a church there will be an inn, or alehouse at least, and hot food and a fire. But Lacey might have the road watched. Taylor, go ahead and make certain the way is ... unencumbered."

"Take the pony," Isobel suggested. "It will be quicker."

Reluctantly, Robert agreed. He held out his arms and she slid into them. "And make clear you are armed; this is no time to make a play of it."

Taylor grinned, throwing his cloak back to reveal his sword and rondel and patting them fondly. "Aye, my lord, I'd best be doing what I'm paid for and, if you'll beg pardon, mistress, that isn't holding ladies' skirts."

Isobel raised a tired smile. "My servant will be pleased to hear it; she feared for her position."

"We'll bide here." Robert looked for somewhere they could rest in the monotonous landscape of sodden strips and ditches. "Be as quick as you can. I do not like the look of that." He nodded towards the thickening clouds creeping perceptibly closer.

"Aye, my lord. I'll be back as soon as it takes me to down a cup or two o' ale." With a grin, Taylor slapped the pony into an ungainly trot.

Huddling closer, Robert dislodged Isobel's hood as he drew his mantle about her. As he replaced it, Isobel felt the merest breath on the crown of her head like a kiss. She raised her face to find him regarding her and that single look warmed her more than the thickest cloak ever could.

They had almost concluded Taylor's jest had been a promise when at last he reappeared, driving the pony at a gallop and leading a dun-coloured animal by its rein. He seemed to be checking over his shoulder every few yards until he was close enough to hail them.

"Better give Crowle a miss, my lord; there's only a cold welcome and sour ale to be had and not much of that." He halted the mud-spattered mare, her flanks heaving, and tugged the other forward. "The churls who thought they'd challenge me were kind enough to give up this nag with a little persuasion, but they might want 'im back." He looked over his shoulder again.

"How many?" Robert asked, taking the stallion by its halter and following Taylor's line of sight.

"Two that I know of, maybe more. But there's been trouble. Your young squire took a beating yestermorn and left Crowle only this day."

"Martin? He's hurt?"

"Not enough to put him in his grave, but surely enough to slow him, the priest said. My lord, the Crowle road isn't safe. The priest says to cross the moor direct using the tracks the peat-cutters use. They'll be flooded in places, but'll take ye straight. He'll point them the wrong way, but they know Mistress Fenton has left her manor, and they'll have guessed where she'll be headed." Taylor wiped his arm across his face, leaving a trail of blood on his forehead.

"You're injured!" Isobel exclaimed.

He examined his arm, and his face puckered. "Nay, mistress, that's not my blood, but we'd best be going, or it might be your'n."

She clambered to her feet, and Robert lifted her bodily onto the light brown horse in front of the high pommel and climbed up behind her.

"The mare is ridden out and cannot keep up; what is Master Taylor to ride?"

"Do not concern yourself, Taylor can look after himself well enough."

"That I can, and I have a job to do tellin' the folk in Crowle how to brew decent ale." The sergeant flashed a grin at her and patted the pony. "I'll be off, my lord. I'll take this lass to a warm stable and keep any dogs off ye back."

"I'll send more men when I can," Robert said. "In the meantime, do not be overly eager to exercise that sword arm."

"I'll be too busy lifting a cup, my lord," Taylor said, raising his hand to his mouth in imitation as he nosed the old pony around and persuaded her back towards the village.

Isobel scanned the land around them, empty bar a few long-legged birds stabbing the thawing peat. "This area is unknown to me. We never used to come this far."

Robert grunted. "I can see why. When not flooded in winter, it will breed gnats and fever in summer." He sensed her tense. "We'll make what we can of it, and it is not so far to Tickhill."

She was not so sure. Scabby land, pocked with scrub and stands of trees, stretched away before them. Unclaimed thatching straw in stooks marked areas of marsh, and patches of open water gleamed like dulled armour under the clouding sky.

Gathering the reins, Robert put both arms around her, securing her against him. "We'll keep to the tracks as far as we can," he said, heeling the horse into a walk. "I want to get some cover between us and anyone who evades Taylor. We'll lose what daylight there is soon enough and have to find shelter somewhere."

"What if they come after us?"

"Then they will have to get past me. And there is always that dagger you have hidden on your belt; do you know how to use it?"

She smiled faintly. Ah, yes, the dagger that had somehow found its way into her things when her back was turned. She saw Buena's fierce eyes, the thrust of the knife, the billow of feathers like blood from the cushion. "I think I know what to do."

"Mm, remind me not to get on the wrong side of you," he murmured into her hood, and tightened his grasp around her. She leaned into him, welcoming the security he brought and the warmth to her back.

The softening ground made the going difficult, and the horse laboured under the additional weight. Where they found a track delineating a boundary, they picked up speed, only to slow again when the path disappeared in undergrowth or under water a quarter mile later.

The wind strengthened, and the clouds that had lain dormant on the horizon encroached on the sun. Exposed to the stiffening breeze, Isobel could no longer feel her wet feet, and the constant jolting as the horse sought its footing on uneven ground wore away at her dwindling reserves. Only the occasional break in the cloud gave any indication of the direction in which they travelled. Isobel sagged sideways as the horse nearly stumbled again.

"We cannot go much farther without a clear road," Robert said, securing her against him. "We will have to take our chances on the main way or risk getting lost." Loosening his cloak, he wrapped it around her, enclosing them both in a tent. "It is not so very far now."

They gained the established hoof-hardened way between Crowle and Thorne as the first sleet began to drive in flurries. "Any out in this weather have no business to be," he remarked. "It'll improve our chances of getting to Thorne without detection, and I doubt Lacey's reach extends that far. We will find lodging there for the night." Sensing encroaching snow and an easier path, the horse broke into an amble.

The moor birds had fallen mute, the wind dropped, so only the hissing of the sleet, the *tok* of metalled shoes on loose stone, and the expelled air of the horse could be heard over her own breaths echoing inside her hood. Concentrating on keeping the sleet out of her eyes, Isobel thought she heard a far-off note that didn't belong in the wide, open space beneath the sky.

"What was that?" Suddenly alert, she tried to look behind them, but Robert's broad shoulders blocked her view.

"Did you hear something?"

She strained into the deepening gloom. "Metal. I thought I heard metal."

He brought the animal to a halt and turned it to face the road down which they had travelled. The horse suddenly snickered, a high-pitched sound, a call. Then a distinct *chink* of metal on metal followed by the shout of a man and a reply from another.

Robert didn't wait to see what materialised from the gathering dusk. "Hold on!" He wheeled the horse around and, kicking hard with his heels, forced it into a gallop. "There's a light ahead. It must be Thorne." Robert checked over his shoulder. "They're gaining ground." He urged the horse, pressing Isobel down onto its neck with the weight of his body as she clung to its mane, trying to keep her balance.

The lights ahead became two, then three, blurred and faint, but lights nonetheless. A cry went up from somewhere behind them.

"They've seen us!" He heeled the horse.

Blindly, they tore down the road, but a sudden sickening scream sliced the night. Isobel felt herself snapping forward out of Robert's arms as she jolted from the saddle, flailing in a frantic attempt to stop herself falling but finding nothing but air. Her breath exploded from her lungs, and she felt her skin rend as she landed on her back with a thud.

She lay, stunned, unable to breathe and with her torn hand burning. With tentative fingers, she touched something cold and hard with multiple sharp points, one of which embedded in her flesh. Gritting her teeth, she yanked it from her hand. Movement near her, great whooshing sounds, snorting, and then Robert's harsh whisper.

"Isobel, are you injured? Isobel!"

She located the rest of her limbs, drew air into punched lungs. "No." She made out Robert's figure pulling on the reins as the animal struggled to get up. Dazed, she said, "What happened?"

"Caltrops," he said, "laid on the road — and we ran straight into their trap."

A shouted command from nearby was lost to the noise of hooves over which the sound of weapons rang clearly. Toil-worn, the horse fell back and, uttering an oath, Robert abandoned the spent animal.

"Isobel, get off the road. Be ready to defend yourself." He hauled her upright as she began to argue. "There's no time. *Hide!*"

She stumbled on numb feet towards coarse hummocks of hedge marking field strips. Invisible brambles tore at her clothes, at her skin. Falling, she dragged herself up again until she could go no farther. She sank down and heard the sound of Robert's shouted challenge.

She peered through wet grasses, the bent stems of sedge and sleet breaking her view. A small group of men in armour, weapons drawn, faced Robert as he blocked the road. He had thrown his leather cloak clear of his sword arm, and he held the weapon in readiness. Strong and well-built as he was, he looked unequal to the men advancing upon him, and she had the impulse to run out of the scant cover, saw herself shouting and yelling, drawing their attention so Robert could escape. They wanted her, not him.

She unsheathed her dagger and began to rise, but reality drove a wedge through her instinct to protect him. He wouldn't save himself, would he? He would shield her and have two people to defend. She hunkered back down, thwarted and at a loss.

What daylight remained made shadow figures of men and horses as they moved to surround Robert. He threw out a challenge, tested the gaps between animals, but had no space in which to manoeuvre.

"Where is she?" a voice demanded, but not one she recognised.

"There's none other, or are you blind as well as insolent?" came Robert's taut reply.

"We'll see." There came a short instruction, and several shapes detached from the group, two melting into the darkness on the further side, others emerging out of the gloom as they left the road and came in her direction. An odd noise accompanied them, a brash rasping, like crickets, then Isobel made out the soldiers sweeping the vegetation with the tip of their swords, coming closer, bearing down.

There was nowhere else to hide. Heart thumping, she crushed herself further into the lank grasses and drew her hood over her head, praying for the obscurity of dusk. A heavy hoof struck the saturated ground just a hand's breath from her head. Horse-breath condensed in drops on her clenched hands.

She tensed for the shout of discovery, the blow of hooves against her skull; but a clash of steel and a man's bray of pain had the advancing soldiers yanking their animals around and returning to the group. Isobel released the breath she held and dared to look. A man lay on the ground, writhing and holding his knee, while his riderless mount skittered nearby. Not Robert, thank God, not him, but where was he?

The wind, once light, gusted. Horses jittered, parted, and she stifled a cry. Robert was on his knees, head bent, his neck exposed, his sword beyond reach. She had seen this before; she had sworn she would never witness it again.

Scalding desperation fuelled her limbs, and she half-crawled, not towards the safety of Thorne, but back the way they had come. Careless of the snagging briar, she made it to a straggle of hawthorn, climbed to her feet and took stock.

She counted perhaps six horses and riders — two others she knew were searching for her, and another pair had again left the company and were combing the side of the road where she recently had lain. Her sole purpose now was to give Robert a chance to fight — anything rather than fall victim to the sword in this obscene position of acute defencelessness. He wouldn't die like that — not for her.

Rising wind drove coarse grained ice that needled her frozen face and drowned the angry exchange. She swiped her eyes free, gauged the distance. Sleet, wind and dark would provide enough cover to do what she must. Wrapping her kerchief around her injured hand, she left her fingers free to grip the caltrop as best she could. Then, hunting around, she found a broken branch.

Isobel was within an oar's span of the nearest horse, its rounded rump flinching, when she detected movement further along the road and lights, dim and dancing but growing stronger. Reinforcements.

Isobel moved stealthily forwards, raised the branch, and *thwack*, hit the nearest horse solidly on its behind. It reared, catching its rider off guard, and he fell in a tumble of metal and curses, but she was already jabbing the next animal, darting under its neck as it shied and towards a third mount.

The branch broke against the soldier's leg as he reached to grab her, but she ducked sideways between the frightened animals. She heard Robert shout, "*Isobel!*", caught sight of him diving for his sword and reaching to drag a soldier from his saddle, but jerked back as a hand captured a length of her hair from behind.

She cried out in rage, swung the caltrop, and felt herself released as the man staggered back with his hands to his face. She whirled around at the sound of clashing metal, saw Robert take down another soldier.

"There are more!" she yelled to him, pointing to where the lights lurched wildly towards them, but he opened his mouth in a silent roar and she turned just as a metal fist made contact with her skull.

CHAPTER TWENTY-EIGHT

Demons with fists knocked merry hell out of the Earl's head, and the residue in his mouth resembled slurry from the privies at the end of summer. Daylight attempted to intrude, and he flung a forearm over his eyes, listening to the sleeping sounds of the woman next to him. He dozed until the need to piss became persistent and, reluctantly, he opened his eyes. He didn't ecognize the canopy over his head for a moment, and it took seconds longer to realise where he was and where he had been the night before.

Cursing himself and the wine equally, he turned his back on his wife and, sitting up, allowed the room to steady before attempting to stand. A half-open shutter let a caustic beam of light cut across the room, low enough in angle to denote the primal hour. Still in shirt and braies, the Earl located his outer garments and negotiated his solitary way across the bailey and back to his own chambers, indifferent to the cold beauty of the dawn.

Bathed and dressed, he felt moderately better, and the crust of the bread he ate removed the remnants of muck on his teeth that scouring with tooth powder had failed to shift. Even his head had cleared enough to recall the night before. But his stomach laboured. He found himself wishing Isobel were there to make him a posset, and then just wishing she were there.

Angelic voices, rising into the vaulted roof of the castle chapel at Christmas Mass, did nothing to ease him, until he recognised that the discomfiture was less to do with his body and more to do with his spirit. He mouthed prayers, wondering at what point he had ceased believing because in the space inside himself where he should have placed faith, he found none.

He pressed his paternoster to his lips, bruising them, squeezing his eyes shut against the images of his life that haunted him, repeating over and over, "*Why have you forsaken me? What else could I do?*" until it became a song, and the song a ceaseless melody that wound itself into his soul.

He became aware of rhythms changing and opened his eyes. The chapel had nearly emptied of his household, except for his wife and a few retainers. Felice looked at him strangely. He tasted iron on his tongue and, wiping his lips with his fingers, found blood. He looked at his paternoster in surprise, and saw the coral and black beads glossed in red. "Leave me."

She reached out to him. "Come now, my lord —" she began.

"Do not touch me," he snarled.

She left him without another word, and a tiny part of him wondered whether things might have been different; but the time for change had passed and his desire to do so with it. In the empty glory of his chapel, he found himself alone by his son's monument. He touched the marble fingers clutching the toy horse and, leaning down, kissed his child's cold forehead. Unvoiced grief, relentless and unforgiving, brought him to his knees, and into the hollow heart of the day he vented his sorrow. He was unsure how long he had been there when shouting from the bailey roused him.

The Earl raised his head and listened, then rose to his feet and crossed to the chapel door, nearly colliding as one of his men ran in.

"My lord! Lord Langton's esquire has returned."

"What of it?" The Earl pushed past him into the sunlight to see Martin being lowered from his horse, bloodied and alone. "Where is my brother? Where's Mistress Fenton?"

*

The Earl looked up as Sawcliffe came into his privy chamber. "Is he recovered enough to talk?"

"His head is cut, and his ribs give him cause for discomfort, but his wrist will mend straight enough. He was assailed on the road from Beaumancote, my lord, by two men bearing no identification."

"A random attack?"

"He believes he was followed. He evaded them for some distance but was waylaid short of Crowle. He only escaped because the priest heard his shouts and raised hue and cry. He set out as soon as he could ride again. He was carrying papers of no import, which were taken, my lord, but he had the foresight to hide this."

He gave the Earl the square of folded paper, sealed with wax as red as the smeared blood that decorated it. The Earl recognised his brother's impatient hand, broke the seal, read the contents, then fed the fire with it. He motioned to a groom. "Have my horse saddled. I want a dozen men armed and ready to ride within the hour. Oh, and rouse Lord Dalton from my daughter's bed; it is time he proved himself and earned his place in *my* affection."

Sawcliffe hovered. "Have you instruction for me, my lord?"

The Earl started to undo the silver-gilt fastenings of his doublet. "Louys — my arming clothes, be quick." Then, addressing Sawcliffe, "Make preparation for some visitors. They might require your especial attention."

Felice met him as he descended the stair to the bailey. "You will not leave, surely? It is Christmas morn, and the festivities are due to begin."

"Treachery has no respect for Christ's day. You can oversee the masque if I have not returned by nightfall; you have done it often enough before now."

"You cannot go, not after last night —"

"*Cannot*, madam?"

"At least leave Dalton. Bess has been barely wed a day. Would you make her a widow so soon?"

"I do not intend to get him killed, Felice, and your consideration for my welfare is touching, as is your concern for my brother. I must find him before any harm befalls him." He left her to mull his sarcasm and marched towards the stables, indifferent to the frost-glazed stone.

She called after him. "And your whore?"

He swung around and stormed back, raising a mailed finger, lips pulled back over his teeth and hissing out, "Do not *ever* call her that again."

She shrank from him. He nodded to his waiting men, then mounted and rode through the gatehouse and out of sight.

Isobel came to as her body shuddered and bumped over rough ground. She dug her heels and attempted to gain a footing but felt herself lifted and thrown face-forward over a hard-skinned saddle. She tried to raise her head enough to gain her bearings, but the horse was already on the move, her chest feeling each bruising bump as it quickened its pace, her chin jarring against the horse's leather-bound flanks as it was led away.

In a rush, the soldier had failed to secure her hands. Using what strength remained, Isobel took hold of the saddle and dragged herself head over heels off the horse, landing with a thump and rolling into a waterlogged ditch. She pulled her dagger free of her twisted clothing and waited for sounds of discovery, but the clash of fighting was diminishing, then ceased altogether, to be replaced by the harsh voices of men and horses. Either Robert had prevailed, or… Sweet Jesu protect him, because without him, without the hope he represented, she had none for herself. Fatigue weighed every muscle, and every bone felt like lead, but, be he alive or dead, she wanted to see him one last time.

She had fallen unnervingly close to her previous position, and she crawled until she could see. Two lanterns had become four — five — and the group of men swollen to a dozen, but Robert was still standing — weary and swaying with exhaustion — but alive.

Through the hardening sleet came a shouted exclamation, and, without warning, one of the armoured men spurred his statuesque horse forward. Robert lifted his sword, but instead of defending himself, ran it back into its scabbard. He had surrendered without a fight. What would they do to him? To *her*?

Isobel retreated as far as the bank allowed. The big horse drew beside Robert, and the armoured man, indistinct in the half-light and his steel back lustrous as he leaned forward, raised his arm. Isobel felt a cry of desperation climb her throat, but the two men exchanged rapid words, and Robert indicated towards the ditch.

She ducked down. The horseman swung his animal around. She kept low, her head bent, keeping the dagger ready but out of sight, hearing the *slup* of hooves sucking wet ground, the snorted breaths of the animal as it came nearer until, when it was nearly on top of her, she moved. It startled.

"Steady!" the Earl soothed, "or we'll both be in the ditch."

"My lord!" she gasped, scrambling soggily to her feet. He seemed mildly gratified at her response.

"You have led me a merry chase. When the rest of the realm is feasting in celebration of Christ's nativity, I am obliged to spend my time in the saddle hunting *you*." His expression slipped as she tried to find something to say, swayed, and would have fallen, but he made a grab for her arm. She held on to him. "Jesu, but you're a mess," he muttered, his eyes glinting in the grey light of dusk. "You will ride with me."

She hadn't a grain of strength left, and the Earl called to one of his men to help lift her in front of him. Her wool skirts clung to her legs and smelled like Alfred after a day running by her father's horse through mud and mire. Cold to her core and shaking, she had nothing left with which to protest when the Earl wrapped steel arms around her and headed his horse back onto the road.

Misshapen bodies lay haphazardly to one side, and several captives were in the process of being disarmed. She was glad to see Taylor nearby, leading a horse on which a swarthy man was bound. The man saw her and spat over the animal's neck.

Taylor jerked the prisoner's tether. "None of that," he growled.

The Earl cast an eye over the prisoner. "If he — or any of the others — tries anything, remind him of his manners; but leave him his tongue — he'll be in need of it if he wants to save his skin."

Taylor gave a short nod. "It'll be my pleasure, my lord, after what he's put me through wi' that foul brew they call ale an' all." Isobel thought he winked at her.

"I would have them walk on their knees if it would not delay us," the Earl responded, "but we must make Tickhill before this weather closes. Brother, you have a fresh mount?" he asked Robert, and Isobel saw he was on a horse next to Lord

Dalton, whose new armour was still brightly dressed and unscathed.

The relief Isobel had initially felt on seeing the Earl curdled on glimpsing his brother — hair sticking to his forehead, his dark eyes focused on the road ahead, avoiding her own. "Move on," the Earl said over her head, spurring his horse into an amble. His breastplate juddered and rattled against her soaking back. "The moor is less wet than you are," he observed wryly. "I will have turned to rust by the time we return."

All iron, she thought, leaning forward to prevent her head from thumping against his metal chest. *Iron heart*.

"We caught up with them shortly after noon," the Earl was saying when Isobel was briefly rattled from sleep by cobbled streets as they approached the castle. She faced sideways where her head had fallen against the Earl's arm, and Robert rode beside them, yellow light from jettied windows reflecting on his face paled by fatigue. "I sent out scouts as soon as I heard from your esquire that you intended to return, but having no news of it thought you waylaid. By the time we reached Crowle, your sergeant had downed one of Lacey's men, but was surrounded by three more." His mouth slid into a smile. "He did not look as pleased as I would have expected when we turned up." His face straightened again. "Taylor told us you planned to cross the moor, and that is where we were headed when we saw the base assembly ahead and thought you one of Lacey's men. Good thing I had no bowman, or I'd have had a bolt through you and asked questions later."

"I am glad you didn't," Robert concurred drily. "As it was, the horse was spent and could carry us no farther."

At the sound of the word *us*, Isobel's eyes fluttered, and the Earl murmured, "I fear to think what would have happened to you if Lacey's men had prevailed — what would have happened to her..." Clamping his mouth shut, he increased his grip around her waist, almost squeezing the breath from her.

Isobel slid into sleep again until the challenge went up from the gatehouse, and the great gate swung open to let them enter the bailey. Braziers blazed and, from a distance, brazen horns signalled the revelry underway in the hall. "I had forgotten the masque," the Earl said under his breath. "I have no stomach for it."

"Nor I," said Robert. "I have not slept for nigh on two days."

"Dalton!" The Earl waited until his son-in-law caught up. "I am too weary for this guising. As it is in honour of your marriage, it is fit you take my place. Ride ahead, if you will; your wife will be waiting."

Dalton's eager eyes touched on Isobel's crumpled form, prevented from slipping from the horse only by the arms holding her securely. "As you wish, my lord. You do me great honour."

"Not so great," the Earl remarked as Dalton broke into a trot and went beyond hearing. "It is many years since my wife longed for *my* return." He caressed Isobel's wet hair with his metalled hand. "You must to your bed," he spoke softly, "and I will to mine."

"Dalton says he is to stand in your place this eve." Felice raged, cold as coal behind the flaming sun masque she wore. "What is that girl doing here? You promised she would be gone. We have a hall full of your affinity waiting for you, and you bring this ... taggle-tail back with you. Am I to be humiliated in front of our guests?"

The Earl lowered Isobel to the waiting groom, then dismounted. Removing his gloves, he tucked them into his belt. "You are the one shouting, madam. I suggest you keep your voice down if you wish to prevent our guests from knowing our business." He beckoned to Taylor who had hauled the prisoner off his horse and now prodded him, none too gently, towards the Earl.

Felice tore the masque from her face, revealing a mouth shrivelled with scorn. "Know our business? They all know you keep that whor… that girl here. You could at least be discreet and not be seen with her." Robert dismounted beside them, and she turned to him, all blazing sun to his mud-drenched drab. "My lord, speak with your brother, for the sake of family honour."

Robert threw the reins to a groom with a bare glance at Isobel. "Forgive me, madam, but there is nothing I can teach my brother about honour." He inclined his head and walked away towards the range of apartments, leaving her standing there.

The Earl finished giving instructions to Taylor and now turned back to Isobel, barely alert and supported in a more or less upright position by the groom. He pressed his hand against her damp forehead. "Faith, I did not know how cold you are."

Felice's lip curled in contempt, and his temper frayed.

"Would you have me leave them out there to be taken by Lacey's men, or to die of cold in the marsh?" Her expression told him everything he suspected and, leaning close so no one else could overhear, he growled, "Not a finger raised against her, Felice, not a hair harmed, or, by my oath, I will have vengeance." Then, taking Isobel, he picked her up, her skirts dragging over his arm. "You have guests to attend to, madam.

I will leave you to your own conscience, and I will take care of mine."

As he mounted the stairs, Isobel tried to throw her mantle off and, in jerks, moved her face against his neck. "Robert," she whimpered.

"Shhh," the Earl murmured, securing her cloak. "He is safe; you are both safe now."

CHAPTER TWENTY-NINE

Waking sometime during the night, Isobel remembered snatches of the previous evening, but her memory remained patchy, like fog, and she felt thirsty. She had stopped shaking at last even if her legs and hands still felt cold and her feet itched and burned. She twitched uncomfortably, her ankles bumping against hard objects. "Ow!"

"My lady must be careful not to hurt herself." Ursula floated into view from somewhere beside the fire bearing a wool-wrapped package, which she placed under the blankets near Isobel's shoulder. It radiated heat. "My lady was very cold when my lord brought her in."

"Lord Langton?" Isobel asked fuzzily.

"My lord, the Earl," Ursula corrected. "He has been twice since to see you, but he did not see me."

Isobel closed her eyes. Had she misconstrued their conversation? Had Robert merely offered companionship through those long hours of travel for want of better company? She felt sure he no longer thought badly of her, that he understood the circumstances in which she found herself, and for that she was immensely grateful. But of one thing she was absolutely certain: he would not oppose his brother in any way, and the Earl was as much the custodian of Robert Langton's loyalty in this matter as he was in any other.

Perhaps when he tires of me, she reflected, *as all great men grow weary and seek fresh pleasure in new flesh, perhaps Robert will wait for me and I'll be free*, and she allowed herself a moment in which it was his mouth that sought hers, and his voice that carried her name, and it was a different tension she sensed run through her, like rivulets of fire.

From Sawcliffe's point of view, events over the last week had gone rather well. His scouts had returned with titbits of information that amounted to more than mere gossip and, intriguingly, what had seemed like predictable friction between the old-order Lord Welles and fast-rising Thomas Burgh was quickly taking a more exciting turn. With Burgh being a particular favourite of the king, where else could Welles turn to keep his footing in Lincolnshire if Burgh was riding roughshod over the county lapping up as many of the offices as the king cared to throw his way? Welles had been loyal to old King Henry before, why not again? To one as experienced in statecraft as Sawcliffe, the board of England appeared like a game, and one man's opportunity was another's downfall. As he saw it, the trick was in thinking two moves ahead, riding the right horse, and knowing when to swap it for another as soon as the one ridden showed signs of flagging. Of course, sometimes the signs were not clear, so survival was largely a matter of knowing when to jump, and where.

At present, secreted in his lord's council chamber bathed in clear winter sun and favoured with the Earl's trust, Sawcliffe thought his future as secure as his earl's, and that depended on which king ruled. And as long as he provided a reliable service to the Earl, he would help ensure the continuity of both king and lord, as ordained by God. That didn't mean he couldn't lay down reserves of goodwill and quarter horses in other stables — that was only prudent in these uncertain times.

He stood slightly behind and to one side of the table in a shaft of sun. It made a warm patch between his shoulders and his body broke the beam, the remaining slivers of lesser light illuminating the Earl who stood examining a map laid before him, his bent head nearly touching Langton's as they conversed.

Sawcliffe was not so sure about the brother. Robert Langton showed a stubborn resistance to being wooed although Sawcliffe endeavoured to play both brothers, especially as the younger had pledged himself to Gloucester, and the young duke was proving an interesting proposition.

Waiting to be summoned to the table, his hands laced in front of him like a monk's, whose ascetic life he had always found attractive, Sawcliffe considered the changing dynamics at the top of the royal tree. After Warwick's attempt to manoeuvre the king had failed last summer, Gloucester had scooped the lands and offices Warwick had been forced to relinquish and was fast building an affinity to rival that of his brother, Clarence. He would be one to watch.

Sawcliffe made a study of great men; they fascinated him, and he put his accrued wisdom to effective use. What drove them? What was their impetus in life? It helped to understand this basic precept: that a man's purpose might drive him to go against wisdom and the safest road. Sawcliffe's motivation lay in self-service, for no one owed him anything, and his only ambition was to die in his bed. These lords, with all the arrogance of their dead ancestors, often failed to see what mattered in life with their notions of loyalty and chivalry that would as quickly consign them to their graves as not.

What was loyalty to him when his lord was dead? He would need to find a new master and he cared not which king that lord served. His priority was survival; personal loyalty was the prerogative of lords and fools. The only loyalty he expected from his own men was in what he paid them and keeping his purse full was a matter of utmost import. His attention came back to the matter in hand as Robert Langton spoke.

"John Neville — Montagu, as we must now call him — holds much of the land here —" Robert pointed to the map — "but since he's had his nose put out of joint when the king granted his Northumberland title to Henry Percy, do you think he can really be trusted?"

Examining the map spread before him, the Earl focused on where the point of his brother's dagger rested, and then on the lands under his own dominion. "Even as Warwick's brother, Montagu is not implicated. But I rule no one out of this mess. I have sent word to the king about Lacey, and it is for him to act on it, although it was he who conferred the office of Justice on him against my advice, and His Grace will not want to be thought misjudged in doing so. But, for my own part, I'll not risk waiting until Lacey raises a sword in my direction. I am ensuring our own manors are alerted and assigning men to reinforce Beaumancote and the Fenton lands along the Trent and Humber. If nothing else, it will send a message to Lacey and anyone else who wants to pick that particular plum."

"But the plum has already been plucked, my lord," Sawcliffe reminded him. "Perhaps if Mistress Fenton were found a match to someone of your own retinue — a loyal gentleman, Master Rigby, perhaps — the fruit would be less tempting, and sour if tasted?" He looked around as Robert snorted. "You wish to comment, my lord?"

"Your matchmaking leaves much to the imagination; her lineage deserves better than the gentleman son of a yeoman, three times her age and lacking teeth as well as dignity. Better if you stick with what you do best."

"My lord has an alternative suggestion?"

The Earl dismissed his secretary's comment. "It is immaterial; Isobel Fenton is not to be discussed."

"And how is Mistress Fenton, my lord? Fully recovered from her ... adventure?"

"A good sight better than the men you are holding in confinement," Robert muttered caustically, letting his dagger drop to the table with a solid *thud*. "You had what you needed; did you have to take it further?"

"Perhaps my lord would rather I had spared them a little discomfort, and risked the lady's life instead? At least this way we have the information, and they lack a thumb with which to hold a sword. A better outcome than the alternative, do you not think?"

"Sawcliffe, hold your tongue," the Earl growled. "You did what was required, but I did not give you leave to debate it with my brother."

"Your pardon, my lords; I wish only to serve."

"Your enthusiasm does you credit," the Earl said with a straight face.

Sawcliffe's eyes narrowed, and his mouth twitched, but he bowed. "My lord, I am yours to command."

"Yet, and despite your *efforts*, we still lack the proof to convict Lacey." The Earl picked up the discarded dagger and examined it. "You report disquiet in Lincolnshire, malcontent, though there is little new in that; it seems much of my discomfort comes out of that region." He frowned at a tiny nick in the blade. "I want you to sow a little of your own."

Sawcliffe's eyebrows soared. "*Sedition*, my lord?"

"Not sedition — rumour. For the sake of keeping discord at bay. Thomas Lacey is likely to abuse his position as Justice of the Peace. He threatened the daughter of a loyal subject, waylaid men in my service and is responsible for the lack of rule around the Humber. Lacey is a disease, and we need to apply a little physic before the sickness spreads." He tested the sharpness of the blade against his thumb.

"Cauterise the problem, my lord?"

The Earl replaced the dagger on the table, the blade momentarily rocking and catching the light. He stilled it. "As much as that would give me satisfaction, it is not the solution at present. The death of Geoffrey Fenton has left a void Lacey is not man enough to satisfy, and it is like to draw interest from others intent on filling it."

"Then what nature of physic would you like me to apply, my lord?"

"Lacey is the heir of a traitor. Old habits and old loyalties die hard. Have people remember that fact, Sawcliffe. Then remind them what happened under the old king and what happens when wives and daughters are not safe in their homes and lawlessness shakes men from their beds. Remind them who has brought peace to this realm. Sometimes true words spoken softly are heard loudest. Speak softly, Sawcliffe."

"My lord, it will require coin."

"Of course; when does it not?"

"Peddling rumour?" Robert queried once Sawcliffe had slid from the chamber.

"Do not make an enemy of that man; you never know when you might need his services and his friendship."

"Friendship? Pray God I never have to call him a friend!" Robert retrieved his dagger and sheathed it.

"Amen to that, but God is not always on our side, so we need men we can turn to instead until God favours our cause again." The Earl's mouth twisted. "If He does."

Robert glanced at his brother. "When did you mislay your faith?"

The Earl brought his thumb and forefinger together across his brow, looking suddenly weary. "When it drowned with my son. God and I have some unfinished business."

Robert leaned across the table and laid his hand on his brother's arm. "Then make it right with Him before you have to face His judgment."

The Earl summoned Isobel to his chambers. When she arrived, Robert was there and he would not meet her eye when he left her alone with his brother.

The Earl drew her towards him, and she turned her head from him.

"Isobel, look at me."

She did as bidden, keeping her expression mute, unreadable, and he held her face in his hand.

"Come," he said, his voice thickening, "I have need of you."

She pulled away. This man was determined to impose his will and his body upon her, depriving her of any chance of happiness. Because of him, Robert slipped like water through her fingers as she faded away into obscurity.

Was this all she had to look forward to; was this to be the sum of her existence? And even had Robert thought of her with any tenderness, that, too, was to be deprived of air and light, the nascent flame snuffed out by his older brother's quenching desire to possess her. If, that is, Robert thought of her at all. What was she, but tainted fruit, flesh corrupted by his brother's sin. Her sin. With a bitter stab of reality, she knew Robert Langton would not wait for her, and that fragment of hope to which she clung withered and died.

Clearly defined by the stronger light of day, the painted figures above her smirked, and she had a sudden urge to punch them, to wipe them out. Their cavorting was meaningless — this was no marriage bed and she no bride. All the hopes and careful plans her parents had fashioned to secure her future, a failed match with Thomas, the trust her father placed in this one man — betrayed, pointless, futile. His shame, her shame. She might as well be dead too.

The Earl lay beside her, so like his brother, so different. In him she saw all that was wrong in her life, and his indifference scalded. Sudden fury, dormant and smouldering, erupted. The hidden dagger whispered from its sheath as she withdrew it.

Careless of her movements, she knelt above him, ready to expunge months of impotent resentment in this single act within her control. Her shame, her life — and with his death, her own. Her. Choice. Eyes flaring, shoulders tensing, she raised her arm. His eyes flicked open, met hers, and his hand whipped around and grabbed her wrist. She struggled to free it from the vice of his grip as, slowly, he pulled her arm until the point of the dagger lay over his heart. He held her eyes with his. "Kill me."

She bared her teeth, willing herself to strike.

"Kill me, Isobel." He let go of her wrist.

Needle-sharp, the dagger dented his skin, the fine sable hair of his chest curling around the tip of the blade. Furious, despairing, she pressed harder, drawing from him a sharp breath as the point pierced his skin, releasing a spreading bead of blood. Fascinated, she froze under the watchful grey eyes that willed her on.

"Kill me. Release me." He closed his eyes, the lines between them smoothing as if already in death.

She gasped and sat back, dropping the knife as pity blunted her desire for blood. Covering her face with her hands, she crumpled inside, searing frustration and contrition drowning out revenge as hot tears forced from behind her lashes. She felt her hands taken and, keeping her eyes tight shut, waited for his anger to engulf her.

"Do you hate me so much?" he asked, regret seeping softly. "What have I done to you?"

She ventured to look at him and found eyes darkened by remorse as he brushed hair dampened with tears from her face.

"Where is my Isobel? What have I done to her?" He leaned forward and very gently kissed her eyelids in turn.

She gulped back the emotion lodged in her throat at this sudden tenderness. Liberating her hands, he captured her face and, sensing the change, his mouth lifted in response. "There she is," he murmured, "my Bel."

"I have failed to woo you as a lover should." Leaning on one elbow, the Earl caressed the ankle nearest to him poking from the tumbled covers. "I had … expectations … demands…" he trailed off, gathering his thoughts, and kissed her toes still reddened and itching from freezing the day before.

"When you sent me back home, you did not do it for me, did you?" she asked. "You wanted to use me to trap Thomas."

His hand hesitated on her ankle. "It is not all as it seems —"

"And to get me out of the way." Her lips compressed, unwilling to let go of her resentment and still angry with him for undermining her potent hate.

"Not all is as it seems, Isobel," he said again. A thread of the intricate embroidery decorating the pillow's border in scrolls had loosened, tickling his neck. He scratched absent-mindedly. "Sometimes we make decisions that go against the desires of our heart." He turned his head and found her looking at him, seemingly more puzzled now than angry. "What is it?"

"Will you not punish me?"

His mouth curled. "Do you want me to?" A flash of alarm told him she didn't understand his jest. He fingered his chest where a small patch of blood matted the tangle of hair. "Would you have killed me, Isobel?"

She glanced sideways at his chest, then down at her hands. "I wanted to."

"And do you now?"

He watched the colour of her face ebb and flow before she finally answered. She shook her head. "No."

"Then you have my answer, also."

EPILOGUE

As Yule came and went, so too did Isobel's remembrance, until all that remained of those brief few days at Beaumancote with Robert was a lingering impression of the dream he had kindled in her of an altogether different life. She took no part in the continuing festivities in the great hall, nor had she any desire to do so. The Earl presided over the merrymaking with his brother at his side. Isobel had seen Robert only once and that fleetingly, but the memory of it hurt like knives and she dared not risk it again. Instead, she begged the Earl to let her leave the tower unescorted to seek fresh air outside. He had not denied her this little freedom.

Isobel found the idle hours her own, and looked for the company of the winter birds in the wilderness garden, where none but she and they occupied the space between land and sky. Snow swathed branches and rendered the garden unsullied. Only five-toed prints declared the passage of a cat as Isobel sought the solitude of the apple tree. She leaned against the trunk. The sun had reached its zenith, and she turned her face towards it, welcoming its warmth.

A part of her had dwindled, she reflected, the part that had clung to her former existence, the Isobel Fenton who, without knowledge of the world, would have willingly, innocently, stepped into marriage with a man who had no regard for her except for the property she inherited. She was no longer that girl and if, in possessing her, the Earl denied her any prospect of happiness with his brother, so too had he prevented a loveless match with Thomas. So here she was, like two-faced

Janus, at the breach of the year, neither one thing or another, hope suspended.

At the thought of the unknown, Isobel felt claws of anxiety. She breathed in clean, raw air and slowly exhaled, once, twice, controlling fear. But Janus, she remembered, was also the god of possibilities, of new beginnings. If she could not find any happiness then at least she could be content and, if not content, resigned, and in resignation, she might be able to accept that just waking to the promise of each day was enough. For now.

Low sun accentuated dimples in the glistening snow. Something caught Isobel's eye beneath the icy surface and she bent down and brushed away loose flakes with her gloved fingers. There undaunted, emerging from the frozen soil like a message, pushed bold green spears of Maids-of-the-Snow — brave little harbingers of hope.

Isobel smiled.

HISTORICAL NOTES

"in the ninth year of King Edward, being the year of our Lord 1469, there arose a great disagreement between the King and his kinsman, Richard, the most illustrious Earl of Warwick; which was not allayed without the shedding of blood of many persons."
Croyland Chronicle, Second Continuation, Part IV

From the middle of the 15th century, England became drawn into an internecine struggle for control of crown and government. Over the previous hundred years, major conflict had been concentrated elsewhere as France and England battled for supremacy in Europe. With England's ultimate defeat and withdrawal from the continent, reduced incomes and sense of esteem focused the minds of the social elite on their political and economic situation on home turf.

England might have weathered the storm of defeat in France had its own ruler maintained a handle on his realm. As it was, Henry VI's grip on the fluid political situation slipped, along with his mental capacities, leaving the country without strong leadership at the highest level. As with any political vacuum, the resulting uncertainty led to a power struggle between the most senior members of the aristocracy and their kin: the Dukes of York and Somerset. In a period when land, offices, and patronage were the foundation of wealth and power, any reduction in these could result in the destruction of individuals and their affinities. So, when York and Somerset vied for power, they did so not merely for personal gain, but in response to threats to the security and future of their family and their wider affinities and, ultimately, their country.

Nor should the importance of bloodlines and the right to rule, God's purpose, vendetta, and personal characteristics be underestimated. There is no simple explanation of a highly complex situation and much has been written about the causes of the bitter struggle for power named the Wars of the Roses by a later generation. As with any civil conflict, memories run deep, with wounds and slights becoming embedded in the personal, regional, and national psyche.

The history reflected in *The Tarnished Crown* series begins some years before the opening chapter. The Duke of York, his son, and their kin were slain at the battle of Wakefield in December 1460, his memory afterwards humiliated by the exhibition of his head, topped by a paper crown. It was left to his eldest son, Edward, Earl of March — now Duke of York — to uphold family honour and power. There could be no half-measures — it was fight or die. Supported by his cousin, Richard Neville, Earl of Warwick, Edward went on to win the crown as Edward IV, the summation of his father's hope. But it left an embittered, factionalised, and defeated enemy, an anointed former king, his determined queen, and their heir, still at large. The Crown of England might have been won by Edward of York, but the battle was far from over. The lives of Isobel Fenton and other fictional characters in *Wheel of Fortune* are unique, but the situations in which they found themselves were not. Memories ran deep and past slights deeper still, and it is into this toxic mix that Isobel, the Earl, and his family are thrown.

GLOSSARY

Alaunt — a type of dog used for the hunt. Medium to large, fleet of foot, heavy-headed, and ferocious, it was used for larger game and baiting.

Allée — in garden design, a (usually) straight path lined either side with trees or large shrubs to create an avenue.

All-night — a call made or a bell rung to sound a sort of curfew in the evening (varying between 8 and 10pm). A light, all-night meal might be left for the lord's sustenance.

All Souls' Day — 2 November.

Arras — a woven hanging (tapestry) of very great value associated with Arras, a town in the Duchy of Burgundy, now northern France.

Aumbry (ambry) — a recessed wall cupboard.

Ave — the (often) smaller beads used in groups of ten — a decade — or five, when repeating the Ave Maria or similar prayers using a chaplet or paternoster. See *beads*.

Ballock dagger — a dagger with a pommel resembling male genitalia.

Bards — an ornament or armour for the neck, breast, or flank of a horse.

Barghest — a huge, ghostly black dog of Yorkshire and Northern folklore.

Barmkin — (north country and Scottish) a small, defendable enclosure.

Beads — a set of beads of varying number used for 'bidding' prayers and personal devotions. Beads could be made from anything and everything, be simple or extravagant, have markers dividing them (aves and gauds), be many or few, terminate in a tassel or cross, be in a single line or circular.

Beads might be worn as a necklace, around the wrist or waist, or carried in a purse or pouch. They were an essential part of everyday devotional life as a Christian.

Bevor — armour; used with a sallet, a bevor protects the neck and chin.

Blanchet — very coarse woollen cloth.

Braies — (long, medium, and short) the medieval equivalent of men's boxer shorts.

Burgher — a town-dweller of standing, often a merchant, who holds land in a town and might be trusted with civic responsibilities.

Burgundian gown — very similar to the houppelande, both types might have deep cuffs and a folded back collar in a contrasting fur or fabric. Low v-necked, high-waisted with tightly fitting sleeves.

Buttery — an area used to store butts of alcohol (from which we get "butler"). Often associated with the pantry (overseen by the pantler).

Caltrop — a multi-spiked weapon designed to present a spike whichever way up it landed and used to impede or wound horses and people.

Caranets — highly decorative roundels or squares made of silver or gold and decorated with gemstones and/or enamels. Used singularly as jewellery and in linked groups on collars of estate by men and women.

Chaperon — elaborate headgear worn by men, often with long 'tails' that could be draped around the neck and shoulders. Gradually lost favour towards the end of the century.

Chaplet — a short set of beads of varying number for saying personal devotional prayers (chaplets).

Chewit/chewette — little sweet, savoury, or mixed pies filled with meat, cheese, peas, or fruits and probably similar to the mince pies we know today.

Chouchou — French for cabbage.

Clarry — a sweetened, spiced wine.

Cockeburr — agrimony (botanical name) widely used in medieval medicine for healing and as a sedative.

Cog — a broad-bottomed ship used extensively for transport and cargo.

Coif — a close-fitting cap, used by men and women, made of linen (or similar) and worn by itself or under other headgear.

Constable — in terms of a castle, the constable was responsible for the maintenance of order and the soldiery retained for its protection.

Cott (cot) — a small house for agricultural workers (cotter/cottager) with an enclosed area for livestock and possibly a barn.

Counterpoint — former name for a counterpane.

Court Baron — a manorial court held to, among other things, resolve disputes between a lord's free tenants.

Cranage — a levy on the use of cranes for loading and unloading goods.

Crenel — the low sections on battlements between merlons.

Cresset — a metal basket or container, filled with flammable material, suspended from a ceiling or mounted on a pole to provide light.

Cuir bouilli — leather which has been rendered tough and very resilient through a process of soaking and heating.

Cuisse — armour; plate of metal, leather, or quilted material to protect the thigh.

Dagged — a toothed decorative edge used with hangings.

Demesne — in feudal terms, the land retained by a lord for his own use rather than that rented to tenants.

Didder — (dialect) to shake, shiver, be jumpy.

Doublet — worn over a shirt by men, a sleeved or sleeveless garment of varying quality, decoration, and fabric, belted at the waist to give the appearance of a short skirt of fabric. Doublets became increasingly short throughout the period, especially for young men.

Douce powder — a (sweet) powder made up of different spices according to personal taste for flavouring drinks and food.

Dun brown — sandy light brown.

Dwale — a medieval medicinal drink for pain relief and for inducing deep sleep. Made to recipes handed down from mother to daughter, master physician to apprentice, it might contain (among other things) lettuce, henbane, opium, belladonna, bile (gall), and various other herbs. It was understood that dwale-induced sleep might result in death if the patient could not be roused.

Ell — a measurement of length roughly from the fingertip to the shoulder of a stretched arm. Mostly used to measure cloth.

Embrasure — a splayed opening in a parapet or wall; an arrow loop in a merlon.

Espiouress — a female spy.

Fardel — a small pack or parcel.

Feoffee — a person entrusted with freehold property (a fief) held for the benefit of the owner.

Fewterers — a keeper of dogs (especially greyhounds) for the hunt.

Fleam — a knife-like tool used in bloodletting.

Gambeson — a quilted, padded jack(et) used as an additional (or the only) defensive layer in combat and for warmth. It could be made of fabric, boiled leather (cuir bouilli), or a combination of materials.

Gaud — a marker bead in sets of beads making up a chaplet or paternoster. Often larger, decorated (as in "gaudy"), or a different colour or texture from the groups of aves.

Glaikit — (dialect) stupid, senseless.

Gleet — a sexually transmitted disease.

Gong-farmer — a highly profitable occupation of gathering human and animal excrement for fertilising fields.

Gonne/gonners — a gun/gunners.

Grains of paradise — a small, brown, popcorn-shaped spice native to West Africa valued for its peppery, gingery, citrusy flavour when ground and added to sweet or savoury dishes and drinks.

Grayne — fine woollen cloth, often dyed red.

Green cheese — freshly made cheese a bit like cottage cheese.

Groat — money, a coin equivalent to four pence.

Guising — dressing up in masks and/or costumes.

Hennin — women's headgear in a short and blunt or long cone shape. Worn over a fabric under-cap and covered in a rich material. It hid the hair entirely and might be worn with or without a veil. Later versions might be split into horns and known as a butterfly hennin. These might be heavily jewelled or decorated.

Hood — worn by all classes and both sexes depending on the weather and the situation.

Hose — single leg or joined with a gusset, men and women's stockings/tights. Some were footed, that is, had a shaped foot, whereas some were more like leggings.

Houppelande — a very fashionable loose-fitting gown, belted at the waist (for men) or underneath the bust (for women). The sleeves were fitted at the shoulder but voluminous lower down. A gown perfectly suited to display the wealth of the wearer in the sheer quantity as well as quality of the cloth used.

Hurdy-gurdy — looking a bit like a violin on its side, a hurdy-gurdy is played using a hand-cranked wheel that rubs against the strings as they are depressed.

Hypocras — a fragrant spiced wine often accompanied by wafers, sweetmeats, and 'banqueting stuffes'.

Jetty — the upper floor/s of a building built out over, and overhanging, the lower.

Jongleurs — entertainers, often travelling groups but sometimes attached to noble or royal courts. Musicians, jugglers, actors, acrobats.

Kendal — a coarse woollen cloth, often dyed green, associated with Kendal, Cumbria.

Ket — (northern colloquial) rotten meat.

Kirtle — the undergarment or kirtle was usually made of a contrasting colour and fabric and was meant to be seen beneath the outer gown.

Lady Day — 25 March.

Lent — an extremely important period in the Christian calendar lasting from Ash Wednesday to Easter Sunday (40 days) in which prayer and a restricted diet played a central role in the preparation for Easter itself.

Luce — a pike (fish).

Manchet — fine, white wheat bread.

Marcher lords — lords with landholdings and responsibilities on the English-Welsh or English-Scottish borders, ostensibly to represent the English Crown and maintain peace along troubled borders.

Maslin — a coarse bread made from mixed cereal grains, ground peas, or similar.

Melee — a confused group of people, or a free-for-all in battle with little overall control.

Merlon — the 'teeth' seen on castle battlements.

Michaelmas — feast of St Michael celebrated on 29 September. It was common practice to mark important events such as marriages or the exchange of contracts, tenancies, etc., on, or with reference to, feast days in the Christian calendar.

Midden — a dump for everyday kitchen, domestic, and garden rubbish. An invaluable source of primary evidence for archaeologists!

Mignon — (French) delicate, pretty.

Misericorde — a long, thin-bladed knife used to kill a downed man on the battlefield. From the French word miséricorde (mercy) the narrow blade could penetrate the narrowest gap in armour. Not to be confused with a misericord, which was a ledged, hinged seat in a church choir stall for support when sitting or standing and often highly decorated. Think in terms of 'mercy' for those standing for long periods of prayer.

Mullion — the vertical stone, brick, or wood element between panes of a window or lancets.

Mural hall/passage — a passage built within the wall of a castle or fortified building.

Murder hole (meurtrière) — an opening in the ceiling of a gatehouse or similar structure of control through which missiles could be fired at attackers.

Murrey — a burgundy colour. Murrey and blue were the colours adopted by the House of York.

Numbles — properly, the edible viscera of animals, but could be used as an archaic reference to men's genitalia.

Nuncheons — a light meal taken around noon.

Palfrey — a lighter-weight horse, smooth of gait, used for riding by high-status women and children as well as men.

Pantler — the person in charge of the pantry where bread and similar foodstuffs were kept.

Pated hanging — a fabric hanging with a decorative edge.

Paternoster — from the Lord's Prayer (Pater Noster), using a set of beads of varying number but often 10, 50, or 150 beads, with gauds or dividing markers, for saying prayers.

Pattens — an overshoe of wood or leather to raise feet out of the mud. Clogs are an example of this.

Pauldron — plate armour covering the shoulder.

Peter's Pence — the plant we now call honesty.

Pleached — tree branches (often lime/linden) grown together to form an avenue.

Pleasance — a formal, fair garden.

Points (point) — the (often) metal pointed end of a tie or lace used to make the threading or the lacing of a garment easier. We use them now on the end of shoelaces.

Pole — (also perch and rod) a unit of measurement equivalent to five and a half yards.

Poleyn — armour, shaped to protect the knee.

Posset — a nourishing, warming, comforting drink made by combining cream or milk with ale or wine, adding sugar or honey, often egg, and flavouring with spices (think of eggnog). Now made as a thicker version and served as a dessert.

Pricker/scout/stalker — someone sent to gain information, especially in covert terms, of battle lines and enemy whereabouts.

Pricket — a stemmed candle holder, more often with a spike with which to secure the candle.

Prie-dieu — (furniture) a kneeling surface used in personal devotions with an upright on which to rest hands or a book.

Quarrel — a crossbow bolt (a short, thick arrow).
Quarter-curtow — a type of field cannon.
Rapere — rape — from to seize, carry off.
Reeve — a manorial office. A reeve oversaw the work undertaken on manorial land.
Rondel dagger — a well-balanced weapon commonly carried by soldiers of middling status, knights, and merchants.
Rosary — prayers of a number of forms said using a string of beads of varying number.
Rouncey — an everyday horse used for riding, occasionally as a pack animal, or as a war horse.
Sallet — armour; a helmet with a fixed visor (used with a bevor) that covers the entire head.
Sard — an orange-coloured semi-precious stone often used in the making of intaglios from antiquity onwards.
Scot's pint/joug — three pints (of ale or beer).
Serpentine — an early type of long-bore cannon used in the field, as a siege weapon, and in defence.
Shawms — a loud, rather penetrating oboe-like instrument. Useful in crowded great halls or in street processions.
Shewel men — scarecrows.
Shift/smock — a linen, silk, or later cotton undergarment worn next to the skin to protect the kirtle and outer gown from sweat.
Smatter/jangle — gossip.
Solar — a private (bed) chamber for the lord and his family.
Squinny — to squint at, to spy.
St Andrew, feast of — 30 November.
Steward — a manorial office; the senior officer retained to manage the manor and estates and to represent the lord in his absence. Often drawn from gentry, the position required a good degree of education and management skills and was

endowed with a great deal of trust by the lord.

Stooks — sheaves of grain stood on end together to keep the heads dry prior to gathering.

Surcoat — a loose, sleeveless outer garment worn by both sexes, later by men to cover armour, often bearing the colours and insignia of the wearer or their lord.

Sweetmeats — delicacies made with honey or sugar such as small cakes, wafers, or preserved and embellished fruits.

Syncope — an illness defined by fainting or loss of consciousness; 'failure of the heart's action'.

Table dormant — a table made for permanent use (i.e. not disassembled like a trestle table), most often reserved for the use of the lord.

Tables — another form of backgammon.

Tawny — an orange colour; think of tawny marmalade.

Trenail (treenail, trennel) — a wooden peg used in building to secure pieces of wood together.

Trencher — a flat object on which food is served. Often made of bread or wood. Bread trenchers could be eaten at the end of the meal or given to the servants or as alms to the poor.

Van/vanguard — the leading part of a battle formation, ahead of the main (middle) and rear (back).

Villein — a feudal tenant subject to a manor or lord to whom he paid dues or gave service in return for land.

Wagtail — euphemism for a woman of loose morals.

Waites (waits) — a band of town musicians employed for civic entertainment. Thought to have had watchmen duties in earlier periods, this aspect became secondary to their role as musicians.

Weld — bright yellow from the plant reseda luteola.

A NOTE TO THE READER

High on the banks of where the river Humber meets the Trent and the Ouse lies the pretty village of Alkborough, on the north-eastern edge of Lincolnshire. There are signs of human occupation dating from the Neolithic period, and the Romans may well have used it as a base from which to move to and fro across the river. Indeed, there are several ancient ferry points to allow access to the Isle of Axholme and the East Riding of Yorkshire. That the position continued to be significant is attested by the outline of what is believed to have been a medieval manor. All that now remain are the lumps and bumps where walls once stood. Known locally as Countess Close, this became the setting for the fictional manor of Beaumancote where we first meet Sir Geoffrey Fenton and his daughter, Isobel. The siting of a fortified manor here is no accident of history, for the steep river cliff affords a panoramic view of the rivers, commanding a stretch of water reaching deep inland in a time when navigable waterways provided means of transportation for goods and people alike. That Geoffrey Fenton, among other things, held offices from the king for the collection of fines and duties on goods gave him far-reaching influence in the region.

Turn around and look south over the gently undulating fields of North Lincolnshire. The yellow soil is fertile here and the vegetation lush and floriferous. Some 36 miles south lies the city of Lincoln, to the west — across the river Trent and the Isle of Axholme — it is a similar distance to Doncaster in Yorkshire. Not far from Doncaster, close to the Great North Road leading up and down the spine of the country, is the small town of Tickhill. Once dominated by its great multi-sided tower of fine crystalline ashlar gleaming white against the green landscape, the castle's motte and bailey would have been a spectacular reminder of local lordship. This is where I placed the Earl and the Langton family, whose sphere of influence stretched across the land like fingers and felt the political pulse.

Standing on top of the now naked motte and looking out over the miles of land, it takes a short leap of the imagination to envisage a time when social and political influence depended on the personal relationships between king and lord, noble and knight, gentleman and yeoman. This interdependency affected all areas and levels of society, from the noble in his castle to the merchants in the towns and the labourers in the fields, and never more so than in the second half of the 15th century. Social, economic, and political wheels turned and turned about, and who knew, when Lady Fortune spun the wheel, which way it would end up?

Through *The Tarnished Crown* series, I returned to my historical roots and a lifelong and enduring passion for the second half of the 15th century — the years of upheaval we now refer to as the Wars of the Roses. I have drawn on contemporary sources and eyewitness accounts, manorial records, court records, Pardon Rolls, letters, and wills. I scoured primary pictorial sources and artefacts, trod the paths of our forefathers, walked ramparts, and surveyed castle ruins. I have talked to other historians, archaeologists, military and weaponry experts, visited museum collections, and watched specialist re-enactors. I experimented with medieval recipes for spiced ales and scoured modern European cuisine to find the remnants of medieval fare. I grow native plants that would be recognised by our ancestors, and I have used Castile soap made to a medieval recipe as the nearest example of the hard soaps used by late-15th-century nobility. I have researched rabbit warrens and dovecotes, wall fruit and exotic imported fare of the period. I grow and harvest the saffron so highly valued at the time. I danced (badly) medieval dances and listened to its music played on authentic instruments. A lifetime of research and experience has fed my senses and imagination and yet I have merely skimmed the surface of what there is to know about this enigmatic period. The search goes on.

If you enjoyed *Wheel of Fortune* and would feel comfortable leaving a review on **Amazon** or **Goodreads** that would be greatly appreciated. If you would like to know about other books in the series and forthcoming releases, why not drop by my website at: **www.cfdunn.co.uk** or connect on with me on **Facebook** or **Instagram**.

C. F. Dunn

Sapere Books is an exciting new publisher of brilliant fiction and popular history.

To find out more about our latest releases and our monthly bargain books visit our website:
saperebooks.com

Printed in Great Britain
by Amazon